Darque Legends:
The Fangs of Solvyngarr
Book Five

DERRIEN RELYEA

When Battle Commander Grifynn found the four matching boot blades in the mysteriously abandoned Keep of St Swiftyn's, he was sure of only one thing. They were exquisitely crafted. When his daughter took the LifeBond with her soon-to-be lifemate, General Gunnarr the Mighty Blue, High Prince of the Highland Dragons, he thought they were the perfect gift.

Now Darque Aalanna Grifynn is Battle Commander of the Dragon Clan, the Resistance Armed Forces, and the LifeBond Teams. With the support of the cursed spirits of the Rashei of St Swiftyn's she makes a shocking discovery. The boot blades were in fact the Magically altered Fangs of Solvyngarr, Gunnarr's grandfather, LifeBond partner and lifemate of her ancestor, Darque Abriya D'Rienne. Ripped from his jaws by his own hand, the four Fangs were to be Abriya's lifeline to draw Sol out of the Void after a most daring and desperate bid to escape the clutches of the Hoard during one of the final battles of the War of Chaos.

But following their successful escape came Abriya's failure to guide her lifemate back to her, for unbeknownst to either, Solvyngarr was not in the Void. Lost in a strange cosmic wilderness, even after Abriya had Passed the Veil they were doomed to an eternity apart.

Nevertheless, 'twas Legend that the Fangs had more than one function: to reunite Abriya and Sol and allow the Battle Commander to open the Book of the Conqueror which would then release the mystic Rashei from their curse, giving the Resistance a new and most powerful ally against the Black and his evil Hoard.

With but one of the Fangs still in her possession not only must Darque find and retrieve those lost since the war began, she must then discover a way to perform the ceremony to draw forth the Mighty Solvyngarr to join Abriya in the Beyond at last. Once the partners are together again, the powerful Fangs would return to the possession of the Battle Commander to ensure the success of the Resistance and her prophesy of their redemption. Or would they?

Darque Legends Novels by Derrien Relyea:
- Darque Legends: The Black War Begins
- Death of Life
- Search for the Wyrdritch
- Battle of Winter's Edge
- The Fangs of Solvyngarr

Coming Soon:
- The Book of the Conqueror (A Darque Legends novel)
- Audio versions of Darque Legends novels (Book 1 expected in 2020)
- A Journey Through Kadoor: The World of Darque Legends
- Darque Ages: The High Races Council (a prequel series)

You can read some of the epic poetry which inspired the Darque Legends series, get updates on the author's activities and hear her read online at https://www.thedragonwarrior.com.

Contents

Acknowledgements

To all those who have helped and supported and encouraged me along the journey of this chapter in my life, I thank you. To my Mom and Dad who are no longer with me, I could never thank you enough. I hope you somehow know how things are going now and know how much I love and miss you both. To my brother Regan and his wife Cathy, the audios are coming as fast as I can get to them! To all my friends and family who have inspired characters in this series, you are amazing, and of course, you all know who you are, both in and out of the story.

To Ariel Frailich, who continues to be my Knight in Shining Armor, toda raba chaver. Please visit him at his website: https://websiteatelier.com.

Dedication

I have had the pleasure of working with many extremely talented people in the world, and some have become fast friends. But one of the women I admire most, is my beautiful and incredibly talented friend and artist, Lisa Dixon http://lisadixonart.com/. Lisa is a passionate and skilled artist in many different medias, but she is equally passionate about her family and her friends. Not only does she produce extraordinary artwork, she is a rancher, has been through the show circuit, helps her husband run a local and internationally acclaimed cattle company, and is always there for her children and their children. Lisa never thinks of her own needs first, going above and beyond for everyone. And times have not always been easy. In fact, she has been through many difficult times indeed, but Lisa never quits, never falters, and continually gives her all. Just look at the covers and the inside pictures she has provided for the Darque Legends series! If that doesn't convince you that this woman is simply amazing, I don't know what will.

Lisa, words are not enough, but words are all I have. Thank you. I dedicate The Fangs of Solvyngarr to you and to our continued collaboration through the many projects I intend to bring to the written page. Long live Darque and the Dragon Clan!

Centuries Past

~~~~~ THE LAST HOLOCAUST ~~~~~

Hadryagg, the Dragon with the amber hues to her scales known only as the Sentinel within the Hoard, plucked the Dragon's Eye from the ashes of the remains with her long talons. 'Twas near all that was left of the one she'd just Flamed into oblivion. Having infiltrated the Hoard only within the past winter, she'd had to be careful to avoid detection while stalking this Dragon. For if her true loyalties became known, she'd no doubt be tortured, violated, and ultimately forced Past the Veil in a manner most revolting.

Extremely rare and priceless beyond measure, a Dragon's Eye was literally the eye of a Dragon killed in battle. Given the powerful pumping of their Life Source rushing Battle Lust through their systems, along with the Magic permeating their bodies to maintain the Healing and Brew their Flame, such a Passing would be dramatic and usually abrupt with these forces still at their peak. As they reached their Final Sleep, their eyes would rapidly shrink and solidify into dazzling gems, becoming the hardest substance known in the world as well as the most stunning. With their brilliant color so condensed, 'twas as if one reached out and captured all the stars in the sky. Squeezing them into the size of a walnut, they lay sparkling in the palm of your hand.

Dragon Eyes could be used to peer through as a monocular to enhance Human vision but were also said to possess mystical powers and enabled some to See into the past, the present, and the future, making them particularly valued by necromancers.

However, the eyes of Dragons were the most vulnerable and therefore, highly unlikely to be intact after a battle. If injured 'twould not survive the Passing and no gem would be created. Nevertheless, Hadryagg knew if she surprised the Dragon upon
~~~~~

the battlefield and killed him quickly enough, all the requirements would be met.

She'd been shocked when she'd first seen this Dragon amongst the Hoard, for his blood red scales were near as rare now, as were the Black's own. But Highlands could sense their futures and Had knew 'twas this exact color she required, caring not for which side he'd pledged his allegiance. No other color would do. The Eye had to be blood red to ensure the prophesy. Though 'twould have been easier to obtain from one she was supposed to be fighting against, than from one of her presumed allies. Still, such would also have been most tragic. Killing one of the Hoard helped salve her conscience about some of the atrocities she'd committed since becoming a spy.

Hadryagg felt no remorse about this battle either, even though it began while assisting her brother, Radryagg, and Prince Maakayyel to escape from the Hoard's clutches after completing a most daring inside mission. Ironically only one Hoard Dragon had seen her involvement in their escape, and that one now lay dead at her feet. But the stalking process, appearing to fight while avoiding the thick of the battle, protecting this Dragon's back, waiting for the right moment, not to mention the ferocity of the Flame storm she'd created to kill him without eye injury, all without being seen by others, had taken its toll. As a result, her Magic was now dangerously depleted.

The battlefield steamed in the falling dusk, the fight still raging all 'round as Hadryagg went swiftly about her work.

Of the three co-conspirators, only Hadryagg was still safe from suspicion. However, 'safe' was a relative term. She, Radryagg, and Maakayyel had successfully entered the Hoard's service many moons past but once in, they'd made a most horrifying discovery and Rad was given a sideline mission by the Prince. One that put them all in much danger.

'Twas no surprise when Maakayyel and Rad were exposed, but with her assistance the pair just managed to escape earlier this evening. However, their exit handed the success of the original mission to her alone. 'Twas a mission she'd accepted knowing 'twould likely last many, many winters and there'd be no backup, for the others could not return. Even the Link would be dangerous, as all Dragons were capable of Hearing.

But Hadryagg was steadfast. She'd not fail the Prince or his sister, the Mighty Maahayyel, the Last Dragon Matriarch. Someone must be on the inside to keep tabs on the Black. And although she'd never envisioned this outcome, thinking 'twould be her brother or the Prince who would ultimately end up staying, that someone turned out to be her.

There had to be a way to win this war and furthering the prophesies would help. Holding tightly to the Eye, she barely spun 'round in time to avoid a fatal attack, but the unremitting barrage of talon strikes that fell upon her took even more of her weakening Magic to repel. Her Healing was slow, her reflexes slower, and she missed the Human running up under her chest, failing to block his stab. As dusk faded into darkness, he shoved his sword deeper into her heart, adding a twist to increase the damage. Roaring in agony, she fell o'er and laid in the bloody dirt at the edge of the field, awaiting the final strike.

But that strike never came. The Human was killed by another and then the battle moved away from her, the sounds becoming more and more distant, the sights fading to mere ghostly images within a mark. Through yet another mark her Healing continued to struggle but she could gain no ground and her strength would soon be gone.

Facing imminent death Hadryagg held onto the Eye, hoping against hope that she'd be able to complete her undertaking to give it to the Human who had yet to be born, to pass along to that Human's granddaughter, the child who would be named Ardyth. The Eye would give Ardyth much support through her span of days and help her achieve her ultimate destiny. Hadryagg knew 'twas a destiny which would further the prophesies and the hope for the success of the Resistance.

As the Sentinel began to lose consciousness, she beheld a love-ly young auburn-haired Human, stepping forth from the tree line. Not dressed as a warrior nor carrying an obvious weapon, the Human moved stealthily from one to another of the victims using the darkness as her cover, eventually making her way to the Dragon. Examining her and finding she was still alive, the Human prayed o'er her in a language she'd heard not in many winters, all the while saying, "My name is Sarai. I'm a physician."

Glancing about, the Human hung her head and noted, "All this is my fault. Well, not all, I suppose. But I did have an unwit-ting involvement. However, if I hadn't done what I did, I wouldn't have this now." Taking a jar from her apron she opened it, dip-ping her fingers into the thick red salve. Then she pushed the salve into the stab wound, deep inside the chest near up to her shoulder, wincing with the Dragon's pain each time she applied more, unable to determine whether 'twas male or female or of what color, let alone knowing for whom the Dragon had fought. She only knew that the poor creature was still alive, suffered ter-ribly, and needed help. And this was all the help she had to give.

Continuing her efforts, she spoke. "I don't know if this will work, but we must try something. I can't be certain, but I have learned that a Dragon dies only if decapitated or if your heart has been completely destroyed, or if you cannot use your Healing. And since life is still in you, there is still hope. However, as I un-derstand the Healing, I theorize that yours is slowed by the de-mand upon it and if we can't boost that process you will soon die anyway. If this does help, your Healing Magic will begin to func-tion soon and if not," she sighed. Replacing the jar in her apron, she sat back upon her heels in the muddy mess, wiping her hands and arms upon her britches afore she finished with deep compas-sion, "then I pray your passage through the Void is painless and you find peace Beyond."

Near jumping to her feet, she crouched and began jogging swiftly toward the trees. Stopping suddenly, she looked back, her unruly shoulder-length curls swirling 'round her face as she hissed in a loud warning whisper, "Oh! And if this DOES work, don't ever mention it to my brother, Yoni. He'd not understand." Then turning back 'round just as swiftly, she disappeared into the forest.

CHAPTER ONE

Hearing The Call

FAST FORWARD
SHAHANALAA

~~~~~ TWO AND A HALF WINTERS PAST ~~~~~

Since the Last Holocaust, the average healthy span of days for a human was slightly more than a century and the Rashei work party had been trapped in Shahanalaa for near half that time. Although the acknowledged leader of their secret society, Myriam, having just entered her eighth decade, was one of the youngest of their group.

'Twas a daunting, terribly dangerous thing they did, putting not only their freedom, but their very lives at risk with every breath they took, to uncover the wickedness spreading within the heart of the Rashei realm, struggling to convince more of their imminent peril if such went unchecked. Neighbors, family, friends of a lifespan, grew leery of each other, and it didn't take long for her followers to realize there was an unusual apathy amongst them. Breeding doubt, the insidious propaganda to ignore what was in front of their eyes, had been more than successful.

Still, there were those who did not sit idly by and simply believe they had nothing to fear. These joined Myriam in their search for the truth afore 'twas too late. What Beryl had failed to accomplish with the destruction of their ancient island homeland Rienne afore taking up residence in the Keep of St Swiftyn's, her great, great, great something granddaughter Koryl was now completing.

Nevertheless, the society's mission failed for most, and now within Shahanalaa Myriam accepted her role as leader. Their primary efforts were focused upon maintaining their gardening,
~~~~~

though on a much smaller scale, for they need no longer feed their entire society, just themselves. At least, 'til the massive door opened again, allowing them back inside the Keep to confirm why it had closed in the first place, and just what had happened to the rest of their people. To make this discovery they were driven to escape.

In the beginning, after they realized they were indeed trapped, they'd tried everything to open the door, even knowing they might yet be affected by the curse (for who knew if 'twas the door or Shahanalaa itself that kept the curse at bay). When those efforts failed they tried to circumvent the entry by digging under or 'round, and when that was unsuccessful, they turned to finding another way into the Keep. Again, all their efforts failed.

'Twas not long afore Myriam attempted to use Abriya's Dragon Sword. After gaining its trust, every day one of the party would take up the Sword to try to cut through the door. But despite the legendary strength and eternal sharpness of the blade, they were not swordsmen and made little progress. 'Twas somewhat depressing.

Still, Myriam kept up their spirits with the certain knowledge that her eldest daughter, Aalanna, had been taken from the Keep prior to the event that locked them in this sanctuary of the Talons. She at least, was still alive, Myriam knew, for her youngest daughter had Seen her. The Battle Commander of the Dragon Clan had kept his word to rescue Aalanna, giving rise to the hope that Grifynn had also kept his word to protect the Book of the Conqueror and the Fangs of Solvyngarr as well.

'Twas but a twist of Fate and sheer good timing that Myriam was inside Shahanalaa when the curse was activated. She'd already hidden the Dragon Sword there but had been unsuccessful in getting the Book out of the Lost Room. That very morning she'd attempted to deliver the Fangs but had not been able to get them out of her chambers without being caught. In desperation she hid them under the bedframe sealed in Blood Wax so they could not be Seen through the scry, just in time to prevent

Koryl from finding them. She'd also left a note of warning to the Battle Commander, if he should return to help as he'd promised, for she'd known such an effort would come too late. Nonetheless, she had to warn him against the bastard Fay, and remind him of his promises. 'Twas all she could do.

When she felt the curse begin to activate, she'd been on her way to join the work party. Sprinting to the door, she barely managed to squeeze through as it closed, slamming with a resounding boom that echoed into the distance behind her. She'd fallen to the ground and even though she'd expected such, 'twas in disbelief that she sat staring at the now solid rock wall while the others stood 'round in equal incredulity.

No word need be said, for 'twas obvious what had happened. The Keep had been compromised. The door would not open again 'til the curse was lifted, and they were stuck 'til such happened, or they found another way out. An unnatural silence lay o'er them like a blanket for many marks as they tried to accept the ominous forecast of their futures.

Nevertheless, there was the comfort of knowing that Shahanalaa was an environment in which they could survive, its remarkable and mayhap Magical attributes including a controlled climate set in the heart of the Raptor's Talons. 'Twas a hunting, fishing, and gardening paradise that the Rashei had protected for centuries.

Not one of them had known for certain that they would be unaffected by the curse within Shahanalaa. But thinking 'twas their only option, they'd all maneuvered their work positions to be there on that morning, hoping their timeline calculations were correct. Unable to convince more of their people and unable to prevent the curse from taking them, at least these forty-eight were not blind to Koryl's activities.

'Twas upon this morning that Kaalanna walked to the door with her granddaughter, Adryanna, born in Shahanalaa a mere seven winters past, and the only one of them who had been successful since their confinement in their specialty method of Seeing the past, the present, and the future: scrying. The failure of the adults was surmised to be due to the curse, and the fact that Adryanna could See was thought to be because she was born this side of the door. 'Twas but a theory, but again, 'twas all they had.

The eldest of them, having gathered o'er one hundred winters, Kaalanna had kept herself fit with daily work. Lifting the great Sword with a grunt, little Adryanna reached forth to help. The child was too small to swing the heavy Sword alone, and she felt her grandmother should no longer try. She frowned as she watched Kaalanna take a deep breath, swinging the Sword o'er head in an arc toward the stone. Suddenly the steel blade seemed as a feather in her hands, and it struck the door with a loud clang, sparks flying. Adryanna was amazed but not as amazed as was Kaalanna, who could not let go the hilt fast enough. The Sword twisted violently out of her hands on the back swing and attacked the door with a vengeance of its own.

As sparks began to fly, wide-eyed, Adryanna pulled Kaalanna away from the tiny flying chips of stone so she would not be further injured. Looking about, the little girl tore the leaves off a native plant growing nearby and handed them to her elder. Kaalanna took the leaves gratefully and crushed them in her hand, squeezing the milky juice onto her wrists, rubbing it in to relieve the pain and reduce bruising as she walked swiftly in search of her daughter Myriam.

Once the twelve survivors were gathered and the pair explained what had happened, 'twas determined that this could only mean that Darque Abriya D'Rienne had returned to the fight and had Called her Sword. Mayhap soon, they could open the door. Good plan or bad, the Sword had taken matters out of their hands and there was nothing they could do to stop it as it tried to answer that Call.

Still, 'twas mystifying, as mystifying as was their situation. How had Koryl managed to place the curse? How had Darque

Abriya returned? The original plan to resurrect the First Warrior at the time of the Last Holocaust had failed, leaving them with a prophesy of her reincarnation through her descendent when the Black would return again, centuries later. But 'twas believed that a Dragon Sword only answered its creator, its 'handler'. So how had Darque Abriya Called to her Sword? Just what was happening out there?

Afore the curse, Myriam Saw the future relationship 'tween the Battle Commander and her daughter Aalanna, knew 'twas their offspring who would fulfill that prophesy of reincarnation for the First Warrior. The Fay had already given the Battle Commander the name by which his first daughter would be called. Darque, the mighty warrior of the Ancients. But even as the reincarnation of the First Warrior, she was not the same person and could not have Called the Sword of her ancestor as long as Darque Abriya had yet to walk Beyond, stuck in the Void, her Lifemate and LifeBond partner still lost to her.

When Kaalanna and Adryanna found Myriam that day, they sat on their heels beside the riverbank with Treygyn, the child's father. The last of the Rashei surrounded the little girl as she scooped up a handful of water. Sitting very still, she peered into it as it settled in her palms. Her auburn hair, so dark that at times 'twas mistaken for black, was braided from her forehead to sweep down the middle of her back, and her skin was golden brown with a healthy sprinkling of freckles from daily outdoor labor. Her blue eyes so like those of her parents were focused upon the water. With steady hands, her high-pitched voice gave away her lack of winters, but her words did not. "You ask once more of what becomes Storrm. As always when I try to See her future, there is nothing."

Myriam swallowed hard. Adryanna sensed this particular scry was not long in coming. The granddaughter she'd never met, must be headed for the Veil. She hoped 'twas not so, but Adryanna's scrying had thus far proven most accurate (aside from the fact that there was no way to prove otherwise for what she'd Seen of the outside world). There seemed a great battle coming, in the caverns of Winter's Edge, and she'd not Seen Storrm since that battle began. If only they could get word to someone, warn Darque, warn Storrm. But 'twas not to be. She felt helpless.

Asking about Storrm was always Myriam's first question for as long as the little girl could remember. And her second? Adryanna furrowed her brows sadly and glanced o'er her shoulders afore she dropped the water and wiped her hands. She was worried about her parents. Myriam and Treygyn were still amongst the youngest of the survivors. Originally ranging from their twenties into sixties then, some of those gathered 'round her had now well o'er ninety winters, and apart from herself, none who yet lived had less than seventy. That placed them all squarely as, or becoming, Elders. They were no longer young, and Adryanna's birth had been a joyous surprise.

Not about to neglect her education, for their entire society was based on scholarly pursuit, all joined in to teach the child, the one they hoped would carry on their heritage. For they knew not if any of them would survive to make 'The Exit', and the fact remained that they knew not the fate of the rest of their society. They faced the real possibility that they were the last, leaving Adryanna their sole legacy, as was her birthright.

Aside from the girl's normal education, she learned the history of the Rashei, their prophesies, their entrapment, and their anticipation of returning to the Keep. Adryanna hoped one day to be able to lead her parents and the remainder of her people back home, although she was well aware she might be the only one left by the time the Sword succeeded. Shivering with that thought, she scooped up more water and stared quietly. "I See my sister, Aalanna, but I See not her lifemate."

Myriam knew in her heart that the Battle Commander must have Passed the Veil as well, for her eldest granddaughter now held his Rank. But 'twas all guesswork. Although Adryanna could See people, she Saw few details surrounding them, and Myriam understood the dangers of trying to make deductions too far away from the facts. As the child gathered her winters, her mystic powers, already strong, would only increase. She must be patient.

Repeating the process of refilling her hands with fresh water, Adryanna addressed the third and fourth questions that need no longer be asked aloud. Confirming she Saw both her other nieces, Darque and Fryya, she sat quietly waiting for the first new question. But as Myriam opened her mouth, Adryanna's eyes widened in revelation and near panting, the little girl turned swiftly to silence her. "Ask no question!" Continuing, she implored, "Tell me what you wish to see."

Myriam folded her hands and gazed at the child with pride in her eyes. Adryanna was a wise one. 'Til now she'd always asked the girl if she could See this or that, one person or another. The success of the scry depended largely on the surrounding emotions and energies. Mayhap 'twould increase the positive and influence the Vision. Licking her dry lips, she altered her course of interest as well as the way 'twas stated. "Show me the future of the door."

The feeling of expectation from those 'round her, near made the child cringe. But trembling fouled the scry and she forced herself to be calm as she broke eye contact with her mother and stared unblinking into the darkening water in her small hands. Drawn deeper and deeper into the murky depths, the scenario that presented itself was more detailed than anything Adryanna had ever Seen afore.

She Saw the Sword as it hacked away within an expanding hollow of the stone, large enough to conceal two adults with the Sword still swinging freely. A huge pile of rock chips and chunks lay at the foot of the door and were scattered for several Dragon-lengths away as with every strike of the Magically enhanced steel more flew in all directions. 'Twas so clear that she near winced as a piece came straight toward her. Forcing herself not to blink, for doing so would stop the Vision, the Sword abruptly broke through the stone and disappeared without fanfare into the flickering torchlit shadows of the corridor beyond. The sudden silence in the scenario was so jarring that she dropped the water. Gasping, she wiped her hands down her legs as she attempted to give the others all the specifics of what she'd Seen.

Scrying took enormous amounts of energy and as Adryanna near collapsed with fatigue, Myriam hugged the slender child tightly and reassured her that all was well and that she need not try again this day. They had chores to do. But afore that, they all returned to the door.

For many marks that first day, they stood in awe and watched the Sword hack away at the massive wall of stone. There was no fear of the Sword's destruction as a Dragon Sword could not be destroyed and the edge would never fail. It reminded Myriam of the stories told her by the Battle Commander, of the Battle Drums and Pipes which played their driving music for the Warriors in the Training Pits of the Dragon's Den.

After endless days, the noise became part of their normal routine and they began to ignore the constant rhythmic echoes of metal on rock, delegating the sounds so created to the back of their minds, only checking on the slow progress of the determined Sword to break through, afore returning to their daily tasks. The Sword would be successful. The door would be broken. But when?

CHAPTER TWO

The Border Of No Return

Rhyah padded his way through the Far Northlands, his massive wolf paws sure-footed in the deepening snow. He'd traveled far and was closing in on the Icelands border when his large sensitive ears picked up the slightest of movements just ahead. With infinite patience he steadied himself, slowing his pace, stepping cautiously toward the target 'til at last he pounced, crashing through the icy crust, sharp teeth chomping firmly upon the mouse. Shaking off the wet slush as he withdrew his huge head, he gulped and swallowed the tiny creature whole. 'Twas the only food he'd had in two days.

The hollow he'd created by catching the mouse provided a place to rest and he sat with his bushy tail wrapped 'round his feet for warmth, for there was little in the way of trees or brush this far north under which to shelter. He had to eat to keep up his strength for once he crossed the border he'd need all and more to survive. But with the lack of shelter, came lack of game.

As he rested, his great yellow eyes scanned into the distance. 'Twas white and barren as far as he could see. The Dragons that Battle Commander Darque of the Resistance had sent to keep watch o'er him when he left the Keep of St Swiftyn's had lost his trail at least a sennight past, and he'd not seen them since.

Not for the first time, he wondered if he'd been fantasizing all along or if 'twas reality, for he'd not had another dream of the lady beckoning him come to her in the Icelands since leaving the Keep. He also wondered how fared Storrm and the other Warriors whom he'd called his friends. His time with the Clan was healing, yet his destiny beckoned him elsewhere. Squinting, he remembered how very fond of Storrm he'd grown.

Nonetheless, the lady in his dreams was the woman his heart desired and 'twas to her that he journeyed.

Rhyah was Fay, and the Fay were the strongest of the Magic bearers. Also known as Shifters, each had their preferred Shift. Rhyah's was the Wolf. His best friend, Corbyn the Raven, was still cursed to serve the Goddess Morrigan. And though he thought that Rhyah was ignorant of such, 'twas understood that by serving Storrm, who just happened to carry the Battle Name of the Goddess, she had not long this side of the Veil.

Dropping his gaze to the snow, Rhyah's sense of guilt for leaving Storrm near o'erwhelmed him once more. However, their mutual understanding of his destiny gave him some comfort. And there was the fact that Storrm did not love him. Their last encounter made that perfectly clear. Besides, she deserved to be with the one who loved her and whom she truly loved: her LifeBond partner, Mystynn the Green.

Gazing all 'round, the Wolf hoped for what he decided would be the last time, that they'd worked out their issues and Storrm was happy, for despite the ominous foretelling of Corbyn's curse, who really knew how long she had? She was a Warrior and Warriors lived with that uncertainty daily. 'Twas not discussed nor seriously considered. They worked hard and they played hard for they knew they'd likely Pass the Veil hard.

Pulling his lips back o'er his wicked fangs into the closest thing to a grin that he could manage in Shift, he recalled how they'd 'played hard' his last night at the Keep. 'Twas one of the most enjoyable nights of his entire, and very lengthy, span of days. A treasured memory. He sighed. 'Twas time to delegate that memory to the past for now he had other business to which to attend and survival this far north would take all his senses, his skills, and his Magic. He could not allow himself such distraction.

Standing up, he shook the wet snow off his thick coat and began to trot northward once again, toward that fog of white that defied even his Fay and wolf vision combined. By his best estimate, he'd arrive at the border of no return in less than a dawn. As he traveled through the last of the clouded daylight and long into the night, he let his mind drift to his dream lady.

Rhyah was certain she was his childhood friend from the Elven Nation, whom he'd met and spent time with only on infrequent delegate visits, for she was of royal breeding. And although he frequented the royal house of the Fay, as his best friend was a Prince, he was a mere peasant in comparison. But she was intelligent, beautiful, charming, sensual, and he'd never forgotten her. In his heart she'd remained his fantasy lover. To think she'd mayhap held the same thoughts of him was the obsession that led him onward, toward the Icelands… and certain death. For the lady in his dreams was Bryanna, who'd grown up to take the throne of the Elven Nation beside the evil Jeeryd, the traitor having aligned himself with the Black afore the Last Holocaust. Her intended, Typeth, had been killed along with his brother Grygoth, and father King Lucien, in an ambush orchestrated by Jeeryd, the king's nephew and last living relative, who then took that throne and the hand of Bryanna.

At the time they were both very young and he could do naught at any rate. Through the following winters he'd kept up with all news of Bryanna, noting her fifteen children with envy. Then the Wyrdritch disappeared during the Last Holocaust and there came no more news 'til his time at the Keep where he learned of the altered Spell that not only hid the Elven Nation, but near destroyed it. On top of that news, he learned Bryanna had joined the ranks of the 'Lost Elves' and the king declared her dead. Taking Alyssa as his new queen, she provided him with an additional two children, bringing the royal brood to seventeen.

Ultimately the Spell was Healed and recreated to be used as protection for the Lairs of the Resistance when the Elven Nation allied themselves with King Gabriel and Darque. Rhyah had experienced that protection firsthand. The Keep of St Swiftyn's, the Bog of St Swiftyn's, and Drekinn Lair now lay under Spell Domes that made them invisible to the outside world, with portals that allowed Gatekeepers to bring in or push away, anyone and anything. Those who'd been so portalled would not realize they'd traveled in this manner and therefore would believe the Lair no longer existed or could not be found.

Panting now, his breath coming in frosty puffs, he continued his thoughts as the marks wore on through the night. There was so much happening outside the Fay Nation, so many changes that those inside still knew nothing about. Yet their own King Bardyn insisted on maintaining total isolation from the outside world. Even if Rhyah returned and tried to reveal to the King what was happening, would Bardyn listen? Should he turn 'round and go back? No. 'Twas his destiny to which he was steadily making way, and once he crossed o'er the border, there'd be no turning back. Nonetheless, if Bryanna were truly there, she'd found a way to survive the fierce environment, and if she could, then so could he.

His shaggy head down, even in Shift he felt like he was pushing his way through a gale. When had the winds become so strong? Nevertheless 'twas not the steady whipping of his furry mane that he felt the most. 'Twas the intense cold. He'd left the last of the scrub brush behind and all that remained was snow and ice in every direction. How long had he been out here? If not for his Fay senses, he'd be hard pressed to know which direction he was traveling. When he could look up, 'twas to a colorless and unforgiving landscape as far as he could see and then he'd have to close his eyes once again to avoid permanent blindness from the icy winds. At least 'twas no longer entirely dark.

Walking now, yet still pushing onward through the increasing whiteout, his mind continued to drift. Why was he so determined to complete this suicide mission? He shook his head. His destiny and determination to fulfill it, were not to be doubted now. Trying to ignore the fatigue along with the increasing difficulty breathing, he directed his thoughts to what he knew of his intended journey's end.

Rhyah's knowledge came from books, rumors, stories told by merchants, and his own dreams of Bryanna in which she Called to him from the depths of the Icelands. During these dreams he could see the surrounding area. 'Twas insanely cold and never thawed. Snow and ice lay like a perpetual blanket o'er the rugged land and could only be challenged by Magic. But everyone knew that Magic required organic energy to fuel, and there was nothing organic in sight. Without organics from which to Draw energy, Magic would be used up in a relatively short time, leaving one open to the elements.

Death came quickly to any who crossed o'er the border to the Icelands. No one who did so, had ever returned to tell the tale. From the distance the Ice Rain phenomenon came to be known. Pelting ice as sharp as daggers would fall during the frequent storms with such force 'twould kill within moments. 'Twas a lonely land. A harsh land. 'Twas not a matter of whether you'd die, but which would force you Past the Veil first: the freezing temperatures or the Ice Rains.

But there was also great beauty to be found there. The snow was always clean and without disturbance and the ice crystals would glisten in the sunlight, especially during the short summers, creating a sparkling prism effect from horizon to horizon. And there were rumored to be massive and intricate caverns of an ice palace carved and modified continually by the legendary Ice Dragons within the most distant mountainous terrain. Who knew if they had a hidden environment in which one might survive? For that matter, who knew if the Ice Dragons truly existed or if 'twas just a children's story? Wasn't there something about needing organics to Draw energy to fuel Magics? How could the Ice Dragons survive out there?

The Wolf looked up briefly to check his position then back down again as he continued onward. Remaining in Shift was draining his Magic and he'd not eaten since that mouse. When was that? He could not be certain, but the lack of decent food further weakened him, as well as the fact that he hadn't stopped to rest. But then, he couldn't at this point, for there was nowhere to do so without freezing solid to the ground. However, staying in Shift had prevented him from freezing already and once he 'crossed o'er, 'twould not be a few days, but a few moments he had left to find her. If he could not, he'd be swept Past the Veil without making his mark in Legend Song. His very name would be forgotten. Not that it mattered to him for truly Rhyah wasn't that kind. He was determined to find her because he loved her and from his dreams, he believed she loved him and that she was Calling him because she needed his help. If he had but a moment to gaze into her forest green eyes once more, touch her long brown hair, he'd Pass a happy man.

Although he knew not why he was so Called to this destiny, surely 'twas not to simply die. Such information as he could confirm would be most helpful to the Battle Commander, and with allies such as the Ice Dragons, the chameleons of the world, able to stand afore anything or anyone without attracting notice, along with their forte Magic of Mesmerizing, able to make someone believe anything they chose (akin to the Memory Magic of the Fay but more attuned to the ancient practice of Human hypnotism only much stronger and more reliable), the Resistance would have three most powerful Dragon Races in allegiance.

After who knew how many marks with such thoughts rambling through his mind, Rhyah plodded along slowly but steadily against the ever increasing cold, ice clumping 'tween his enormous pads, his mane and tail frozen into a spray of hard spikes, his lashes stuck together so tightly he could no longer open his eyes without causing major injury, his very breath beginning to freeze upon his tongue, he abruptly realized he was long past the border. His Fay Magic had always been strong and had protected him for near a league into the region afore it began to fail. But he could go no further.

He must find Bryanna but to stop moving was to die. Maintaining his forward momentum against the wind as best he could, he ripped his eyes open. The pain of tearing the delicate surrounding tissues immediately disappeared, the drops of blood frozen afore they could trickle down his muzzle as he looked all 'round him, peering into the distance. Southward was the white of the never-ending snows from whence he'd come. Northward was a grayness into which he must continue.

Wait. A grayness? Squinting as his vision began to fade, he focused his Magical efforts to protect his eyes. 'Twas yet another danger to be faced as he grasped the reality of what he saw afore him. There in the distance, blowing toward him so fast he could already feel the frozen daggers slicing into his sensitive nose as shards of glass, came an Ice Rain.

<center>~~~~~ A SENNIGHT LATER ~~~~~</center>

Naked and lying on a smooth flat surface, he sensed the soft voice in the distance was apparently in conversation with one whom he initially could not hear. 'Twas most definitely a feminine voice but held a quality which he could not decipher for 'twas a voice he'd never heard afore. 'Twas not Elven, nor Sprite or Fay. And for certain 'twas not Human. Mayhap 'twas Dragon? He tried to shake his head but found he was too weak. Still, if 'twas Dragon, the voice was not that of a Highland Dragon, nor of a Water Dragon. Those he knew well.

Barely able to open his eyes, he squinted as he tried to scan the area. Although Rhyah recalled the injury to his eyelids when last he opened them, there was no pain now. What there was, was a prism of soft colors permeating an enormous white space that seemed to glisten in a diffused light. 'Twas unlike anything the Fay had ever seen afore and simply breathtaking in its beauty. But he could see nothing else. Had he been blinded? Was this the other side of the Veil?

Rhyah had always assumed that being blind meant total darkness. Struggling to raise his hand in front of his face, 'twas as if he were in total darkness, but 'twas not darkness with which he was surrounded. Yet he could not see his own hand. The Wolf could feel the surface under his body but could not decide if 'twas hard or soft, hot or cold. His senses were muted and yet seemed to be running amok at the same time. Even so, 'twas not uncomfortable.

"He wakes!" exclaimed another voice near to him. Mayhap standing beside Rhyah now, this voice was extremely excited, and 'twas clearly Elven. Brows furrowed, confusion became doubt as he knew she was beside him, yet he saw her not. He was getting a headache and there seemed no explanation as to why his memory and his senses were so hazy. And though Rhyah thought he'd wake up Past the Veil, he decided this was not the Beyond. So where was he, what had happened to him and just how did he get here?

All Rhyah could remember was the driving force of the Ice Rain blinding him, forcing him to the ground in agonizing pain as he was o'erwhelmed by the ferocity of the sudden storm. Being carved to pieces by the falling daggers of ice, he lost his Shift and laid naked in the bloody snow awaiting the Veil, as there was nothing he could do to prevent that passage, disappointed that he'd not seen her again. And then… Rhyah barely shook his head as he tried to remember what happened next.

Her voice dripping with disappointment, she spoke again. "He remembers not." If Rhyah had the energy, he'd smile, for in his imagination he envisioned her ruby red lips in that delectable pout that was so very typical of... where was he? So close now that her warm sweet breath caressed his cheek, Rhyah longed to see her face.

But although the statement was obviously about him 'twas not directed to him and with his eyelids growing heavier Rhyah thought he heard the first voice reply, now standing to his other side, "The Fay was damaged not by the alteration, only by the Rains. 'Tis merely fatigue as he heals and adjusts." As if apologizing, the Dragon told the Elf, "This process may well take some time, as it did with you."

Reflectively, she replied, "Then he has become like me? He can never return to the warmth of Kadoor?"

The voice was wary, with a hesitance Rhyah would later consider odd. "Yes. He can never return."

Was he a prisoner then? And to what precisely must he adjust?

There was a long period of silence afore the Dragon added, "I thought 'twould please you, to have another here. Are you not lonely? We had little time to debate the alteration. Was I wrong?"

Immediately, the Elf responded. "You were not wrong. He would have died. I just wish he could have made his own decision."

"Are you sorry that I altered you?"

"Oh no! Please, think not that I would have my life any other way. You saved me from more than an Ice Rain."

'Twas a perplexing conversation to which he was made privy, but his vision began to fade and afore Rhyah could formulate his next thought, he slipped into unconsciousness again.

CHAPTER THREE

Walkyr's Down!

THE KEEP OF ST SWIFTYN'S
ONE OF THREE LAIRS OF THE RESISTANCE
DEEP IN BYNDYNN FOREST IN THE RAPTOR'S TALONS

~~~~~ NEAR TWO WINTERS LATER ~~~~~

Despite her youth, Battle Commander Darque Aalanna Grifynn was known as an exceptional leader and strategist as well as highly respected for her extraordinary fighting skills and swordsmanship. Equally known for her quick temper and lack of height, with her long red hair and deep blue eyes she didn't quite fit the picture for such Rank. Nonetheless, the Warriors of the Dragon Clan had readily accepted her field promotion when her father was killed in action at the beginning of the war. She'd just as readily performed her final duty as Second, acting as Death Avenger, killing the one who'd delivered the fatal strike to Grifynn and saving her mother at the same time.

Darque's swordsmanship was unsurpassed. Yet despite her many qualities, not to mention the fact that she was the answer to the prophesy, 'And there will be a girl child born to the Race of Man, of Dragon Blood and Dragon Seed, with flaming red hair and piercing blue eyes who will take up the Sword and lead the Races from near extinction into a New Beginning', she was still young, having just seen twenty-two winters. Not that age meant anything to her any longer, for she looked not a day older than the seventeen she had when she'd taken the LifeBond with her lifemate, Gunnarr the Mighty Blue, High Prince of the Highland Dragons.

'Twas a time of war and she had much riding upon her young shoulders. She was proud and did not want to fail her people, but she'd made mistakes, lives had been lost. She had to admit that
~~~~~

she was not so proud as to allow her own feelings to interfere with the success of the Resistance.

However, she'd been through so much in the past few winters that she sometimes wondered if she were truly 'the one'. Mayhap her prophesy merely referred to her role thus far and her usefulness in her current capacity would reach an end. Would she step down if such were prophesied? Of course she would, for she truly did place the success of the Resistance above her own. If someone else could lead better than she, then so be it. Her fighting skills were legendary already, she would find her way elsewhere. But she wasn't looking for a replacement just yet.

These thoughts and more, jumbled their way through Darque's mind. Her muscled arms covered by leather bracers tooled with ancient runes of protection and blessings, were crossed o'er her rather well-endowed breasts held down by a leather width. Her long, thick, wavy hair was braided 'round her face in three lengths to join together into one single braid dropping to the back of her knees.

Sitting at her desk in her office, Darque's eyes gleamed with determination as she pondered the past winter's events. Up 'til Walkyr the Clan Seer and her own little sister Fryya, had taken the Oath and joined the Brotherhood, Darque had been the shortest Warrior. But she was not in the least, average. The others held high esteem for their Commander, and her buxom curves and singular beauty were not the reason. She was good. The best of the best. A swordsman to be admired. Her aggressively offensive approach, boldly taking full advantage of her stature along with incredible speed and strength, made it difficult to beat her in any practice session and she'd suffered few serious injuries in the realities of the war thus far. Having already led them through many a battle, her Warriors would follow Darque to the Veil without question or regret.

Still, she wondered about recent revelations. Glancing up at the bookshelf 'cross the large room, she bit her bottom lip as she stared at Storrm's Sword. Dragon Swords could slice through Dragon scale, making them a Warrior's most valuable asset in battle. Thus far, there were only fourteen known Swords in existence. One had belonged to the First Warrior, Darque Abriya D'Rienne, her ancestor and lifemate of Solvyngarr, during the War of Chaos. The door to Shahanalaa was recently found but remained closed. However there was a constant, vaguely soft tapping sound from the area, doubtless metal on stone, and this fueled the speculation that Abriya's Sword was inside as it had not been located elsewhere and had not come to the Warrior's Call afore the Battle to Draw the Domes.

The other thirteen Swords were created for First Flight soon after the first LifeBond. Ariel's Sword had accepted her betrothed, Rygyl, after her death in battle. Storrm's Sword had not moved from the top of the bookshelf in her office, despite other Warriors Calling to it with Darque's approval, since the day of Storrm's funeral. Darque refused to Call. She could not touch her little sister's Sword. Mayhap one day. But for now, her only solace for the endless heartache of Storrm's loss was immersing herself in work and training.

She leaned upon the desk she'd had made to match the one her father used at the castle of the Warrior Brotherhood, the Dragon's Den of Drekinn Lair, even to size. Her feet rested upon the matching platform she'd had built after taking Command, to prevent her from dangling as when she was a child. Her father had been a big man. The paperwork she should be wading through was piling up in the middle of the desk, also matching that at the Den. 'Twas a part of being Battle Commander that she detested and was the reason she'd missed morning katas. Again.

She sighed. Swordsmanship was her passion, fighting was her forte, and the effects of age would not stop her for many, many winters as her 'Bond with Gunnarr not only allowed them to Share the MindLink, the Healing, enhanced senses, speed, and strength, but also the longevity of the Dragon Race. Musing, she wondered what would have happened if Storrm had been first born? She glanced once more to the bookshelf and took a deep breath. Scratching her eyebrow, she realized 'twould have merely delayed her Command, for their positions would have been reversed and upon Storrm's Passing, Darque would have been promoted.

And here she sat, waiting for Tammra Dayo to arrive per her summons. Tall even for an Elf, the stunning, broad-shouldered, black-haired Commander of the Ancients, once the leader of the Elven forces during the War of Chaos, was now Commander of the Kreegaren Elves, the infamous Assassins from the Rol Dan. Separated from the Elven Nation as Lost Elves after the Last Holocaust, they were now a distinct entity, recently swearing allegiance to the Resistance.

Tammra's following of o'er two thousand now based and rotated from the Kreegaren Keep in the Sakyn Forest beyond the frozen wasteland at the eastern border of the Rol Dan, through Drekinn Lair and the Keep of St Swiftyn's. The Bog Lair was built and maintained as a Training facility for the Flights and was now connected to the Keep underground via a single tunnel built and protected by their allies, the Borkahn, known as Trolls afore the Last Holocaust.

But the assistance of the Borkahn was limited as they were still fighting their own civil war, with the last two major factions divided 'tween those of Roack who had aligned himself with the Black, and those of Gorch, father of Crytcha. The 'Stone Child' who was about sixteen to anyone's best guess, stood near twice as tall as most of the other children, and resided with the Resistance for her own safety. Her new family included her 'sister' Flyrra, Captain Natanamia, and the Eagle Warrior, Kayarr.

Darque smiled. That family was a mixed lot for certain. Flyrra the half-breed Elf and Sprite with huge, black, almond-shaped eyes, a triangular face and sparkling silver hair giving her the appearance of a giant wasp, was Claimed (as was Crytcha) by the lithe, pale-skinned, green-eyed, blonde Sprite Captain (who was her aunt by blood), along with her lifemate, the black-haired dark-skinned Warrior from the Eagle Clan (of which there were but twelve remaining), whose eyes would change color with his mood from menacing darkest browns to calm greens.

Among other issues Darque wanted to discuss with Tammra was the fact that she and her ancestor, Darque Abriya, lived and fought together in the War of Chaos. She hoped the Elf would be able to give her some answers as to what had happened then. How had the war ended? What could she be doing differently to help bring an end to the war this time? She also hoped that Tammra could give her some insight about the Fangs of Solvyngarr, which they desperately needed to find and retrieve.

She'd considered long and hard about having Ardyth channel Abriya again, allowing the spirit Warrior to manifest long enough to answer all her questions. But 'twas a Gift not to be taken lightly nor to be o'er used as 'twas dangerous. She recalled the last time Ardyth had channeled Abriya they'd near been unable to separate.

Such thinking brought back questions about Abriya's Sword. The First Warrior had Called, but the Sword had yet to answer. She'd tried having her mother Aalanna, a pure blood Rashei, scry the region behind the door, but she could See nothing and could not be certain if 'twas the door or the curse affecting her attempts. Were the sounds they heard coming from the other side of the door to Shahanalaa really the Sword still trying to break through? Only time would tell.

Shaking her head to clear her mind of the confusing jumble of thoughts and needs and must-haves now, she was certain only that Tammra's expertise and vast experience would be appreciated. Since Storrm's Passing, Darque had not had much time for herself or for her lifemate and she felt drained. Mayhap the Elven Commander could bring some order to her rampant emotions.

~~~~~ **THE WARD OF THE KEEP** ~~~~~

Despite the fact that summer was waning with fall just 'round the corner, hard work made one sweat even in the chill of dawn, but 'twould become quite warm by mid-day. As Fryya wiped her brow with her forearm, her hip-length bushy mop of copper-red curls broke free of their leather strip once again, fluttering annoyingly about her face in the early morning breeze. Her blue eyes, so like her sister Darque's, flashed impatiently while she rolled lengths 'round her dirty fingers, forcing it behind her ears, expertly weaving and then tying the two remaining leather pieces through the strands to create an unruly bun at the back of her neck afore she returned to sharpening and cleaning her weapons. 'Twas a chore of which she never tired. She'd been told 'twas a familial trait (along with the habit of biting her lower lip when concentrating).

Glancing for the umpteenth time to Walkyr the Clan Seer, her Dragon Clan Warrior brother, constant companion-in-mischief, and best friend, she was filled with wonder at their good fortune. The two youngest ever to take the Oath and join the Brotherhood o'er two full winters past, they'd earned their rights by fighting in the war since the beginning and the first LifeBond.

Fryya had gathered o'er eleven winters, Walkyr ten. They were still small for their winters compared to the other children of the Clan. But 'tween them they were close to the same height and weight and with hard Training under their belts, they now matched each other's skills in both swordsmanship and martial arts. 'Twas not bragging to say they'd become formidable enemies of the Hoard.

'Twas more than a shared dream to take the 'Bond with one of the mighty Highland Dragons. 'Twas their shared belief 'twould save Walkyr's life. Fryya had been talking non-stop since dawn's rays allowed them to see without a torch. Not that Fryya needed one, as her hybrid Dragon/Human status made her night vision quite exceptional. She was trying to get Walkyr to agree with her
~~~~~

plan to 'crash' the upcoming fourth LifeBond ceremony, allowing them to make the attempt.

"I'm fine!" Walkyr exclaimed with a hard edge to his voice as he caught Fryya's quick glance during one of her infrequent quiet moments. Her incessant chatter was so reminiscent of her sister Storrm, that he sometimes had to look twice. Even Fryya's facial features closely resembled Storrm's and she was already near as tall as was her elder sister, Darque. But that wasn't saying much.

Walkyr's shoulder length, straight, mahogany brown hair marked him as an Outlander despite his pale blue eyes. But the thirteenth child of subsistence farmers had been readily handed o'er to the Dragon Clan Seer, Kallyr, and his lifemate, Shayla, to train as a Seer and take o'er once Kallyr retired. He'd been raised with the Clan since he was weaned and everyone considered him such, including Walkyr himself.

"I feel no approaching Visions," he stated with less rancor, knowing her concern was for his wellbeing. His Visions were not coming as often since Storrm's Passing, but for the past few winters, when they did, as one had just the prior sennight, they'd cause him to experience seizure-like activity and he'd be in the clinic for marks, sometimes days, with Fryya and the Healers unsure he'd even survive.

The entire situation made him feel useless. A failure to his station and to the Battle Commander. Vision details were lost in the time it took to be imparted and what good was a Clan Seer who couldn't tell you everything he'd Seen? Since he was a toddler he'd been hailed as the most powerful Seer in all Kadoor. Now?

Walkyr sighed. "You can stop watching o'er me like a mother Kahyah," he continued, referencing the huge, sentient, Night Beasts of their allies, the Daggogh, standing shoulder-to-shoulder with their human hunting partners, looking like a mix 'tween the ancient big cats and wolves that lived afore the time of the Last Holocaust. Which of course, they were.

Purposely avoiding looking at her partner, Fryya's gaze swept 'cross the Ward to watch Captain Natanamia helping Tiyya train with her lifemate, Thorrn. Tiyya had been so quiet since losing their baby last winter. Thorrn had tried everything to help her return to her once vivacious self. Warriors didn't get pregnant often and when they did 'twas a time of celebration, even though the child would be fostered for their own safety while their Warrior mother and father continued with their duties. The parents of such children participated as much as possible in their raising and part of their pay was diverted toward education and living expenses.

No one had the same childhood. Vivid memories flashed in Fryya's mind of how she was raised in the castle of the High King, her mother a prisoner she was not allowed to visit (although she managed). She oft' times wished she'd been born and raised as a Warrior like her sisters, however, Aalanna did her best to provide what training she could. Nonetheless, Darque and Storrm were raised by the entire Clan, their father ever absent attending to his duties as Battle Commander, so mayhap 'twould not have been that different. Everyone had a tale to tell when it came to their upbringing.

She continued to chew on her bottom lip thinking about Tiyya. 'Twas sad, but 'twas no sadder than most of life since the war began. Still, 'twas not a sword wound that would not heal, 'twas a festering wound in the Warrior's soul with which she dealt. Yet if Tiyya would not allow others to help, she must heal herself and soon. 'Twas her decision. If her focus were not on her fighting skills, the Clan could lose a Warrior unnecessarily, and that would be as tragic as the loss of her baby.

Watching Tiyya spar with the others, Fryya thought she saw a quick smile, and even heard the pretty Warrior laugh at some joke or other while blocking an incoming strike. And then Tiyya spun swiftly about to avoid another from her second and third opponents. 'Twas the most engaged the young woman had been in ages. 'Twas as if the Warrior had turned a corner. With her strawberry blonde hair pulled up and braided and the sheen of sweat upon her skin, Tiyya's large dark freckles looked like she'd been splattered head to toe by one of the artists shaking out their paintbrush. Fryya nodded her head approvingly. Tiyya appeared to be on the mend at last.

Returning her attention to Walkyr, Fryya replied haughtily, her nose wrinkled in irritation, her eyes focused now solely upon her weapons. "My ORDERS are to watch o'er you like a mother Kahyah, remember?" She longed for the 'old days' when they had total freedom to come and go as they pleased, when Walkyr's Visions weren't so important to the war effort, nor so harmful to him. They'd had fun then. Now all she did was worry about losing her best friend.

Without Walkyr, Fryya was all alone. Her older sisters were not only raised together, they were near inseparable, but now that Storrm had Passed the Veil, Darque kept to herself. 'Twas only natural, since she was a decade Fryya's elder and had so much on her shoulders, but it left Fryya feeling that she was no more important than any other Warrior to Darque.

Not that she should be. Their own mother was oft' times too busy to visit as both Fryya and Walkyr now lived in the area of the Keep designated as the Warrior Barracks and had strict daily schedules to attend. However, since the day she and Walkyr met they'd become near joined at the hip. Darque had not separated them and in fact, had them working together as a Team. She grinned. 'Twas a bonus the boy was cute. She knew Walkyr thought she was, too.

Suddenly she noticed Walkyr hadn't responded to her taunt and she spun toward him, fearing the worst. The Vision had struck hard and fast and Walkyr was rigid, falling forward toward the gray stone of the Ward. She barely reached forth quickly enough to keep him from cracking his head wide open, succeeding in grabbing his tunic and turning him to land on his shoulder instead. Scrambling into position to protect his head in her lap while he thrashed upon the ground, 'twas a mere few heartbeats later that she realized he'd stopped breathing. Yelling for back-up, her youthful voice rang through the air both firm and commanding, "ONE WARRIOR DOWN, WALKYR'S DOWN!" 'Twas not the first time she'd heard those words, but 'twas the first time they'd come from her mouth.

Instantly, Tiyya, Thorrn, Natanamia and several other Warriors training in the Ward, sheathed their weapons and rushed o'er to assist, grabbing the boy up by his arms and legs and carrying him swiftly to the clinic. Fryya was shaking near as hard as was her best friend by the time they got there. In their haste, the Warriors slammed him upon his back on one of the racks. Such action seemed to help in that he stopped shaking, but he was still not breathing. Stepping aside, the Warriors allowed the two resident Healers access.

Senior Healer Chynnar was a human girl, a refugee from the beginning, and with just thirteen winters at that time, had answered Shayla's call for Apprentices. Having excelled in her new profession, Shayla promoted her after the last battle, assigning her to the Keep. Although extremely intelligent and constantly seeking new information, she was initially lanky and socially awkward with stringy brown hair and nondescript features. Now closing in on eighteen winters, she was blossoming into a young woman of delicate beauty.

Kelseacyr, called Kelsey to those who knew her, was the child of an Elven Skald, and although she too, had come to the Dragon Clan as a refugee at the beginning of the war, she'd tried to hide her true appearance then, not certain the Humans could be trusted. With long curly brown hair, brown eyes, and an ever-youthful face, she was quite petite and even shorter than the Battle Commander, but the gentleness of her appearance was deceiving. Her Elven martial arts training, along with her command of a sword and blade made her one to watch. With the war's progression, Kelsey came out of hiding, dropping her glamour to reveal her true bloodline and declare her allegiance to the Resistance. She even had her own War Dog, Bullaga, who followed her everywhere when he wasn't visiting Walkyr's Horace or Fryya's Drys. But with her vast experience and extensive knowledge in the medical field, her main interests now leaned toward research. And since mentoring Chynnar, either could handle both their Human and Magic bearing clientele. They made a good team.

Watching them work on Walkyr, Fryya was apprehensive. Chynnar immediately began using the Kiss of Life but the boy still hadn't started to breathe, and he was turning blue. Looking up at her Elven partner, Kelsey nodded and then took o'er. They'd discussed this attempt long ago, not sure 'twould work on other than a trauma injury, and Magic could not bring back life once 'twas gone. But they had to try something.

Nonetheless, Kelsey must be careful. The energies of Magic could create or destroy and if not kept in balance, 'twould result in disaster. The diminutive Skald leaned close, her delicately pointed ears poking through her spiral curls as she barely touched Walkyr's forehead with the tip of one slim finger, imparting a miniscule spark of Healing energy afore stepping back to wait anxiously with the others.

Within a few heartbeats Walkyr's chest rose, and he gasped, surprising them all. Then with breath stuttering, his eyes opened, his color began to return, and he looked about, bewildered. Noting he was in the clinic, with an impish grin he joked bravely, "Does this mean I have the rest of the day off?"

Surviving a hearty laugh of relief that came with a slap on the back from every Warrior present, Walkyr watched them all file out of the clinic, except for the youngest one still standing there with a grim expression upon her face. His Warrior brothers and sisters were truly grateful 'twas not his time to Pass, but like everyone else now, they expected such to occur at any moment due to the increasing violence of the boy Seer's Visions. The entire

Healer staff, including all Apprentices, were working to find a solution, spending as much of their time on this one duty as they spent on everything else combined o'er the past few moons.

Exhausted beyond belief, Walkyr struggled to keep his eyes open. He had to make report. He had to tell the Battle Commander what he'd Seen. 'Twas a vast number of large, multi-colored pearls, rare and exquisite, being harvested by a very young girl diving all alone. She was quite small but athletically built and an excellent swimmer, holding her breath in the cold waters seemingly forever while she stuffed the pearls into her pouch. Such an ability was a true Gift. Somehow that girl was familiar, but try as he might, he could name her not. Mayhap 'twas because she reminded him of the Battle Commander, but he knew for certain 'twas not Darque.

Still there was something very crucial about this Vision. Presenting as if 'twas of the utmost importance in the here and now, 'twas also laced with antiquity as would be Seen in an event of the past. He shook his head when he felt Chynnar's hand upon his shoulder. "She must know, Healer. Darque must hear this Vision." Chynnar stayed with the boy as he related the details, and taking careful notes as was her habit, she brushed his cheek with her knuckles when he could say no more, comforting him in the knowledge that he'd done his duty. Gazing up at her smiling face, he fell fast asleep.

CHAPTER FOUR

We Are One

Kelseacyr left Walkyr in Chynnar's care and returned to her adjacent study while the boy Seer related the details of his Vision. She was so close to a definitive answer. Having access these past winters to both pureblood Elf and Sprite living at the Keep, had helped her complete the puzzle. Working with the assistance of Synahmarr the Dragon Matriarch, and Corbyn the Raven, as well as Clan Healer Shayla who had lived since afore the Last Holocaust when she was a prominent physician working with DNA, also helped. After so much speculation, this last test should either confirm or deny… 'Twas truth!

Excitedly, she ran into the adjoining chamber of the clinic to share the news with Chynnar, who laughed aloud at her mentor's enthusiasm afore watching the Elven Skald race out of the clinic heading toward the Battle Commander's office to make report.

Chynnar just shook her head and walked out of the room leaving Walkyr to sleep, with Horace and Drys standing o'er his rack, and Fryya ever at his side. The elder Dog, Bullaga, ambled o'er to join the other two and laid down for a nap as Chynnar considered what to do. Returning to her research, she decided that if the Commander didn't show up soon on her usual rounds, she'd send Fryya to Darque with her notes of the Seer's Vision later.

Kelsey was so excited, she didn't even bother allowing the Standing Guard to announce her arrival, pushing past the burly Warrior and bursting through the heavy door into Darque's office, leaving the guard sputtering behind her. "WE ARE ONE!" she exclaimed breathlessly in her musical voice afore coming to a sudden halt, eyeing the Commander's other visitors. She could deny not, the high tension permeating the room. Something was very wrong. Backing down, both hands in the air with palms forward, her eyes wide and shoulders to her ears, Kelsey turned to leave, stammering softly, "Pardon my intrusion. I'll come back later."

Darque had shifted her attention from her other visitors to Kelsey when the Elf burst in and her eyes now fixed upon the guard stepping up behind the Skald who was backing into him. Just as he was about to lay hand upon her, his plan to forcibly remove the intruder, Darque gave a slight shake of her head to dismiss the disgruntled guard afore he could do such. The entire sequence of events was amusing but the situation was not. With a slight smile upon her face, she raised her hand to stop Kelsey's voluntary exit, stating, "No, we're near finished. Please, just sit down for a moment as we wrap this up. I know what you have to say is very important."

Kelsey took a deep breath and then sat in the huge wing-backed, leather upholstered, hand-carved Dragon chair usually positioned opposite Darque's desk, but which had been pushed to the bookshelves lining the far walls to accommodate her other visitors, all of whom were standing in a semi-circle 'round the Battle Commander.

As 'twas whenever she entered, she, as did the others, felt the slight sense of déjà vu at the copied furnishings in the Keep's office. Darque found it both a tribute to her father and comforting to herself to be in familiar surroundings when she worked at either location on any given day.

Standing in front of her desk, one hip hiked up to lean upon the edge of the hand-rubbed oak, Darque crossed her muscular arms o'er her chest. Without thinking, Kelsey glanced down at her own, much smaller figure, and frowned afore her eyes darted back up hoping that no one was looking her way. As she gazed from one to the next 'twas with considerable gratitude that she confirmed her self-scrutiny had gone unnoticed.

Shifting in her seat, Kelsey observed the others with rising interest. In front of Darque stood the Warrior Regynn. Of average height yet heavily muscled, with long shaggy blonde hair and a perpetual tan, he had a frown on his face, his own leather braced arms also crossed o'er his chest in a posture that spoke of defiance.

To Regynn's right stood Caleichante, her pale skin and almond-shaped eyes a'glow with a golden shimmer, her long snow-white hair pulled back in its classic single tail with a black criss-crossed leather strip, revealing sharply pointed ears.

Flanking Calei were the Sprite brothers, Ardryyn and Kryllyn, equally pale with blonde hair and green eyes. They all stood afore Darque; emotions intense from whatever they'd been discussing just prior to Kelsey's abrupt entry.

Then Darque took a deep breath and facing the Sprite trio, she stated, "You have your orders. Any questions?"

Calei answered for the three of them, her jaw set and obviously not happy. "None, Sir."

Sighing, Darque replied, "I know you want to return to your Team, Calei, but they shall have to make do without you for a while, as this new situation will require your presence elsewhere. Besides, the news you've brought has me far more concerned for you than for your Team. I'll send a Water Dragon to inform them about the change in plans." Without a pause, she'd Spoken to Gunnar to make that arrangement, while continuing, "Take whom you will and be safe in your journey. You must get to the Island of Dreams and find a solution afore 'tis too late." She took a moment as her gaze encompassed the three Sprites. "Report as soon as possible. Assure Lord Rohar that the Resistance forces will supply whatever support deemed necessary."

Gunnarr Responded to her request within a few moments, *"Pyth and Dyrth have agreed to take the message to King's Gate."*

"Good, thank you. They should leave immediately."

"They have already done so, my jewel."

Calei nodded but said nothing more. She had to agree. Though she'd returned to Drekinn Lair to make report to Darque on her Team's successful infiltration of King's Gate Village, they'd also made significant progress toward infiltrating Evanntyr Castle itself and she was eager to get back to them and to her lifemate, Graasyn. 'Twas a crucial time for the Team and they'd be exiting soon. She'd left him with his son, Bastyen, and her sister-by-vows, Diadranei, the Elf with powerful Empathy, one of only two Elves known to bear this type of Magic. The foursome were the most successful Stealth Team of the entire Resistance. Dia had Felt the Passing of Storrm last winter but they'd not been able to safely leave at that time and doing so would have changed nothing.

Calei had just managed to arrive the prior evening, Dancing her way through the Razor's Edge to Drekinn Lair. Discovering Darque was at the Keep, she'd also discovered her brethren, Ardryyn and Kryllyn. Requiring some respite from the journey, after sending word to the Battle Commander that she'd arrive by morning, she'd spent most of the night drinking with Regynn and the brothers as they relived their first meeting o'er fifty winters past.

During their evening, they'd accidentally made the disturbing discovery that there were three more barrels of poison left in the ship they'd scuttled on that past mission. The barrels must have been protected by a powerful Spell that prevented them from being seen afore they'd sunk the pirate ship, and now 'twas likely at its end and might already have begun to fail. The poison could be released at any time and they had to remove the barrels or neutralize them afore the Spell deteriorated enough to allow the seawater to reach the powder, activating the potent poison. The Island of Dreams and the Grotto housing thousands of Water Dragon eggs as they incubated, were in imminent danger once more.

Immediately after making this discovery, the three traveled swiftly to the Keep via Regynn's 'Bond, the big Green, Sydrayyah. Still feeling the effects of their raucous evening, the Sprites felt 'twas the better part of valor to simply ride, rather than Dance. But carrying all four riders made it impossible for Syd to use the native Magic of the Highlands to enlarge space to the point of moving the air 'round them, allowing them to fly so fast, 'twas as if using the mythical Magic of teleportation. Using the 'timefold' phenomenon, they'd have arrived within half a mark of their departure, but travel was slow without. Still, Sydrayyah was a very large Highland and she flew them with all haste. Arriving just a mark prior, here they stood.

Calei was disappointed with the order, but she saw the logic and the need. She could not be in two places at the same time. Accepting her mission she turned to leave, the brothers folding in and closing the heavy iron hinged and strapped oak door behind them.

Regynn stood unmoving, his eyes boring into Darque's. "I should be going on this mission. 'Twas my faulty memory that caused this mess."

Snorting at the very idea of him having a faulty memory, she then replied, "No Regynn, I need you here."

Unaware of her true line of thinking, he was insulted and questioned, "You don't think I'd survive, do you?"

Her sharp blue eyes flickered to the floor and back to the Warrior. "I DO need you here, but you must realize that Sydrayyah is not a Water Dragon and although you are still an excellent swimmer, you cannot swim into the deep, and you have no experience working there. Syd flies through the air, not through the sea. You would be without her assistance, working with Water Dragons that you knew not how to ride effectively, and with whom you could not Communicate. No, Regynn, this is a mission for the Sprites. The dangers they will soon face are not ones we can solve with our swords," and then referencing his vast knowledge and intellect, she finished, "nor with any logic."

Regynn started to respond, but then closed his mouth and looked quite contrite. Rubbing his chin, he replied, "You're correct. I'd be a hindrance."

Grimacing she replied, "Regynn, you could never be a hindrance, but you would certainly not be in your element. And as I said, I do need you here. I'll meet you in the Library within the mark." Concluding their discussion, her gaze swept toward Kelsey and back to the Warrior.

Darque watched as the Elder Warrior made his exit, knowing his thoughts were already upon his next project, assisting Master Tyrza to organize and catalog the vast library of the Keep, as well as praying he could help with her research. After what seemed marks to the Elf, Darque turned her full attention to Kelsey still sitting in the big leather chair.

As Kelsey stood up and walked toward the Battle Commander, her posture exuded her enthusiasm. Still, she felt compelled to apologize once again, for her rude and unexpected arrival. "I'm sorry, Darque, I was just so excited!"

Darque grinned as she pushed aside the weight of her orders and the deadly mission to which she'd just sent her friends. "You've done it, then?"

"WE'VE done it! I could not have managed alone. I had much assistance," she stated while nodding her head, her long spiral curls bouncing, giving credit to all those who'd helped her achieve this scientific success. "Yes. We've determined the link 'tween the Sprites and the Elves." Nodding her head, she continued, "I completed the last test just a half mark past. 'Tis conclusive. We are one Race, Darque! Not cousins, not different in any way! Well, except for our coloring, the Elves all dark-haired and dark-eyed and the Sprites all fair. No doubt isolation from each other for so long has maintained that. And there's our opposing affinities for the light of the sun and the dark of the night, which I believe to be a learned behavior. But in every way, we have determined the Sprites and Elves are one people!"

Darque was just as happy for Kelsey, as was Kelsey for her success. Shifting her weight so that she now sat fully on the edge of the broad work desk, she placed her hands on either side of her hips, swinging her booted feet softly, creating a firm tapping rhythm that she oft' times found helpful to her concentration. She'd need to recall Calei and have her include the notification to Lord Rohar and decide whom to send word of the breakthrough information to Queen Alyssa of the Elven Nation in the Wyrdritch.

Then she frowned and furrowed her brows as a stray thought suddenly occurred to her and 'twas perplexing. Thinking about the scrawny adolescent, Flyrra, with her odd features and sparkling silver hair, she found herself still staring at the now bewildered Elf. Voicing her puzzlement, she began, "Kelsey, if the Sprites and Elves are one Race, then Flyrra cannot be considered of mixed blood as she was conceived by rape of her Sprite mother by an Elf in allegiance to the Hoard. Yet we know she's a half-breed." Darque considered her own thoughts. Mayhap the mix of genes for fair and dark hair and eyes? No. There was more to this story than they yet knew. "So, what other Race is in the mix to have created such extreme features and coloring?"

After less than a quarter mark of discussion of this phenomenon, Kelsey left the Battle Commander with a new research project, while the Battle Commander steered herself toward the library to set Regynn upon his.

<div align="center">~~~~~ BACK IN THE WARD ~~~~~</div>

Captain Natanamia finished cleaning up and headed to the Mess Hall. Even though Tiyya and Thorrn were thankful for her suggestions during training, her thoughts were not with the Warriors this morning and for that, she felt guilty. She should have been paying more attention. If only she could tell them why she was so distracted. 'Twas something about the look in Tiyya's eyes, the grip she used upon the hilt of her sword, switching fluidly from either hand to a slip and spin as needed. 'Twas poetry in motion. That one was well on her way back to level. The Human was tougher than she thought. 'Twas so like another she knew and had trained.

She wondered where her First Mate was now and if Aiisabeau had succeeded in her mission. Of course, 'twas a lose-lose situation no matter the outcome, so how would her success be measured with such a task? Furrowing her brows, she absentmindedly rubbed the fresh bruise on her left bicep. Served her right for being slow to react.

Although her Sprite team knew of their friend's departure afore they arrived at the Keep, they knew not the reason why. As far as she knew, aside from herself and Aiisabeau, only Lord Rohar and Corbyn the Raven were aware of the undertaking. Such had been her first major command decision. 'Twas dangerous but 'tween her and Corbyn, just as necessary and could only be done alone. A solitary infiltrator might succeed where more would fail miserably. She shook her head. Even with the battles she'd commanded since, Aiisabeau could end up being the first person she'd sent to their death.

Natanamia's thoughts drifted as she continued walking toward the Mess Hall. It seemed as yesterday, had o'er two winters already passed? She'd been placed in command of a seven-member team to travel to the Keep of St Swiftyn's to ally with Darque and the Resistance. However, shortly after making landfall upon the mainland, the tall outspoken Sprite whom she'd named her First Mate, sat down beside her at the fire. A surprise visitor, Corbyn the Fay, was perched upon her shoulder in his preferred Shift as the Raven, his beady black eyes a'glimmer. In his beak were two rolled parchments, which he gave to Aiisabeau. Without a word, she handed Natan the parchment with her name upon it, bearing the seal of Lord Rohar, tucking the other into the pouch at her waistband. That one must be handed o'er to someone else.

Natan had been puzzled but once she broke the seal and read the words therein, puzzlement turned to shock. Aiisabeau had been ordered to a separate and most clandestine mission. Alone she would travel, and alone she would live, facing immense hardship and personal danger while trying to fulfill those orders.

Corbyn had contacted Aiisabeau upon his arrival less than a quarter mark prior with the parchments he'd received from Lord Rohar and told her just enough to allow her to prepare for her departure that night. She was already packed and well-armed as usual. Natanamia kept her expression carefully neutral as she handed the orders to her First Mate, observing quietly while she read them. Warned to remain silent, Aiisabeau finished reading, tossed the parchment into the fire and watched as it burned to ash. Then she nodded with a reassuring smile to her Captain and took her leave into the darkness as Corbyn flew away in the opposite direction to who knew where.

Natanamia could have cancelled the orders, she was in command, 'twas her team, and they were officially outside the Lord's influence at that time, traveling to give their allegiance to the Resistance. But she could sense her friend's excitement and not only did Natanamia deem the mission most important, she knew the outspoken Sprite was perfect for the task.

She passed someone in the hallway and afore she knew it, brushed up against his shoulder. Not even aware of whom she'd just jostled, she mumbled an apology and continued walking and thinking. The fact that Lord Rohar had not sent a roster of her team to Darque, now made sense. Eight Elite Sprite Guardsmen left the island and within the moon seven arrived at the Keep. No one said a word. As of the moment her team were made aware of Aiisabeau's abrupt departure, 'twas as if she'd never existed.

Natan smirked. Princess Anastasia would be proud of her. Such decisions were not quite as difficult as she'd originally thought, however, melancholic moments like this one made her wonder about her coping skills. She needed to forget about what she could not control and do a better job with what she could. Darque made such decisions every day, only the Battle Commander did so on a much broader scale. How did she cope?

Natanamia removed the hair picks and allowed her thick blonde hair to fall down her back as she rounded the corner and entered the Mess Hall. Looking for Kayarr, she speculated as to when she would hear something, anything, about her First Mate and good friend. O'er two winters. Was Aiisabeau still this side of the Veil?

CHAPTER FIVE

A Sprite In The Wyrdritch

DEEP IN THE FOREST OUTSIDE OF HAVEN

~~~~~ A SECLUDED CLEARING ~~~~~

'Twas early Fall and the leaves were turning. Surrounded by brilliant oranges, yellows, reds, golds, and browns, painted against the lush background of the evergreens in the forest, would be breathtaking for most, but Coltyn had no eye for such beauty.

His baby-faced features denying the fact that he'd recently gathered eleven winters, Coltyn faked a missed sidestep and ducked as if stumbling, avoiding the expected incoming swing. Immediately, the youngest Elven Prince, tall for his winters, lean, brown-haired, and brown-eyed, took a firmer grip upon the hilt of his short sword and made an awkward jab toward his opponent, who easily blocked and then flipped the boy's weapon out of his right hand. Smoothly, Coltyn drew his dagger with his left hand as he watched his sword fly away with an equally faked surprised expression on his face, then completed the rightward turn and stepped forward again, shifting his weight quickly to thrust the dagger toward the tall Sprite who was his Trainer. Blocking this newly brandished weapon as easily as she had his sword, he caught the smirk on her face. At least he had the sequence. However his timing was a tad off, and he was worried.

Crouched o'er, his hands on his knees and panting from the afternoon's workout, Coltyn looked to his Trainer seeking approval of the moves they'd practiced all afternoon. Even though he had yet to reach age, sometimes when he looked at the tall blonde he wished he were a few winters older, as did most of his friends. But he knew Aiisabeau would only laugh if he'd admitted to such, calling it exactly what 'twas: a childhood infatuation. Mayhap 'twas her pale hair and blue eyes, giving her an exotic appearance, that made her so alluring. Nonetheless, although she was mysteriously attractive, he knew the difference 'tween lust and love and could never think of her like that anyway, for he held much respect for her, along with much admiration of her skills. Waiting for her to make a comment, any comment, he shook his head to regain his focus and blurted his own assessment of his performance. "I missed my stab. I was too slow."

Aiisabeau's voice held no condemnation, only encouragement, as she flashed a brilliant smile. Coltyn was growing so fast! The fact that he was now near her own height, gave her hope that the plan would work. But 'twas still dangerous. As was the situation. Even so, she could see no other option. "You've done well today, my Prince. Nevertheless, 'tis not our goal to acquire injury and 'twill be the result if we continue training with such fatigue. I think 'tis time to clean up for evening meal."

He frowned, a tangled string of questions spewing forth. "But what if I need this tonight? What if he doesn't wait? What if he finds out they're coming?"

Aiisabeau's smile faded as she glanced to the ground to quickly gather her thoughts. Looking back to the boy she stated, "If such occurs, we do what is needed, when 'tis needed, and depend on Battle Lust to fuel our strength." She suspected the next attempt would come just prior to the arrival of their visitors, due any time now. 'Twas clearly what Coltyn was thinking as well. "You will do fine," she said reassuringly as she winked at the handsome boy and then reached forth and ruffled his shaggy hair, dripping with sweat, cut to shoulder length, and layered away from his youthful face as per his personal preferences. He claimed that having longer hair like that of his brothers, got in the way of his training. And he took his training very seriously. She could have asked not for a better student.

The series of moves she'd been teaching him o'er the past sennight, were exacting and purposeful. For this to have any chance of success Coltyn must perform them with flawless timing. After endless marks of observations to learn the favored techniques of the likely suspects, she'd chosen this path and this maneuver. Coltyn would be facing the sword of a far more experienced and taller opponent near twice his weight, and nothing but a feint would succeed. But her concerns were not so much for his performance as they were for the unknown factors.

Which one was the spy? From the past attempt, she'd deduced his plan was not to kill the boy but to take him as an offering to the Black. Nevertheless, if that plan had changed with the difficulty they'd encountered, the spy may now be ready to sacrifice the boy himself. And if Coltyn were truly surprised by his identity and hesitated, 'twould be disastrous. Should she tell him more of her plan?

With resignation in his voice, he replied, "Aiisabeau? I will not falter. I understand whom you suspect, as I've had my own suspicions since he tried to take me. Although I could see him not, it could only have been one of the Guard. And that means, 'twas likely one of my brothers."

Making her decision she firmly responded, "I've chosen this maneuver because I believe he will attack when we are alone, so that no matter the outcome, I will be charged as the spy. This maneuver will allow you to avoid killing and to provide adequate distraction so I can rescue you, setting up the plan. Our word alone will not convince the Council and mayhap not even the Queen if 'tis one of the Princes. I am still doubted, held in low regard by many, and you are the youngest of the royal family. Although I want to avoid him taking you, our only chance is if we can make him reveal himself. This encounter is expected, but if it goes awry, you cannot hesitate. Even if you must force him Past the Veil. For if need arise and you do not, he WILL force YOU Past."

Nodding, the boy's expression was all business. "This is war. I understand. I can and will do what I must," Coltyn responded just as firmly, but his eyes shifted focus to the ground at her feet, as he fingered his dagger nervously.

Aiisabeau placed her hand upon his arm and waited for his gaze to meet hers again. Softly, she stated, "You are young, and 'tis the worst betrayal we fight against. You don't have to like it; you just have to do it. For yourself, your family, your Queen, and your Nation."

Taking a deep breath, the boy pulled back his square shoulders and looked her straight in the eye, responding clearly and with resolve, "I can. And I will."

Aiisabeau hoped he would not be forced to such at his age, but it could happen. She thought about the past winters and how things had come to this. Arriving at the Wyrdritch with her orders, she'd presented them to Alyssa in front of the Council. The Queen took the scroll, unsealed it, and read silently, her expression skeptical at best.

Soon after King Jeeryd died, Alyssa had discovered evidence to suggest there was someone else in contact with the Sorcerer, the evil necromancer of the Black and his Hoard, and then someone had attempted to kidnap Coltyn. Since she had no solid proof, she'd tried to keep the attempt 'tween herself and the boy, and without anyone's knowledge or approval, secretly appealed to Corbyn the Raven. His response was for her to keep close watch and that he would send help.

The beautiful Sprite warrior was not exactly the 'help' she'd expected. However, quickly realizing 'twas a brilliant strategy she announced that Aiisabeau had come as Ambassador from Lord Rohar to learn and teach, assisting the two Nations to understand each other so they'd be better prepared for the Reunion, as well as to prepare the way for the Royal visit within the next two winters.

Alyssa had always suspected that someone in her castle had been helping the mad king Jeeryd afore he died, and within a few short moons that someone began to undermine her leadership, threatening her rule as well as her family. She'd heard rumors and there'd been increasing occurrences, but none as despicable as the attempted kidnapping, making her fear for their very lives. Which was why she'd delayed the Call to Return. There was a spy in Haven, and no one was safe 'til that one was identified and neutralized.

Shortly after her arrival, Aiisabeau was given the position as Coltyn's Trainer, for all his brothers still at Haven, Thyrazin, Fyrdien, Irylane, Beralarr, Enlyrod, Dyrachin, and Englyrim, were in the Queen's Guard. Thyrazin had since become Captain, a position that involved more traveling than the others, complaining that this prevented him from identifying the spy within their ranks. And he was not happy about having to monitor a Sprite in their midst. He was not certain that Aiisabeau was not involved, and rumors abounded. As Captain of the Queen's Guard, he was obliged to protect her, but he liked it not. To ease his misgivings, the Queen reminded her Captain that having Aiisabeau as Coltyn's Trainer would keep her under tight scrutiny. Thyrazin also was not certain he trusted his brothers while he was gone, so he made any outside trips as short and as random as possible. The claims that the attempt to kidnap Coltyn had been orchestrated from within had made his blood boil and he'd given his vow to the Queen that he would be the one to ferret out and neutralize the spy.

Smiling once more, the boy nodded his head and grabbed his gear to follow Aiisabeau back to Haven from the surrounding woods where they'd been working in secret. 'Twould not do for their training to be observed. Dancing swiftly, they both reached the castle at the same time, afore going their separate ways to clean up.

KING'S GATE VILLAGE

ALONG THE SOUTHERN SLIPPES OF THE RAZOR'S EDGE

~~~~~ **EVANNTYR CASTLE** ~~~~~

</div>

Head back and eyes closed, the Sorcerer ran his fingers through his hair ensuring 'twas rinsed clean as he stood naked, his softening middle aged body drenched by the buckets of wa-
~~~~~

ter pouring down from above. He could yet swing sword with the best, however, a fact of which he was quite proud.

He'd just returned to the castle from a most interesting and mayhap productive rendezvous. The request for his audience had been long coming yet still something of a surprise as he'd heard nothing from the Wyrdritch since it disappeared after the Last Holocaust. Nothing 'til just last winter.

Unsure of the intent of the self-described Hoard spy, the Sorcerer had delayed the meeting for many moons. 'Twas intriguing to believe that he yet had a grip upon the Elven Nation, no longer through Jeeryd but through his son, whom he'd met afore they'd been silenced at the time of the devastation. This boy had been the only one of his brood whom Jeeryd trusted to be his liaison with the Hoard. After all, 'twas most difficult to do everything one's self, and for the new King to remain unchallenged required occasional assistance.

Through the many winters of their past arrangement, the boy had been sent alone by the father several times, to deliver information and to seek guidance as well as support. 'Twas in fact eye opening as 'twas soon revealed that Jeeryd had no real taste for what he must do once he got what he wanted: the crown and the hand of Bryanna. The boy had felt the wrath of the Sorcerer but was pitied and not truly punished. 'Twas then that the boy's future desires were made clear by his actions, even to the point of his willingness to betray his father if asked to do so.

'Twas interesting that the disappearance of the Wyrdritch occurred just afore the Black intended to conquer the Elven Nation, using this boy to gain entry. Such an event saved Jeeryd and his people from the Hoard's rightful dominance. However, the boy's former loyalties had remained in the back of the Sorcerer's mind.

Just how tight a grip did he have? Jeeryd had been a useful tool but not particularly intelligent, which served the Sorcerer's purposes at the time. But the light of ambition beyond being King, shone in the boy's eyes upon their initial meeting, and faded not through all those following. 'Twas not just greed as was in the heart of his father, but true motivation to climb higher into the hierarchy of the Hoard, where Jeeryd cared not and would not.

Standing perfectly still under the pouring water, the Sorcerer considered the information he'd obtained from the recent meeting. When he'd asked about the reason behind the lengthy silence of the Elven Nation, he'd felt no subterfuge. But instead of revealing what had happened to the Wyrdritch, the boy blamed Jeeryd's insanity. Still, the Sorcerer knew for a fact that the Wyrdritch had seemingly ceased to exist and after the boy made his initial contact, he'd sent his own minions to search for it again, to no avail. The Wyrdritch still could not be found.

Obviously, the Elf kept secrets, which to the Sorcerer equated to lies. But such was to be expected in any negotiation. 'Twould do nothing but alienate the Elven Prince to argue or insist upon more information afore he was ready to give it. He had to impress his power upon the young man and ensure his loyalties were to the Sorcerer alone. He would not suffer another shallow-minded fool like his father. However, with no other option available, if he wanted to control the Elven Nation he must foster this contact for the time being.

The Elf had told him many things, despite nothing about the disappearance. The Sorcerer suspected 'twas some kind of new Protection Spell, for he continued to believe that the Lairs of the Resistance survived, even though they too, could not be found. The situations were just too similar.

Nevertheless, if he had to gain knowledge through deception 'twould not be difficult, for deception was his forte. So when the Elf told him that Bryanna had died and Jeeryd took another Queen, adding two more to the royal brood, he was cautious. The youngest Prince would have gathered eleven winters by now. After their relatively brief discussion, the Sorcerer had steered toward a compromise. He would believe the Prince if he brought him a live sacrifice.

The corners of the Sorcerer's mouth had lifted a tad and his eyes narrowed at the slight display of astonishment he'd felt emanating from the Elf upon this suggestion. He knew the Elf had killed afore, to help his father keep the crown, but thus far, not one of his own. The Sorcerer pushed further. "Your youngest brother shall be the proof of your loyalty. Bring me Prince Coltyn. Alive."

The Elf's emotions disappeared behind a mask of his own creation and simply nodding, he then stated eloquently, "As you will," afore taking his leave.

The Sorcerer's choice of sacrificial lamb was twofold. The youngest was likely the most precious to the new Queen and she would do anything to get him back. This had been the Sorcerer's experience with mothers throughout the ages. Once he had the Queen in his pocket, he'd no longer need her stepson.

And there was the fact that the blood of an Elven Prince was most powerful in conjures and Spells. He was still trying to draw the spirit of Battle Commander Grifynn away from Aalanna, his lifemate and anchor at the Keep. Nothing thus far had allowed such. And many times he'd tried unsuccessfully to capture the Heir Apparent, Myrrdin. If this Elven Prince failed to produce his little brother, 'twas no matter. The Sorcerer had no problem with using the blood of this Prince.

"Enough," he said, and the water stopped pouring. His blinded assistants helped properly dry and then dress him, afore returning to clean up as the Sorcerer carefully replaced his hood upon his head. His assistants could never reveal what they could not see, but they could and did provide him with the shower he enjoyed daily, the buckets of heated water poured gently o'er him as he stood in the privacy of his chambers. He'd blinded them himself. One did not need one's eyes for such chores. And the fear that he would do worse to them if they failed him, kept them perfectly aligned with the Sorcerer's demands.

Gazing in the mirror o'er the chest of drawers in the corner, he ensured his thinning, iron-gray hair was tucked away from prying eyes. 'Twould never do for others to note that silver sparkle that appeared at random moments. He'd hoped by the time his hair had completed its change from dark brown to gray, that the sparkle effect would be eliminated. But no such luck. And no amount of Magical intervention had dimmed that annoying effect for long (besides the fact that such took up an enormous amount of energy he would rather use elsewhere).

He'd oft' times speculated about why the purebloods with whom he'd been raised did not show such, along with wondering why he'd shown any aging at all. His half-brothers still looked near as young as they did when they'd come of age as did most others of Magic bearing bloodlines. He sneered in self-loathing. Another reason to believe half breeds were weaker and more inferior.

But then there was the other half breed he knew personally. Very personally. Not only had she shown no such signs of aging the last time he'd seen her, but she knew nothing of her own bloodline. Why was that? Magic bearer blood should show itself early in life, as did his own. But since the war began he'd heard many stories of those who'd only now discovered they shared the blood of another Race without prior knowledge of same. He had to suppose 'twas something to do with the power of the Magic bearer parent. No, more likely 'twas the inferiority of the other parent.

But he honestly knew not, and since one could not choose one's parents, 'twas not his fault. However, such reminders still angered him and grumbling to himself, he left his chambers and began the short trek toward the dungeons where he could vent that anger on one of the hapless peasants held there, all caught in some minor offense or other.

His mind filled with intense hatred toward his half breed past collaborator and with plans to find her wherever she had taken refuge, he abruptly noted the passing of the new weapons crafters from the village, being escorted by the guard down the hallway to their scheduled audience with High King Shytin. His lip curled with intense distrust. His intuition told him that those men and their females were more than they pretended to be, but if using glamour to conceal their true lineage, 'twas most powerful. Scowling, he continued to the dungeons, but in the back of his mind he was already making plans to find out more about these merchants.

THE ISLAND OF DREAMS
~~~~~ NEAR THE NORTHERN CLIFFS~~~~~

</div>

'Twas early Fall and that meant they must finish harvesting their summer crops, leaving only the gourds and a variety of squash and pumpkins to fully ripen afore being brought inside. 'Twould be turning cold soon and they'd need more wood, but the Sprite was confident they'd have enough and with plenty of time to spare.

The toddler struggled to pull the carrot from the well-maintained and orderly garden row. Leahnyah laughed when she watched the little girl finally succeed in not only pulling the stubborn vegetable but falling backwards on her butt. With her arms and legs flailing, she had the funniest expression of shock plastered upon her pretty face. Then the girl smiled, which only made her more adorable, and keeping a firm grip on her carrot, she clapped her chubby hands. Rolling o'er with determination, she set her feet wide, her hands pushing in the dirt to help her balance so she could stand up, afore she brought the carrot to the only mother she'd ever known.

The Elder Skald of the Sprites squinted as she thought about the girl. She had only recently gathered a single winter, yet 'twas as if she were near three times that age. Again, she realized how lucky the child was that Leahnyah lived such a solitary, reclusive existence in one of the least populated portions of the northern region of the Island of Dreams. The Skald had retired to this place many winters past. In her youth she'd practiced the medici-
~~~~~

nal arts near Dream Hold in the southernmost tip of the island, where they would not have been able to hide.

And she reminded herself how lucky she was to have been given this chance at her age. Having spent her entire span of days treating the poor and the rich, peasants, mariners, guardsmen, and royal family members alike, she'd never seemed to find the time to settle down and have her own family. Though she enjoyed the solitude of her retirement, 'twas at times lonely.

When Islyth, Lord Myrrdin's Water Dragon Tie, showed up one day with a newborn tied to her chest by way of a bloody leather shirt, she'd asked not why, how, or from where. She'd simply taken the baby and began to raise her as her own. Near nine moons after the baby arrived so had Lord Myrrdin to make an explanation of sorts and to leave a bag of gems that would fund her and the baby's upkeep for a full span of days.

Thus far, she'd spent not a single gem of her fortune. She had no need. Leahnyah was still a good hunter, trapper, and gardener, as well as a skilled survivalist, and she was enjoying teaching her 'daughter' these skills. In her youth she'd been a good warrior and Myrrdin had impressed upon her that the child would need those skills as well. Nevertheless, 'twas Leahnyah's thinking that the baby would also need a stake when she eventually struck out on her own, which was inevitable whether she herself were still alive or not. And so the bag of gems remained untouched.

The Skald had named the child Leah, after her own mother, but 'twas not her given name. That had to remain a secret, as did her very existence. If word of her survival leaked, Leah would be hunted. She smiled as Leah handed her the carrot, which was near as long as her little arm, brushed the dirt off her hands then turned about deliberately and marched back to the next carrot in the row, to begin the whole process once more.

The unexpected flash of silver momentarily blinded the Skald, making her blink her watering eyes. As the little girl continued waddling away, she peered at Leah's full head of shoulder length, curly red hair, and furrowed her brows. There seemed nothing out of the ordinary now. Must have been the shifting sunlight catching her hair at just the right angle.

She chewed the inside of her cheek as she mused. Leah was of mixed blood, that much she knew for certain. As of now, she knew of no other tri-bloods in the world. And of course there could be no other ever, with this child's combination of Dragon, Human, and Fay, for having the blood of the Dragon came from an alteration of her Human mother's DNA, not from a mating. Dragon and Man were known to have mated but could not procreate. There were but three known to be in existence who carried such a bloodline: this child's mother was Past the Veil and another was mated to a Dragon but of course could not reproduce unless she did so with a Human, which was not likely since their mating was a lifelong commitment. However, there was the third...

She sighed. Just because one carried mixed blood, did not give one any Magical ability. That was up to the Fates themselves. And some didn't show their Gifts 'til later in life, or even lost what they'd started out with, as they came of age. She'd noted not a single event thus far, to indicate Leah had any Magic bearer blood, except for the 'tell' of the Fay: the occasional lightning like flashes in her eyes, along with her rapid growth and delicately pointed ears, which were not so sharp that she could not pass as Human. In fact, the child was becoming the mirror image of her Warrior mother.

The little girl looked to Leahnyah expectantly afore attempting to pull another carrot. Smiling and nodding approval of Leah's choice, the child's face brightened and then with her blue eyes focused upon the task once more, the Skald continued to ponder. Myrrdin had warned that if the baby began to show Magical abilities, Leahnyah was to do her best to keep it under control. She would have to teach the child how to handle whatever came, alone. No mentor could be called upon. There could be no one else involved in her upbringing, for the danger to them both was far too great.

Nonetheless, the child had grown fast in the womb and was continuing to do so, and such would make it less likely that anyone would believe she was who she was even now. Mayhap her aging process was a gift of the Fates or mayhap the gods themselves, helping Leahnyah keep her safe, and in her Healer opinion, would stop once she came of age, if not sooner, allowing the child to begin a more normal aging process.

'Twas a shame Leah's mother had been forced Past the Veil in battle. Ahh, the ravages of war. Sighing again, the elder Skald stood from her bench at the edge of the garden, picked up their full harvest basket with a bit of effort, and called the child to come with her inside. There was much left to do afore dusk.

CHAPTER SIX

The Search Begins

~~~~~ THE KEEP ~~~~~

Entering the library, Darque soon located Regynn standing at one of several massive central worktables covered with large piles of scrolls, books, parchments, and all manner of things, spilling onto the hand tied rug o'er the stone flooring. The big Warrior had a grin of pure delight upon his face, as he surveyed what Darque would have described as little more than a big mess. Although Regynn was a highly skilled fighter both brave and sure, 'twas in the use of his equally impressive intellect that he truly shined. Having taken on the position of Clan Historian upon his retirement from active duty many winters past, he'd become one of Darque's most valued advisors.

Waiting a few moments for his attention, she finally stated impatiently, "I'm here."

"Huh?" he questioned while shifting his focus, his eyes ultimately resting upon the Commander. With sudden clarity and raised brows he exclaimed, "OH!" And then just as suddenly his brows furrowed as he asked, "What was it you wanted me to do?"

To ensure his full attention she steered him to the clearest space available, a relatively small table off to the side which only had a few piles of parchments upon its gleaming hand-rubbed wooden surface. Pulling out the two nearest stools, they sat and Darque began to brief him on his next investigation. "Tell me what you know of the Fangs of Solvyngarr."

His facial expression made him seem distant as he sorted and restacked the parchments, giving them a little more space. Darque knew him well enough to remain quiet as the moments dragged by 'til the Warrior eventually leaned one thick forearm upon the table, his hazel eyes now locked to hers as he began. "I've
~~~~~

been researching this since last winter and I've found some interesting information, but nothing that can be considered to be factual. 'Tis said there were originally four of the Fangs, forged in Flight of Fire Keep of the Highlands, in the depths of Fire Heart Mountain. But these were no ordinary blades, for the rumors suggest they were the actual fangs of the Mighty Solvyngarr, removed himself, given to Darque Abriya D'Rienne, his LifeBond and lifemate, in a daring move to allow him to escape the clutches of their captors by slipping into the Void and leaving her on this side of the Veil. His sudden and violent disappearance would lead their enemies to believe he'd managed to sneak past them, causing much chaos. Their situation was dire and Solvyngarr could not get out through any ordinary means, but without him, she could, and using this to their advantage she was able to get out and complete their mission. The Fangs were to be his lifeline once the task was done. She was to forge the blades from them using the Magic they Shared, and then in a conjuring ceremony, draw him back to her through their 'Bond." His eyes now gleamed with moisture as 'twas a highly emotional tale for one in the 'Bond, knowing the ties that bound them were unbreakable and being torn apart in such a manner would have been devastating.

Swallowing hard, as did Darque herself, he continued, his voice low and ominous, "But something went wrong. She was unsuccessful in her attempt to draw him back from the Void and I have a theory as to why. Knowing how the 'Bond works, that even when Darque Abriya was Past the Veil and they were still apart and knowing Solvyngarr was the 7th son of a 7th son, I believe Sol slipped mistakenly into the Otherworld instead of the Void. Although he would not have understood this at the time, 'twould have been the only place he could go without taking her, even with his powerful Magic, despite the abilities of a Highland. And then there were delays along with the actual escape, the travel to Fire Heart, the forging, the ceremony. Yet another factor with the shearing of the LifeBond in such a manner would be that Darque

Abriya would've grown weaker. And although very slowly, she began to age as soon as he disappeared, making her not the same person she was when they were separated. Once she failed to draw him from the Void, where he was not, they were doomed to be apart forever."

A sad silence hung 'tween them for several long breaths afore Darque responded. "The Otherworld. Of course. The Healers of the People of the Razor's Edge, the Daggogh, use some kind of potion to allow them in, but 'tis always a dangerous journey, not for the naive." Sadly, she recalled what happened to Mikkal, her friend and fellow Warrior, who'd accidentally slipped into the Otherworld with disastrous results. Lifting her chin, she pushed those thoughts back and continued with the current discussion. "I've always wondered why they were not able to join again once she was Past the Veil. 'Tis so simple. If she'd known then where he was, mayhap she'd have been successful."

Circumspectly, Regynn replied, "'Tis not likely, as she would not have had the strength to perform the conjure by the time she made the attempt. You and I both know how hard 'tis on us when we are separated, and how much harder it gets the longer we are so. Recall how difficult 'twas when your mother drew forth the spirit of Grifynn, and Aalanna had everything required for that process. Still 'tis only a theory but I agree: if he'd been alive and stuck in the Void waiting for her to Pass, then in the 'Bond he'd also have Passed which should have reunited them, thus strengthening my theory substantially."

Considering all this information, Darque then proceeded to lay out the task she had in mind. Discussing the Fangs for half a mark, she concluded, "They must be found, for their purpose is multi-fold. Not only will they free Darque Abriya and Solvyngarr from their a'cursed separation, but we can then proceed to use them to open the Book of the Conqueror which will release the Rashei from Koryl's curse which will then open the door of Shahanalaa. If we can't do this, we lose out on a most powerful ally AND we will be hard-pressed to feed our growing population in safety from the Hoard."

The mystics known as the Witch Women of Kadoor who once lived in the Keep of St Swiftyn's had been cursed to another existence, roaming the Keep as spirits who seemed to have no knowledge of their own plight nor the ability to communicate with each other or others of their own kind. 'Twas a tragic non-existence to which they'd been suddenly pushed, their entire population disappearing in the blink of an eye. The spirits and the unexpected abandonment of the Keep o'er half a century past led to many rumors, myths, and fears 'til Darque and the Resistance took up residence and soon thereafter, made the shocking discovery.

Breaking through her drifting thoughts, Regynn asked, "You still have one of the Fangs in your possession, correct?"

His voice brought her back to the present as she replied. "Yes. And I gave one to Fryya afore the Battle of Ice Mist Falls, and one to Aalanna at Evanntyr," she grimaced in disgust afore continuing, "when I had to leave her there alone, to be rescued by another." The memories of the battles to which she'd raced with Storrm at her side, near brought tears to her eyes for many reasons, but she swallowed them back again.

Regynn's brows furrowed. "That's only three. What did you do with the other?"

"The other?" Darque's expression flowed from confusion to determination as she recalled the first blade she'd lost. 'Twas during their first kill, the Hoard Dragon relentless in his attack. Gunnarr held steady in flight as she'd leaped off his shoulders to land on the shoulders of their enemy, climbing laboriously amid defensive flying maneuvers, savage fighting, and showers of blood, to plunge the blade repeatedly into the Dragon's eye to slow his Healing, allowing Gunnarr to finish the kill after she'd leaped back aboard, losing the blade in the process. Returning to the scene of the battle the next day, the blade was nowhere to be found and she knew not what had happened to it. "Yes. That one will be the most difficult to locate. But mayhap in the end, not the most difficult to retrieve. One can but hope."

Cracking his knuckles and nodding his head while he pondered, his shaggy hair pulled back in a classic tail secured with a thin brown leather strip, Regynn asked, "That was in the Battle of Kaddart, when you rescued Fryya, was it not?"

Thoughtfully, she replied, "Why yes, 'twas."

"Who else knew how that blade was lost?"

Darque's mind drifted back past shadowy and painful memories, to the battle. Biting her bottom lip, she recalled a discussion with her father. He'd sent another Team to investigate after she and Gunnarr had returned, leaving her out of the mission. At the time she'd thought it quite inappropriate and was angered. As Second in Command she should have led that mission and felt that such action meant he'd been disappointed in her failure to uncover evidence of High King Shytin's role in the massacre, as well as her failure to recover her missing blade.

Grifynn had given the Fangs to her as a gift upon taking the LifeBond. Mayhap he knew something that could help thcm now. His spirit resided in the main Altar Room of the Keep, where Aalanna had completed his conjure and was now his anchor to this side of the Veil. Although just a spirit, Aalanna could see him and speak with him but could not touch him and Grifynn could not return Beyond 'til the Sorcerer was destroyed, as he was ever vulnerable now. If the Black's necromancer were successful in snatching him away from Aalanna, his spirit would be enslaved, forced to assist the Hoard against Darque and the Resistance.

As Darque got up to leave, Regynn was already deep in thought. Knowing the task was in good hands she shrugged her shoulders and left without saying a word. Regynn wouldn't have noticed anyway.

FLIGHT OF FIRE KEEP

IN THE MIDDLE OF THE OCEAN KNOWN

AS THE DRAGON'S TEARS

~~~~~ **HOME OF THE HIGHLANDS** ~~~~~

The Dragon Matriarch, Synahmarr, her russet scales a'shimmer, stood once again outside the nursery sands, peering intently at each one of her thirteen eggs. Laid o'er two winters past, the largest batch of eggs known to Memory, she'd thought the biggest one, which had rolled itself 'cross the sands to the far wall and then ceased moving, there to remain to this day, would have hatched by now. Were they the Black's as was her Memory of his Claiming? She'd been held captive for so long, rescued by Darque and her aunt Maahayyel when she successfully passed her rule, but by so doing the Last Dragon Matriarch lost her life with the energies produced to fuel those events.

Corbyn the Raven had finally convinced Synahmarr to lay the eggs she'd known she'd borne, reassuring her that the Memory of the Claiming was false, an alteration by the Sorcerer after they'd discovered their plans went awry and someone else had already Claimed the Princess. 'Twas believed that Dragons only bore eggs with their lifemates, but she'd been unable to escape at that time and with her altered Memory, she knew not to whom she was mated. If Corbyn were correct, her lifemate was either Past the Veil by now or mayhap still out there somewhere, unable, or unwilling, to come to her.

Listening closely, Synahmarr heard naught, no shell cracking, no internal rustling, no Voices through the Link. Apart from the one repositioning itself, her children had been immobile and silent since being laid. Mayhap they were not viable after all. She'd avoided laying for so many centuries, refusing to do so in captivity, and then she'd thought the worst…

She cocked her great head at the Message. Taniyyah had finally arrived. But she was without her LifeBond, Thorrn. Tan's request for audience near a sennight past, was urgent and yet mysterious. Why was she alone?

"Come," Syn said quietly to her ever-present Human companion and liaison from the Resistance, the tall flaxen-haired
~~~~~

Warrior Mynx. Though they shared not the 'Bond, their history together forged a special Link that closely resembled such and Syn was positive if they ever participated in the ceremony, they were sure to take. This one Human knew more about her than she knew about herself, for she'd been with her since afore her escape from Evanntyr, when she was so weakened from her self-induced stasis, she hardly knew who she was, let alone what was going on 'round her. Mynx was credited with not only saving Syn's life but with alerting the Mighty Maahayyel to her niece's status and whereabouts, making that rescue and the passing of the Matriarchy possible. Syn considered the girl to be her best friend and closest confidant, and the feeling was mutual.

Mynx was assigned the post shortly after her twin brother, Mace, Passed the Veil in his attempt to LifeBond with Maddokyn. The Magic was powerful and dangerous, and everyone knew the risks. This time the Warrior's Blood Call went Beyond to a Dragon who had died previously in battle and therefore could not cross through the Veil as more than a spirit, which would have rejected the LifeBond and Mace would have died. They were at a stalemate for Mace could not cross to her without dying, and if he'd backed down from the Magic to try to save his own life, all those touched by the ceremony that night would have perished as well. Once he understood the gravity of the situation, he'd hesitated not and allowed Maddokyn to pull him through the Magical fire straight into the Beyond, so that the others could continue unscathed. Third Flight had been named after him, and Synahmarr was working to alter the LifeBond Magic in preparation to accommodate the increasing potential of such happening again.

The upcoming Fourth LifeBond ceremony would still include the possibility of Dragons reaching out from Past the Veil, but with the alterations they'd be able to attach themselves to the skin of their partners, much like an intricate tattoo. Once Called forth, they would detach and be as in life for such time as they were able to maintain their strength afore required to return to their partner. And, just as in the LifeBond with a living partner, the Human would Share in the MindLink (the telepathy of the Magic bearers most strong in the Highlands), and in their other Magics, such as the Healing. They would also have an elongated lifespan as well as enhanced strength, speed, and reflexes. And if the Human partner were killed or eventually died as did everyone, he would Pass to join his Dragon partner Beyond, still together as were the others, for the LifeBond was forever.

The changes to the greatest Greater Magic Spell of all time were proving complicated to achieve but would be necessary, as the war put them all at increasing risk of drawing their partners from Beyond and Darque wanted no more failures. Such was the power of the new Matriarch. Her alteration of the Ancient Magic of the LifeBond would soon be complete.

Mynx could feel the sadness and uncertainty emanating from her good friend. As she turned and fell into step at the Matriarch's massive shoulder, she reached out and touched her. With sincerity she stated, "Mayhap they are still adjusting to no longer being in stasis. After all, you were in that state of being for centuries, maintaining your own life functions at their lowest point just to survive 'til you could make good your escape." She held back momentarily but Syn noticed and making eye contact, Mynx near whispered, "You knew you were bearing, but you thought they were another's and though I know you tried, your emotions would have been less than favorable about their very existence. Mayhap this too, is still affecting them."

'Twas exactly why the Matriarch cared about this Human so. She was totally honest, disregarding the Dragon's royal status as well as her potential response. Mynx simply stated, without condemnation, her highly insightful opinions, leaving Syn to consider them or toss them aside with no repercussions.

The massive Dragon nodded her head but did not respond as she considered. Usually Syn had to admit that Mynx was correct. Mayhap she was the reason her children had yet to hatch. Of course, there was naught she could do to change the fact that she was in stasis for so long, nor the fact she had waited o'er another winter to lay after being rescued. All she could hope for was that the one who'd Claimed her would return soon to make his Claim known. As for the rest, she would have to make a better effort to believe they were of another's seed and not the Black's and attempt to Communicate with them a little more than she had thus far. She'd been hesitant, simply staring at the eggs as they lay in the heated sands, her emotions bewildering.

But the pressure was enormous, and she was buried in doubt. Synahmarr was the answer to the Death of Life prophesy and if she failed to bear 'twas foretold that her Race would go extinct. And because of that prophesy, 'twas believed that since the time of the War of Chaos long afore the Last Holocaust, the Highlands had become sterile, with only the Matriarch able to bear eggs. However, Corbyn the Raven had worked with the Human Healer, Shayla of the Dragon Clan, along with some others, to make the relatively recent and bold assertion that 'twas not some kind of Spell.

Dragons mated for life and so many, still in their prime, were forced Past the Veil during the war. They became reclusive in the time 'tween the War of Chaos and the Last Holocaust and even more so from then 'til the Hoard returned, starting the Black War just a few winters past. Yet if 'twas truth, and 'twas not a Spell, surely one of the remaining mated pairs of Highlands would come to bear soon. Then her own eggs would matter not. At least, not as much as they did now. Her young would still be needed to fill the Rank and carry on the Matriarchy.

The burden she bore was so heavy, tears began to roll down her long muzzle and one fell on Mynx's upturned face. Wiping it away with the back of one hand, she looked anxiously to her friend. "Did I cause you pain with my words? I meant not to hurt you. I want never to do that."

As they walked, Syn sighed. "The truth can be painful, my child. You spoke the truth, as is your way." She paused in thought. "You want never to hurt me? Lay not such a burden upon yourself. I wish to hear your honest opinions, always." Then waving one great paw about, she finished, "Your insight helps me focus and keeps me sane in the insanity of our present lives."

Hurrying along now, their path led toward the massive conference room. Syn let Mynx ride up the huge stone stairway by standing on one of her front paws, the Warrior grasping 'round the Dragon's thick elbow. 'Twas as hugging the trunk of a tree. As Flight of Fire Keep was made for the Highlands, not for Humans, and everything was gigantic compared to Mynx, they'd recently installed a rope system allowing her to repel the stairs as a series of cliffs. She could have pulled her way up but riding with Syn was a rapid transport technique they'd perfected through the past winter. 'Twas one they each enjoyed.

<p style="text-align:center">~~~~~ LESS THAN A HALF MARK LATER ~~~~~</p>

Synahmarr was in shock. She could not close her muzzle. Her bottom jaw simply hung there, her eyes unblinking as she stared at the orange-gold scales of Taniyyah, a'glitter in the sunlight streaming through the tall, narrow, open stone windows built into the eastern wall of the Conference Room.

Taniyyah dared not move a muscle as she faced her Matriarch's scrutiny. She'd revealed her secret. Now she nervously sat and feared the worst reprisal. Why had she come? Why had she not simply taken care of the deed alone in the wilderness? Surely she could have hidden…

Their eyes momentarily locked one to the other, Taniyyah broke eye contact as Synahmarr finally began to blink. Multiple times. Then she found her jaw closing and as she straightened out her long neck, standing and rising to her full height, she towered o'er Tan, whose eyes now fixed upon the stone floor in front of her large paws. Her heart pounding, Taniyyah lifted her gaze to

Synahmarr, following an unnerving silence she could tolerate no longer.

In the Matriarch's eyes swirled a crowd of emotions. Fear, confusion, hatred, jealousy, astonishment, and envy took their place amongst relief, excitement, and great joy. Huge tears welled up in Synahmarr's eyes, spilling o'er and rolling off the sides of her muzzle to splash upon the floor.

Shaking, the Matriarch found her tongue at last and reached forward to Taniyyah, assisting her to stand up as the other kept her gaze locked upon Syn. In her slow, regal voice, Synahmarr asked, "You are certain? There can be no mistake?" Suddenly everyone understood why Synahmarr feared. If Taniyyah's lifemate was now Past the Veil, this too, would be a dead end. "You and which Dragon?" Syn questioned. "Who has made his Claim upon you?"

Tan had been reluctant to bring this news to the Matriarch, knowing how difficult 'twould be, but also had been reluctant to talk about it with her 'Bond, for Thorrn and Tiyya had lost their baby afore 'twas born. She wanted not to cause any more pain. But the time was now. And she wanted to do it here at Flight of Fire Keep, as in days of old. As was her right. Tan's voice trembled but became clearer as she spoke. "I was Claimed by your cousin, Prince Shasynn, in 'Bond with the Warrior Tiyya. And yes, I am certain. I bear eggs, my Matriarch."

Abruptly Synahmarr lost her balance and sat down hard. 'Twas Tan's turn to assist Syn back to her feet. The Matriarch's eggs had been laid but not yet proven viable. Nevertheless once Synahmarr laid, others began to have hope, following closely the research showing that their infertility was caused by a combination of propaganda, stress, their increasingly reclusive nature, and lifemates lost to the war resulting in a significant decline in mating flights.

Taniyyah smiled shyly and with deep emotion said, "With your blessings, I desire to lay my eggs here upon the ancient

Nursery Sands of my lifemate's home. Matriarch, the Great Drought has lifted. I believe as do so many others, that with your return the Death of Life has been averted."

THE KEEP OF ST SWIFTYN'S

~~~~~ ATOP THE RAMPARTS ~~~~~

</div>

Maakayyel sat back on his thick haunches to rest from the morning's efforts. Folding his long wings aside his flanks and wrapping his tail 'round his feet, one could see the similarities in his mannerisms to those of his nephew, General Gunnarr the Mighty Blue.

The sole surviving sibling of his hatching with both his elder sisters Kaahayyel and Maahayyel now gone, the enormous Dragon sat in his preferred location atop the southern edge of the walls of the Keep. Along this side of the outer wall was a large, fertile common area usually occupied by Master Tyrza and her classes of children playing, along with those other residents of the Keep looking for a safe outing during their free moments. Covering the wall itself was an abundance of very large blackberries that grew within his reach to snack on at will. He loved blackberries but afore coming to live at the Keep he'd had to search extensively for the delectable fruit.

Now he'd discovered that not only did they taste good, the tart sweetness helped him to focus his Link. Aside from that, he'd also discovered that he could send forth his Message further from this place on the wall than anywhere else he'd attempted. Today, he was trying to reach out near to the Sakyn Forest, far beyond the Rol Dan. 'Twas not his first try, but he was optimistic he'd soon be able to Communicate with the one he was certain had Heard and ignored all his past efforts.

'Twas a surprise when Prince Maakayyel had taken the LifeBond with the Warrior Aspynn during the third LifeBond ceremony. One of the eldest Dragons left in the world, soon to be considered an Ancient, he'd understood the mechanics of the
~~~~~

'Bond Magic, but once entered, 'twas so much more. 'Twas a remarkably powerful and delightful experience in his opinion, and it made him feel youthful and energetic again, bringing him back from the abyss of apathy into which so many of his Kind had fallen.

Maakayyel's Link was the strongest of all the Highlands, able to Send and Receive further than any other noted thus far, and once this fact was recognized, he'd been assigned to lead the Communications section with Rolf and Nalwynn based at Drekinn Lair and Axyl and Haniyyah supporting him at the Bog and the Keep. Communications had been running quite smoothly since he'd taken charge.

The renowned Dragon's partner was a skilled Warrior who was also extraordinarily intellectual and while he performed his duties, Aspynn trained for battle or assisted him as needed. But in their spare time they visited the library of the Keep, enthusiastically reading, learning, debating, and taking much pleasure in their discoveries.

One rainy afternoon they'd been researching in a part of the library that had notes about what happened just afore the Last Holocaust. 'Twas this day's readings that provoked old memories and brought Maakayyel full circle to the mission he'd been assigned at the time. His good friends, brother and sister Dragons, Hadryagg and Radryagg, were recruited to join him in his clandestine undertaking. Though they'd been initially successful, things had quickly fallen apart with a most unexpected and alarming discovery, and all their plans had gone awry.

Maakayyel had lost touch with Hadryagg after he and her brother escaped the Hoard pursuit and then Radryagg retreated into seclusion, his heart heavy with self-doubt. His friends had acted upon Maakayyel's orders and he felt responsible for their fates. If alive, Hadryagg was still in the Hoard, a spy without a contact. And Rad? Well, the best friend of his youth had shown up for the First LifeBond and then for the Second, bringing with him others to stand for the Magic only to retreat again to his secluded home once he discovered Synahmarr was still alive. They'd thought her dead, killed by the Black himself, but somehow she'd survived. Maakayyel had tried to talk with Radryagg, but the other wouldn't listen, blaming himself for the Matriarch's long imprisonment.

But Maakayyel knew that even if Synahmarr hadn't loved Radryagg, she'd understood and had agreed to the Claiming to prevent being taken by the Black. 'Twas only after her escape that they'd learned of her altered Memory, the rage such knowledge produced, pushing Rad further away. Synahmarr wouldn't even remember his Claim. 'Twould be his word alone she would have to accept, and Radryagg's boundless guilt may or may not persuade her to believe such a remarkable tale.

'Twas with great daring they'd carried out the Claim under the Black's very nose, but the situation denied them a full Mating Flight, requiring the actual deed be performed upon the ground not unlike Human mating. Through the following winters Rad and Maakayyel had speculated as to whether Synahmarr would even have had any eggs with such an unorthodox Claiming. But Synahmarr produced the biggest batch of eggs in history, a total of thirteen. They lay in the Nursery Sands of Flight of Fire Keep at this very moment.

The Prince was saddened. 'Twas not like his courageous friend to hide. No, Maakayyel knew Rad was not hiding from others, but from his own heart. He'd been in love with Synahmarr since they'd been hatchlings and he could not go through her loss a second time. If she rejected him for leaving her in such dire circumstances, or if she simply did not return his love, there'd be no living with the pain.

Eating another paw full of ripe berries, Maakayyel licked the juices off his talons, then stood up and took a mighty breath afore trying once more to Send his Message to the wastelands fronting the Sakyn Forest. Such a dismal place, depressing and ugly.

And cold. He shivered with that imagery but kept up his barrage of Messages. He felt he had to reach out to his best friend, he must help him face the past. And the future. 'Twas the least he could do for the anguish he'd already caused. Surely soon…

Abruptly, he Heard a weak, very distant response, coming from the middle of the wastelands. Success! The deep Voice responded, "*Shut up.*"

Maakayyel laughed, for the brusque Retort was so typical of Radryagg. Mayhap there was yet hope. "*A nice greeting for an old friend!*"

After an elongated silence, wherein the Prince began to think he'd lost the other, he Heard a sigh and then with sarcasm Rad Responded, "*I know nothing nice about being old.*" The tone was not angry, and this made Maakayyel optimistic. Again, there was a gap of silence, and Maakayyel simply waited. Soon, Radryagg continued, curtly stating, "*I heard you were in the 'Bond. It seems to agree with you. Are you trying to recruit me for the fourth ceremony?*"

"*No. I am not recruiting you for the 'Bond.*"

"*A new mission, then?*" Rad questioned cynically.

Maakayyel sighed. "*I want you to stop being an idiot and go see her.*"

Now Rad exploded in self-pity and anger, "*It has been too long! How do you expect me to face her now? Not only did I fail her in her greatest need, she is now my Matriarch!*"

Maakayyel understood and his heart went out to the friend of his youth. Like a tidal wave the pain hit him, and he allowed his words to simply flow in Response. "*I know who she is. And I know that you saved her life; for the Black would have killed her. We both know she would never have allowed his Claim! You did not fail her. You followed MY orders to Claim her afore did the Black, and then HER orders as Heir Apparent to the Matriarchy to leave, as there was no hope of her escape from the castle.*" Understanding was now waning thin, and the Prince became demanding as he continued, "And now I order you to do the right thing once more. If you will not go to your lifemate for that reason alone, then go to her to ease her mind about the sire of her children! Our Matriarch should not suffer forever because of your sense of guilt!"

CHAPTER SEVEN

Surprise Guests

DARQUE'S OFFICE AT THE KEEP

~~~~~ SHORTLY LATER ~~~~~

'Twas near midday as Darque stared unseeing at the never-ending pile of paperwork upon her desk, her mind elsewhere. Specifically, upon the details of Walkyr's recent Vision as just conveyed by Chynnar. Pearls. He'd Seen a young girl with a pouch full of abnormally large and most colorful pearls in her sole possession. Walkyr had never seen such a treasure. And he'd impressed upon the Healer that the Vision had the taste of antiquity, therefore, he was certain 'twas a past event of utmost importance. Sadly, although the girl seemed familiar to the Seer, he recognized her not from anyone he now knew.

Nevertheless, all thoughts of pearls and whether she knew of anyone with such a stash, vanished when she glanced up at the Standing Guard announcing her latest guests. Breaking into a wide smile, she leaped out of her chair and near ran to the trio whom she'd not seen in much too long, embracing each warmly in turn. "M'Lord Myrrdin! Welcome to the Keep!" She quickly Spoke to Gunnarr, *"Stop Calei and her troops from leaving. We have special guests!"*

Gunnarr's low rumbling voice resounded through her mind as he Responded to her request, *"No need, my sweetness. Calei and the brothers were gathering their Team in the Ward when they witnessed Myrrdin's arrival. They are on their way to you at this moment."*

Returning her thoughts and attention to those afore her, she continued, "Princess Anastasia, Prince Kevon, welcome back!" 'Twas then she noted yet another amongst their party, standing quietly behind his comrades. Although she'd never met the man, his identity was clear by his regal manner and the look in his sharp eyes, as well as his resemblance to Kevon. Astonished, she exclaimed, "M'Lord Rohar!" Sweeping her hands outward to encompass the entire group, she asked, "What brings you here at this time?"

Lord Rohar stepped forward and greeted Darque with an informal arm grasp. Tall, blonde, wearing a short well-groomed beard and simple clothing that did little to hide his true status, the Lord of the Sprites was a commanding presence despite his attempt at blending in with the others. Pulling Darque closer, he whispered in her ear that he wanted no special treatment. He was traveling incognito with the company, on a diplomatic visit to the Elven Nation that he felt was long o'er due. Darque assured him that no royal recognition would be forthcoming as per his wish, and he was safe within the confines of the Spell Dome o'er the Keep.

As the Lord stepped back slightly behind Myrrdin once more, Darque stood in front of her desk observing the travelers. Myrrdin was the eldest of the royal Elven brood of seventeen, and Anastasia was next to the youngest. 'Twas amazing that although they shared not the same mother, the two could not be mistaken as unrelated. But then again, Elves and the other Magic bearing Races tended to be very attractive people sharing many similar characteristics such as pale skin, pointed ears, and almond shaped eyes. After exchanging pleasantries, Darque hiked her hip upon the edge of the desk and faced her visitors with much interest.

Myrrdin was the first to speak. "I'm escorting Ana and Kevon back to the Wyrdritch. 'Tis time I met my stepmother and see my siblings once again. I'm certain there has been much change since afore the Retreat." His easy-going smile disappeared as he continued. "And they prepare for the Call to Return. Apart from the Kreegare, the Elves still outside the Wyrdritch know not they can now go home, and 'twill take considerable Magic to accomplish a world-wide Communication of this type. Unfamiliar as I am with the level of expertise and strength of Queen Alyssa," he cleared his throat, as her title was now tenuous, "as the Heir

Apparent to the throne," at which time he actually scowled, "at the very least 'twould be inappropriate for me not to attend such an undertaking, and to assist if required."

Myrrdin had not set foot inside the homeland of the Elven Nation since being forced to escape imprisonment and a death sentence placed upon him by his own father afore the Retreat. And now that the Elves had sworn fealty to King Gabriel of the Resistance, bringing their forces, such as they currently were, under Battle Commander Darque, he had to figure out how NOT to be forced to take the throne. King Jeeryd had Passed the Veil and Queen Bryanna was still missing. Since 'twas determined she had not become one of the Assassins of the Rol Dan this placed Alyssa's claim to the throne in jeopardy. If could be proven that Bryanna yet lived, then Alyssa would have to forfeit the throne to her. And even if they could not prove Bryanna was still this side of the Veil, 'twas HIS throne 'til such time as that proof was available. Then of course, Bryanna would have to return to TAKE the throne, and who knew what she was doing now, or where she was? 'Twas a complicated matter. Nonetheless, his life and his heart were forever entwined with the Sprite Nation on the Island of Dreams where he'd taken refuge shortly after his escape, spending o'er half his length of days thus far with his adopted Nation. He wanted nothing to do with the throne and wished only to continue sailing upon the high seas as Ship's Master.

Such thoughts brought him back to their present situation. The pride of the Sprite Fleet, his flagship the Krakken, was scuttled in a desperate battle o'er a winter past, and now rested upon the edge of the crevasse of the Leviathans in the Ocean of Fears. She was safe there, but could she ever be raised again? 'Twas in the deepest region of the deepest ocean, and the creatures guarding her were the most lethal menace of the seas.

His heart 'ached, for he knew not how to get her back. Yet several items were still aboard. For one, the bottle of Drekinn Whiskey b'Spelled to sit in the middle of the table in his personal cabin. He and Caleichante had made a promise involving that bottle. However, that was not a secret as were some others. His eyes drifted to the Battle Commander while he considered what lay in his safe. And even more important, the deception that involved the transfer of certain 'property' he'd taken part in, just afore the battle. Did she see the truth in his eyes?

That deception was a promise he'd keep to the Veil if need be, for 'twas made to his good friend, Corbyn the Raven. Nonetheless it involved Darque and 'twas far more personal than sharing a bottle of whiskey. The child's safety was paramount, and all would surface in time. Darque might never forgive them, but she'd come to understand. He sighed. Would he ever manage to keep all these promises? For certain not if the Krakken remained where she now lay.

As he straightened up, his glance caught Ana's eyes. She was watching him with growing awareness upon her young face and he willed her to keep what she Felt under wraps. He'd forgotten the power of his little sister's Empathy Magic. Just allowing all these thoughts to come to consciousness, gave her the knowledge he'd meant to keep to himself. But thankfully, although she had little ability to prevent it, Anastasia was very tightlipped about information she gained through her Magic. She respected privacy and recognized the danger of sharing such. Myrrdin nodded his appreciation.

Darque's piercing blue eyes shifted from one to the other of the pair, knowing something had just passed 'tween them and that something likely involved her. With her brows slightly furrowed she considered whether 'twas important enough to divert their current conversation. Finally choosing to file the odd moment in her memories, she realized several heartbeats of silence had passed and her guests were all looking at her keenly. Mayhap she'd learn one day of what just happened.

Smiling, she turned her focus to Anastasia. Sixteenth in line to the throne, her little brother Coltyn just four winters behind, the stunning Princess Anastasia had been to the Keep afore, as had the handsome and equally youthful Sprite Heir Apparent, Kevon, standing at her shoulder. Tall and lean, both already towered o'er the Battle Commander. Ana's long brown hair reached past her hips now, and although pulled back, Kevon's blonde hair fell to his waist.

Having each reached age gathering o'er fifteen winters, they'd been promised one to the other in a ceremony to bind the Sprites and the Elves once more as allies, and Darque wondered if the news of their true lineage would alter that binding. Although Ana and Kevon were quite mature for their winters, they'd not been of age at the time of the decree. Extremely good friends and 'promised' to mate, they had yet to go through a formal vows' ceremony, but such was not expected for several more winters. However, they'd gone through much else together, and Darque knew even if they never took those vows, they'd always be close friends. She sighed as both grinned broadly, renewing her confidence in the alignment of the Sprites and Elves as allies to each other and to the Resistance.

A loud knock interrupted her musings and the Standing Guard announced the return of Calei, Ardryyn, and Kryllyn. Their expressions reflected a combined mix of warm welcome for their brethren and leery anticipation of the reasons therein. Lord Rohar was acknowledged but with the way he tucked his chin and stepped back, his position was made clear.

Myrrdin and Calei had not seen each other since she'd disembarked from the Krakken on her journey so long ago, and with hesitance he told her of the ship's loss. She knew the heartbreak he felt and forgave him the inability to fulfill their promise, stating they could and would share a new bottle of Drekinn Whiskey afore she left again. But Myrrdin was not appeased. 'Twas the bottle sitting on the table in his cabin which they must share to fulfill the promise, but 'twas nothing to be done.

O'er the next mark Calei's mission was discussed. Ana, Kevon, and Lord Rohar listened attentively but said little. Lord Rohar was torn, for the danger to the Island of Dreams was great, but 'twas finally decided he must continue to the Wyrdritch on his original undertaking while Myrrdin returned to the Sprite Nation with Calei and the brothers.

Myrrdin's new ship, the Lytle, was not quite as large as had been the Krakken but after much work refitting her o'er the past winter, he'd managed to make her near as fast and she was well armed. The Team would Dance back to Port O'Drekinn where the Lytle was anchored, and then sail swiftly back to the island where they'd make report to the Elite Guard and determine how to proceed. Calei chose the other Sprites o'er the Elves from Captain Natanamia's mixed command primarily because they all had Water Dragon Ties and knew how to ride. Their Team now consisted of Myrrdin, Caleichante, Lyrianei, Kalisadei, Ardryyn, Kryllyn, and sisters Datyniah and Dalakiah. Natan would lead the rest of her team, the Elven Princes Orasynth, Malyrist, and the twins, Gylrann and Gylragg, to escort Lord Rohar, Anastasia, and Kevon safely to the Wyrdritch.

'Twould be the first time the brothers had returned to Haven since being sent to represent the Elven Nation in alliance to the Resistance, and although Queen Alyssa knew of Laratyn's death near two winters past, they'd yet to share the customary ceremonial Reverence Gathering of the Elves. Myrrdin and the middle brother, Leisalarr, who was now Second in Command to Tammra Dayo of the Kreegaren Assassins, would not be present, but all the rest would and 'twould be their best opportunity for such a Gathering.

'Twas at the moment Ana turned to leave, that Darque thought she saw it. Or rather, she thought she didn't see it. For the briefest instant, Darque saw Ana's eyes change shape, their up-ward lift shifting downward. Shaking her head, she decided she was tired and had imagined the whole thing. But then again, so many things had become normal in the past few winters, little would surprise her. And honestly, Ana was beautiful no matter what shape were her eyes.

<div align="center">~~~~~ IN THE HALLWAY ~~~~~</div>

"She noticed, I know she did," Ana whispered anxiously to Kevon, as they ducked into a small sitting alcove along the corridor, allowing Lord Rohar to continue on ahead. "I'm losing my birth glamour."

"No worries. 'Tis intact again." Kevon whispered back to her, after checking to make sure he wasn't going to be caught in a lie. "But you know, I'm becoming rather drawn to that look. 'Tis quite attractive in an exotic way," he teased her while waggling his eyebrows.

But Ana was more serious. "I've tried but I can't seem to place a new glamour 'til this one is completely worn out. 'Tis not like an ordinary glamour. I wonder if my mother knew this would happen. Mayhap she thought 'twould fall off all at once. And just how did she keep hers intact?"

"Stop worrying. I don't care," stated the young Prince firmly.

"But if anyone else knows," Ana said with growing anxiety.

"We shall face all that comes, together. And if anyone else knew, we'd have heard the rumors by now. Besides, we've discussed the ramifications, and our responses," he said while flashing that glorious smile that always made her forget all her concerns.

To answer his unasked question, she repeated the information about her mother that she already knew, along with what they'd discovered not long after she'd arrived on the Island of Dreams. "Alyssa's hair is naturally blonde, and Rohar's is naturally brown. They both use glamour to fit in with their people."

"Yes. And that means?"

"That me having Human shaped eyes, means nothing more than the royal leaders of the Elves and Sprites hiding THEIR true appearances."

"And?" he questioned, remembering the new information to which they'd just been made privy, a smile of pure triumph lighting up his face.

Ana also smiled when she put it together. "Of course! 'Twill merely be more proof for the doubters, that we are one Race."

Kevon nodded with bold resolve and taking her by the elbow he steered her down the hallway after the others. He would not allow anyone to bully his girl. Ever.

Walking swiftly to catch up with Myrrdin and Rohar just entering the Mess Hall, they eagerly sought out Leisalarr and his lifemate Dyraserrah, a good friend of Ana's. Their reunion was long o'erdue and they wasted not a moment, eagerly catching up on all the events of the past few winters afore everyone would take their leave in opposite directions.

THAT EVENING

THE KEEP OF ST SWIFTYN'S

~~~~~ THE CHAMBERS OF ARDYTH, AXYL,

BRYYNN, AND HANIYYAH ~~~~~

</div>

The Warrior Axyl had eaten quickly, then stood up just as quickly as he'd told his lifemate Ardyth, that he'd be 'right back' afore dashing out of the Mess Hall to run some unknown errand.

Axyl was a huge, muscle bound Warrior, one of the brawniest of the Brotherhood, in 'Bond with the petite Green, Haniyyah, the smallest adult Dragon anyone had ever seen. Though Axyl had never been conceited, he was quite good-looking and popular with the females throughout his span of days, 'til he and Han were ambushed some winters past. As a result of the brutal attack, the Warrior was now covered head to toe with countless scars from fang, talon, and Flame. His confidence and pride took a beating, not from the ugly scars, but because they showed ev-
~~~~~

eryone how he'd not been able to protect his 'Bond, she having saved them both. And due to the severity of their injuries he'd been unable to participate in the quick to follow, Battle for the Dragon Clan.

Feeling as if he'd failed everyone, he'd retreated into himself for some time afore meeting Ardyth at the Draw of the Domes. Her undying love and support gave him back his robust nature and protecting her returned his confidence in his fighting prowess. They'd shared vows shortly afterward, and his Haniyyah would soon be Claimed by Ardyth's Dragon, Bryynn, who had yet to reach his full growth but now stood taller than the Green. Still, 'twas estimated that he would not grow much more.

As 'twas with some other working relationships, though Ardyth and Bryynn were not in the 'Bond at present, they were sure to take if they ever participated in the ceremony. However, 'twas not certain that Ardyth's Gift as Seer of the Dead, along with her ability to channel their spirits, would be adversely affected if they did so, and therefore, they'd made the painful decision to avoid such. Ardyth was not a Warrior and although she could take care of herself in the average fight, such as occurred in the battles in which she'd participated since joining the Resistance required the skills of those she channeled. Therefore, Ardyth and Axyl lived with the certain knowledge that she would eventually age to the point that to those who didn't know her, she'd appear to be his great grandmother, and would Pass the Veil afore him, if he was not killed in battle himself. 'Twas a subject never broached aloud.

Bryynn was newly hatched when he'd met Ardyth and the two of them had become inseparable. The blood red Dragon was the '7th Egg', the '7th Prince', the '7th son of a 7th son', the youngest of the sons of the Mighty Maahayyel, and had the amazing special Magics of Absorption and Amplification. He could benefit from another's skills or Magics by 'absorbing' them, as well as amplifying or enhancing another's Magic or abilities.

Bryynn's Gifts had come in quite handy in the past and allowed Ardyth to increase her own Gift, for Seer of the Dead was an ability extremely rare even within the Rashei community. But even more rare, with their association Ardyth had increased her ability to channel the spirits with whom she could freely engage. And as her appearance so closely resembled that of the Battle Commander, Ardyth had successfully channeled Darque Abriya, allowing the First Warrior to participate in the Battle to Draw the Domes. Abriya had Called to her Dragon Sword, but in the end they'd used Darque's, for her own had yet to appear. Ardyth had also rapid-channeled spirit after spirit during the Battle of Darden Caverns, allowing them to take their revenge upon the Hoard afore they finally crossed the Veil for good.

Ardyth was orphaned at the time she'd gathered just eight winters, and 'twas her treasure that kept her from being killed with the rest of her village. That treasure, a vast number of large, multicolored pearls, she'd kept in a pouch wrapped 'round her waist for the many winters she'd roamed the wilderness. That pouch had seen better days, and Axyl had decided she needed a replacement.

Leaving the Mess Hall and returning to their quarters, Ardyth was greeted shortly after by her lifemate, grinning ear to ear, holding something behind his back. She was so excited to see what 'twas, that she stood on tiptoe and held his shoulders, trying to peek 'round one side then the other afore he finally relented. Laughing at her antics, he pulled forth a glass bowl. The bowl was created by the Master Craftsmen specializing in the making of glass. He'd designed it himself, with some assist from both Haniyyah and Bryynn to ensure she'd be happy with the result.

Ardyth's blue eyes gleamed with emotion as she reached for the beautiful bowl. 'Twas large and heavy, somewhat oval shaped and shallow, with a slightly irregular edge (not quite a ruffle as Ardyth was not exactly into 'frillies'), and 'twas a lovely pale sage with random streaks of equally pale blue, reminding her of the ocean, and home. She could not speak as she simply gaped at Axyl, waiting for an explanation.

"That pouch has been repaired so many times, 'tis not even the same pouch. Why not put them on display? They're pretty and you enjoy looking at them. They make you happy. They should be where you can have easy access and where they can be seen," he stated cautiously as he waited for her approval.

Although the pearls had made her both happy and sad in the past, she loved seeing them and the pouch was so worn now, 'twas difficult to take them out to enjoy. Just the other day as she'd been trying to repair it once more, she'd mentioned that she'd once dreamed of giving them a more elegant holder, one in which they could be displayed. Ardyth's grandmother had taught her how to weave and sew and as a result she was a good seamstress, could make clothing and fishnets with equal talent, and her grandmother was proud of her skill. But she'd had little in the way of aesthetic personal items in her nomadic lifestyle since then, and the pouch had been merely functional to begin with. 'Twas also true she need no longer hide them from others, for she was no longer alone, traveling the wilds of Kadoor. No one would try to kill her to steal them here.

Much to Axyl's relief, Ardyth was delighted. Taking the bowl from his trembling hands she set it upon their table in the main living area. 'Twas perfect upon the thick slab of oak with natural bark edging and hand rubbed surface that gleamed, accenting the gleam of the bowl. Near running to their sleeping area in her excitement, she carefully took the tattered pouch from where it lay, and bringing it back she just as carefully poured the contents into the bowl.

Then as an afterthought she reached 'tween her breasts for the Dragon's Eye that always hung there upon its leather strap. Holding it provided comfort, and 'twas the only thing aside from the pearls that she had left from her childhood. She held it gently as her thoughts returned to that time. 'Twas a gift from her grandmother, who told her that she'd received the Eye when she was but a child from a Dragon with amber hues to her scales. The Dragon foretold she would have a granddaughter one day, whom they must name Ardyth. "'Twas to Ardyth, the Eye must be passed," the Dragon had insisted.

And just as was also foretold, the Eye had assisted much, leading her to her blood red partner Bryynn, to the Resistance, to her Gift, and to the love of her life.

<center>~~~~~ THE FOLLOWING DAWN ~~~~~</center>

The Gatekeeper was perplexed. The huge gray wolf had paced back and forth just outside the invisible barrier of the Spell Dome for o'er a mark afore coming to an abrupt halt precisely at the end of the bridge. The Spell Dome covered the entire mountain, including the natural bridge leading to the Ward Gate, its Magical roots deep in the surrounding soil and rock. The shaggy beast had been sitting on the ground seemingly staring at the barrier since just after midnight as if willing someone to take notice. Believing he presented no danger and knowing he could not see inside the barrier, they'd left the wolf alone.

But 'twas becoming most peculiar. Motionless for marks, the wolf simply sat and gazed straight ahead. Ryygg, the Night Beast hunting partner of Gheryh of the Daggogh, had come to the Ward just afore daybreak as if his presence had been requested. And after watching the wolf for but a few breaths, Ryygg demanded to be let out the massive gate onto the bridge o'er the river that swept past the mountain in which the Keep was carved.

Since she was not able to speak with Ryygg, the Gatekeeper called for Gheryh to come and translate, and once she and Ryygg conferred, Gheryh became very excited and told the Gatekeeper to let the Kahyah onto the bridge, afore running back inside the Keep. 'Twas most confusing. But Gheryh was Danah of the People, ruling alongside her mate, Kyrag of the Gordatch, Danoh of the People, strong allies of the Resistance. The Gatekeeper was compelled to do as she was told.

When the huge Kahyah walked 'cross the bridge to stand just opposite the wolf, the wolf's ears pricked up as if he'd heard something. That was also quite odd, as the Dome did not allow sound to travel through the barrier from the inside. The Gatekeeper became alarmed. That was no wolf. Preparing to send it away from the Keep, she was prevented from opening a portal by the return of Gheryh, now accompanied by Darque, Myrrdin, and Ana. Kevon came running up behind them shortly after, never far from his best friend.

That boy had the most remarkable blue eyes, the Gatekeeper thought to herself. "I know," stated Ana aloud with an impish grin on her face, startling the Gatekeeper as the Princess walked gracefully past. "Kevon's eyes are quite remarkable," she continued, while grinning at the Prince walking beside her, who grinned back. The Gatekeeper merely widened her own eyes in astonishment at this display of the powers of the Princess, not knowing quite what to think.

'Twas a rule amongst those in the Resistance, that no one's mind would be invaded without permission by those who had access to the Link. Private thoughts would remain private. "No," stated Darque patiently, watching the rest of them as they filed out of the Ward, making their way rapidly to the far end of the bridge. "She uses not the Link. She has not the ability to read your mind. She is like Diadranei. 'Tis your emotions that give her all the information she needs to interpret your thoughts." Then reassuring the Gatekeeper that all was well, Darque followed Ana, Kevon, Gheryh, and Myrrdin onto the bridge toward the wolf now standing opposite Ryygg as if trying to communicate with the Night Beast he should not be able to see, let alone know was there.

Night Beasts were near the size of a small pony, and the creature Ryygg faced was near half his size. 'Twas amazingly large for a mountain wolf. With his shaggy gray mane and ears pricked as if listening closely, she noted that although he appeared exhausted, his yellow eyes reflected an urgency along with incredible intelligence.

Darque had to think about that notion. Why would she associate such intelligence with a mountain wolf? Suddenly she gasped and pushing past the others, stepped forward and raised one hand as if to touch the barrier as she gaped at the wolf. Without even looking back, she reached behind her and grabbed Ana's hand, yanking the girl to her side. "What's he saying? Who is this?" she questioned the Elf, desperately hoping the wolf was who she thought he was. At the same time, 'twould be tragic. Why did he not simply Shift? He could communicate more effectively as Fay, or even as a human.

Ana's musical voice rang through the edgy silence. With tension mounting, she struggled to understand the wolf through the barrier. She spoke haltingly as she interpreted the emotions she felt, into language. "His name is Rhyah and he desperately wants to speak with you. With all of us. But he has little time left and must hurry."

Darque turned rapidly to signal the Gatekeeper to portal Rhyah to the Ward. The wolf leaped up. With his head lowered as if to fight, fangs flashing and snarling, he began to back away from the barrier. Ana grabbed Darque's shoulder quickly, declaring, "do not bring him through the portal!" Her hand o'er her mouth and her heart pounding, she turned back to the wolf who was slowly stepping further and further away but had ceased his aggressive posturing. Her breath stuttered with the power of the emotion with which she'd been suddenly assailed as Rhyah 'told' her that he would have been forced Past the Veil if she'd not prevented his transportation. Firmly, she stated, "He must remain outside."

<center>~~~~~ SHORTLY LATER ~~~~~</center>

Darque was hesitant to allow the Prince and Princess out of the Keep 'til she realized how silly was that notion. 'Twould be herself in the most danger if something happened, for the others could simply Dance away. After all, 'twas how they'd arrived. And Myrrdin had reported that through their journey they'd seen nothing to suggest the Hoard were currently active in this area and for now, there was little of which to be concerned. What they need be concerned about was the message Rhyah came to deliver, for could be nothing else. He'd obviously not come to vacation, and he'd not tried to return since leaving so long ago. With that sure knowledge, deep resentment grew in her heart for the Fay.

O'er two winters past, he, and her sister Storrm, had a developing relationship, and when everyone thought they'd share vows, he'd departed after the pair spent one night together. Storrm revealed not the details, just that they both knew his destiny lay elsewhere and saying their private farewells, he left, not to be seen again. 'Til today. There'd been no way to find him, no way to communicate with him. Did he know he'd fathered her child? Did he know both were forced Past the Veil half a winter later?

The bitterness she felt was vile and she swallowed hard. Such thoughts, such emotions, would serve no useful purpose. Rhyah was a good man. He'd been good to her sister. She had to admit that 'twas Storrm who'd not allowed the relationship to blossom. 'Twas Storrm who'd pushed the Fay out of her life for she did not love him. 'Twas her LifeBond partner, Mystynn the Green, Gunner's brother, whom she'd truly loved.

Yet she could not help but wonder if things would have been different if Rhyah had not left. Shaking her head she knew one could not fool the Fates. Storrm's life had followed a prophesy as surely as did her own. She sighed. At least they'd parted as friends afore the Fay accepted his destiny to travel to the Icelands. A suicide mission at best. 'Twas a final destiny Darque felt he'd have sidelined if Storrm had been the least bit favorable toward him. She'd seen the admiration in his eyes for her sister every time he looked at her. But all Storrm felt was a deep friendship for Rhyah, something they apparently settled that last night.

Darque had ordered Dragons to follow the Fay to try to keep him safe while hoping beyond hope that he'd regain his senses, turn back to the Keep, and not cross the border of no return. But they'd lost him in the Far Northlands, his trail as cold as was the environment. So. If Rhyah had successfully crossed into the Icelands, he'd not be alive today. But why had he not returned to the Keep 'til now and why would he not Shift? 'Twould be good if Corbyn the Raven were here for he might be able to figure out why Rhyah was.

Rhyah's best friend and Heir Apparent to the throne of the Fay, Corbyn was still serving the Goddess Morrigan as his curse for a murder for which he was falsely accused but for which he continued to feel responsible. Having spent some time at the Keep after Storrm's death Corbyn abruptly disappeared o'er a moon past, after having thanked Darque graciously for their hospitality for so long, but stating he had urgent business elsewhere to which he must attend. They'd heard nothing since, and given the nature of his 'service', she'd kept close watch on her Warriors. To her relief, no raven had become anyone's recent companion.

She took a deep breath as she finished arming up in preparation for the meeting in the deep forest of the mountains outside the Keep.

<p style="text-align:center">~~~~~ A QUARTER MARK LATER ~~~~~</p>

Darque met up with the group in the Ward and they walked to the barrier afore being portalled out of the Dome. The portal was extremely short, and they found it to be somewhat jarring. Keeping their eyes and ears open, they stood for a time, scanning the area, and regaining their bearings while waiting for the Wolf to show himself.

Shortly, they saw his yellow eyes gleaming from behind a huge oak tree, and checking their perimeter, they walked briskly to him. The Wolf stepped out fully from behind the tree, but he seemed unsure of himself as he faced them. He moved not as

Ana left the others fanned out behind her while she approached. Rhyah appeared significantly older and more ragged than he had less than a mark prior. Darque wondered what was wrong with him. Was he dying? Diseased? Was it safe to be so close?

As the Wolf he could not communicate through other means than Empathy and their conversation appeared one-sided to the rest, yet 'twas clear Ana and Rhyah were in an active discussion of some importance. Ana used a combination of Pushed emotion and speaking out loud, to try to convey her responses and questions clearly and oft' times seemed to be repeating what Rhyah was 'telling her' not only to clarify his thoughts but so the others might be able to follow along somewhat.

Toward the end of less than half a mark, Darque heard her sister's name come up in the conversation and the wolf hung his head. When next he lifted it, tears rolled down his muzzle, dripping off his nose onto the dirt at his paws. Watching those tears roll, Darque became very much aware that Rhyah's mane was thinning afore their eyes, his muzzle turning white. 'Twas so clear now that Darque knew 'twas not their imaginations and in an attempt to comfort the Wolf at the knowledge that Storrm was Beyond, Ana tried to reach forth and touch him. In response to her innocent action, the Wolf leaped back, spun swiftly 'round, and ran off, looking o'er his shoulder once as Ana yelled, "But we leave on the 'morrow!" Still, the Wolf slowed not, disappearing into the trees.

Darque looked quizzically to the Elven girl as Ana told her not to bother sending Dragons to find Rhyah this time, for the Wolf had been told he could touch no other living creature while in this Shift. Besides, Anastasia knew where he was going and 'twas imperative he travel there with all haste. And, though she could not be certain he'd understood, she'd attempted to Push the thought that she was heading to the Wyrdritch and Diadranei was working in the Razor's Edge, expected to return soon. 'Twas all she could do.

CHAPTER EIGHT

Escape From King's Gate

Regynn caught up with Darque in the Ward soon after she bid the travelers fare winds and safe journey, setting Myrrdin, Caleichante, and the rest of the Sprites on their mission to the Island of Dreams while Captain Natanamia along with the Elven Princes, took Lord Rohar, Prince Kevon, and Princess Anastasia to the Wyrdritch. Each had their mission and she'd included passing along the information about Elves and Sprites being one Race.

'Twas scarcely two dawns since Darque set Regynn upon his task to locate the Fangs. Mysterious in his countenance, he led her through the Keep toward the Altar Room where the spirit of Grifynn was anchored by Aalanna to this side of the Veil. Darque's father was Battle Commander afore she'd taken her rightful promotion upon his Passing. His spirit now doomed to forever float above the waters of the largest scrying bowl in the whole of the Keep of St Swiftyn's where his lifemate had successfully drawn him from Beyond in her first conjure, 'twas now common knowledge that he could not return to the other side 'til the Sorcerer was no more.

Regynn placed his hand upon Darque's back, gently urging her toward Grifynn, waiting in the corner of the huge room. Her mother stood beside the bowl as Darque stood at the threshold looking curiously o'er her shoulder at the big Warrior who would apparently not be following. His words made her wonder. "You should hear these stories from your parent's own lips. I could not do justice to the re-telling."

On their way to the Altar Room, Darque had considered Ana's report about the Fay's visit. Rhyah had traveled o'er a moon trying to locate Diadranei, but once he'd determined another with her Empathy Magic was at the Keep, he'd tried to get someone's attention so he could pass along his message to the Princess. He'd been in much danger and 'twas his understanding that if he'd been transported inside, he'd have Passed the Veil in agony. Ana was good, but not as powerful yet as was her mentor, Dia, elongating their exchange. Rhyah had impressed upon her that he'd indeed successfully penetrated the Icelands and that the Ice Dragons were no myth. He'd taken a huge risk to travel back as he'd somehow been altered to survive there, no longer able to survive elsewhere, and outside of his Shift he'd have turned to a solid pillar of ice as soon as he'd crossed o'er the border. Along with that horrifying revelation, he revealed that Ana was correct in her earlier discovery. Queen Bryanna was also in the Icelands, also altered. However, there was something he'd needed to give her but had not known how to do so. Traveling as the Wolf to find someone, anyone who could understand him, he'd learned much. Not only that he COULD travel in Shift outside the Icelands, but for how long afore he had to return. Bryanna was Elven and could not Shift as effectively as the Fay, therefore, she was stuck. The Ice Dragons could travel, but the Elven Queen had never done so with the Empress Bronwyn, to whom they were both Tied by the alteration. Rhyah indicated that this method of travel was a possibility discussed but not yet attempted. After all, there were just the two of them and any such experimentation could result in their deaths.

'Twas all rather confusing and Ana was doing her best but Rhyah abruptly ended the 'conversation' as he was running out of time and needed to return or die. She'd tried to 'tell' him that they were leaving soon for the Wyrdritch but was unsure if he'd 'heard'. But if he did manage to return, traveling to the Wyrdritch would take him longer than to the Keep, along with the time 'twould take to get back again. And she still knew not for certain what he'd wanted to give them.

Darque sighed. The girl and those with whom she traveled were on their way even now to the Elven Nation. Her mind reeling with all that had happened o'er the past two dawns, she frowned as she returned her attention to the big Warrior. Regynn, unable to spin a tale? Why, he could give the Bards a run for their coin! Warily she asked, "What stories?"

Regynn said not a word as he shook his head. Sighing deeply he gave the Battle Commander a gentle push o'er the threshold afore he turned and left her alone with her parents. Walking back to the Library where he had a meeting planned with Darque's little sister, he pondered how the Battle Commander would handle the truth, and then how they'd handle the recoveries, for Lord Myrrdin and his Team had just departed on a very dangerous mission from which he may not return, and with the exception of Calei's report, there'd been no contact with her Stealth Team.

MEANWHILE

~~~~~ KING'S GATE VILLAGE ~~~~~

</div>

Not that long ago 'twas discovered that when the Elves were forced to Retreat to survive the devastation that was certain to occur with the Last Holocaust they'd not only found refuge amongst Humans but had mated. This was only an issue if the resultant child of such a mating had Human characteristics, necessitating abandonment for the child's own safety as well as the parent's, for the longevity of an Elf would eventually give away their existence. Such children knew not their legacy, simply believing that their occasional Gifts were normal, or did not realize what they had was a Gift at all.

After the War of Chaos 'til the Last Holocaust, Humans hunted Elves and Sprites. Humans lived a much shorter span of days and became fearful with time, thinking the Magic bearers were blood suckers and butchers, calling them Vampyr, recalling their skin to skin energy Draws to the death, used to their advantage in the war. And, Elves did not trust Humans, not only for being hunted and
~~~~~

vilified after once being trusted allies, but blaming them for the destruction of their homeland, forcing them to the Retreat.

Therefore, 'twas thought that such half breed children would never be accepted by the Elven Nation and 'twas best they never know their heritage. But times change, and in the past four winters the Wyrdritch had been Healed and the Elven Nation were now allied once again with Humans.

Such was the case with the Stealth Team of father and son Warriors Graasyn and Bastyen. During their first mission with Diadranei, her Empathy Magic not only disclosed their mixed blood, but uncovered their previously unacknowledged and shared Gift which gave them the ability to see Allure. Graasyn (who it turned out, was a true 'half breed' with one Human and one Elven parent) could see the Allure of glamour surrounding a Magic bearer, and Bastyen (whose mother was an Elf, making him a mere quarter Human) saw through that Allure to the reality which lay under the glamour. Once they understood what they were seeing, having taken for granted the unusual characteristics of such all their lives, they'd developed signals to allow them to work together, keeping them safe from such deception. Other half breeds had been discovered since then, and all were different in their inherited abilities, some having none. Darque had Shayla's staff working on learning more about them, and 'twas becoming rather enlightening.

Bastyen had since shared vows with Diadranei, and she and Caleichante, the Sprite who'd shared vows with Graasyn, joined forces to form the most successful Stealth Team in the Resistance. In this latest mission, they'd been living incognito for near three winters, establishing themselves as the finest weapons crafters along the Southern Slippes. Their cover story was sound. No one would be able to follow their backtrail, for they had extensive experience in creating such cover stories.

Having arrived via ship from the Far Northlands to this village (taking o'er half a winter of their mission), the tale they wove about trying to increase their presence and their market was extremely credible and they took great care not to produce anything akin to that of the Dragon Clan. With her forte Empathy Magic, Diadranei was able to meet the high demands of their customers, creating both functional as well as unusual and ornate scabbards and sheathes to their delight, while Bastyen, Graasyn, and Caleichante were all excellent weapons makers. Soon their weapons and accessories were sought after by the High King himself. After so many moons striving to achieve such, they'd finally managed to get inside Evanntyr Castle.

Still, they had to be cautious. King Shytin's Adviser, the Sorcerer, cared not about skill or contracts. A known subordinate to the Black, he was a depraved prick and lived for the torture of others, feeding on the terror, pain, and despair he inflicted. He especially enjoyed taking the villagers' loved ones, and beautiful women oft' times caught his eye. Though he had long been impotent, rape knew many forms, and such fueled his evil cravings. To avoid danger of this happening to Dia and Calei, when they'd first arrived in the village they'd both worn an aging glamour, but such Magic might be perceived by the Sorcerer and once they broke into the High King's market they had new concerns.

'Twas about that same time that Calei left to make report to Darque and now that she'd been sent on another mission and would not return in the near future, 'twas decided to have Dia use her Magic and Suggest to all that both 'older women' had moved away and that she, being a relatively new employee trained by her predecessor to continue meeting their needs, was but an afterthought to their sight, not worthy of notice.

Dia did not accompany the men when they went to the castle for contract negotiations, staying behind to manage the shop, but 'twas still a gamble as the Sorcerer actively sought out those he thought might be groveling or trying to hide from his attentions. Truth be known, no one was safe from his wicked desires. Terror was his goal, pain the fuel for his increasingly dark Magic. Nonetheless,

Diadranei's Magic was stronger, enabling her to feel the evil emanating from the Sorcerer most foul, giving her enough advance warning to avoid the scrutiny of the King's Agents. Thus far.

Their original mission to keep tabs on the Hoard, discover the extent of damage and repair to the castle from Synahmarr's dramatic escape, and seek the whereabouts of the Queen Mother, Koryl, would be coming to an end soon. Confirming that Koryl had not been seen in several winters and that Shytin was indeed a puppet on the strings of a true master, the Sorcerer himself, they did everything they could to determine what had happened to the Hoard after Darque destroyed the Lair of the Black in the Battle of Darden Caverns near two winters past. But even speculation was slim and no new information had presented itself. As for the castle reconstruction, they'd yet managed to enter, but had taken extensive note of all external changes.

They were now very close to the King's business ventures and 'twas decided 'twould not be wise to remain much longer. Their attempts to elicit information about the Hoard would soon be noticed by the Sorcerer and they need vacate afore they were all taken to the Pits of Hades, his 'playground' in the dungeons of the castle.

THAT MORNING

~~~~~ **THE WEAPONS SHOP** ~~~~~

</div>

Diadranei was working diligently on a new design for a special-order scabbard, when the jingling of the bell hanging o'er the front door alerted her to a customer's presence. Setting her project upon the table, she wiped her small hands down her ankle length skirt to smooth out the wrinkles caused by sitting for so long, afore reaching for the curtain separating their display area in the front portion of the shop from their combined work and living space in the back.

She'd been fully absorbed in the project trying not to think about Bastyen and Graasyn, who'd left afore dawn to complete
~~~~~

the negotiation for the contract with the High King that they'd begun the other day. Such would be considered a very good thing for an ordinary shopkeeper, but not for the Stealth Team as 'twas not just a contract being negotiated. They were also following up on a last slim lead to the Black's new lair and learning what had and what had not changed with the reconstruction inside the castle. 'Twas a most dangerous time for them.

Caleichante had left to make report to the Battle Commander o'er a fortnight past and when Darque sent a pair of Water Dragons recently to tell them the Sprite would not return to King's Gate, Dia was on her own. Making friends with both Dragons, she'd come to look forward to their daily visits, worried they might be seen. But the shop was not far from the ocean and as a function of their Magic, if a Water Dragon was wet he was near invisible. Such was not the perfect disguise for if one knew what one was looking at or for, 'twas not impossible to see them, however most were still unaware of the very existence of the creatures. But with both men gone oft' times of late, she was less lonely with the company of Pyth and Dyrth and she wondered what they might be doing this morning, smiling at their imagined antics while playing in the ocean.

Her long slim fingers reached forth to touch the heavy curtain and immediately her silver-gray eyes flashed as she was hit hard with a sensation of evil intent. Dropping her hands and turning swiftly, she ran to the back door fronting the alley behind the shop, followed now by crashing and yelling while four big men in uniform destroyed the shop in their haste to catch her.

With Elven strength and added adrenaline, Dia pushed the heavy door open and could not stop herself as her momentum threw her into the hands of two more uniformed men, laughing and kicking her, pulling her long black hair, and tearing off her skirt in their enthusiastic examination to ensure she had no weapons. When the others joined them, they dragged Dia by her hair through the back alley and into King's Gate as she tried desperately all the while to keep her feet, with nothing to protect the bare skin of her long legs.

Diadranei had been well liked, her shop visited frequently and much respected. But this day, no one helped her. No one said a word as they paraded by, unwilling to make eye contact, stepping aside quickly, or hiding within their homes and shops so as not to be taken themselves. They knew the woman's fate. These were the Sorcerer's men. Such as these invaded their homes in the middle of the night, taking family and friends at the will of their superior, dumping their hapless victims into the Pits of Hades, never to be seen again.

Chastising herself for falling into this trap, she held onto her head to keep the men from ripping all her hair out of her scalp, tears of pain and anger falling from her eyes as she was dragged toward Evanntyr. The palms of her hands, along with her thighs, knees, and elbows were bleeding and she had a laceration 'cross her left cheek, with bruises everywhere. She'd hit the back of her head during the scuffle in the alley, and now 'twas pounding, her vision blurry.

But all she could think about was the safety of Bastyen and Graasyn. Had they been detained at the castle or had they already left?

<div align="center">~~~~~ BACK AT THE SHOP ~~~~~</div>

Bastyen and Graasyn were forced to slip away after a brief scuffle when their escorts attempted to take them prisoner shortly after entering the castle. 'Twas not that difficult and keeping true to their extensive experience in stealth techniques, they'd quietly and efficiently walked away, leaving a few bodies in their wake. Now they had to collect Dia afore departing the village. That would take speed to accomplish afore the bodies were found.

Both men were stunned when they approached the shop from the alley. 'Twas silent as a tomb and no one was about, which was typical when someone had been taken by the King's Agents. No one wanted to be 'round if they decided to come back. Their hearts racing, they knew they'd all been targeted at the same time, and ending their mission suddenly became much more complicated.

Sprinting inside they saw everything was broken. Glass display cases, wooden shelving, and weapons they'd had for sale were strewn about. The heavy curtains were torn down and lay in a heap on the floor. But crawling through the midst of the mess were Pyth and Dyrth, squinting their enormous slit eyes, sniffing here, there, and everywhere.

Averaging the size of a War Horse, they laid their scaled bellies to the floor, widening and flattening their thick torsos. With each turn they dragged their long tails through the debris, sweeping it 'round and creating even more of a mess. As soon as they noted the Humans, they stood up on their short stocky hind legs and pressed their wrinkled noses against each other, front paws touching as if in greeting. But instead of expressing joy, they were huffing and puffing, snorting furiously. Bastyen was about to accuse them of destroying the shop when Graasyn grabbed his shoulder and shook his head, telling him 'twas not the fault of the Water Dragons. Quickly Graasyn asked, "Did you see them take her? Can you help us get her back?"

Now the Water Dragons faced the men and dropping to all fours, they invited Bastyen and Graasyn to mount and ride. Water Dragons had a difficult time thinking in Human languages, as well as the difficulty producing those sounds with their short muzzles, sharp teeth and long, slim tongues, giving them a childlike lisp. Pyth pulled her lips away from her fangs, her tongue flicking in and out of her mouth, saliva splattering in all directions while she spoke to them. She was clearly upset. "Bad Men. We see not. Strong scent. They hurt Dia! We hurt them back, get Dia back!" Dyrth simply nodded his massive triangular head in agreement. Even though they'd not known her for long, the Elf was their friend and a Water Dragon never forgot a friend. They were pissed.

Their expressions made Bastyen smile wickedly, understanding what the King's Agents were facing. Water Dragons fought with their claws, fangs, razor sharp serrated dorsal ridge, and with their spit. They were able to spew forth a focused stream of water with enough power to cut through rock. And their precision? They'd carved the names of those Warriors who had Passed the Veil since the Black War began, upon the stone walls of the Training Pits of the Dragon's Den, now known as the Wall of Valor. His eyes locked on Dyrth's, he asked, "You have enough water?"

His tongue swept forth and flicked about, tasting the air afore he sucked it back inside his mouth like a string of spaghetti, drops of saliva spraying everywhere. With nostrils flaring and an intense shine in his reptilian eyes, Dyrth growled, "Guts full."

~~~~~~~~~~

Bastyen and Graasyn declined to ride the Dragons, instead dousing them with water afore following them through the back alleys as their strong sense of smell allowed them to track the King's Agents with all haste. 'Twas good, for they had little time, and if they couldn't catch up soon they'd be trying to get Dia out of Evanntyr, a much more difficult endeavor. Their plan included making the rescue outside the walls then circling back to the docks and escaping by way of the ocean via Pyth and Dyrth. But since the Water Dragons were slow on land, once the Agents' route was established the pair led their Human friends through a short cut.

Nearing the southeastern walls of the castle, they finally sighted their prey. Dia was still struggling to keep her hair on her head and to keep from being dragged along on her knees, her predicament further angering her friends. But she was clearly also intent upon slowing them down, and in this, she'd done well.

Since Synahmarr's dramatic and destructive escape from Evanntyr, the castle had been somewhat restored, adding to the
~~~~~~~~~~

northern and southeastern edges of the walls, and closing off and stabilizing the southwestern section that had crumbled down the steep cliffs into the Fears, including the Witch's Dungeons and the Well of Evanntyr.

However, High King Shytin was not his father, and the King's Advisor, the Sorcerer, cared not for upkeep of the castle, therefore, 'twas not the best workmanship. 'Twas in the opinions of the Warriors downright shoddy, as well as horribly unfit for security purposes. Trees and brush had not been adequately cleared nor kept away from the new walls, and the walls themselves hid those walking near, from the guards above. Aside from the fact that those new walls would not hold back a siege from an army, 'twould allow access to the old walls surrounding the Ward which had been damaged by the severe quake-like shaking during the escape to the point that they too, might not hold for long against a force of any substance.

The main castle structure, however, had been adequately rebuilt and reinforced, as the Warriors noted in their recent visits. The Sorcerer's Pits of Hades had been repaired, and from what little they'd been able to glean from the peasants and kitchen staff, with only one entrance/exit through a deep stairwell, 'twould be impossible to effect an escape from there.

Consequently, 'twas now or never as the Warriors prepared to race to Diadranei's rescue. But afore they could take a single step, Pyth slid her huge bulk in their path, preventing them from moving. Turning her short muzzle to them, she growled, "No! Stand back."

Turning in unison, they watched Dyrth draw a breath quickly followed by a steady stream of water spurting forth. Afore the King's Agents were aware that they had attackers, the one covering their flank was sliced in half vertically, the blood spraying into the air and raining down o'er his companions as he fell apart. The other men leaped away as if about to be bitten by a venomous snake, and chaos erupted. All but the one still holding Dia panicked as their comrade's demise became clear and ran toward the gates of the wall, screaming in terror, seeking backup.

His eyes glued to the grisly mess, his face covered with his friend's blood, the last man shook uncontrollably, unable to free his grasp in Diadranei's hair. He could see the Warriors approaching him now, but since the Water Dragons were still wet, he knew not what was, nor from where had come, the killing strike. The people of King's Gate were superstitious and greatly feared Magic, and this could only be such. Voiceless and with his eyes widening, Dia pried his fingers open so she could distance herself to allow access for the Water Dragons or her partners, afore the fleeing Agents brought reinforcements.

As soon as Dia began to scoot away from her captor, Pyth finished him. Seeing the lance-like stream coming from out of nowhere, he simply stood motionless, frozen in horror. The spear of water pierced straight through his heart and he fell o'er backwards with the force of the attack, an expression of shock still upon his face.

Bastyen raced o'er and lifted Diadranei to her feet, performing a quick field triage in the process. The lacerations and abrasions on her face, arms, and legs were bleeding along with extensive bruising, and she had probable internal injuries and a possible concussion. Yet other than using the Healing properties contained in the bag of thick, amber colored Dragon saliva every Warrior now carried with him, they could not adequately treat her in their current situation and would have to get out of King's Gate afore doing anything further.

Graasyn assisted Bastyen with Dia and then following the Water Dragons, they ran, the sounds of Agents in close pursuit. Their encounter had taken only a mere few heartbeats and 'twas the easiest fight in which the Warriors had ever been involved, but the chase was on and they could not allow themselves to be captured again. Now they were known. Now there was a price upon their heads.

But despite Pyth and Dyrth sliding along as quickly as they could, it soon became clear they could not avoid recapture by skirting 'round Evanntyr into Wyndsyr Forest, nor could they get through the port district to the docks without being seen, not to mention that the Water Dragons were drying off, becoming visible, and running out of water for defense.

Backed up to a stone wall, they discovered to their dismay that they'd come near full circle, chased by the King's Agents and some villagers who'd tagged along for possible reward. Graasyn and Bastyen were out of ideas and were close to preparing for a final assault where they now stood, when Diadranei put up her hand. "Wait," she panted. "There is one more option, if you have the stomach for it, for 'twill be terrifying."

The Water Dragons appeared quite puzzled with their predicament as they sat and listened to the Elf. Graasyn and Bastyen were ready to hear her suggestion, as were Pyth and Dyrth. Any chance to escape, was welcome at this point.

As Dia took several breaths, Bastyen gave her a look and gestured with one hand to hurry, the sounds of their pursuers coming ever closer. Without further delay Dia stated, "Pyth and Dyrth have been wondering why we haven't just jumped off the cliffs into the Fears." Her glance toward the increasing noise of the incoming Agents, she continued, "At this point, I think 'twould be worth a try."

They now stood upon the highest peak of the cliffs of the Southern Slippes in this region and the matching expressions that 'crossed the Warriors faces were near comical. Dia quickly understood what they were thinking. "No, not just jump! We mount the Water Dragons and THEY jump." Dia looked to Pyth and Dyrth and back to her partners. "They've already decided they can make it from this height without us, and they believe they can take us with them." She paused afore adding, "With minimal difficulty."

"Oh great," stated both Bastyen and Graasyn together, but having no other choice, they all ran toward the cliffs where the Witch's Dungeons had fallen, and with their pursuers close behind, they got a quick lesson on how to ride a Water Dragon, needing only to maintain skin to skin contact. Dia's legs were already bare and taking a deep breath Bastyen and Graasyn ripped off what remained of their torn shirts and mounted. Pyth was smaller than her friend, so she took Graasyn, while Dia and Bastyen mounted Dyrth.

The Water Dragons slid to the very edge, glanced one to the other and nodding, they dove, pushing hard out and away from the rocks with all four of their short stocky legs, afore plunging near an eighth of a league to the cold waters below, their short leathery wings spread to soar as far away from the cliff face as was possible, their riders unsuccessfully trying not to hold too tightly, their screams blown backwards with the force of the driving wind.

Although Dia knew the Magic of the Water Dragons, 'twas the first time she'd ever ridden one, as 'twas for the others. And so when they hit the water, all three passengers closed their eyes tightly and held their breath, hoping they'd not be smashed upon any rocks that might be lurking just under the surface, as well as hoping they'd not all committed themselves to drowning as their method of escape.

CHAPTER NINE

First Deployment

LATER THAT EVENING

~~~~~ DARQUE'S OFFICE IN THE KEEP ~~~~~

Just a short time earlier, Darque had slowly walked from the Altar Room back to her office, trying to process everything. Her parents had filled her mind with so much new information, so many revelations. Speaking with them for several marks, her emotions ran through a gamut of highs and lows. Anger, frustration, astonishment, sorrow, and pride had all swept through her leaving an emotional exhaustion in its wake.

When Gunnarr failed to coax her back to their quarters, he'd brought her food and drink and sat with her in the office as she repeated everything she'd learned, helping her to link all the information together into an accurate timeline to discover the whereabouts of the three missing Fangs. Or at least, two of them.

As Gunnarr listened, Darque began with the blade she'd given to her mother at the Battle of Evanntyr so long ago, ensuring Aalanna would not be taken alive. With the battle still raging, she and Storrm needed to return to Drekinn to lead the Brotherhood against the Hoard attacking while their leaders were away. She'd gone to rescue Aalanna, but her mother had refused to leave Grifynn. There was nothing she could do. Giving her the blade, they'd said their goodbyes and Darque never expected to see it or her mother again.

But Grifynn made Aalanna promise not to commit suicide, telling her that she must live to further the prophesies. When he'd Passed, Aalanna had ducked into the walls of the castle, making her way eventually to find Sarai's lab. For a short time after the Last Holocaust 'twas the work study of Shayla the Healer. Inside, she'd been startled when Larkin found her, and she'd left
~~~~~

the blade upon the desk under peeled Blood Wax from unfolding the Royal Birthing Certificate she'd found on the bookshelves. On a side note, that certificate now resided in the Library of the Keep, as 'twas the documented proof of the First Born, Gabriel, the True King of Kadoor, making High King Shytin a usurper.

Therefore, if the Blood Wax had still been effective, preventing Koryl from scrying its location, and the lab had not been located by Shytin or the Sorcerer since Aalanna escaped, nor fallen into the Ocean of Fears with the rise of Synahmarr, then the blade would still be there. The front entrance was in a dark and unused corner upon one of the many landings of the Grand Staircase, hidden under an ancient tapestry.

Darque chewed her bottom lip. 'Twas possible the blade was still safe there, but Evanntyr had been compromised and was now considered a Lair of the Hoard. How by the Ancients were they to retrieve it from that wasp's nest of evil? She was reminded of a story told her by King Gabriel of a time when he, Gheryh, and Ryygg had slipped through the nest of the giant wasps of Abysmal Gorge, using only a sage smudge. What could they use as their smudge to enter Evanntyr?

Moving on to the second blade, 'twas actually the first one she'd lost. The one she'd dropped at the Battle of Kaddart, where she and Gunnarr made their first kill. But such memories were another story. Right now, she was more interested in what happened to that blade, than in recalling the details of the battle. She and Gunnarr had returned to the scene the following dawn and searched painstakingly, but to no avail. The blade had never turned up. Yet, to her utter astonishment, Grifynn just supplied the rest of the story.

Apparently the blade was found just prior to their return by Brannyn the Falcon, brother of Corbyn and now Darque's somewhat erratic contact within the Hoard. Brannyn watched them for o'er a mark, knowing for what they'd searched. Eventually, he'd used it to communicate with Grifynn, offering him the chance to rescue Aalanna from the clutches of the cruel King Shytin. 'Twas a slim chance, but one that the Battle Commander grabbed onto with both hands.

Darque had visibly flinched as Grifynn described plunging the blade into his own heart to set the Spell into motion, a Spell that would assist him to get to Evanntyr alive and give him time to save his lifemate, but from which he would not survive. Even knowing his own fate, he'd done what he must without hesitation.

Once the Spell was set he gave the blade as his passage to Myrrdin, the Ship's Master of the Krakken, and he was on his way. The rest was known to her. 'Twas after that battle that she'd given her mother the next blade.

Therefore, Myrrdin was now in possession of the blade she'd lost at Kaddart. Mayhap he knew not of its origins, nor of its importance, but she knew in her heart that he would have kept it safe. All she had to do was ask for it. Relief washed o'er her as she reveled in the ease with which that one would be retrieved. At least 'til she recalled that the Krakken now sat at the bottom of the Ocean of Fears and the blade was likely still in the safe.

But afore her thoughts could go any further, in burst Regynn. Jerking her head up, her eyes wide, she began to laugh at the look of triumph upon his face, her reaction causing an equally impressive look of confusion upon his. Taking a deep breath and exhaling slowly, she gathered her wits as her Warrior did the same.

The third 'lost' Fang was given to Fryya and although Darque could have interviewed her little sister herself, she'd not had the time. She knew Fryya felt that Darque had abandoned her, but the girl was now a Warrior and Darque was Battle Commander. Still, she promised herself that she'd try to spend more time with her youngest sister soon. In the meantime, what more complications could Regynn add to the mix? Clasping her hands together, her elbows upon the desk, she leaned forward. "What have you for me, now?" she questioned.

Without preamble, Regynn began, "I've spent several marks confirming Fryya's account of the Battle of Ice Mist Falls, where she dropped the blade you gave her. The closest eyewitnesses were Kydra and Ragnyrr but since they're currently away from the Keep, I rounded up others. 'Twas not likely to have fallen into one of the bodies of water by their descriptions and unless the Hoard have found it since, 'tis probably still where it lay when 'twas dropped." Regynn knew Darque's doubts about sending her youngest Warriors out in the field, but he also knew they needed the experience. "And I have a suggestion," he stated, his eyes a'gleam with satisfaction, stepping closer to the desk, waving to General Gunnarr to join them in the huddle. 'Twould be the perfect first assignment for the Daring Duo.

<div align="center">~~~~~ LATER ~~~~~</div>

Warriors Walkyr and Fryya stood at Battle Ease in front of Darque's desk, awaiting orders with such eager anticipation they could not wipe the grins off their faces. Darque had glanced up occasionally while they stood, then pretended to be engrossed in her paperwork, leaving them to practice patience. She was reminded of herself by their antics, when she'd stood so afore her father, waiting her turn to speak. The more she fidgeted, the longer he'd make her wait. 'Twas both a sad and satisfying memory.

Nonetheless, she was very proud of Fryya and Walkyr and was as impatient to give them their orders as they were to receive them. Giving credit where credit was due, the suggestion had come from another, but 'twas still her responsibility if anything went wrong. A sobering thought. So she'd added to the suggestion, ready to take care of that as soon as these two were off.

Finally deciding they'd waited long enough, she put the quill pen back in the holder then gathered up her papers and pushed the pile to the side of the huge desk. She cleared her throat and faced the pair. "I'm sending you to locate and bring back the blade I gave Fryya that was lost at Ice Mist."

The mention of losing it made Fryya furrow her brows and look down with a pout upon her face. "I'm sorry I left it there," she began, but Darque stopped her, lifting her hand, palm out.

"I am well aware of the circumstances of that loss," she stated, not wanting Fryya to apologize for something out of her control. "'Twas in the midst of battle and if you'd not done what you did, you'd not be here today. I have no condemnation for the loss, for 'twas not a'purpose." Darque noted Fryya still hadn't looked up, appearing as a chastised puppy. Shaking her head she continued, "I stated a simple fact. You lost it there. However, 'tis up to you to stop chiding yourself or fearing what others think about what life throws at us." Darque wanted her little sister to have the confidence of their linage, but the girl had not been raised in the Clan and she could sense Fryya's self-doubts.

"But I made a promise," she stated miserably, while scratching her shoulder. Seemed lately every time she became emotional, her skin felt tight. And thick. A truly odd, prickly sensation that would spread down her arms and back, as well as 'cross her shoulders.

Darque noted Fryya's discomfort but chose not to mention it, as she replied, "You promised to use it well and keep it close. You did that to the best of your ability. You used it to save your life and to affect your first kill. Nothing more do I expect."

Fryya nodded and met Darque's gaze once more, the former eagerness returning along with the lessening of the bizarre skin sensation. Darque smiled her approval and then began again, "You're to leave within the mark for Ice Mist Falls. Search and retrieve if still there, then return as quickly as possible. Remember many winters have passed and it might be well hidden by now, under silt and debris or washed away from the original landing site. Use your training. I expect you to do a thorough search. When you return, with or without the Fang, you will make full report."

They nodded, and with fists to chests they exclaimed together, "So be it, Commander!" afore taking their leave, their excitement near causing sparks to fly through the air. Just as they started to shut the heavy door behind them, Darque added as an afterthought, "And watch your backs, 'tis not known if the Hoard has penetrated this far into the Talons again. But remember with the fading of the old Aversion Spell o'er the forests, comes the ability of all Dragons to enter!"

"Yes Sir!" they both chimed in and then shut the door. Turning about swiftly, they near ran into Warrior Rygyl as he approached the office. First stepping one way and then the other in unison, Rygyl shook his head and then grabbed Fryya's shoulders and set her to one side as he stepped to the other. With Walkyr close behind his partner, they finally passed each other. Apologizing profusely, Walkyr and Fryya ran down the hallway to pack for their first mission.

Chuckling as he allowed the standing guard to open the door, Rygyl stepped in and leaned out to watch the two of them run down the hallway. Then as the door shut with a resounding thud, he stepped up to face his Commander. He grinned rakishly as Darque eyed his double scabbard, each of his Dragon Swords strapped 'cross his back. She knew how swiftly he could pull them and strike. Rygyl had both his own Sword and Ariel's and with them he'd become one of her most skillful, and lethal, swordsmen.

But he oft' times felt guilty. A Dragon Sword was permeated with Magic along with the essence of the one who Drew it during the ceremony, giving it a personality of sorts. 'Twas still an inanimate object, but 'twould not lose its edge, 'twould assist its Handler in the fight, could be Called back to you if dropped or otherwise lost, and was so sharp 'twould cut through Dragon scale, giving the swordsman the opportunity to make a swift kill. Although one still must be a good swordsman, with such a weapon one had a distinct advantage fighting against the Highlands of the Hoard. Without it, 'twas possible but much harder to make the kills.

Rygyl felt every Warrior should have a Dragon Sword of his own, and since another Draw for their creation was not in the immediate future, for Darque had decided another LifeBond was more important, he'd recently made the decision that he needed to share. But though he'd started to experiment, thus far Ariel's Sword would not settle into another's hand. Ariel had been a quiet introverted woman, very gifted and stylish in her swordsmanship. She could have been a Stealth Ops Warrior but had chosen to volunteer for the LifeBond and the rest was history. He was confident, however, that someday the Sword would find the one it wanted to be its Handler. And that meant that someday, he'd have to let it go.

He shrugged off the emotions that thought caused, for he'd finally come to accept his loss. Facing his Commander, he gave her his full attention while she explained his mission and gave her orders. When she was done, he sat down in the Dragon wingback chair and flipped his hand dismissively. "A veritable walk in Far Meadow. Of course I can follow them without being seen. My question, if I may be allowed to ask, is why?"

Wanting to keep the two safe, Darque hoped she'd thought of all angles. This mission was the least complicated, the most straightforward, and therefore the simplest she could envision, and 'twas perfect for their initiation into their chosen professions. Standing up, she walked slowly 'round the desk, hiking her hip onto the edge and crossing her leather braced arms o'er her rather ample chest creating a delectable cleavage to which Rygyl's eyes were now glued.

The Warriors of the Dragon Clan were not much on following rules and like her father afore her, Darque cared not, as long as they showed proper loyalty and respect. She'd rarely had to put any of them in their place since taking Command and had done so quite effectively when required. They were randy, disorderly, and tough, but none would fail her now and all would fight with her at their backs, to the Veil itself. Although she'd never been attracted to other than her lifemate, such attention was flattering.

She huffed and rolled her eyes. "Yes, you may ask. 'Tis a simple mission, but I want to test them. They've never been out on their own afore, strictly speaking they're not of age, and I want to see how they work together and without backup. Obviously, I can't see this without someone watching. AND I am concerned about their safety. With the Aversion Spell near dissipated, the Hoard is sure to notice, and will soon become a greater threat in the deep of the Talons. Besides, 'twas where the Sorcerer and King Shytin lost many of their minions in our ambush and 'twould not be outside of the norm for him to send someone to investigate. If they've found Ice Mist and evidence of the battle, this could become more complicated than a simple retrieval mission."

The thoughts that had flashed through his mind when he'd looked at Darque's bountiful figure made him aware that it had been a while, and he could use some relief. He determined that he'd find such if possible, afore he left on this duty. If no willing partners presented themselves, he could handle it alone, though 'twas rare that he'd had to do so.

Then the burly Warrior nodded, smiled, stood up, and after stating, "So be it, Commander," he took his leave, already thinking of a number of likely partners whom he might be able to contact within the next half mark.

Walking away he shrugged his shoulders. A simple mission? No mission was ever simple. So, was Darque trying to convince him or herself? Laughing out loud he drew odd looks from the few other Warriors and Den staff he passed in the hallway while he wandered to his quarters to pack, Telling Tegrynn about the mission and his plans for the next couple of marks. No need to hustle as he was highly confident he could easily track the pair with a head start, even if he hadn't already known where they were going.

~~~~~~~~~~

Her fingers laced behind her head, Darque leaned back in her chair and rested her booted feet upon the desk crossed at the ankles as she contemplated what else had occurred in her office. Given their hybrid status, Darque had recently learned that she was able to alter her skin to form Dragon scale in the heat of Battle Lust. She
~~~~~~~~~~

and Gunnarr had been attempting to do this upon command but had been unable to produce the effect at will thus far.

As she'd surreptitiously watched her little sister, the last known of their hybrid line with the Passing of Storrm and her unborn niece, she came to the conclusion that Fryya was also exhibiting this 'scaling up' phenomenon. But Fryya had only gathered eleven winters, and her emotional status standing in the office was far from Battle Lust levels. Chewing her bottom lip, she knew in her heart that Fryya was clearly going to be able to master this Gift to her advantage, and soon.

Darque was proud of her little sister and admired her swordsmanship, bravery, and loyalty. She loved her dearly and admitted to herself that she'd been protective from afar, because she was afraid of losing her, too. Nevertheless, since Storrm Passed, Darque had been avoiding the child altogether. She tried to tell herself that she was merely avoiding showing any familial bias as had her father in his treatment of his daughters growing up. His lack of personal and parental attention had made her strong and eager to please. Such had fueled her desire to become the best swordsman of his entire Brotherhood, but she'd still wanted her father to just be her father, a relationship for which they'd rarely found time.

She closed her eyes as the truth ran through her awareness. Her lack of attention wasn't her desire to harden the child to Warrior life. 'Twas the fact that Fryya looked more like Storrm than her. Seeing her little sister caused her heart to turn o'er in anguish and guilt at not being there in time to save Storrm. The smells, the sounds, the sights of the vicious battle where her sister was lost, would flash through her consciousness every time she laid eyes upon Fryya.

But with time and maintaining a busy workload, those issues were being pushed under the rug. Darque sighed. Hoping for the best for the Daring Duo, she promised herself that things would change when they returned to the Keep. If they returned. Biting her lip and putting her feet back on the floor she sat upright and wondered if she should have sent another Team for the blade.

Gunnarr had been sitting by the bookshelves, encased in what appeared to be a giant bubble that was a feature of their Magic allowing the huge Dragons to push aside the physical and to occupy small spaces. Those used to seeing it had no difficulty but for those who had no experience the illusion caused some visual distortions as they at times appeared to be occupying the same space as those 'round them. But 'twas this Magic that they used to fly through the timefold, coming as close to teleportation as reality allowed.

Now the bubble shimmered as he ambled closer. He sensed her emotions and his deep resonating voice rumbled forth, "They will return, my treasure, and there will be time enough to spend with her. But you cannot shelter her forever. You are more than her sister; you are her Battle Commander and have acted appropriately. Besides, you must take care of YOU, to be effective in taking care of the Resistance."

'Twas out of her hands now. The Team's safety and success lay squarely in their skill and what the Fates had in store. At that specific moment, one of the General's guts growled in protest and Darque laughed. "And just when was your last hunt? Seems to me, we both need to take care of ourselves."

Gunnarr said nothing but he yearned for when they could take time to 'take care of themselves' and just enjoy each other's company now and then. He sighed. Such seemed not to be forthcoming in their current lives. There was always something more to do.

Her mind still whirling with paperwork, strategies, and orders she needed to issue, Darque completely missed his emotions. 'Twas getting late and they were both hungry. Taking Gunnarr's elbow they walked together to the Mess Hall, after which he left the Keep on a much needed outing.

~~~~~~~~~~

Within the mark Walkyr and Fryya reported to the Gatekeepers, ready to leave on their mission. 'Twas good to leave so late, as the night disguised their exit should anyone be watching the area. And since Darque had given them the use of the two War Horses stabled at the Keep, they'd present a lot to see. The Horses once belonged to Graasyn and Bastyen but after arriving there from a previous mission Darque decided that the two massive beasts would stay at the Keep instead of being returned to Drekinn.

The Horses now provided for the needs of the community (usually being ridden to and from the Bog Lair) as well as providing teaching opportunities for the children with their care and upkeep. The Clan had been good farmers and breeders of fine animals, and such skills should not be lost. Darque knew their occupation of the Keep was not forever and she was already feeling the pressure of some to return to their homes in the Outlands, as well as to return to start rebuilding Drekinn. Under the Domes, such would now be safe. She shook her head as she pondered how safe 'twould be for those who wanted to return to the Outlands and the villages and subsistence farms that had been destroyed by the Hoard.

A'horseback, travel to Ice Mist Falls would be faster than a'foot, but mindful of the Battle Commander's warnings, the pair quite admirably covered their trail to avoid anyone who might be in the forests, both from those on the ground and those flying o'er head, lengthening the time 'twould take to get to their destination. After being frequently frustrated with the amount of effort he was having to expend trying to follow them, Rygyl estimated 'twould take about a moon to get to Ice Mist and silently admired not only how hard Walkyr and Fryya worked but how successful they were.
~~~~~~~~~~

He'd ordered Tegrynn to stay out of sight while he tracked the pair on the ground. When just a fortnight into the trip, he lost their trail for the third time, instead of spending another day or two trying to pick it up again, he decided to go straight to Ice Mist. Figuring the timing at another fortnight, as long as they continued on the chosen path, he traveled leisurely aboard his Dragon partner, trying to ascertain if the Hoard had infiltrated into the Talons, hoping the pair didn't get into any trouble without him.

Arriving o'er a sennight afore expecting the Team, Rygyl knew where the blade had been lost, and with that in mind, he set up his 'camp' where he could watch the two youngest Warriors complete their search without them knowing he was present. He spent the extra time making a systematic inspection of the surrounding area being careful not to leave any indication of his activities but found not the blade. Not that he'd been searching specifically for it. But he did find evidence to suggest the Hoard had been there, probably less than a full winter after the ambush, but he found nothing to suggest current occupation.

He did not expect to find Tyrrsyn's Thumper (his Clan Shield covered with Dragon scale) which the Warrior had lost in the battle, because he knew it had later been taken by Ardyth and Bryynn. Tyrrsyn had gifted the Thumper to Ardyth in appreciation for all they'd done in the next battle and he'd been given a new one since that time. The Warriors had reported losing more than a few Clan blades, though no swords or other shields, and mayhap the Hoard had already found and taken them. Clan steel was prized and brought a high price on the black market.

In the meantime Tegrynn kept out of sight, watching from a distant mountain peak, Listening to her partner's reports of progress. Rygyl prayed the Hoard hadn't found the Fang, as he settled in to wait for the arrival of Walkyr and Fryya.

CHAPTER TEN

Four Different Directions

TWO DAWNS LATER

~~~~~ EVANNTYR ~~~~~

The Sorcerer made his orders quite clear. He recalled when they'd discovered the evidence of ambush at Ice Mist Falls near six moons after losing contact with them. He'd been quite angry that they'd found so little to tell the story. A mere handful of Clan blades. The presence of the Thumper was recognized but 'twas gone, for his senses told him that the 7th Prince had found it prior to their arrival.

But regardless of what they'd not found, what they HAD found was something of great importance. After near a moon searching the area thoroughly, they'd found where one of the Fangs of Solvyngarr had lain for a time. The Sorcerer had secretly visited the Keep of St Swiftyn's with Koryl many winters past and knew of the treasures guarded in the Lost Room.

Koryl had thought to use him and his Magic to help with her curse, but he'd ended up using her instead. Nevertheless, he knew not where the witch was now, and that infuriated him. She'd somehow taken the Book of the Conqueror from the Lost Room, and for a while he'd thought she also had the Fangs in her possession. But discovering Darque had them confirmed Koryl did not. Still, the Book had not been found. Yet without the Fangs, 'twould do little good.

When he'd placed his hand o'er the grass where the Fang had been, the sensation was so strong, 'twas clear it had been taken recently. But by whom? Or, since he could sense not a Human presence, by what? And how by the Ancients, had the Fang come to be at Ice Mist Falls? Surely no one would use it in battle. Try as
~~~~~

he might, he could not sense the answers and after a time, he decided the best plan was no plan. He would retreat.

Eventually he decided to send troops back to the site to reconnoiter. Mayhap they would uncover more information, something they'd missed the first time. The perpetrator of theft always returned to the scene of his crime, and in his convoluted thinking he considered the taking of the Fang as theft. All he needed was one good clue as to what had happened there.

Facing the five Hoardsmen and two Dragons, he stated ominously, "Return not with empty hands. If not the blade I seek, then I require information of its whereabouts." His narrow eyes narrowed further and curling his lip, he made his vile promise. "This alone will allow you safe homecoming."

NEAR A FORTNIGHT LATER

~~~~~ APPROACHING ICE MIST FALLS ~~~~~

</div>

Walkyr was pissed at both himself and their situation. "Do it! Tie me to the damn saddle! We have to leave!"

Fryya had found her friend thrashing in the underbrush when she'd returned from scrounging root stock to supplement their supplies. The rabbit they'd caught was still roasting nicely on the spit. She'd left Walkyr behind as he was a better cook than she was, preferring the hunt to the chores that followed, and although she knew 'twas a risk, she'd thought 'twas not great.

Walkyr's Visions were lately coming as a complete surprise. Without warning, he jerked forward and fell into the edge of the firepit. The resultant burn on his sword hand jolted him to the awareness required to roll out of the way of further injury afore the Vision took complete control of his body.

'Twas the first fire they'd made since leaving the Keep, as they were certain they were being followed 'til now. Once that threat appeared to have ended, they'd treated themselves to some real food, deciding 'twas mayhap a native of the Talons going their
~~~~~

way briefly and now off on his own. Yet both of them had attempted to discover the identity of the follower without success.

But despite her partner's desire to leave immediately, along with his uncharacteristic attitude, Fryya kept a more level head, which was truly odd. Usually 'twas the other way 'round. Insisting she treat and dress the burn and that they finish their meal and clean up afore departing, giving Walkyr time to recover as well as much needed nourishment, he finally had to admit she was correct. However, he was still concerned.

Brushing o'er the entire area with a leafy branch afore randomly tossing handfuls of leaf litter, 'twould take much skill to note anyone had passed through recently. Their Horses loaded, they steered away from Ice Mist, taking a roundabout route to leave a false trail as of a wandering horse or local traveler. The thick mulch of the forest floor would help to disguise the size of their hooves, and every so often one of them would leap down and run back to cover here and there, disguising the trail even more, afterwards catching up with both Horses and their partner. She knew 'twas taking twice as long to get to their destination as was normal, but they were determined not to fail the Commander. They had to get there safely to do the search and then they could hard ride back.

Typically they traveled in silence, for the forest might have ears to hear, but Fryya needed to know about Walkyr's Vision. "So? What did you See? Why in such a hurry to leave?"

Walkyr appeared pensive for a moment afore he replied, "I Saw Rygyl."

Surprised, Fryya responded, "He's the one following us?"

Again, Walkyr hesitated. "No, he's ahead of us. I Saw him at Ice Mist."

Indignantly she questioned, "But why? Trying to beat us to the blade?" Fryya liked the burly Warrior and had greatly envied his skill with double Swords. 'Twas awe inspiring to watch in Training. She could only imagine what 'twould be like to see in battle. And it went without saying such would not be a good thing with which to find yourself at odds. Noting the lengthening time 'twas taking for Walkyr to respond, she eyed him apprehensively. "There's more?"

He took a deep breath. "Yes, there's more. He wasn't searching. He seemed to be waiting for someone."

"Us?" But 'twas puzzling because why would he be ahead of them if he weren't looking for the blade himself? Mayhap he was the one following but if so, he'd get there after them, or, he'd have flown on Tegrynn. And therefore for whom was he waiting and who had sent him? Was he working on orders, or on his own?

"Honestly, I couldn't tell. 'Twas most peculiar." He paused afore he finally continued after catching 'that look' on Fryya's face. "Alright! I also Saw at least five Hoardsmen and two Dragons in route to Ice Mist from the Razor's Edge."

Fryya gasped with the possibilities that burst into her mind. No Warrior had ever broken their Oath, but the war had brought many changes and the one lesson they'd all learned was the hardest: that anyone could fail, anyone could make bad choices, anyone could betray them. Putting one's faith in others was always a dance of uncertainty. Still, she shook her head. "Surely he's not gone o'er to the Black. Not Rygyl."

"All I know is that we have to beat the Hoard party to Ice Mist Falls if we're to obtain the blade. And with Rygyl there already and not knowing why, we have our work cut out for us. Several scenarios come to mind. If he came for the blade, he may be waiting for us to find it for him, afore trying to take it away. If he has already found it, he may intend to give it to the Hoard. But no matter what, we must accept this mission has suddenly gone from simple to extremely complicated. We face competition, as well as strong potential for a fight."

Fryya nodded her head solemnly. They were near their destination, and now they needed to rethink their original plans. One hand holding her reins, the other now resting on the grip of her sword, she stated summarily, "A triad. Us, Rygyl, and the Hoard."

<center>~~~~~ MEANWHILE ~~~~~</center>

Myrrdin and Calei pushed hard and the party moved quickly, making no unnecessary stops or diversions on their way back to Port O'Drekinn while still allowing them all to keep up their strength. Within a fortnight they arrived where lay the Lytle at anchor. 'Twould take near another fortnight to sail to the island.

As soon as they climbed the gangway to board, Myrrdin's Tie, Islyth, soared out of the sea, her short leathery wings spread wide as she landed in a belly flop on the deck, splashing water everywhere. Her long tail provided stability for her enthusiastic greeting as she quickly sat up on her short hind legs. Her huge saucer-shaped paws pressed back to back at the wrists held firmly to her chest gave her that adorable look that was so off beam as she swayed her long, green scaled body side to side, opposite the swaying of her slightly triangular head, (her heavily muscled jaws enhancing that shape) with her enormous slit eyes flashing and nostrils flaring in pure eagerness.

'Twas a tad mesmerizing and Calei had to shake her head to regain her focus. Delighted to see Caleichante again, Islyth assured the Sprite she had taken very good care of her Tie, Schlynn, after which the oldest Water Dragon Calei had ever known, leaned o'er the railing and slipped back into the sea, promising to bring her wayward friend as soon as possible, as well as to summon the rest of their Ties.

It took less than a dawn for all their Water Dragons to report to that summons and following alongside the ship, they set sail for the Island of Dreams. 'Twas an adventure in the making and all Water Dragons were up for an adventure, therefore 'twas no real surprise to find the rolling waters surrounding the ship, teeming with Water Dragons by the time they approached the island. Though 'twas sometimes difficult to get the cooperation of a Water Dragon, as they preferred not to be told what to do ('twas an art to discuss matters with them, as they needed to be made to think 'twas their own idea), once Myrrdin had impressed upon Islyth that they, along with their eggs and the island, were in grave danger, literally hundreds came to help.

Standing on the quarterdeck, Myrrdin watched the Water Dragons dance and fly through the waters in their wake, soaring and diving happily as if they had not a care in the world. If he'd been Human and seen such, he might mistake them for so many whales, or dolphins, or other sea creatures. He spoke to Calei, but his eyes did not leave the waters, his voice troubled. "They should not be here; they are in grave danger. Did I not tell Islyth that?"

Her musical voice matched his, though not in timber. "They protect their own. 'Tis their nature. They will not back down in the face of peril. They do what they must without thought for their own safety. You know this."

Their need was urgent, and secrecy was not in the plan. There was no time for such. The arrival of the Lytle followed by the massive procession of Water Dragons, was a sight to be remembered by every citizen who happened to be near, and rumors began to fly even as they docked. Disembarking, the party followed Myrrdin and Calei to Dream Hold leaving the port more than crowded with Water Dragons, effectively blocking any other ships that might be trying to make port.

Since there was no royal presence they called an emergency meeting with the Sprite Elite Guard, for their participation would be required in any decision made. Captain Naftaleah was happy to see them, yet leery of the news they brought. Despite the fact that the former Captain, Caleichante, had not set foot on the island since leaving with Kevon, greetings were brief and somewhat stilted. Myrrdin sat at the right hand of the head of the table, his First Mate, Lyran at his side, flanked by Caleichante, Lyrianei, Kalisadei, Ardryyn, Kryllyn, Datyniah, and Dalakiah. Naftaleah sat at the head, and her six primary Elite Guardsmen, fanned out behind her, rounded out the participants.

It took not long for them to explain the threat. All were silent as Naftaleah sat back, crossed her arms, and furrowed her brows in concentration. She agreed with Myrrdin and Calei that the danger affecting them was a task for the Guard. They'd not call upon the Assembly, as this required speed, not diplomacy.

To clarify, she summarized aloud, "Fifty or sixty winters for the Spell to fail and the poison in those three barrels still in that scuttled ship, to be exposed to the waters, which will activate it." She continued after seeing the slight nod of Myrrdin's head. "Those three barrels are enough to destroy the entire batch of Water Dragon eggs incubating in the Grotto as well as most of the organics upon the island, including our citizens." Again, she paused for the nodded confirmation, uncrossing her arms and running one long finger back and forth 'cross her bottom lip as she considered her next words. "And they have been there for just o'er fifty winters now, therefore, the Spell could fail at any moment." To which she received yet another nod to confirm.

Now leaning forward, she continued, "If the Spell fails, it fails. All we can do is try to prevent the disaster. They must be moved. But 1) they may be wet already and 'twould kill those trying to dive for them, 2) they cannot be neutralized mid-ocean as we would have not the organics from which to Draw energy to perform the neutralization, 3) we could not keep the powder inside dry when opened to neutralize in that situation, and 4) we cannot bring them here, as the poison might be activated while trying to raise and transport it and 'twould kill us all. As for the other option, even sacrificing a ship to haul it away could be a suicide mission for the crew and no guarantee they could haul it far enough away afore it activated. We need more speed than any ship, including the Lytle, can provide."

Naftaleah was truly perceptive and although what she'd said had already been thought of by the others, bringing it all to light aloud was somewhat deflating. 'Twas true. They could not do it mid-ocean and they could not bring it to the docks, as well as the absurd notion of someone volunteering to take it away and surely die. Afore Myrrdin stood up, everyone knowing he was about to be that volunteer, Naftaleah raised her hand to stop him. "There's yet another possibility, Ship's Master. The risks are the same, but it may well be the answer to more than one problem."

THE DRAGON'S DEN OF DREKINN LAIR
~~~~~ MEANWHILE ~~~~~

</div>

The Stealth Team had arrived via their Water Dragons at the castle of the Warrior Brotherhood through the Well of Drekinn in the dungeons. Quickly recognized, the Guards escorted the three directly to Darque who was currently at the Den. Her Seconds in Command, Kydra and Ragnyrr were deployed to locate the lost Warriors as well as any refugees of the Hoard's vicious attacks and while they were away, her acting Seconds, Tyndall and Fyndarr, with her acting Thirds, Daayn and Kashiyann, were assisting her with the Command rotations through the Keep, the Bog, and Drekinn.

Darque continued to struggle with the decision to permanently replace Kydra and Ragnyrr as Seconds. Although Kydra tried to keep such knowledge from her, Darque knew that Ragnyrr had been plagued with guilt and depression since losing his cousins and mother in the big battles and Kydra was trying to help him heal. But Darque suspected she was making little progress. Kydra had requested their mission be extended again and again, and Darque knew they were making little progress with that as well.

But there was always so much to do that she barely had time to think, and she and Gunnarr had not had a moment to themselves for many moons. His discontent with the situation was growing but she felt trapped and to salve her conscience she buried herself in her duties.
~~~~~

When the Stealth Team arrived Darque told them of Calei's mission, confirming she'd heard nothing since they'd left. Graasyn remained silent, but Dia sensed his near stifling emotional state of helplessness.

Then they made report on their mission to King's Gate. While there they'd only been able to confirm that Koryl had disappeared and was still being sought by the Sorcerer. She was likely traveling as an Oracle and might have been in Tupry for a while. As for the Black's new Lair, no one said or knew anything. They'd been frustrated with such a lack of factual information. They had, however, been able to study some of the new architectural repairs upon the castle.

As for their escape, once they hit the water and discovered to their great relief that they'd not been smashed upon any rocks nor had they drowned, they were delighted to also learn they could breathe while the Water Dragons near flew them through the Ocean of Fears away from King's Gate. Skirting along the dangerous shoreline of the Southern Slippes they avoided the even more dangerous Leviathans out in the open waters, making their way to the Sea of Dreams and then up the coast to Drekinn. Water Dragons could freely enter the Domes by way of the wells, and so they wasted no time trying to attract the attention of a Gatekeeper to portal them through the barrier.

Darque's Communications Teams and the People of the Daggogh and Gordatch acting as her transient spies in Wyndsyr Forest learned of the Stealth Team's hasty departure, as well as that the King's Agents had completely missed their escape route, unable to fathom the idea that anyone would simply leap off the cliffs let alone that they might have survived such a fall. Consequently, they Agents spent many marks and then many days searching the port district and the surrounding forest, taking countless to the Pits of Hades for the Sorcerer to question about the current location of the fugitives. The citizens of the village knew that giving him others upon whom to vent his anger had the added benefit of keeping the Sorcerer's focus away from them and so, lies and betrayal were rampant.

These people had been their neighbors, their customers, their friends. But they'd also betrayed Dia, lifted not a finger to help when she was taken, slammed doors in their faces when they were on the run, and pointed out which way they'd gone to their pursuers. Mayhap 'twas fear but the Team felt no remorse. You either fought against evil or you became its pawn. Such was the Oath of the Warrior Brotherhood. Such was the watchword of the Clan.

Darque leaned forward in her chair, waving at them to stand down. After they made themselves comfortable, she took a deep breath. Then she cleared her throat. Then she scratched behind one ear. She was clearly uncomfortable with what she was about to say. The Stealth Team glanced at each other with growing apprehension and when they noted Dia's eyebrows rising, they knew they were about to hear something they'd rather not.

Squinting, Darque finally blurted forth, "There is still something quite valuable at Evanntyr and I'm sending you back." All three simply stared at her in disbelief. She sighed and leaned back again, rubbing her eyes. She was so tired. She needed a break.

Graasyn stood up and placed one hand upon her desk, leaning o'er with an incredulous look on his face. "What?"

Darque knew he was asking if she had completely lost her mind. But she gave him the benefit of the doubt. Mayhap he was asking what the very valuable thing was. No matter, she'd figured out 'the smudge' to get them back inside. Catching his eye, she stated, "Well, at least I have a plan. Sort of." Shrugging her shoulders, she continued, "Take it or leave it, but you must go back. Oh! And I suggest you try to convince Pyth and Dyrth to go along if they will. I have a feeling they'll be quite helpful."

<div align="center">~~~~~~~~~~</div>

After hearing about the mission and the plan she had in mind, they were rather impressed. Like her father afore her, Darque was a good strategist. Bastyen and Graasyn had not been all that happy to return, but even afore they knew the insanity of the mission, none of them would have refused the Battle Commander.

One of the Fangs was still at Evanntyr Castle and must be retrieved. And that meant, they had to get back inside without getting killed or captured. Not long afore they'd returned to Drekinn, Darque heard from her spies that the Sorcerer had placed high prices upon their heads. But he wanted the Stealth Team alive. Especially Diadranei, as 'twas alleged she was a Magic bearer.

Darque's plan was for the men to disguise themselves as King's Agents and take Diadranei in for the reward as if they'd found her in the forest. 'Twas not a bad plan but the Stealth Team made it better. King's Agents were not well trained and held in low regard by the Sorcerer and Shytin. Going disguised as Bounty Hunters would be a safer option for them all and 'twould get them further inside. Bounty Hunters could come and go without fear of being held by the Sorcerer because he appreciated their assistance, along with a healthy respect for their profession. He was no fighter and knew not entirely of what they were capable. No one was even certain if they were human. Thus, there grew a truce of mutual tolerance that neither would break. This also had they discovered during the winters they'd spent there. This trivial information suddenly proved to be very useful indeed.

THE ICELANDS

CRYSTAL CAVERNS

~~~~~ CASTLE OF THE ICE DRAGONS ~~~~~

</div>

Bryanna's eyes filled with tears of joy mixed with concern as she brushed snow off the fur 'cross her lover's forehead. The Empress Bronwyn cradled the Wolf to her chest and once
~~~~~

Bryanna was seated upon the Dragon's shoulders they took wing back to the castle.

They'd found him lying in the frozen snowpack barely 'cross the border, still in Shift. Bryanna had waited and watched and prayed for Rhyah's safe return. Daily, they'd set out and searched the border, and o'er two moons later he'd finally been found. 'Twas a good sign he'd been able to maintain his Shift, for this showed he still had strength left him to survive the ordeal.

The alteration of their bodies and their Life Forces allowed Bryanna and Rhyah to endure the harsh environment of the Icelands, but in so doing, they'd been informed that they'd lost the ability to survive elsewhere. According to Bronwyn, if he'd been unable to maintain his Shift he'd not have survived the travel back to the Icelands. Now that he was 'cross the border, he should be able to recover.

When Rhyah first arrived near three winters past, he'd discussed their situation at length with Bryanna. The Empress Bronwyn impressed upon him that she'd altered them so that they could live, but unwittingly she'd sentenced them to a lifespan of captivity. The Ice Dragons could cross the border freely, though they would weaken as their bodies warmed, and required returning to the ice and cold of their homeland to replenish their strength and their Magic. 'Twas not unlike others, for all Magic bearers had a Link to Kadoor and the Ice Dragons' Link was the Icelands, their Magic requiring not organics, but the frigid cold of the ice itself.

But the border of no return was a boundary Bryanna and Rhyah could not cross. For if they did, Bronwyn told them they'd instantly turn into a pillar of ice. For many moons Rhyah had wanted to test the boundary, to test their imprisonment. The Fay were powerful and valued their freedom, and as his preferred Shift was the Wolf, he felt an ever-increasing restlessness filling his heart and soul. But he also loved Bryanna and if he died she would once again be alone here, her heart broken.

She'd not argued with his desires, she'd fully supported him. She'd felt guilty that he was now trapped as was she. Bryanna loved Rhyah with all her heart, and all she wanted was for him to be happy. If that meant he would leave her, then so be it. Her unusual Tie to the Empress had elongated even her Elven span of days and she would spend them in misery without Rhyah. But knowing he had done what he wanted, would be her solace.

Frequently Bronwyn would leave for up to moons at a time, returning with treasures of all types from the far corners of the world. And then one day she returned with the Fang. Bryanna identified it positively and with great wonder. She knew it required not only protection but to be returned to its rightful owner. However, the Ice Dragons were a bit different in their thinking. Bronwyn had 'given' the treasure to Bryanna, therefore, she could not take it back to hand it o'er to another. And Bronwyn reminded them that even if anyone could come and get it, given the unique properties of the alteration they could touch no other living creature than each other and the Ice Dragons, without turning into that block of ice, therefore, neither could Bryanna hand it o'er to anyone. What were they to do?

Nevertheless, the Fay were the strongest Magic bearers and Rhyah's senses told him something was wrong. And because of this feeling, he became convinced that the alteration would not affect him the same way when he was in Shift. Bryanna was Elven and though Magic was Magic, some were more skilled in different types, each having their forte Magics, and the Fay were the best Shifters. So 'twould be up to him to make the attempt. If he could leave the Icelands in Shift and get to the Empath Diadranei, he could communicate as the Wolf with her, telling her they had the Fang. Then mayhap they'd have time to discuss further how to make the exchange.

Although there must be another option, he just couldn't see it. Mayhap he was too close to the problem. For many moons he'd thought about his plan. Would it work? If not, the Fang would lay in the castle of the Ice Dragons forever, just another treasure in the stash of the Empress.

Then one night as they lay completely satiated in each other's arms after making love for marks, he gazed into her eyes and she knew he was leaving. She gulped back her tears. "Must you go?" she'd asked him. He'd nodded his head and caressed her cheek with his knuckles, the sadness he felt, reflected in his eyes. "Yes," he'd replied. Lowering his face to hers, he'd kissed her deeply, passionately, filling her with all the love he had to give, hoping 'twould not be the last time, but knowing if 'twas, this would be her last memory of him. If he changed to ice when he stepped 'cross the border, even that would be destroyed by the light of the sun within a few dawns. He did not want her to see that. "Stay here," he'd demanded. And once she nodded her promise to do so, he'd stood up and prepared to have Bronwyn fly him to the border. Turning to his heart's desire, he whispered, "I love you." And then mounting, Bronwyn reluctantly flew him out of the caves of ice into the near constant blizzard.

Much to her relief the Empress had returned shortly later, telling her that Rhyah had made his Shift just afore crossing the border. Taking one cautious step at a time, the Wolf had soon bounded forward with ever increasing speed, both the Empress and the Fay surprised and delighted by his success, but neither knowing how much time he had.

Such had never been done afore. After having planned, discussed, and theorized for moons, the Empress hoped for Bryanna's sake that Rhyah would succeed. She yelled her warnings, echoing behind him as he disappeared into the distance, "Return as soon as you feel the effects for you surely will! And do not enter past Magical borders or protections! AND do not touch ANY LIVING CREATURE!"

Now her lover had returned to her safely, intact and exhilarated with what he'd done. Bryanna said nothing for she was not so excited. Such a success meant that he could do something she could not and once more she would be alone, if not always, then much of the time, for she felt his wanderlust growing.

'Twas late and Rhyah had slept most of the day since they'd found him at the border. During those few marks, the aging process reversed, his injuries healed, and his strength was regained. Barely falling below the junction 'tween her thighs, the blouse she wore was laced at the top, while Rhyah lay naked in all his masculine glory. He was so handsome, her hand reached forth to touch him, to convince herself that he was real. But she pulled back. She didn't want to wake him.

As Bryanna leaned o'er, his eyes suddenly opened and she stared at him, searching for answers, confirmation of his love, needing to know if his success had made him want to leave for good, but so very grateful he was back, that he'd survived. The mixed emotions must have shone through the open windows to her soul, for Rhyah stared at her with equal intensity as he pulled her down to lie next to him on their ice bed. "You are not happy for my return?" he questioned; afraid he'd done something that had diminished her love for him.

Her brows furrowed with concern, she sucked her bottom lip into her mouth, holding it there with perfect white teeth. Then Rhyah rolled onto her, locking her legs 'tween his, and with one hand holding the nape of her neck he kissed her, drawing her lip into his own mouth, his tongue intertwining with hers, conquering her doubts. She was so beautiful; he was stunned at the power of her love.

With his kiss, her heart pounded within her chest as if 'twould burst forth. She felt his free hand slowly unlace her blouse and push impatiently inside the fabric to release her firm breasts, cupping them, kneading them, bringing them to the diffused light of the caverns so he could gaze upon their beauty. His tongue slid painstakingly down her chin and neck as her body arched upwards, begging him to take them in his mouth. As her breath shortened and stuttered he teased her, licking, and swirling his tongue o'er the soft skin of her breasts, closer and closer, afore at last he encircled the hardening pink nipples. Bryanna gasped as he lowered his head ever so slowly and gently suckled.

Breathless, his heartrate accelerating, he strained to control his actions, forcing himself to slow down as he brushed his other hand from her neck 'cross her shoulder, caressing down her arm, afore drifting to her flat belly. With the intensity of the emotions his vision began to change, and he felt his canines elongating as if he were about to Shift involuntarily, something that had never happened afore. The taste of her skin, her mouth, her moisture, was intoxicating.

Nipping at her breasts, he could feel the heat of her body increasing and if not altered, 'twould have melted the bed upon which they laid. But his own body temperature was rising to an unbelievable level, the length of time he'd been without her, far too long, and he could wait no longer.

Bryanna whimpered in yearning, and the sound fed his feral need. The plan to be slow and gentle vanished. Ripping her blouse open to give him free access, he shoved his hand 'tween her thighs, parting the coarse curls with his long fingers, invading her depths as he reveled in the tightness of her walls, slipping in two fingers, then a third while her sweet hot juices covered his hand. Still staring at his lover he brought his fingers to his mouth and licked them greedily.

She was ready for him and he lost all control. Aggressively pushing her legs apart with his knees, he knelt 'tween them as he grabbed her hips and pulled her up his thighs. His buttocks tight, his stiff cock plunged inside her, deep and hard. Yanking her to him and holding tightly for added leverage with each push, he set a quickening rhythm that would take them o'er the edge of ecstasy within moments. With one final thrust, Bryanna climaxed screaming his name, her juices spurting forth prompting Rhyah's release, his hot seed filling her in spasms of pure joy.

~~~~~ THE FOLLOWING DAWN ~~~~~

Near feral, struggling for control, Rhyah realized he'd been much rougher than he'd planned but once he saw the look on Bryanna's face, the encouraging smile she gave him, he'd repeated the performance 'til both were completely satisfied. They'd slept in each other's arms for the remainder of the night.

'Twas now morning and he told her of his travel to the Keep of St Swiftyn's, his search for Diadranei. But she was not there. Sensing another Empath, he sat at the barrier trying to figure out how to contact her. 'Twas Anastasia. That one was still young and therefore not as powerful as Dia, not to mention that she should have been on the Island of Dreams, but he'd take what he could get.

He was convinced Ana understood him or that she could figure it out given what he'd conveyed. She'd also told him she was leaving for the Wyrdritch, but he'd been in need of leaving himself. There'd been no time to clearly divulge that the Fang was in the Icelands, and no time to devise a plan. His experiment was successful in that he learned he could survive in Shift for a time, but as for imparting their message, 'twas disappointing.

While Rhyah talked about what had happened, Bryanna remembered something from her own past. She recalled seeing a young girl suddenly appear in the Icelands, and then just as suddenly turn about and dive into thin air, disappearing. She'd been riding Bronwyn at the time and they'd flown quickly toward the girl, Bryanna waving to get her attention. From the girl's description, Rhyah confirmed that 'twas Anastasia, her youngest stepdaughter. Still holding Bryanna, his gaze upon the crystalline ceiling high o'er head, he asked mischievously, "So, you are certain 'twas not your imagination?"

Punching him in the arm, she sat up and tried to reach for what was left of her blouse, but Rhyah playfully pulled her back to his side, laughing. "Yes," she said. "I am certain of what I saw. 'Twas long ago, and I know the girl saw me afore she turned and
~~~~~

disappeared again, diving into nothingness, the same way she'd appeared. From nowhere."

Rhyah considered what Bryanna had seen. By the timing, 'twas afore the Protection Spell o'er the Wyrdritch had been Healed, and that meant that the portals were uncontrolled, not like they were now, and were randomly pulling Elves out of the Wyrdritch, which was how Bryanna had arrived in the Icelands in the first place. She and Bronwyn had patrolled frequently, hoping they'd find anyone else who might be drawn through a portal afore 'twas too late, hoping to save them, but none ever came. 'Twas as much of a surprise to find Rhyah the way they did, as 'twas for Bryanna to see Anastasia. Mayhap if she'd had the presence of mind to turn and dive back through the portal by which she'd come, she'd not have near died, forcing Bronwyn to alter her to save her life, leaving her stranded.

But no one knew what was happening back then with the portals, 'til Anastasia began experimenting. 'Twas no one's fault and now that Bryanna had the love of her life with her, she felt less like a caged animal, making this life easier to bear. Suddenly she noticed Rhyah looking at her with the strangest expression on his face. "What are you thinking now?" she asked cautiously.

"I'm thinking that Crystal Caverns is not as cold as 'tis outside."

With a knowing look, Bryanna replied, "No, 'tis not, and yes, with adequate clothing, even a Human might survive for a few marks here, mayhap even a few dawns. But no, no one can trek this far into the Icelands. The other Dragon Races cannot move quickly enough in this intense cold and would eventually freeze solid afore they could get here. And even by Ice Dragon, no one unaltered can survive long enough to fly here for flight increases the cold. And then there's the Ice Rains which can occur at any moment. Dancing requires organics, of which we have none, and since true teleportation is a myth and not reality with Magic, there is no way to enter the kingdom of the Ice Dragons and live, other than to be altered. I've already thought of all this, discussing it at length with Bronwyn, and she has confirmed my thoughts."

Teleportation? Picturing Anastasia and the portals of the Spell Domes his mind was awhirl. "But if one were to portal directly inside Crystal Caverns, one could survive the journey both here and back again as did Anastasia," he continued, her eyes widening at the realization that he could be correct. That just might work.

Then her heart dropped. She could see it in his eyes, felt it with her senses. He was going back. Back to give Anastasia the coordinates for Crystal Caverns. With flaring emotions, for such would expose the Ice Dragons to the outside world in their own homeland, she let him hug her to his chest as she wept quietly.

Oh, she knew it had to be done, for she'd been a Queen of the Elven Nation, teething on diplomacy and foreign policy strategies. The Fang must be taken back to Darque. But her tears fell for another reason. The Ice Dragons she'd come to love and respect, were being dragged into the Black War. The Magic was out there. The portals existed. If the Sorcerer learned of such, he might eventually duplicate it and there'd be nowhere to hide. They needed Darque and Darque needed them.

NEAR A FORTNIGHT LATER

~~~~~ ICE MIST FALLS ~~~~~

</div>

The Daring Duo had been very careful approaching the area a'foot, leaving the Horses to free graze a league distant. The forest floor was covered with a new layer of fallen leaves, the scrub was thick but bare and provided less camouflage than at other times. When they found the lone Hoardsman on guard, they'd jumped him from behind and afore he could cry out to warn his comrades, they'd silenced him forever. Covering his body with brush so as not to alert the others too quickly, 'twas clear they had to do the same to the rest of them, to complete their mission.
~~~~~

Neither wanted to return empty handed. But in all the battles in which they'd participated thus far, they'd been part of a much bigger presence, surrounded by their fellow Warriors. Still, this was why Darque had sent them here, to get experience, to learn to fight as a solo Team. Fryya was excited. Walkyr was cautious.

'Twas apparent the Hoardsmen had not expected company as they'd actually set up a full camp with a fire. Swords in hands, the pair crouched behind the underbrush trying to get a good look at those they must soon face. Listening carefully, they'd heard nothing about an expected encounter. It seemed the Hoardsmen were here for the same reason as were they.

Fryya leaned o'er to her partner and whispered, "Mayhap they are waiting for Rygyl, but I think not." She adjusted her position wondering where the huge Warrior was now, and continued, her plan taking into consideration the fact that she was a winter elder of her friend and that as always, she wanted to protect him. "I'll take the one on the far side of the fire, he's the biggest, and you get the smaller two o'er there." She pointed confidently toward the south side of the small camp, never doubting her friend could take more than one at a time.

"What about the Dragons?" Walkyr whispered.

"Dragons?" Fryya was a tad confused, then suddenly remembered that Walkyr had Seen two of the huge beasts along with the Hoardsmen afore flippantly exclaiming, "We'll take care of them when they show up!"

Still on their hands and knees, Walkyr had to grab onto Fryya's ankle to stop her from forging ahead into the clearing to set forth her plan. Harshly, he hissed, "Wait!"

Glaring at him o'er her shoulder, she asked, just as harshly, "Why?"

"Aren't you forgetting something else?"

Exasperated, she asked, "What?"

"I Saw FIVE Hoardsmen," Walkyr whispered softly.

"So? We took out one back there," Fryya began, using her thumb o'er her shoulder to point toward where they'd left his body afore she continued, "and the other three stand afore us!"

Walkyr sighed as he finally got her to pull back and kneel beside him. Shaking his head, he stated with mild sarcasm, "Did you pay any attention in class?"

Having been raised as an Outlander, Fryya was still defensive about her shortcomings. She'd missed out on Early Childhood Training and had worked very hard to catch up with her age group once she'd been rescued and integrated into the Clan. She'd quickly decided that fighting skill was what she needed most to become a Warrior as were her elder sisters. A touch of agitation laced through her voice as she replied, "I was particularly good at swordsmanship and survival, as I recall."

Walkyr's original Claim father, Kallyr, had personally tutored the pair on their academics and he knew that Fryya was not stupid, she was merely being hasty. And she was not thinking. She had the intelligence of both her sisters, mayhap more so given her upbringing. Slowly, patiently, he said, "Fryya, we killed one, and we now see three more. That means what?"

Doing the figures quickly in her head, the girl immediately took offense and grimaced in growing awareness. Deflated, she said, "Four. It means there's one missing." She'd been impulsive, she knew it. She just wanted so much for Darque to be proud of her, she wanted so much to be successful in this mission. She frowned in apology to Walkyr who merely smiled and nodded his understanding. He loved that girl no matter what, she was more than his best friend and he would stand beside her through any trial, anywhere, anytime. To the Veil. He just preferred that to happen a long time in the future and not tonight.

They needed to back off, they were too close to the camp with one of the enemy missing not to mention the two Dragons they had yet to locate. Training taught them that first and foremost, one had to know where ALL of one's enemies were, afore attacking the main body. And Dragons could be difficult to see at night, especially if their scales were a darker color, or one of the blues that ranged through plums, lavenders, purples, mauves, lilacs, violets, and grays. Highlands were many different colors. However, all Dragons had a sparkle to their scales that would sometimes glint in the sunlight. The trick to spotting them at night was to highlight that sparkle by the light of fire or torch, which also meant one had to be near within reach. Thankfully, the Hoardsmens' fire was very large.

Glancing o'er their shoulders then to the men, they began to slowly creep backwards, when suddenly Walkyr felt a strong hand grab his ankle, jerking him off the ground and slinging him far away from Fryya. The hard landing knocked the wind out of him, and he huffed and rolled o'er to catch his breath afore swiftly regaining his feet. The Hoardsman was wrestling with Fryya and he ran toward them as fast as he could.

Thinking the children were just children was the man's first mistake. The second was not paying attention to their weapons, clearly marking them as proficient fighters. Fryya had the man impaled upon her sword afore he could get a solid grip on her throat and now she struggled to get out of his grasp. Refusing to let go the hilt of her sword, for that would give the enemy her weapon, she felt that odd sensation of thickening skin 'round her neck, 'cross her shoulders and down her arms. She sensed that without this change, her throat would've been crushed.

Walkyr knew from personal experience that the man had strong hands, and that grip stayed Fryya from pulling her boot blade as she worked at prying his hand away from her throat with one hand while her feet dangled just off the ground, allowing her no leverage. The Hoardsman's other hand was trying to force her to release her grip upon the sword so he could yank it out.

Walkyr swung his own sword as he ran forward and struck true, hamstringing the man. Blood was already trickling out of the corners of his mouth from Fryya's stab, as he dropped forcefully to his knees, a look of pure astonishment upon his face at being bested by such an unlikely pair. Releasing his grasp upon Fryya's neck, she coughed, her eyes watering, and in one smooth movement she regained her feet and yanked the sword from his gut to join Walkyr who was slitting his throat with a boot blade to keep him silent afore they finished him.

Granted, the man had little chance against the pair with his chosen tactics, but he'd caused some minor injuries aside from opening the burn not yet healed on Walkyr's sword hand, and the commotion of the skirmish alerted his comrades to their presence despite their best efforts. They were in trouble. 'Twas difficult to swing sword in the midst of such thick brush, and the others were heading toward them anyway, so glancing one to the other, together they leaped o'er the body of their second kill and charged into the fray. Speed was their only ally now.

<p style="text-align:center">~~~~~ MEANWHILE ~~~~~</p>

Rygyl had kept a dark camp since his arrival, unsure when the Daring Duo would appear and wanting not to alert them to his presence. When the Hoardsmen came with their Dragons just three nights past, he was somewhat shocked but remained undetected as he made every effort to keep tabs on them while still watching for Fryya and Walkyr. Tegrynn was little assistance in the latter effort as her raptor's vision could not see much through the surrounding heavy forest.

'Twas clear the Hoardsmen expected to be alone as they'd set up an open camp. After an extensive observation Rygyl concluded there were five humans and two Dragons. No one new had shown up, nor had the men said anything indicating they were expecting reinforcements. But the Dragons had flown off to the northwest shortly after arriving, leaving the men alone. Tegrynn kept a wary eye out but went not so far as to follow for she felt confident they were hunting after their long journey, a notion with which Rygyl agreed.

'Twas just shy of a fortnight since he'd arrived and estimated Walkyr and Fryya would be here at any time. He needed to get to them afore they ran into the Hoardsmen or a'foul of the Dragons, for who knew when or if they'd return? He'd considered simply hitting the men all at once, but they were never all at the camp at the same time and too many things could go wrong, especially if the Dragons decided to return at that moment. And he didn't want to pick them off one by one for that would alert them to his presence, making them even more cautious, which in turn would make it that much more difficult to finish them off. He felt the weight Darque had placed upon his shoulders to protect Walkyr and Fryya, even if they'd not been his Warrior brother and sister in arms. But 'twould be wiser to wait for their assistance.

Circling the camp slowly, 'twas long past dusk and getting quite dark when just as he realized not one, but two of the Hoardsmen were missing, he heard rustling to the east, a good distance away from the camp. Noting none of the remaining Hoardsmen seemed interested, likely thinking 'twas an animal, he skirted the camp and getting there as quickly as possible, he found one of the Hoardsman dead under some brush. Four left with one unknown position and 'twas obviously the Daring Duo who'd done the deed. They were here and he'd missed them. Now where had they gone?

Fuming, he zig zagged his way back toward the camp. Convinced the pair were somewhere in the surrounding brush, he had to find them afore they did anything rash or were found by the Hoard. 'Twas at that moment he heard the commotion off to his right.

CHAPTER ELEVEN

Kidnapped

~~~~~ HAVEN ~~~~~

Coltyn rubbed the sleep from his eyes as he tried to wake up. His mind was foggy, and he could barely remember going to bed earlier, but he recalled evening meal and that his drink had tasted funny. Feeling ill shortly after, Aiisabeau helped him back to his room and that was the last of his memory. Except that he was certain it hadn't been that long ago.

Squeezing his eyes closed tightly then opening them very wide to bring him back to why he'd awakened, he was surprised to see his brother Fyrdien, who had been shaking him. Urgently Fyrdien exclaimed in a hushed voice, "Wake up little brother, hurry, there's no time to lose!"

Coltyn pretended to still be drugged, as the Spell placed upon him to increase his resistance to such was taking effect and his senses were clearing fast. Fyrdien? No, he couldn't be the one. Sitting up with feigned difficulty, he struggled to slow down his heartbeat.

Fyrdien's eyes were kind as they met Coltyn's. With confusion spreading o'er the boy's face, Fyrdien reached out to help him climb down from the high bed while Coltyn mumbled, "What's going on? Why are you here?"

"There's danger a'foot my brother, I need take you to a place of safety," he whispered.

Coltyn was leery about the entire situation. 'Twas disconcertingly similar to the first kidnap attempt and he tried to reach for his sword kept beside his bed at all times. Thinking he was falling, Fyrdien grabbed the boy and although he was not much taller than Coltyn, tossed him o'er his shoulder with relative ease. Coltyn could not reach his sword without openly struggling and
~~~~~

wasn't sure what to do. That sword was his main chance to defend himself. With these thoughts running rampant through his mind, Coltyn saw someone coming up behind Fyrdien from the darkness of the hallway outside his open door.

Days later, Coltyn would remember how the hallway should have been lit by torch, and that someone much bigger than they, had rushed in and hit them both on the head with something hard. He'd fallen off his brother's shoulder to the floor like falling off a cliff, only without enough sense to be afraid. Granted, he was somewhat certain that he wasn't the intended target and had simply been in the way of the object used against Fyrdien as he'd lifted his head to look at the attacker. Landing in a heap upon his now unconscious brother, he too, began slowly losing consciousness as he watched his elder brother Thyrazin, kneel beside them and lean o'er to check if Coltyn was dead or alive. The disgust upon his brother's face at the added inconvenience Coltyn had caused, was the last thing he remembered.

<p style="text-align:center">~~~~~ THE HALLWAY ~~~~~</p>

Having been on constant alert since the boy was drugged earlier that evening, Aiisabeau remained hidden in the shadows outside Coltyn's room yet far enough away to not alert the one she knew was coming for him.

When Fyrdien showed up, extinguishing the hallway torches at the boy's doorway, she was surprised. The 4th Prince in line to the throne could only be described as kind, trusting, and supportive. If any one of the Princes was the spy, she'd have put him at the bottom of the list. But then she saw the new movement out of the corner of her eye. Thyrazin! The one she'd truly expected to show up.

She could do nothing but watch and wait as she prayed Coltyn would not be harmed in the taking. Her heart in her throat, she listened to the quiet scuffling from the boy's room, and then within mere moments, Thyrazin left the room and headed stealthily down the hallway, Coltyn hanging limply o'er his shoulder. Following, she glanced into the room as she passed, only to see Fyrdien on the floor. Her Sprite vision allowed her to see the blood trickling from the back of his head, but she knew not the severity of his injury and could not take the time to make that determination. Coltyn's life was at stake. Still, she was confident that Thyrazin would not kill him unless forced to such and therefore she sidestepped, changed directions, and rushed into the room to grab the boy's sword afore continuing to follow.

This side trip told her more than she wanted to know. The boy's blood was upon the floor as well as was Fyrdien's. She was not far behind, for she carried not a near full grown boy o'er her shoulder and tracking the tiny droplets of blood made it even easier.

Aiisabeau had already memorized every Dance signature of all the royals, along with a few others she thought might be on the 'spy list'. So, finding herself without a trail, alone in the darkness, and far outside of Haven shortly later, she feared not. Casting about, she soon located Captain Thyrazin's signature near the dense underbrush. But all it told her was his departure point. If she followed, she might run right into the Elven Prince.

Her plan had included this scenario. She'd placed a Spell upon Coltyn moons past, that helped him to shirk off any drug he might consume such as happened last night. 'Twould not occur quickly, however. It merely gave him a sort of immunity to long lasting ill effects. All had not gone as she'd hoped, but Coltyn should have been awake and alert, faking otherwise, able to put their swordfight scenario into play as soon as she followed. But she'd not planned on him being hit on the head.

Standing very still, she quickly considered all her options. Charging in brazenly she could end up in a trap or at least in an immediate fight with Coltyn as helpless hostage. Aiisabeau's swordsmanship was superior to that of the Elven Prince but Thyrazin outweighed her by far, and with his reach longer than hers, she could not guarantee her success in a simple face to face meeting. However, Thyrazin would not be expecting company and such would be to her advantage. But she knew not where this Dance had taken them and again, she'd be taking a huge risk knowing Coltyn was likely not able to assist as was the original plan.

Where was Thyrazin going? For certain 'twas to the Black or to the Sorcerer. But he would have to get a Gatekeeper to let him out of the Spell Dome covering the Wyrdritch. So, to escape through a portal with Coltyn she'd already determined that he had a Gatekeeper in his pocket. She thought very hard about the time she'd met all the Gatekeepers when she'd first arrived. Most were very direct and straightforward. Then there was one who had avoided her. Discrimination was the excuse apologetically provided by the others. That one had no love of Sprites and opposed the Reunion. But they'd shrugged it off while she'd filed the memory for future need. That need was now.

Aiisabeau's blue eyes hardened. If she were wrong, Coltyn might be lost. Reaching for the old oak, she Drew her energy and Danced.

<div align="center">~~~~~ THE SOUTHERN EDGE OF THE SPELL
DOME O'ER THE WYRDRITCH ~~~~~</div>

His hands and ankles securely bound, Coltyn leaned against the enormous tree trunk and stared at Thyrazin, willing him to look his way. His head hurt, he was dizzy and even if Thyrazin hadn't disarmed him, he was too well wrapped to get to anything, anyway. Mayhap if he could coax his brother close enough, he could grab his sword. He snorted. His hands were tied behind his back, so how would he do that? Unless he could slide his hands in front of him again and loosen his ties. But 'twould take some time, time he'd not have. And what would he do when Aiisabeau came? She'd be on her own against Thyrazin.

"Why?" Coltyn asked with sarcasm. "Why take me? What do you think to accomplish? What good am I to you?"

Thyrazin seemed not to hear for several moments, then he turned to face Coltyn, an evil sneer upon his lips. His voice felt near slimy as he stated, "Through you, I will sit the throne of the Elven Nation. As is my right."

Shivering with the effects of his brother's words, the boy replied curtly, "I believe that Alyssa sits the throne, and then there's Myrrdin and Persephone ahead of your claim."

Laughing, Thyrazin countered, "Jeeryd promised me the throne when I had less winters than do you now. Myrrdin aligned himself with the Sprites, he is no more than a traitor. And Persephone? A mere female with weak Magic. No, Jeeryd promised ME the throne."

Stalling for time, Coltyn continued. "But why take me? I'm last in the succession, I am no threat to you."

A far away expression crossed the Captain's face. "Jeeryd died afore he could name me as his heir and 'twill take a bit of doing to gain it now." Then, his face a mask of hatred, he stated, "You are correct. You are nothing. A half-brother. An afterthought. Therefore, I feel no guilt handing you o'er to the Sorcerer. But even so, you do have some value, for you carry the blood of an Elven Prince. You are the price for my crown." The flash of surprise and betrayal on the boy's face pleased Thyrazin.

"You can't even get me through the Dome," Coltyn said with scorn, hoping to push his brother into revealing more information for he was infinitely curious, and he needed to give Aiisabeau time to find them.

"I pay well." Thyrazin stopped what he was doing and with narrowed eyes he continued, so agitated that spittle formed at the corners of his mouth. "Your presence has been requested and all I need do, is obey. Then, like my father afore, the throne will be handed to me and your filthy mixed blood mother and sister will die as will you, by the hand of the Sorcerer."

Coltyn was shocked. Being a precocious child, he'd discovered winters past that his mother and Anastasia used glamour to hide certain 'faults' in their appearance. 'Twas entirely possible he, too, wore such a birth glamour. But Alyssa and Ana were both beautiful and he'd never truly considered what those faults meant 'til Thyrazin's words brought sudden clarity.

Nevertheless, loyalty to family and friends was Coltyn's highest virtue and Thyrazin had crossed the line. He no longer thought of the 3rd Prince as family, therefore his words meant little. Who cared if he and his sister and mother were of mixed blood? Since the Last Holocaust, most of the Elven Nation had probably become a mix of some percentage or other. The truth would reveal itself when Alyssa completed the Call to Return. Many of those Elves outside the Wyrdritch had been living amongst the Humans for centuries, just to survive, or with the Sprites like Myrrdin, or were descendants of those who went into the Retreat. Was there anything wrong with that? Did such make the purebloods more worthy or mean they'd betrayed the Elven Nation? No.

Anastasia had been promised to Prince Kevon to secure the alliance with the Sprites, a destiny both righteous and by her own choice. For 'twas one's choices that set one's fate and he was about to set his own. He'd not go willingly to be handed o'er to the Evil One, precipitating the attack on his family, friends, the very Nation of the Elves. He would fight to his last breath.

~~~~~~~~~~

Aiisabeau crouched behind a large rock not far from where Coltyn sat. She'd Danced to the general area and after discovering Thyrazin had taken Coltyn away from his point of arrival, she picked up Thyrazin's physical trail that eventually led to this small clearing in which he held the boy. Watching, waiting for her moment, she first confirmed Coltyn was alert and able to fight. Then came confirming Thyrazin was working alone, except for the potential of the Gatekeeper that his words confirmed he planned to bribe.
~~~~~~~~~~

Crawling painstakingly ever closer to the boy and crouching behind the tree, she soon had his hands freed and gave him his sword and her own blade, the one he'd been using in practice. She could not cut the ties on his ankles. He'd have to do that himself. The boy had moved not a muscle, pretending to ignore his brother who had been mumbling to himself as he walked away, repeatedly checking his weapons and pockets. Aiisabeau noted all, along with their locations.

Then Thyrazin pulled out a small pouch from his vest pocket and weighed it in his hand with a satisfied smirk as he began walking back toward Coltyn. "You asked how I would get you out? This pays for our passage, and ultimately, my throne!" he exclaimed, just afore Aiisabeau burst out from behind the tree to confront the startled Elf.

Coltyn wasted no time and cutting the ties on his ankles with the blade, he leaped up and ran toward Thyrazin, sliding the blade into the sash at his waist. Thyrazin pulled his own sword and when Coltyn closed in, his training took o'er. Faking a missed sidestep to avoid Thyrazin's first slow strike, he then shifted and stabbed awkwardly, his brother now following the sequence Coltyn was orchestrating as if learning the steps of a new ballroom dance.

The fight should have brought in any stragglers who might stand with Thyrazin, and with no one coming out of the brush, Aiisabeau closed in just as Thyrazin disarmed the boy. Coltyn watched his sword fly out of his hand and then completed the rightward spin to step forward with the blade.

Thyrazin was not the best swordsman Aiisabeau had ever seen, and along with the fact that he'd wanted the boy alive, he was completely taken by Coltyn's pretense, missing the swift turn and the newly brandished weapon, totally shocked at the boy having any weapons at all. Coltyn was feeling the intensity of the moment and his every sense was heightened as he stepped forward aggressively with blinding speed. Thyrazin tried to turn away presenting his left side to the boy, and afore Aiisabeau's eyes, Coltyn stabbed his brother in the chest.

<center>~~~~~ MOMENTS LATER ~~~~~</center>

Coltyn's voice trembled with guilt, realizing what he'd done as the adrenaline from the fight diminished. Thyrazin had disappeared as soon as he was stabbed, taking the blade with him. "You knew that would happen! You knew I'd stab him!" he accused the Sprite.

Aiisabeau looked away then back to the boy and said, "Oh yes. I knew. Or I thought 'twould happen as it did. 'Twas part of the plan. You were in full Battle Mode and had little control of your actions. You performed the sequence perfectly, simply from practice. You had to be the one who did the deed, and it had to be with my blade. There was no other way to prove..." her voice trailed off.

Now the boy was regaining his senses, and his control. In a lower voice he demanded, "Prove what?"

"That Thyrazin is the spy and that I am not."

"But you aren't the spy! You didn't take me from the castle, you didn't try to give me to the Sorcerer!"

"Coltyn, we don't have time for this. We must leave. NOW!"

"Back to the castle? But Thyrazin is still out here! He'll try again! We may never have a better chance to stop him!"

"No. Thyrazin has returned to the castle, which is why we will not." She sighed. The look of confusion on Coltyn's face made her sad for his now lost youth. "Returning to the castle will do no good. At least follow me away from here, and I promise I will tell you the plan when we reach my safe camp."

As Coltyn nodded in agreement, he reached for the closest organic from which to Draw his energy for another Dance, but Aiisabeau stopped him. "No. We aren't certain when he will return, but I've arranged to give us some time. We leave here a'foot. We cover our trail. 'Tis the only way," she said, remembering another Sprite and her highly successful disappearance using these same tactics. Would it work for her? "No Magic," she emphasized to the still confused boy.

THAT AFTERNOON

SEVERAL LEAGUES NORTH OF HAVEN

~~~~~ MID-FOREST ~~~~~

</div>

Coltyn stirred the coals of their small fire. "Are you certain we are safe here?"

Aiisabeau smiled and nodded as she finished skinning the rabbits, handing them o'er to the boy to spit and set 'cross the fire. "I established this camp ages past. 'Tis secure."

Coltyn nodded, realizing this 'plan' was well thought out and had been in place far longer than he'd been privy. Considering his role, he was a tad upset that he'd not been informed from the beginning on how things were going to occur, and he frowned. Quietly, he stated, "I missed his heart. I should have finished him."

"'That would have sealed my fate and spoiled everything," she replied without hesitation, near as if she'd expected him to say such a thing.

Once more, Coltyn was confused. He was getting tired of the feeling. "Killing the spy would have sealed your fate? None of this is making sense. What are you talking about?"

As the rabbits roasted, their delectable scent wafting through the air making her mouth water, Aiisabeau sat back against a rock and began to braid long grasses into twine. 'Twas an exercise she'd learned as a child, one that the Dragon Clan taught their own children using their long coarse hair. Through her time in the Guard she found such activity calming. It also kept her fingers nimble and increased her concentration.

"I promised to tell you the plan," she stated, still braiding the grasses. "After Jeeryd's death Alyssa could trust no one amongst her own people. The Queen summoned Corbyn the Raven for as-
~~~~~

sist to rout the spy. Corbyn sent me." Aiisabeau watched the boy's eyes as he listened attentively. Tossing aside the braided length of grass, her senses picked up no fear, only interest and surprise. The Fay Heir Apparent was well respected throughout the world, despite his curse. "I soon discovered evidence that corroborated Alyssa's own fears that the spy not only had access to Haven, but was in her Guard, and so, 'twas likely one of the Princes. To protect you she made me your Trainer so I could have easy access to Haven and the Guard. I quickly concluded she was correct in that 'twas one of your brothers."

Coltyn cut her off. "Did you suspect Fyrdien?"

She hesitated a moment. "No. He was the one I did not suspect, but 'twould not have been wise to discount his involvement entirely." Coltyn remembered his feeling of surprise when Fyrdien came for him last night. He nodded and fell silent as he waited for more. Soon, Aiisabeau resumed. "I learned their fighting styles, movements, strengths, and weaknesses. I memorized their Dance signatures."

The boy's eyes widened. "You can do that?"

She laughed. "Yes. A high-level skill taught to the Elite Guard, but near anyone could learn eventually." Noting Coltyn was listening again, she continued, "Once I felt I had a grip on who might be the spy and how they might attack next, I placed the Spell for you to avoid long term effects of any drug and I taught you the fight sequence. I was surprised at the strength of what was slipped to you that night but was confident you would quickly sleep it off. Unfortunately, I did not catch the one who did that, leading me to suspect he had help in the kitchens." She considered how many might be in the 'employ' of Prince Thyrazin for there seemed many who opposed the Reunion. "After taking you back to your bedchambers, I hid in the hallway outside your door 'til I saw Fyrdien. But afore I could act against him, Thyrazin followed."

Coltyn was somewhat impatient. "I know that part, but that's not the plan. That's what happened."

Aiisabeau was proud of her student. He would not be fooled. Grinning, she continued again, "Thyrazin is likely back at the castle at this moment, informing everyone that I am the spy. He will tell them that I kidnapped you in the night, near killing Fyrdien in the process, and Fyrdien will not be able to contest that, for he did not see his brother coming up behind him."

"But I did!"

"Your word will not be taken o'er that of the Captain of the Queen's Guard, especially after having been 'ill'. Nor will mine," she added afore Coltyn could protest further. "He will say he followed me to rescue you, and that I ambushed him. The proof of my guilt is my blade in his chest." Aiisabeau saw the light of understanding come to the boy's face and she smiled. "The fight sequence I taught you, took into account your height differences, where he would step to avoid your strike and how you would then be forced to approach. Your stab was close to his shoulder. You were not supposed to kill him, my Prince."

He was amazed at her expertise but curious. Knowing Aiisabeau had framed herself a'purpose, he asked, "But how goes the plan AFTER this point? What now?"

"Thyrazin has been emboldened by this turn of events, but although she knew not the perpetrator, the Queen already expected this very scenario. Now he has but one option. He must kill us both so neither can shed light upon his involvement, and so that he can focus the blame upon the Sprite Nation. We need make Thyrazin show himself for what he is. For that to happen, we need only wait for Lord Rohar and his entourage to arrive."

Coltyn was silent for several moments. Testing the rabbits and deciding they were ready, he used his blade to cut off a piece and hold it as he began to pull the meat apart. Eating it gingerly, he licked the hot juices running down his fingers as he handed some to Aiisabeau. As the silence lengthened, making it clear that she would impart no more information at this time, he asked softly, "Do you think Fyrdien is still alive?"

MEANWHILE
~~~~~ ICE MIST FALLS ~~~~~

'Twas as the Warrior's worst nightmare unfolding in front of his stricken eyes. The Daring Duo yelling the war cry of the Brotherhood, brandishing their weapons, crashing through the brush toward the last three Hoardsmen who were running toward the pair, swords in hands, yelling just as loudly, while off in the distance he heard the beating of incoming wings. NOW the Dragons decide to return? If the whole situation hadn't been so horrifying, he'd have laughed.

And then he did. Snorting and shaking his shaggy head, he set his jaw and prepared to support the Team, realizing this was no worse than what the pair had faced during the battle to Draw the Domes. However, he still ran to catch up to them as quickly as possible.

Walkyr was ahead of Fryya when they clashed with the Hoardsmen and the fight was on. Swords at ready, the young Warriors took advantage of their size difference against the much taller enemy, ducking easily out of their swinging swords time and again, 'til they could get in close enough to use their own. Fryya went after the bigger man as they'd planned afore, letting Walkyr go after the other two, and both let the Battle Lust rule.

Fryya was ruthless in her fighting technique, taking after Darque, seeing no need to 'fight fair' and nothing was off limits. After all, the average man was o'er head and shoulders taller than either she or Walkyr, and the most sensitive target was at the most convenient level.

Blocking and spinning away from the man's first strike attempts, Fryya had him with a perfectly timed stab, then ducked quickly as his sword came sweeping downward while he screamed in agony. Stepping in again, she repeated the act, surely castrating him, and this time he dropped to his knees, where she cut his throat. A fast kill. 'Twas the only way she and her partner could survive a battle. Taking too much time would only use up their energy. Though they were strong, 'twas not even arguable that they could match the strength of a grown man for long.

Spinning 'round, her eyes sought her partner and she raced o'er to attack one of his opponents from behind, giving Walkyr time to block and strike the other, cleaving that one's skull. Without stopping, he swung and sliced through the other's guts afore he'd even had time to face Fryya, spilling them o'er the ground, the hapless man dropping his sword and trying to hold his entrails together with his hands. He gaped unbelievingly at the pair afore his eyes glazed o'er as he fell forward, dead.

The entire encounter took little more than a few heartbeats, and as the Daring Duo looked about, they heard a muffled 'whoosh' just as they felt the backbeat of huge leathery wings, sparks scattering from the fire. Clearly about to land, Fryya yelled a pointless warning into the hard gusts, "INCOMING!"

The first Dragon landed along the eastern edge of the clearing, right in front of Rygyl, bringing him to an abrupt halt. Both Swords drawn and ready, Rygyl used his expertise and the enhanced blades to perfection, slicing upwards through the scales with the Sword in his right hand afore the Dragon could use his sharp talons to slice through the Warrior. With a long open slash through the hard scales, in less than a heartbeat Rygyl stabbed upwards with the other Sword, cutting through the heavy ribcage that surrounded the heart and hitting his target with all his strength. Twisting the blade then carving 'round in a highly practiced maneuver, he tried to sever the organ from the veins and lungs. But the Dragon fell flat on his face, forcing an early withdrawal of the blade, the huge head just missing him. Falling to his butt and scooting backwards as quickly as he could, Rygyl knew the Dragon was not finished and if he didn't complete the kill, the Healing would negate all his efforts. 'Twas then that Tegrynn came screaming down from the heavens to land atop the Dragon. Using her talons and fangs, she decapitated the beast in a blood splattering fury. Now, he was finished. With the focus of his own fight complete, he remembered the second Dragon. "The other one! Get the other one!" he shouted, pointing 'cross the clearing toward Walkyr and Fryya.

Scrambling to his feet Rygyl raced toward them, and the sight he beheld would be forever emblazoned in his mind. That Dragon had near squashed the pair in his landing, and both were still on the ground in front of the massive beast. Walkyr's sword was stuck in the unscaled portion of the Dragon's belly, having stabbed forward as it landed, which action made the vile creature rear backwards, preventing the Warriors from being landed upon. But the Dragon's Healing had been quick and now the sword was embedded in his leathery hide while he prepared to Flame the pair Past the Veil.

As Dragons Brew their Flame, the Magical substance they mix with their fiery breath, they first inhale deeply. Then lowering their chests and elongating their necks, they spew it forth in a steady stream of fire as if belching. Or as Fryya once noted vividly, "'Tis as projectile vomit!"

Time slowed as Rygyl ran the short distance 'tween them, the Lust building to unbearable intensity at the thought he'd be too late to intervene. Then he saw something amazing. Fryya's skin changed as she spun 'round to crouch o'er Walkyr, covering him with her body like a shield, her shoulders, back, and arms now fully scaled as of a Dragon, just afore the Flame burst forth, engulfing the pair. Tegrynn was but a fraction of a candle drip too late to prevent that occurrence as she attacked the beast from behind.

Her wings beating fully outstretched for stability, Tegrynn yanked the Hoard Dragon's head upwards with her long talons, cutting off the stream of Flame. At the same time, Rygyl felt Ariel's Sword pulling him forward faster than his feet could keep up, and still too far away to attack the Dragon in time, he suddenly realized what he must do.

As Fryya collapsed onto her partner limply, Rygyl yelled to Walkyr, now peeking from under her arm. Walkyr held out his left hand in response, pushed Fryya away with his right while Ariel's Sword was tossed to him. Catching it smoothly mid-air, he sliced up and 'cross in a wide arc, his target the elongated neck with the beast's head pulled away. The Dragon Sword sliced through that neck with fair ease, and the blood rained down upon the pair, bringing Fryya to her senses as she rolled to her hands and knees to watch the end of the action afore her astonished eyes.

<div align="center">~~~~~ THAT EVENING ~~~~~</div>

They'd taken o'er the enemy camp after cleaning up a tad in the frigid waters. Fryya had returned to normal and what injury they thought she had, simply flaked off as if shedding her skin while she'd washed. 'Twas to everyone's relief, including Fryya. Even her bushy mane of unruly red hair, appeared untouched.

With the death of the Hoard Dragon they were able to re-trieve Walkyr's sword, along with salvaging from both carcasses, which included the fangs, talons, and most of their scales. Such salvage was useful in the war effort and all such bounty would be handed o'er to Alric the Weapon's Master upon their return, for him to create more Thumpers and fashion into weaponry for the rest of the Warriors.

Nevertheless, Ariel's Sword had not returned to Rygyl and Walkyr was ill at ease 'til the Warrior reassured him. With a knowing smile the big man shook his head and stated, "The Sword has chosen. I pray 'twill serve you well, my brother."

Rygyl could feel Fryya's fluctuating emotions about the Sword's new allegiance. The young girl had dreamed of having her own Dragon Sword since the first Draw. But even if there was another, 'twas determined that she and Walkyr would not survive that Magic. She'd have to wait 'til she reached her full growth in another four or five winters to even attempt such, and now she'd be standing alone.

Yet, Fryya knew Walkyr needed the Sword more than she. She had her Gift, now he had his, and she was happy for him. They were both highly skilled, but she had the advantage of being enhanced like her sisters by her hybrid status and had always secretly enjoyed protecting her friend. However, with a Dragon Sword, he wouldn't need her as much. If at all.

Yet after her amazing transformation she was a bit confused. Still brooding, she asked, "What did happen to me out there?"

Rygyl did not mention Fryya's feelings about the Sword. She would have to work it out for herself. The pair's loyalty to each other was strong. She'd get past it. "You scaled up," he answered simply. Seeing the quizzical expression on Fryya's face, he continued. "Darque is showing such capability and has been attempting to make it happen when called forth. But thus far, she's had minimal success, only feeling the change come upon her when in full Battle Lust." Again, Fryya appeared somewhat confused and he summarized, "You're able to transform your skin to something like Dragon scale. This appears to be a phenomenon of your Dragon blood."

Waving her hand in dismissal, she replied, "Oh, I believe you. 'Tis not that. I was just thinking. This has been happening at varying degrees for the past few moons, whenever I'm feeling high emotion." She grinned and shrugged, fully aware that most thought her a highly emotional girl. "But this didn't start with the Battle Lust. 'Twas not 'til I saw that Dragon about to Flame Walkyr, and I just let it come o'er me without considering the consequences. I felt an inner peace, as if I knew 'twould keep us safe."

Rygyl considered her words. "Mayhap the lifesaving desire is what will turn the tables for Darque as well."

Walkyr remained silent as Fryya thought about the fight. After a few moments she asked, "Rygyl? Do you think Storrm was able to do this?"

Gauging the girl's fortitude to hear his opinion he answered truthfully. "We know not. 'Tis possible she was showing the ability afore she Passed, but she never said anything and there's no evidence to prove such."

Fryya then looked to Walkyr who nodded his support of what she was about to say. Shifting her gaze back to the big Warrior, she stated, "Yes. There is."

'Twas obvious they'd discussed this 'tween them at some point. She had a theory. He wanted to hear it. "What do you mean?" he asked with sincere curiosity.

Now her gaze fell to her hands in her lap, and she began quietly speaking, "Storrm was Flamed at close range. She should have been unrecognizable, near ash. Yet she was still mostly intact. Her hair, her skin, her face. She'd fought a good fight, but when we found her she was…" she paused. Of the three Aalanna Grifynn siblings, Fryya had always considered herself the 'ugly duckling'. Trying to find the right words, she finally concluded in a near whisper, "She was still beautiful."

Rygyl remembered clearly when they'd found the Second in Command, and although he'd not thought her condition odd at the time, he had to admit that it did suggest Storrm had begun to scale up as well. However, sensing the pain in Fryya's admission as well as having dredged up the memory aloud, Rygyl placed his large calloused hand upon her shoulder. "Aye, lass. That she was." He paused a moment for emphasis, then winking at Walkyr, he finished, "But no more beautiful than are you. Trust me. Many's the Warrior envious of our brother, Walkyr."

Walkyr's eyes glistened with gratitude as he acknowledged the other's statement. He had to agree. His partner was the most beautiful girl in the world, and he was the luckiest Warrior in the Brotherhood.

CHAPTER TWELVE

The Trap Is Set

~~~~~ HAVEN ~~~~~

Thyrazin had returned to Haven post haste, and with much dramatic flair made report to the Queen while he was being treated by the Skald. As predicted, he blamed Aiisabeau for kidnapping Coltyn and brashly declared she was working on Lord Rohar's orders. To strengthen his claim, he accused the Sprites who'd visited winters past, Calei and Kevon, of setting the betrayal in motion and now the Sprites and all who followed them, including Anastasia and his younger brothers, were coming to take the boy to the Black. He demanded he be given free rein to stop them.

'Twas this very scenario they had to root out of the Nation. The distrust of the Sprites, the lack of support for the Reunion. Just such a conspiracy theory had been simmering in rumors and whispers in the courtyards and now here 'twas out in the open. Now they could stop it in its tracks.

Trying not to exude her true feelings, Alyssa then told her Guard that she would entertain their visitors afore taking them prisoner. They'd be charged with espionage and with Coltyn's kidnapping. Thyrazin pushed her to allow him to throw them in the dungeons immediately, but Alyssa's word prevailed. They would wait for the banquet. Privately, Alyssa knew she would have to rely on Anastasia's senses to keep her safe during the time afore the banquet, in which their visitors would be in the greatest danger. She also needed time alone with Ana to assure herself that her daughter was not being duped into believing a lie.

In the meantime, she ordered her Guard to continue in their efforts to locate Aiisabeau and Coltyn, and to affect a rescue. Alyssa knew such would draw out her stepson. His thinking would be that even if Aiisabeau knew 'twas him, if he could still
~~~~~

find them, he could kill them both and strengthen his accusations against Rohar, and they would then be able to use the Lord as a hostage for negotiation with the Sprite Nation to avoid outright war.

~~~~~~~~~~

Lord Rohar and his entourage had arrived the following dawn and were given luxurious guest quarters. After cleaning up and unpacking, he'd been called straight to a private greeting with the Queen as would be expected for such a visit. Captain Natanamia and the Elven Princes under her command were taken on a tour of Haven, leaving Kevon and Anastasia being hustled hither and yon, endlessly attending to diplomatic duties in which they saw not, any of the others.

Ana was troubled. She'd already noted that Thyrazin was favoring his left arm. As Captain of the Guard, he'd requested her attendance alone shortly after arrival, but the Song she Heard suddenly emitting from her older brother grated her senses and Ana had stated she preferred to show Kevon the castle and would see him after the banquet. Throughout the day, she'd avoided Thyrazin as much as possible. Such did not go unnoted by the Queen.

Anastasia knew all the activity was a diversion. None of them were allowed to freely roam the corridors of Haven, not even those born within its walls. And she in particular, was being kept distant from the staff of the castle, while those accompanying the pair were shrouded as if b'Spelled to avoid her senses. Still, although she could sense not their emotions, she could Hear the Song of the castle itself, and 'twas most odd. But of even more significance, she knew not why she had yet to see her little brother. Finally returning to their quarters, Ana had to leave Kevon at the door of her room.

They'd been told the official greeting would occur at the dinner banquet to be held this evening in their honor. For the formal
~~~~~~~~~~

event she'd brought with her a stunning, low cut, strap sleeved, silk evening gown in her favorite sky blue with pearl accents and matching ankle boots. On the Island of Dreams, which she now considered her home, boots had become her staple footwear as she needed solid support for climbing cliffs, shelling on the beaches, playing with the Water Dragons, and riding the beautiful Sprite-bred horses with the fiery eyes that matched their tempers. She didn't like dress heels.

Braiding a section of her hair into a headband, she secured it with mother of pearl combs allowing the rest to flow down her back, afore stepping out to join the others. She could sense they had questions, but she had no answers to give. Lord Rohar shook his head covertly afore she could ask what they thought was going on.

Walking into the ornate banquet room she was all smiles, for this was her homecoming. 'Twas near three winters since she'd seen her mother and she was very excited. As the others were seated in the front tables closest to the Queen, Ana stepped up to the Queen and gave her a hug with tears in her eyes.

But as they touched for the first time, Ana's smile faded to an anxious frown. No one could see their expressions as Alyssa barely narrowed her eyes and gaining all the information she required at that moment, she shook her head afore holding her daughter at arm's length.

Although unprepared, Ana understood her role immediately and plastered the smile back on her face afore anyone noticed. She also understood she was not to ask about her little brother and why he was missing from the formal greetings. What was happening, she wondered with growing apprehension. The emotion she gathered from her mother was that of extreme wariness, the Song she Heard was not of welcome and goodwill, but of mystery and intrigue. Ana had to bite her tongue not to say anything as they exchanged certain knowledge of something horrible about to occur. In a very low voice, Alyssa stated, "Smile to the others and then take your place at the Queen's table."

Ana wanted to protest, but the heat in her mother's eyes brooked no argument. She cast a glance o'er her shoulder at Kevon and 'twas the look on her face in that instant that made the young man afraid for her safety, mayhap the safety of them all. But afore he could say anything, with weapons brandished the Queen's Guard trooped through the banquet room, surrounding the visitors, including the youngest Elven Princes. There was nothing they could do.

"Take them to the dungeons!" Thyrazin spit hatefully through clenched teeth. The Guard obeyed and quickly marched them all out of the Banquet Hall. Ana was appalled, sensing wonder from the others at her own involvement in this turn of events.

Ana was ushered to sit beside the Queen as they awaited the Guard's return. The other banquet guests were dispersed, and the hall now stood empty except for Alyssa, Ana, and Prince Dyrachin. 'Twas he who had insisted the Queen needed protection and should not be left alone, which action infuriated Thyrazin for he'd hoped to eliminate Ana and cared not if Alyssa were in the way. But Dyrachin had stood his ground.

Although Aiisabeau's plan was going mostly as she'd predicted, with her disappearance Alyssa could not initially be certain just who was the spy, for Fyrdien had also been injured. But Alyssa knew the trap had been laid when Coltyn and Aiisabeau failed to be found the previous night, and given her daughter's Magic, she was certain the Sprite Lord was not to be doubted or Ana would have notified her immediately upon arrival.

When Thyrazin had returned with his tale of espionage and accused the Sprite of kidnapping Coltyn, Alyssa's emotions exploded within her heart. Thyrazin brazenly lied that despite his best efforts, the cowardly infiltrator had taken the young Prince and fled, and with her blade in his chest he'd been unable to follow.

Alyssa was not fooled, but others might be, and taking her visitors into custody was their only means to keep them safe and to eventually prove their innocence. This she'd revealed to Lord

Rohar, who had been expecting this very outcome upon their arrival. Since none but the Queen's Guard carried weapons other than personal daggers in Haven, Alyssa returned the Lord's weapons to him in private and using her own Magic as opposed to his, disguised the fact to all eyes.

To put his vile plan into action, Thyrazin would have required assistance and she'd already begun rounding up the Gatekeepers as well as the kitchen staff and anyone else who might have been involved. She also knew that Anastasia was the only one of them who could tell without a shadow of a doubt, who was guilty and who was not.

What Thyrazin soon learned was that the dungeons were the safest place in Haven for their visitors. No spy would try to kill those who were imprisoned, implicating himself, and even if someone did, she'd detailed Aiisabeau's plan to Rohar, whom Corbyn had insisted she could trust. No one else had been warned, for the plan required true surprise and indignation to fool the Captain.

Thyrazin was not happy that Ana had been singled out to remain free, as 'twas clear the Queen trusted her daughter as well as her daughter's Magic. He'd made every effort to cast doubt upon the girl, needing to implicate her as well. With the mass arrests that followed, it became clear he could not get Coltyn out of the Wyrdritch now, but at least he could save himself. He felt no concern about betraying the Sorcerer, who could do nothing to him for failing to bring him the boy for he knew not the secret of the Spell Domes and could not touch the Elven Nation within. In Thyrazin's mind he could yet rise to the throne with the untimely deaths of those who might challenge. After all, this situation would require fighting and deaths were to be expected.

Everything was falling into place for Thyrazin, though 'twas not exactly how he'd envisioned such. He just needed to find Aiisabeau and Coltyn. Alone. He could then kill the bitch and the boy and bring their bodies back to Haven, full of sorrow at losing his little brother and whomever else he could manage to kill along the way, again blaming Aiisabeau, but pleased he'd gotten revenge upon the one who'd done the deed. He'd be hailed a hero of the Nation, and the Reunion of Sprite and Elf would be prevented. He near drooled at that thought.

Reporting to the Queen, he told her he was leaving immediately for the search. He would be able to locate his little brother anywhere Aiisabeau took him. But he insisted on going alone to minimize the danger. Alyssa played her part well but ordered him to take another along. Fuming, he altered his plans again for he could not argue with the Queen.

After a brief period of self-pity, he realized 'twould not be so bad. He would simply kill whomever she sent with him afore he found Coltyn. There'd be no witnesses to dispute his story. And to make matters easier and eliminate any other contenders to the throne, he requested that Fyrdien, Irylane, Beralarr, Enlyrod, Dyrachin and Englyrim all join him, for in his increasingly disordered rationale, although they were younger and had little challenge to his claim, having no other left was his strongest position. Such had been his father's rationale when he'd orchestrated the ambush that killed King Lucien and his sons the Princes Typeth and Grygoth.

The fight to rescue Coltyn would provide plenty of cover to kill his own if they made it that far. There were but two ahead of Thyrazin in line, but he considered not Persephone, for he believed her Magic so inferior that she'd never sit the throne and she was an easy target he could take care at will, as was Anastasia. Myrrdin was another question, but with the Sprites implicated, his eldest brother would be considered a traitor and his former death sentence could be reinstated. The rest of his brothers would not survive the dungeons, nor would that other Sprite, Captain Natanamia. Since 'twas clear the younger Elven Princes were in league with the Sprites as well, 'twould be simple to kill them all!

Sinking deeper into his own greed and evil, he saw not the absurdity of such outlandish plans.

Alyssa was repulsed at the level to which her stepson had fallen. Gathering herself, she reminded him that Fyrdien was not yet recovered and still in the care of the Skald, which only made Thyrazin smile inappropriately, causing her to squint. But the light of madness shining in her Captain's eyes told the story of his bloodthirsty desires and she hid her emotions from his awareness.

Alyssa delayed as long as she could without raising Thyrazin's suspicions, giving Aiisabeau and Coltyn time to recover and close the trap. Finally she had to make her choice, hoping for the best. She assigned Dyrachin and Beralarr to accompany Thyrazin on the hunt, requiring the others to remain for her protection as well as for the protection of those in the dungeons. These two brothers were the least likely to jump to conclusions. Fair and even tempered, they sought out facts afore acting. Thyrazin reluctantly agreed with her decision, his mind trying to adjust and alter his plans with each unexpected change.

Alyssa hoped her stepsons' attributes would not become detriments, as she was unable to speak with them privately afore they left Haven. Relying on Dyrachin and Beralarr to realize the truth of what was happening afore 'twas too late, she bid them good chase.

~~~~~ AIISABEAU'S CAMP ~~~~~

It had taken them several marks to get to the campsite, and they'd had little time to recuperate from both the fight and the hard foot travel that followed. But she could wait no longer, and after he'd fallen asleep just a mark prior she reached forth to shake Coltyn's shoulder while stating, "Hurry, we must return to the south." The boy near leaped up at her touch. "Sorry!" she laughed. "'Twould seem you have fully recovered." Then securing her arms, she watched the boy follow her lead.

Coltyn didn't ask questions. Listening intensely, he Cast forth his senses and embraced that which he found there. "We go to get caught. To leave a trail for Thyrazin to follow us back here."

She was so proud of her student. Once again he showed her how much he'd learned o'er the past few winters. How much he'd grown and matured. "Yes. But your life is precious. We must not lose you. 'Twill be very dangerous."

Coltyn snorted. "No more so than what's already occurred." As he made ready to leave, he continued thoughtfully, "Thyrazin depends heavily on his Magic, thinking others do, as well. He would never have thought to try to follow a physical trail. So he'd be stumped if he returned to where he left us afore we do, trying to find my Dance signature. He must know mine, being Captain of the Guard, but I doubt he had the foresight to learn yours. Even though he hated you."

Again, Aiisabeau was pleased that the boy's reasoning was so insightful. Groaning at the reference to Thyrazin's feelings toward her, she replied, "He hates everyone. Including himself. He is a slave to greed and prejudice. Now come, timing is everything, you know," she said with a wink.

Coltyn grinned and Drawing their energy from the nearby branches of the trees, they both Danced away.

~~~~~ LATER ~~~~~

It took a true expert to determine the subtle nuances of Dance signatures such as whether 'twas incoming or outgoing, and the timing of such, and since Aiisabeau felt their enemy had not this expertise, they'd Danced from her camp back to Thyrazin's camp in a hopscotch pattern of short distances and then away from it using the same thread of energy after having arrived mere moments afore Thyrazin's return. Then they'd set themselves up along the path to keep tabs on Thyrazin as he appeared at each stop.

Watching the Captain arrive at their first stop leaving his camp, she was surprised to see Dyrachin and Beralarr with him.
~~~~~

Alyssa must have used that decision to give them more time. Still, she didn't want to kill the brothers; she'd grown rather fond of them in these past winters with the Elves. But as always, she'd do what must be done to follow her orders and protect her charge and to do that, she had to take down Thyrazin and anyone who tried to get 'tween her and the boy.

Coltyn's voice was sad, as Thyrazin located their departure point and they watched his brothers disappear. Turning to Aiisabeau, he asked, "Do you think they're in league with him?"

Standing up and brushing off her hands, she replied briskly, "No. I do not. They are likely unaware of his true intent and are in as much danger as are we. But we trust no one."

"I understand," Coltyn said with a slight sigh, as he stood up and looked gloomily to his Trainer.

Aiisabeau was in full Battle Mode and in her opinion the boy's attitude revealed he had not caught up to that same level. To rectify that, she determined that he required increased respect of the peril. Turning to face him, her voice was hard. "There is now a price upon your head and the spy must kill you to prevent his own capture. No one gets close to you; do you understand THAT?" She relented when she saw the deflated expression cross the boy's face. Sighing she stated, "Not 'til we have this all sorted out. Even if they fight with you against Thyrazin, you must not let them touch you. My intent is to take Thyrazin back to Haven alive. But if something happens to me, Dance back to Haven without delay and present yourself to the Queen. Tell her alone, all that has transpired. Make use of Anastasia's Magic, she will know who is lying and who is not. If Dyrachin and Beralarr show up, place them under her scrutiny as well. Then once everyone in league with Thyrazin is identified, free those in the dungeons."

Coltyn nodded, his full attention upon the task and her orders. "But how do I get into Haven without being seen?"

Aiisabeau smiled. "Am I to suppose you never sneaked into your sister's dressing chambers?"

His blushing cheeks made her laugh. He'd not been in his sister's bedchambers since he was a little boy, let alone her dressing chambers, but suddenly he understood. "Are you saying the ivy is still there? I can Dance directly to her room, then sneak to the Queen's chambers!"

Coltyn could think of nothing more to say, and Aiisabeau fell silent. Within the span of a few short breaths, she turned to him. "They should have arrived at our campsite by now and will be Casting to find the next signature, which of course they will not find. With no one about and just one incoming/outgoing signature they will initially be confused and Thyrazin will become angry. 'Twill work in our favor, but to get the upper hand we must surprise them afore they figure it out."

<center>~~~~~ THE ISLAND OF DREAMS ~~~~~</center>

With an expression of resolution upon each of their companion's faces, Captain Naftaleah stood up and took Myrrdin's arm in grasp, her other hand upon his shoulder. Both tall and slim, they stood otherwise in stark contrast. Their foreheads touching in a moment of silent gratitude, his dark hair threaded through her blonde hair as it hung down 'tween them afore they looked up. Now Myrrdin's dark eyes stared into Naftaleah's pale green.

His voice just as musical as the others but with much greater depth when he spoke, he made his decision regarding the Sprite Captain's 'other option' for removal of the threat. "If we're to be successful we have no time to waste. And we'll require the assist of the Water Dragons. Have your team aboard the Lytle within the mark. I go there now, to speak with Islyth."

Lyran fell into step behind Myrrdin as he took his leave along with Caleichante and the rest of her Sprites. Naftaleah and her six Guardsmen left the conference room for the armory to prepare as for war. Lyrianei, Kalisadei, Ardryyn, Kryllyn, Datyniah, and Dalakiah Called to their Water Dragons to meet them at the ship. Islyth and Schlynn were already there waiting.

'Twould be a most daring operation. The poison would be harmful near anywhere they tried to take it, destroying all life within several square leagues 'til dissipating into the sheer amount of water in which 'twas dissolved. Sprites and Elves were most attuned to nature and 'twas traumatizing to consider the resulting initial damage. Therefore, first and foremost, they had to get it as far away from any inhabited areas as possible.

'Twas also well known by now, that the Krakken lay upon the edge of the crevasse of the Leviathans in the Ocean of Fears. Even if the terrifying creatures had not existed, that crevasse was so deep it had never been explored, the pressure too great for the adventurous Water Dragons. 'Twould take considerable Magic to swim to that edge and taking along their Ties would stretch them close to their limits.

Leviathans were enormous creatures and of the known three (for no one had survived to tell the tale if they'd seen more) one was near a quarter league long in the body with a tangle of even longer, poisoned spiked tentacles sprouting from 'round their massive perfectly round jaws. These they used to reach forth to capture their prey, stunning them and then dragging them helplessly to be stuffed into the beast's mouth. If enough poison were injected, the doomed victim would die afore being crushed and swallowed. They seemed to have no eyes and no separation 'tween head and body, but sightings were rare and by necessity, brief.

The gigantic creatures were the largest to live in any of the world's oceans and had been rumored to have been released from their underwater prison at the time of the Last Holocaust, when 'twas theorized that the huge crevasse opened. From historical records which were admittedly few and vague, those ships that had been in the area at the time were 'swallowed', never to be seen again, and 'twas surmised that 'twas more likely by the suction of the opening itself than by becoming a victim of the beasts. These ships and crews were considered the lucky ones.

For those unlucky, the Leviathans were relatively colorless, exposing to the naked eye most of their internal organs and vessels, extremely fast, flexible, and terrifying, rising randomly from the crevasse to destroy with ease. Few ships had ever escaped the trio and 'twas rare for a Water Dragon to do so, despite their impressive speed, with the exception of Islyth who had done so more than a few times. Her experience made her the reigning expert, and she provided guidance to the others as they prepared for the task upon which they were about to embark. 'Twould be the ultimate test of their skill, speed, Magic, and courage.

To eradicate the Leviathans was everyone's dream, for 'twould make the Ocean of Fears safer for the Mariners as well as for the Water Dragons. Leviathans were said to be responsible for near all shipwrecks and subsequent deaths in the Fears, and for hundreds of Dragon deaths. But no weapon ever used against them thus far, seemed to have any effect.

'Twas Naftaleah's idea that the poison might kill them, or at a minimum, provide a temporary stunning effect. Such would offer Lord Myrrdin his best chance to raise the Krakken from her watery grave and would add to their arsenal of weapons against the creatures, mayhap causing permanent damage to the Leviathans as well as dumping the poison in the most appropriate place, causing the least amount of damage. 'Twas theory in all but the fact that the crevasse was the perfect location for the soon to be activated poison. Yet all agreed 'twould be worth their efforts along with any losses certain to occur, and the plan was set in motion.

<center>~~~~~ THE WYRDRITCH ~~~~~</center>

Thyrazin stood at the backs of his brothers surreptitiously drawing his blade when Aiisabeau and Coltyn burst upon the campsite several Dragon lengths behind them. With their weapons drawn and yelling the war cries of the Sprite and Elven Nations, chaos ensued. Thyrazin was already committed to his vile deed and stabbed Dyrachin afore turning about to face the pair, while screaming to Beralarr that 'twas the Sprite once more. Dyrachin dropped to the ground in agonizing pain, frothy blood gushing forth from the flank wound that pierced his lung, while Beralarr's eyes flashed from the incoming threat to the one that just injured his brother, trying to make sense of what was happening.

Relying on the confusion with hope that Aiisabeau would take out Beralarr for him, Thyrazin charged forward, his face a mask of fury at this unexpected interruption. He'd wanted to continue the chase alone after having killed Dyrachin and Beralarr. But his plans kept changing and now his hands were full.

Beralarr could not watch both Thyrazin and Dyrachin and had to choose quickly. Ripping off his shirt, he did the best he could under the circumstances, to field dress his brother's wound afore jumping up to assist Thyrazin with the Sprite and to rescue Coltyn.

But Beralarr was no fool. Quickly but methodically he put together the sequence of events in the span of a few heartbeats noting Coltyn clearly fighting shoulder to shoulder with the one they'd been informed had kidnapped him, along with seeing Thyrazin turn away from them, his blade already in hand, just as Dyrachin fell. Beralarr confirmed in his mind that the Sprite could not have thrown her blade and hit Dyrachin with such speed coming in from the Dance, as well as the certainty that Thyrazin's position would have blocked such, causing him to have taken the blade and therefore, the guilty party was Thyrazin.

Despite his elder brother's screams to help him, combined with his vile profaning of the Sprite, Beralarr jumped into the swordplay 'tween Coltyn, Aiisabeau, and Thyrazin, joining forces with the Sprite and his little brother, forcing the elder Prince to surrender within a few strikes after surrounding him.

Thyrazin stood in the middle of his opponents, bloody, exhausted, and panting, sword tip in the dirt, initially refusing to disarm. Unable to convince Beralarr of his 'mistake' in choosing sides, he then threatened him with charges, of being named a traitor when they returned to Haven, and that obviously Coltyn had succumbed to the Sprite's evil intentions as well. "Can you not see the true traitor here? Am I the only sane Elf in the entire Wyrdritch?" Thyrazin roared.

Aiisabeau wisely said nothing and merely watched Beralarr's eyes as he struggled to prove to himself, the truth of the matter. Thyrazin continued his rush of ideas, his thought processes becoming less and less logical, spittle forming in the corners of his mouth, his eyes blazing with fury, his own words convicting him. Coltyn also stood silently waiting for Beralarr to come to his conclusion, for if he chose against the Sprite, the fight would be reignited. In the meantime, all kept their swords at ready, pointing at the Captain of the Queen's Guard, mindful that Thyrazin might yet try to escape.

'Twas several long moments afore Beralarr finally spoke, clearly sorrowful but fully aware of the truth. With disgust and in a low voice, he simply said, "You are the only INSANE Elf here, and my eyes now rest upon the traitor."

<center>~~~~~ ICE MIST FALLS ~~~~~</center>

The three Warriors had spent o'er a sennight thoroughly searching the specific area where Fryya had dropped the Fang afore moving methodically outward to the surrounding areas and found nothing. Though the forest had many evergreens, so too, did it have many deciduous trees and the fallen leaves did lie thick upon the ground, making their search a little more difficult. But Fryya had stubbornly pushed them to stay and keep looking, with the notion that the Fang might be under more than this, having laid here since the ambush.

Now sitting at the fire trying to get warm, she was simply irritated. Rygyl sat back and ate the grilled fish Walkyr had prepared for supper. Using natural seasonings available in the area, 'twas amazingly flavorsome as well as moist. Walkyr could have been a Master Chef. During the past few days, Rygyl learned that there was more to the Seer than most knew.

Now Rygyl's deep voice broke the quiet of the evening. "Are we finally in agreement that we've done the best we can and are certain 'tis here no longer?" Amused by the look on Fryya's face, he licked the juices from his fingers and continued, "Our next step is to determine where 'tis now."

As usual, Fryya was the first to speak. Still unwilling to accept the Fang was not here, she sarcastically questioned, "And just how do you propose we do that?" She pulled her cloak higher about her neck. Lately, the nights had been getting much colder, for 'twas mid-fall.

Walkyr handed Fryya her portion of the fish, and then casually answered, "We ask Tegrynn."

Rygyl grinned ear to ear as both he and the Seer turned to Fryya, a mystified expression upon her face that threatened to bring together both her eyebrows into one. The two men had to clear their throats to keep from laughing for 'twas so comical.

Tegrynn was sitting nearby, nonchalantly cleaning her talons. She'd done little since the first day. After less than half a mark assisting in the search, she'd returned to their camp and thereafter spent her time generally lazing about. She cocked her head at the suggestion, for she'd been waiting for them to ask since that day, but Rygyl had prevented her from interfering. The young Warriors were not in 'Bond and Dragon senses were not their first thought. They still depended upon their own. 'Twas Rygyl's firm belief that experience was the best teacher.

Nevertheless, the big Warrior was surprised at Walkyr's suggestion. How long had he suspected?

Walkyr replied as if to his unasked question, "For a while now, I've figured Tegrynn knew something. I just didn't know what 'til you said that bit about where 'twas." He looked to Fryya.

Now fully engaged in the hope that the Dragon would know where the Fang was, enabling them to collect it forthwith and return triumphant to the Keep, she near burst with excitement, asking, "Well, Tegrynn? What happened to the Fang?"

Tegrynn was pleased she could finally share her knowledge. She'd found the exact place the Fang had been for near six moons after the ambush. But though Bryynn and Ardyth were here at one time and had found Tyrrsyn's Thumper, she knew 'twas not them who'd found the Fang. With her teeth flashing, she replied in her rumbling but definitely feminine voice, "Bronwyn. 'Twas the Empress of the Ice Dragons who took the Fang. And that means she's collected it for her stash. 'Twill be in the Icelands now."

Rygyl already knew this through their Link and had been spending his time pretending to search while he was really trying to come up with a solution of how they were to retrieve the Fang from the Empress. But now that the Daring Duo had finally figured it out, 'twas time to return to the Keep, inform Darque, and make a plan. Fryya sulked as they packed up the camp, and though she was unusually quiet, both her companions knew her heart was heavy with grief, for she felt that she'd failed her first mission, her partner, her sister, and herself.

'Twas as they were preparing to leave that Fryya remembered one who'd penetrated the land of perpetual ice and snow. Somehow he'd survived and returned in Shift, wanting to give them something. It had to be the Fang! For the entire trip back to the Keep, Fryya said naught, so absorbed was she with trying to figure a way to contact Rhyah to work out the exchange.

CHAPTER THIRTEEN

Battle Of The Leviathans

~~~~~ THE SEA OF DREAMS ~~~~~

Once all had come aboard the Lytle, with Calei to guide them Myrrdin set sail for the place they'd scuttled the pirate ship o'er fifty winters past. 'Twas not far from the island and they arrived within a mark. The Water Dragons had been fully briefed on the mission and the dangers, and not one had retreated. Islyth had become their leader, with Schlynn at her side, and she now sent down several of her friends to check out the wreck and report their findings.

Her nose wrinkled, nostrils flaring, and long tongue slipping in and out past her sharp fangs, Islyth spoke aloud with Myrrdin. "Found. Ship lies on side covers hole. Must make new one."

Myrrdin didn't like that. "Can you not push the ship o'er to open the original hole?"

"Barrels move more," she began afore Myrrdin interrupted.

"Of course. 'Twould be as shaking them up. Alright. Cut a new path to the Hold and then report what's there. If it seems safe, enter, and try to retrieve the barrels, then come back for us."

The Water Dragons could swim through the shell of the ship easier without riders but Myrrdin's real concern was that the Spell covering the barrels that was hiding them from their vision, might hide them from the Water Dragons as well. This presented several issues. If they could not see them, they would have difficulty finding and transporting them. But on the other hand, it also meant that the Spell still held strong.

'Twas anticipated that whoever carried the barrels would be too close to flee the poison once activated. Islyth was the fastest Water Dragon, Schlynn a close second, with Schlyth, Schlynn's hatchmate, coming in third. They'd volunteered to carry the bar-
~~~~~

rels, while Schlett, another hatchmate, would swim along in case of need to transfer.

Myrrdin would be riding Islyth and Caleichante, her Tie, Schlynn. Schlyth and Schlett were Tied to Captain Natanamia, who was on her own mission, and Captain Naftaleah respectively, therefore Schlyth would carry his barrel alone while Naftaleah and Schlett would try to protect their flanks. The rest of the Water Dragons both with and without riders, would form a giant hollow spearhead cutting through the water to allow the ones carrying the barrels to draft off them from inside, using far less effort. This would help them keep the barrels steady and save their strength for when they got to the crevasse.

The Water Dragons swam into the murky sea deep down to the shipwreck and began to spit-carve through the hull. Islyth chose a site opposite the Hold as she remembered it, as she was fearful that they might cut into the barrels themselves. She too, wondered what 'twould mean if they could see them.

The Warrior Regynn once told Islyth that the powder was used in fluids of all kinds and would initially show up as a milky streak, swirling about as stirred 'til completely dissolved. Once dissolved, 'twas invisible and quite deadly to whomever came into contact with it 'til it lost its strength with time, becoming completely undetectable. Increasing the amount of fluid in which 'twas, also decreased its potency. Therefore, along with the longer 'twas activated, so too, the larger the amount of fluid, the weaker it became. But the poison from the Rol Dan was so strong, 'twould take but a few grains of powder in a full bottle of wine, to kill near instantly if consumed within a mark.

Such was the reasoning behind having thirty barrels of the poison sent to the island in the first place. The barrels had been packed full but in such a manner as to keep their contents dry against minimal to moderate exposure to water. The original plan was for the barrels to be destroyed with the ship close to the island, completely immersing the powder so that 'twould dissolve quickly, at its most destructive.

If the plan had gone as expected, the ship would have been sunk, the Hold and the barrels within, destroyed, quickly dissolving all the powder, carried by the currents to surround the island and infiltrate the Grotto. Such devastation could have annihilated both the Sprite Nation and the Water Dragons. Therefore, 'twas surmised that if the weakening Spell held long enough for them to safely deliver the barrels to the crevasse, the pressure would break them open and whatever was near them would be affected, if not killed. But the poison would quickly dissipate mid-ocean and at such a depth. They'd have to hit their targets very accurately.

'Twas Islyth's idea that even if the barrels were compromised along the way to the crevasse if they could avoid the 'streak' of powder as it dissolved they might still have time to deliver and retreat afore 'twould be too late. She was counting on her phenomenal speed to get the job done.

Cutting through the hull, 'twas Islyth who entered first, swimming through the darkness initially using her senses to guide her to the cargo hold. The ship had been old and decrepit when 'twas sunk, and o'er fifty winters underwater had not been kind. Soon Islyth could see the Allure from the old Spell, using it like a beacon to guide them. As they made their way through the cramped rooms, corridors, and stairwells, it became obvious 'twas the Spell alone that kept the ship's carcass from total collapse. She warned her companions not to touch any of the old timbers, and to create no wake to stir the ship to further ruin.

Swimming slowly and very carefully they finally made it to their destination. The doors were hanging open and as she swam down into the hold, Islyth told her companions to stay back and exit quickly if anything went wrong. Peering about she surveyed the damage they'd done so long ago. She used her Magic to enhance her already excellent vision as she squinted in the semi-darkness. She saw the twenty-seven barrels that had been neu-tralized, stacked up in a huge pile, lying on their sides or tops, lids off, falling apart against the hull of the ship. If she'd not known what they'd carried, the scene would make little sense. Empty barrels. Twenty-seven of them. But where were the three miss-ing ones? And why was there an increasing light within the hold?

Then she realized what was happening. The Allure was bright-ening because 'twas fading. Spells gave off a burst of energy to-ward the end of their power, one last shine afore the light died out, but 'twas a visual phenomenon only afforded a Magic bear-er, or those with the Gift. Seeing the Allure brightly enough for them to follow to the hold, meant the Spell was ending. However, she saw not the barrels yet, only the light of Allure surrounding each of them.

As her companions quickly realized the same thing, they swam toward the ovals of light and could feel the invisible barrels within with their huge round paws. Each Water Dragon clutched a barrel to their chest, and without further delay they swiftly ex-ited the shell of the ship, which completely collapsed upon itself in their wake as they removed the Allure.

Their massive heads broke the surface of the water and as Islyth made quick report to Myrrdin, the team leaped o'er the railing and mounted their Ties. They had not long to get to the crevasse.

Even swimming deeply, the sea churned as hundreds of Water Dragons created their conical spearhead and protecting their brethren in their midst they made for the middle of the Ocean of Fears. First Mate Lyran commanded the Lytle and would follow but watching the Water Dragons pull away from the ship he won-dered if the Lytle would arrive in time for the initial encounter. Whatever happened, might happen afore they got there. Roaring his orders into the winds, his crew hustled to set sail.

Lyran was correct in his thoughts and it soon became obvi-ous the Lytle was unable to keep up with the Water Dragons, despite his best effort. 'Twas truly amazing for singly, a Water Dragon was not this fast. Only Islyth had ever been faster than the Krakken but with all of them together in this formation of theirs, they were moving up to ten times that speed. They had to be using their Magic, 'twas no other explanation. But if they did that, they'd be weakened by the time they got there, and poorly equipped to flee or fight the Leviathans should they rise.

'Twas also clear the Lytle's speed was being enhanced and he had to thank the draft off the spearhead for that, and for being Magically included. Otherwise, 'twould take a full moon or more to arrive at the crevasse at their greatest speed. At this rate, 'twould take a mere day, mayhap two. He set his jaw. The Lytle would provide what support she could. He could do no less for his Captain and the courageous Water Dragons.

SEVERAL MARKS LATER

~~~~~ ENTERING THE OCEAN OF FEARS ~~~~~

</div>

The surrounding Water Dragons were of all ages and abilities and some dropped off during the charge to the Fears due to intense fatigue, forced to do so, unable to keep up with the extreme pace. Without the Magic of the huge number of Water Dragons focused through the formation, they would lose speed, and that meant many of them would die when the poison dissolved. As they lost their strength, so too, their Magic, and dropping back, they left the formation but continued to follow. 'Twas these stragglers that found themselves alongside the Lytle as they entered the Ocean of Fears, Lyran's Tie, Kath, among them.

Lyran had been Myrrdin's First Mate since the beginning. Meeting the Elven Prince as dock workers, he then helped Myrrdin with the Krakken when 'twas first dragged into Port O'Dreams by Water Dragons who'd found the wrecked ship half sunk after being scourged by pirates. Once the pride of the Sprite Fleet, the Krakken had been misused, mistreated, and mismanaged, falling into disrepair. A mere shadow of her former glory,
~~~~~

when the pirates attacked, the Captain abandoned her, returning to the island by way of his Tie and leaving the ship, and his crew, to their fate.

Although Lyran was much older, he and Myrrdin became close friends while working the docks, and Myrrdin had scraped and saved his coin. Driving a hard bargain with the owners, Myrrdin purchased the Krakken and through the winters that followed, refitted her, replacing the stripped and stolen hand carved woodwork, brass fittings, and elaborate décor, as well as arming her and making her better than she had ever been. Lyran had even designed her banner, presenting it to Myrrdin upon the day they first set sail together. Faster, more powerful, the ship became the pride of the Sprite Nation again, with Myrrdin as her Captain and Lyran as First Mate. They'd sailed together since that day.

Now Lyran comforted Kath with the reassurance that she'd done her best and 'twas no shame in fatiguing with such an enormous effort. But Kath was desperate to rejoin the others, her greatest desire to help raise the Krakken, to be a part of the adventure of a lifespan. Lyran was not sure how this adventure would play out, for his Tie was near as old as was Islyth but not near as fast. However, his own loyalty to the Ship's Master a mirror of Kath's to him, he could deny her not and as they followed the main body of Water Dragons, he encouraged his Tie and the stragglers to feed and rejuvenate themselves along the way, for the battle to come. Their participation might yet be needed.

~~~~~ IN THE MIDDLE OF THE OCEAN OF FEARS ~~~~~

Water Dragons were known to be highly distractible with short attention spans. Playing, feeding, and spending time with their Ties, were the driving forces in their existence. But with the danger to their eggs, along with the danger imposed to the Sprite Nation who'd saved them from extinction at the time of the Last Holocaust, they were united and focused on the mission. And
~~~~~

of course, they all loved Myrrdin and 'twas an adventure. Water Dragons loved adventures.

Islyth swam steadily onward, trailed closely by Schlynn with Caleichante, Schlyth, and Schlett with Naftaleah. Myrrdin urged her to a steady pace, letting the formation help increase her speed, rationing her Magic for what was to come.

Carrying the barrels turned out to be more difficult than the Water Dragons had expected, as they were awkward and created a drag through the water. They had to clutch them tightly to their chests to lessen that drag. This was using up their energy quicker than anticipated and even with the formation surrounding them, they were becoming fatigued. Still, they swam onward through the open waters, maintaining a close watch on the Allure enveloping the barrels, hoping they'd not lose the protection of the Spell too soon. If they did, the barrels would have to be abandoned as they sought to distance themselves quickly enough to avoid the poison, losing their only opportunity to raise the Krakken.

Myrrdin could Hear his Tie's thoughts and lying flat against to her body, he patted her shoulder, reassuring her they would succeed. Islyth narrowed her green eyes, the gold flecks flashing with resolve as she continued swimming.

<center>~~~~~ DREKINN LAIR ~~~~~</center>

Diadranei had improved daily o'er the past fortnight, regaining both her health and the strength of her Magic. Her capture had left her bruised and weakened, though without major injury, but she was no Warrior and their escape had been perilous. They'd decided to remain at the Den long enough to allow her to fully heal, as well as prepare for their roles in the upcoming mission which would require some research along with some special training.

The mated Daggogh pair, Larken and Matana, now living with their Night Beasts at Drekinn Lair, were quite helpful.

They'd spent near four decades living in Evanntyr and knew every secret passage, every cleverly disguised lever to open said passage, and every method of entry and exit. Obviously, they knew not about what changed with the reconstruction but from what information Bastyen and Graasyn imparted it seemed they'd simply sealed up the side of the castle that had crumbled into the Fears, along with the partially added wall extending the castle grounds further northwesterly. Of course, this confirmed that the Well of Evanntyr was no more, and that meant the easiest method of gaining entry or exit was no longer an option.

Matana drew detailed maps of Evanntyr both inside and out, along with separate maps of the tunnels which ran 'tween most of the walls of the entire castle. The Stealth Team spent many marks memorizing them. But Diadranei's skill was in Empathy and when 'twas clear she was struggling, Darque sent Bryynn to assist. Using his Magic to enhance her memory of the maps, Dia was able to keep up with the others.

Bryynn also laid out a visual Spell in the Training Pits comparable to creating a physical maze, that allowed the Team to experience Evanntyr as if they were there. Day after day they would navigate through the grounds and in and out of the castle with particular focus on the Great Hall and Grand Staircase where could be found the 'front' entrance to Sarai's lab.

Larken and Matana gave no quarter in their study 'til at last Larken felt confident they'd be able to find their way about with or without a torch and even while being chased. The man turned out be a hard taskmaster for which they were most grateful.

Although they'd thought they knew much about disguise from their Stealth Training along with many winters of practice, they quickly learned that Larken was a master far above their modest level of expertise. He'd been the Court Jongleur during the time they'd lived there, hiding his true allegiance and appearance, and working as a spy for the Daggogh and their cousins the Gordatch, known as the People of the Raptor's Talons and the Razor's Edge. When they weren't trying to race through the Spell's visual corridors or memorizing yet another section of the castle so they could not only get in and out but could locate Sarai's lab from any direction under any conditions, Larken taught them the art of disguise.

Diadranei and Caleichante need not be a part of these sessions but they attended anyway, ever curious, and willing to learn. All knowledge was worthy, and they soon realized that they could use most of what they were learning to enhance the effectiveness of their glamours, making them more believable. Simple mistakes led to exposure, which Dia also realized was what might have happened in King's Gate.

'Twas one afternoon as Dia returned to their quarters for a break, that Shayla approached her with a special request. After the Healer explained, she said, "I could not ask this of the men. They care not for such things, but 'tis most important to me, and mayhap to the war effort."

"I understand," Dia responded with a smile.

"Then you'll try?"

Diadranei could sense the longing in her words and exclaimed, "Of course! I see no difficulty. Once we're inside the lab, 'twill take no more time or effort than collecting the Fang itself."

Shayla sighed in relief but was also concerned. She and her brother, Grifynn, had used her Blood Crystal to give them similar abilities shared 'tween LifeBond partners without that partner, the most significant being her health and longevity. She'd been using the substance since she'd created it just afore the Last Holocaust and had even used it upon a Dragon on that battlefield. The one who'd been heart struck and should have Passed the Veil. She'd never learned what happened to that Dragon. But after treating the Teams wounded in battle for serious injury their Dragons could not Heal, along with others not in the 'Bond, she was using up her current supplies of the Blood Crystal faster than she could make it and recently discovered she was also running out of ingredients. If she could no longer create the Blood Crystal, 'twould impact the Resistance greatly, as well as the impact 'twould have upon herself. Nevertheless, she'd decided long ago that she needed to refine the substance, creating one that would be easily replenished, more effective, with fewer side effects. For this she required her research notes but when they'd unexpectedly been forced to abandon Evanntyr, she'd had to leave everything behind. Still, she didn't want anyone to get hurt trying to do her a favor. "This means much to me, but do not risk your lives, for your lives are more important than that for which I have asked."

Diadranei nodded her reassurance, bid the Healer good afternoon, and retreated to her bed to rest afore evening meal. Her Empathy was exhausting her as she Felt a struggle of monumental proportions happening mid-ocean. 'Twas curious, but 'twas also far away and she need maintain her focus upon her own mission. The Stealth Team would be leaving at dawn.

CHAPTER FOURTEEN
Raising The Krakken

They could see the darker waters far beneath them, signaling they were within a league of the crevasse. Thus far, they'd seen no indication of the Leviathans, but keeping close watch, the formation began to dive deeper and deeper into the ocean, closing in on their target.

Halfway there, Islyth Heard a cry of alarm. Glancing o'er her shoulder, what she saw made her shiver. The barrel that Schlyth carried suddenly appeared as a ghostly mirage but was becoming more visible with each passing moment. Her eyes flashed to the same visual of her own barrel as well as the one carried by Schlynn and Calei. The Spell was fading. The poison would soon be activated as the surrounding waters soaked through the wooden slats, the increasing pressure of their dive speeding up that process.

Turning her focus again to the crevasse intent on getting there in time, she saw another danger. The glowing, poison spiked tentacles of one of the Leviathans were creeping up through the darkness of the depths. 'Twas rising.

As the formation separated to allow the barrel carriers through, the rest of the Water Dragons prepared to fight. Never in their history had so many of them gathered to attack a common enemy. Communicating with Myrrdin, Islyth made her plan. Telling Calei and Schlynn, she and Myrrdin accepted no argument. Islyth was the fastest. She would go in first. Then glancing once more toward Schlyth, she suddenly had yet another problem.

There afore her eyes came a thread of white from the failing barrel. Schlyth set his jaw, moved the barrel gripped with his sharp talons to his side and continued swimming toward the rising Leviathan with the others, the tiny ribbon trailing off behind them. But 'twas clear he wouldn't make it in time. If that poison dissolved in their midst, 'twould be the Water Dragons 'round them who died.

Islyth hesitated not. Myrrdin held on, strengthening her with his own Magic, encouraging her to do what she had only a few heartbeats left to do. While Schlyth held the barrel out to his side, still avoiding the increasing white ribbon trailing from it, Islyth suddenly swam past him, catching one talon on the soft wood slats, and dragging it out of his grasp and making certain the streak was not in his path. Aiming directly at the rising creature, Islyth put her head down and charged forward. Schlynn and Calei raced on toward the Leviathan, hoping they could drop their barrel directly into the middle of the tentacles, which might end up in the creature's giant maw.

But even carrying two barrels, Islyth was the faster. Passing Schlynn and Calei, swimming diagonally to their position so that the whitish streak was dragged away from everyone, she used her back leg to push Schlynn out of her way, while the other Dragons began to distance themselves from the streak. Schlynn turned o'er backwards and dove deeper to avoid the dissolving poison.

Not only did the two Water Dragons and their riders have to avoid the poison leaking into the waters, but they had to avoid the rising Leviathan, its long tentacles reaching out in a circle of death, seeking its prey. In a commanding Voice, Islyth Spoke with Schlynn, "Follow not! Drop and go!" Islyth knew there were at least two more of the Leviathans in the crevasse, and she knew Schlynn would not be able to follow them and avoid the poison as both barrels were crushed by the pressure. Calei adjusted their target and they swam away from the Leviathan.

Weaving her way 'tween those tentacles, Islyth brought the barrels directly o'er the middle afore she dropped them and backed away. The white streak became a huge cloud as both barrels were taken into the creature's mouth and the tentacles thrashed wildly about. Islyth was stung several times while navigating through the forest of flesh, the poison spiked tips digging deep into her scaly hide, each sting weakening her further. At least the poison of the barrels was staying relatively contained and Myrrdin surmised later that 'twas due to the intense pressure. All Myrrdin could do now was duck and hack at the tentacles, cutting them off as they attached, his sword flashing in the murky depths.

As Islyth entered the mass of tentacles, Schlynn and Calei rode just outside of their reach and dropped the third barrel into the crevasse, while Schlett, Naftaleah and the other Water Dragons swam for the Krakken. 'Twas no time to waste.

It took many of them to cut through the massive chains that kept her from sliding o'er the edge. The Krakken had been 'laid to rest' using numerous chains along with her anchor and once cut loose the ship rocked perilously in the strong current. But the Leviathan's reaching tentacles were close and if they didn't move her now, the flailing creature might drag the ship down with it afore the poison took full effect.

Hundreds of Water Dragons grabbed hold of the chains and then each other, creating a living chain of sorts, pulling hard for the surface, their efforts led by Lyrianei, Kalisadei, Ardryyn, Kryllyn, Datyniah and Dalakiah. 'Twas clear to all now that the first Leviathan, thought to be the largest, was showing definite effects of the poison, the tentacles less agitated, some beginning to float aimlessly about. The creature had not fully emerged from the crevasse, but the other two did.

The strength of the Water Dragons was near drained from the formation. Rocking the Krakken back and forth assisted by the current itself, Islyth, Schlynn, Schlyth and Schlett managed to clear the silt from the hull, and it began to list upon the ocean floor with the currents created by all the activity. 'Twas with their hard-won success, joining the others on the chains and attaching to each other, towing with all their might, that they saw the second Leviathan rise aside the drooping tentacles of the first. The poison spikes stretched forth to latch onto the ship, starting a huge tug of war for her possession. The Water Dragons could not fight and keep hold of the Krakken and with their Magical limits soon to be reached, they would not win. She'd be lost forever in the crevasse.

As Myrrdin prepared himself to order the Water Dragons to abandon their efforts, to let go the Krakken and swim to safety, they saw the stragglers just catching up, led by Kath. The brown and silver Water Dragon now commanded a legion of near a hundred others, and instead of joining the chain still trying to pull the Krakken off the edge and toward the surface so far above, they dove for the creature trying to stop them.

Kath was alone, Lyran still in the Lytle. He'd been afraid 'twould be the last time he saw his Tie, but Kath was adamant. If she were to Pass the Veil, let it be while helping Lyran. If the Leviathans had risen, the Lytle was in danger and she wanted to protect them both. They'd traveled as quickly as possible, feeding along the way, and drafting off the ship as it sliced through the waters. Racing onward Magically assisted, the Lytle arrived shortly after the battle began. The plan included hitching the Krakken to the Lytle to drag her out of the Fears, for her masts and sails had been destroyed in the battle. She'd be difficult to get afloat, but with the Magic of her preparation Spell and some assist from the Water Dragons, she could be dragged to safety. Without such assist, she'd be dead in the water.

Kath and Lyran had been together for most of Lyran's long span of days. But 'twas Lyran's duty to stay aboard to Command the Lytle and 'twas Kath's dream to go down fighting. As he lost sight of her in the depths, he prayed the poison had done its job, and his girl would be safe.

PORT O'DREAMS

A FORTNIGHT LATER

~~~~~ THE KRAKKEN: QUARTERS OF THE SHIP'S MASTER ~~~~~

First Mate Lyran had been promoted to Ship's Master but he refused to work for anyone else. Myrrdin, grateful for his loyalty, gave him full Command of the Lytle. Such a time would normally be accompanied by much celebration, however, Lyran was still in mourning for losing Kath in the battle. The new Captain had known in his heart that she would not return to him. A Tie created a working relationship 'tween the different Races, Sprite and Dragon, and although 'twas not as the LifeBond, 'twas still devastating when broken. The loss of Myrrdin himself, would have been the only greater loss Lyran could imagine. Myrrdin was as his own son.

In the Grotto, one large batch of Water Dragon eggs were showing signs of hatching soon, and Captain Naftaleah, currently recovering from multiple fractures and pressure sickness sustained from her daring transfer in the depths, insisted to the Assembly that Lyran be placed first on the list to Tie with one of the new hatchlings. She, having had a Water Dragon, was not originally on that list herself, but Myrrdin knew she would be. The Ship's Master had some hefty influence. 'Twas a secret as she needed time to mourn Schlett, but he wanted her to be surprised, as well. Naftaleah would soon Tie again.

In the meantime, Pyth and Dyrth had returned to the Sea of Dreams, seeking their friends. 'Twas soon enough that they learned of the raising of the Krakken, proud of the part played by those who were lost and distressed they'd not been a part of it themselves. But after telling the tale of their own absence, the journey to, and escape from Evanntyr with the Stealth Team, Pyth and Dyrth became heroes as well. Adventure was adventure, after all.

The Krakken had been b'Spelled in the operation known as 'The Final Sleep', in which Myrrdin and Lyran had prepared her
~~~~~

to be scuttled, ending the Sorcerer's evil Spell hold upon her. Unsure if he'd ever see her again, Myrrdin's Spell of Protection soaked into every surface under the top decks after sacrificing the masts, sails, and railings above to fool their attackers, afore Islyth and Schlynn had spit carved the hole that took her down. Even though she was full of water, her interior remained intact and untouched, protected by the Spell. All she needed was cleaning, refitting, and exterior repair once she was dragged home.

The entire Sprite Nation seemed to be in attendance as the news of their bold exploit spread far and wide. Cheering and much fanfare met them at the docks as the surviving Water Dragons filled the bay. 'Twas a sight to be remembered, the mighty beasts rising out of the water using their strong tails as if standing upon the surface afore diving back under to rise again with much excitement, clapping their huge round paws and chattering loudly in their native tongue.

Although Myrrdin was very emotional to have the Krakken returned to him, he was just as emotional when he saw how many Water Dragons they'd lost. Watching helplessly as they fought to protect him, the ship, and the others of their Kind, he'd seen them die. And of the hundred stragglers who'd taken it upon themselves to attack the Leviathan, less than half returned. Among the last of those lost was Kath.

Myrrdin had known Kath near as long as he'd known Lyran, and the loss was great. But no greater than the loss of Naftaleah's Schlett, who, while dying of the poison spikes dug deeply into his hide, demanded Naftaleah go with Schlyth. If not, she would not have escaped the tentacles herself, and when she'd lost contact with her Water Dragon, the pressure of the depths would have killed her instantly. 'Twas the first known such transfer from one to another Water Dragon mid-water, and although Naftaleah was heartbroken, she could sense her Tie was near the Veil and did as he demanded, feeling horrible guilt and an instant of extreme crushing pressure as she left Schlett afore being drawn under the Magic of Schlyth. With tears in her eyes, they watched Schlett pulled toward the edge of the crevasse, being dragged down by the many tentacles wrapped 'round his body like a net of chains as the Leviathan retreated from the unexpected onslaught of so many attackers trying to deny its catch.

'Twas also how they'd lost Kath. There was no stronger bite than the jaws of a Water Dragon, nor a harder head for battering. Fearlessly, she'd hit here, there, and everywhere, using her razor sharp serrated dorsal ridge to cut at the tentacles in their classic 'spinning saw' technique, tucking their tails to their noses and spinning backwards, the ridge becoming a saw blade. Attacking relentlessly, she was successful in keeping the focus of both remaining Leviathans on her and not on the rising Krakken, taking no heed to her increasing exhaustion.

Joining the effort to free Schlett, she used her last bit of Magic and strength to try to cut his body loose afore she realized he was already dead. In a daze from being unable to deal with the increasing pressure 'round her, Kath stubbornly tried to push his body toward the surface afore the third Leviathan entangled it. And then she just stopped. As the other Water Dragons watched in grief from afar, Kath's heart failed her, the pressure too great, the battle too strenuous, her Magic gone. As her body began to sink, she too was grabbed by the flailing tentacles. Once o'er the edge, she was not seen again.

Many Water Dragons fought that day, spitting, cutting, biting, and clawing. The poison had stunned one Leviathan and slowed the others. Once it rose, the Water Dragon attack intimidated the second afore the third finally showed itself. Weakening, they continued to fight, trying to keep the third Leviathan occupied while the Krakken broke the surface, was hooked up to the Lytle, and set sail to the Sea of Dreams with many Water Dragons keeping her afloat to speed the retreat. However, those who remained were spent. By the time the Krakken was clear of the Ocean of Fears and the fight could be abandoned, the death toll was near a third of all who had participated. But the Leviathans would not leave the deepest part of the Fears and so the rest were safe.

Once secure in port, Lyran shoved a broom stick into a crack in what was left of the quarterdeck and helped Myrrdin tie on the Krakken's banner. Tears near filled the eyes of the Ship's Master once more as he stood and gazed at the beautiful flag unfurling in the breeze. The Krakken was home at last.

The next thing they had to do was patch the hole in her side and pump all the remaining water out so she could float on her own. That had been accomplished by much volunteer labor from those who knew and loved the Elven Ship's Master and his ship. When that repair was complete, Myrrdin chose to rest and to honor the lost with a day of mourning.

Such was the atmosphere when Caleichante finally walked into his quarters again. It had been so very long and so much had happened in that time. Looking all 'round her, she was ever amazed at how beautiful was the Krakken, how meticulous had been her design, the lavish ornamentation. The ship was Myrrdin's mistress and he'd spared no expense upon her. Calei had spent many moons aboard preparing for her search mission with Kevon. 'Twas a time of desperation, and countless conflicting emotions flooded her mind as she noted the bottle of Drekinn Whiskey still sitting in the middle of the small table.

His voice broke into her thoughts as they sat down once more at that table, the bottle finally opened and shared 'tween them as per their long ago promise. Tipping his glass toward hers, he said, "A promise kept and a new one made. To our future. May we never wait so long to see each other again."

Her smile lit up the room as she met his glass with hers and nodded. "May we never wait so long again."

For the next several marks through the night, Caleichante wove the tale of the mission upon which she'd embarked after they'd left from the Krakken, giving Myrrdin much pleasure and more detail than anyone else to whom she'd shared the quest.

The whiskey flowed as he laughed with her triumphs and cried with her anguish. And then 'twas Myrrdin's turn. He shared with her all that had happened in the Battle for the Krakken, the activation of 'the Final Sleep', the pain, and the struggles.

Just as dawn broke through the eastern skies, Myrrdin's thoughts turned to what lay in his safe. 'Twas the Fang Grifynn had given him as passage to Evanntyr so many winters past. Mayhap 'twas time to return it to its rightful owner. Sharing that story as well, he then stated, "The work on the Krakken can continue without me. 'Twould do Lyran good to keep busy and at any rate, my homecoming has long been delayed. I must travel back to the Wyrdritch in time for the Call to Return. Mayhap you would care to join me as far as the Keep. I know you are eager to return to your Team and your lifemate." Then with a sly smile, he concluded, "And I would very much like to meet the man who captured your heart."

CHAPTER FIFTEEN

An Icy Deception

THE WYRDRITCH
O'ER A FORTNIGHT AFTER COLTYN'S RESCUE

~~~~~ HAVEN ~~~~~

Anastasia glanced up at Kevon, sitting 'cross the table with his golden blonde head buried in one of the many histories of the Elves in their newest batch of books taken from the massive shelves of the library. She reflected upon the breakneck events of the past fortnight. Such chaotic emotion and disorder with which she'd had to deal.

As soon as Thyrazin, Beralarr, and Dyrachin Danced away, Alyssa had Anastasia 'test' all those she'd had taken into custody throughout Haven and the Wyrdritch who might have been working with Thyrazin, and clear Lord Rohar and his entourage. Much to Alyssa's relief, 'twas a mere handful of Elves identified as accomplices. Those were imprisoned while physical evidence was gathered, for Magic senses alone were not enough to condemn.

In the meantime, she waited for the return of her youngest. 'Twas not long and once Aiisabeau, Coltyn, and Beralarr returned with Thyrazin and the still unconscious Dyrachin, the injured Elf was immediately taken to the Skald, while Thyrazin was just as immediately placed in the dungeons recently vacated by Lord Rohar, Captain Natanamia, Prince Kevon, and the Elven Princes Orasynth, Malyrist, Gylrann and Gylragg. For those who might still doubt their innocence, the proof was in the mounting evidence against Thyrazin as well as his insane rantings that also had the advantage of strengthening the innocence or guilt of those Ana had 'tested'.

Fyrdien survived his head wound but was still on the mend, however, Dyrachin's wound was too severe and he succumbed
~~~~~

within a dawn to a collapsed lung and much loss of his Life Source, never having regained consciousness. He Passed the Veil with his stepmother and most of his siblings at his side.

Due to the tragic events 'twas decided that the Call to Return would be delayed 'til such time as the raw emotions of the Nation could calm down. Nevertheless, plans were in the making so they could be ready by the winter solstice if not afore. Alyssa wanted the Elves still out there, to 'come in from the cold' and not have to wait a moment longer than necessary. They had less than two full moons to achieve this goal.

By the end of the first sennight the Elven royals held their private Remembrance Ceremony for both Laratyn and Dyrachin. Aside from the deceased, the only family members missing were Myrrdin, Leisalarr, and of course, Thyrazin. If it hadn't been such a somber occasion Ana would have described it as charming, with all the candles, incense, and melodic formal chants in Ancient Tongue, along with endless marks of dancing and bottomless glasses of mead which accompanied any such ceremony for the Magic bearers. She and Persephone wore lovely ritual gowns with tight bodices and gathered skirts of multiple layers of delicate and iridescent pastels cut in the shape of petals giving them the appearance of blooming flowers, while the males wore loose fitting cloaks in greens and browns that symbolized the soil from which the flowers bloomed. The Celebration of Life lasted from dusk to dawn and Anastasia had slept through most of the following day while Lord Rohar and the rest of them met with Queen Alyssa to offer what assistance they could, to ensure the success of both the Call to Return and the Reunion of their peoples.

After the ceremony Alyssa declared the Dome secure and the Nation safe again from the Black and the Sorcerer. With so much behind them 'twas just a few dawns past that she and Kevon were reunited, at which time Ana felt drawn to the library. She'd shown Kevon the picture of her stepmother, Queen Bryanna, riding upon the horse, waving to the one looking at the painting, while she described her prior experiments with the portals afore the Protection Spell had been Healed by Persephone, which had created the Spell Domes.

In one of her first attempts she'd found herself in the Icelands and realizing her danger she'd turned and dived back through the collapsing portal to return to the Wyrdritch. 'Twas a close call and had led her to theorize at the time (a theory that was later proven by the discovery of the Kreegare in the Rol Dan) that all of the Lost Elves had been drawn through such a portal and might yet be out there if conditions at their destination were conducive to life, which the Icelands were not. But in the instant she'd turned about, she'd glimpsed a figure flying toward her riding an Ice Dragon, waving for her attention. And once she'd found the picture of the Queen on the horse, she was certain 'twas Bryanna and she was still alive. With the return of Rhyah the Wolf at the Keep, Ana had been trying to figure out how to get back to the Icelands safely. She now believed the Fay was trying to tell her that he had the Fang lost at Ice Mist Falls, and if he'd found a way to survive, so could she.

Given all this information Kevon agreed with Ana that some research was in order. While experimenting with the portals so long ago, Ana had hoped to find the Lost Elves. They'd since learned that many had been thrust to the Rol Dan, becoming Kreegaren Assassins, but the census they were undertaking indicated there were many more out there still unaccounted for. The Elven Nation was once one of the largest forces upon the entire world. Of course, the Call to Return could very well accomplish finding them, however, now she had real hope to find at least one. Toward this effort, 'twas their desire to learn all they could about the Icelands and the Ice Dragons.

Piling up tall stacks of large, heavy books, along with heaps of scrolls and literally thousands of single parchments, they would study all day and long into the nights, re-shelving, and re-stacking, afore continuing their self-appointed task as they worked their way methodically through the library.

Kevon had been fascinated with the differences he found there. Being a Prince of the Sprite Nation, he'd spent much time in the Library of Dream Hold as well as visiting others upon the island. In the Elven library, there was little from the time of the Last Holocaust to the time the Protection Spell had been Healed. As the Sprite library had continued to flourish during that period, this difference proved in his mind that the morphing of the Spell had been negatively affecting all within the Wyrdritch.

Yet even more amazing were the clear differences in information from afore and after the Separation when the Sprites had left the Wyrdritch, with the Sprites having little information from prior. He'd been taught that the Sprites had been unable to take anything with them and so their history was cloudy and from memory. Now he realized that could not have had such a stark affect since the memories of Magic bearers were long and quite accurate. Disturbingly, he understood the differences could not be anything less than personal perspective colored by rampant emotions. 'Twas at least comforting to note that even for the Elves, the Separation had been traumatic.

They'd been at this for marks and Kevon was getting tired. While he was vowing to himself that such inaccuracies and contradictions in their mutual histories would be corrected within his span of days, his drifting thoughts came to an abrupt halt. Staring at the words, he read the passage again. Then with furrowed brows, he read it once more. Chills ran up the back of his neck as he ran his finger under the lines of script to help him keep his place while he read it a fourth time. With growing excitement, he exclaimed, "Ana! Come here! Look at this!"

The book was very old and very large, the pages yellowed and fragile, the edges crumbling. 'Twas from long afore the Separation, and 'twas written in Ancient Tongue. They were both fluent with speaking and translating the oral language, but there were nuances within the written words that could be misinterpreted. So although Kevon was excited, he was also leery and wanted Anastasia to confirm.

Making her way 'round the table, she sat beside him, and he watched her closely as she read to herself. With much impatience he questioned, "Well? Does it say what I think it says?"

Turning her head and catching his gaze, she broke into a huge grin. Elated, 'twas difficult to keep her voice down as she declared, "I think it says what you think it says! The Ice Dragons once lived at the Keep of St Swiftyn's!"

SHORTLY LATER

~~~~~ **QUEEN ALYSSA'S CHAMBERS** ~~~~~

</div>

"But mother! This information might be most helpful to the Resistance!" Ana exclaimed, pointing to the passage in the book that lay opened upon the table.

Alyssa frowned in thought. "This history is among our most ancient, and although it does APPEAR to INFER that the Ice Dragons MIGHT have been the first inhabitants of the mountain now known as the Keep of St Swiftyn's, I see not how, even if 'tis true, this can be of any assistance to the Battle Commander now."

Ana pursed her lips in frustration at her mother's tactful way of telling her she wasn't certain 'twas truth. "But the passage states," she began.

No longer looking at the book, Alyssa replied, "'Twas a brief paragraph that referred to the Ice Dragons in a manner consistent with what we might think of today, as saying they 'lived' there. But in reality, Anastasia, there was little factual information, even less detail, and 'twas a mere reference only. Surely you see that. I fear your desire to find just such information has clouded your judgment."

Anastasia was most disappointed. Closing the book and holding it to her chest, she glanced to Persephone as the tall, lithe young woman walked into the chambers for a meeting with the
~~~~~

Queen. No, 'walked' was not quite the right word. More like, 'glided' or 'floated' into the room, as Persephone was the most graceful and delicate Elf Ana had ever known.

As Persephone passed her little sister, she reached out and gently touched Ana's shoulder. Ana looked up and caught the encouraging wink, afore she turned and left to find Kevon. They required more. They had to convince her mother of the need to return to the Keep and give this information to Darque. And if they couldn't convince Alyssa, they'd not convince the Battle Commander, either. Ana knew somehow this information was key to retrieving the Fang. She just had to make the others believe.

<center>~~~~~ BACK IN THE LIBRARY ~~~~~</center>

In less than a mark, Persephone approached the pair pouring o'er more volumes of ancient history, trying to find more references to the Ice Dragons, along with anything they could find about the Keep's origins. Now that they'd identified the correct section of the library to search (meaning, the correct century), they were piling up open books marked with their discoveries. Still, they were all 'mere references', but with enough of them Kevon assured her they would be successful.

Persephone's Song was mystifying. Ana turned her full attention to her sister and Heard the urgency. "What is it? What's happened?"

Her slim hand gesturing to the pair to follow, Persephone insisted, "Come quickly. The Wolf is outside the barrier."

<center>~~~~~ LATER~~~~~</center>

Kevon and Ana had dropped everything and leaped up from their chairs, racing after Persephone who led the way to Ana's dressing chambers and the ivy. Following her sister, they all Drew their energy afore they Danced to the western edge of the barrier of the Spell Dome.

Ana knew Rhyah had something most important to tell her. The distance traveled from the Icelands to the Wyrdritch was farther than to the Keep and he couldn't possibly have much time left to return safely. They had to hurry.

Yet she was slightly confused. Why hadn't he stopped at the Keep to confer with Diadranei? Or was she still on her mission in King's Gate? Then she had another thought. Mayhap Dia was not the one for whom he searched. She wished she knew what had happened since the last time they'd seen the Wolf. But she doubted there'd be enough time for such a conversation now.

And she was correct. When they'd reached the barrier and found Rhyah, his coat was already showing the 'aging' effect. He was fatigued and hungry but could not stop for such luxuries as rest and food. He'd had one mission and afore he'd run away, he'd accomplished it. Finding Anastasia, confirming she was his primary target, not Diadranei, he'd given her the coordinates to the Castle of the Ice Dragons, Crystal Caverns. She was positive he knew she'd once portalled 'cross the border of no return by accident and he'd tried again to tell her that the Fang was with the Empress. All she had to do was come and get it.

Rhyah had given her the information and left immediately. Now Ana and Kevon stood afore the Queen, waiting for her response to the ridiculous sounding notion. With irritation in her voice, Alyssa stated, "The location of the castle of the Ice Dragons has been a well-guarded secret for eons. I still don't understand why Rhyah would tell you."

Ana squinted. She'd been explaining why for near half a mark and they had little time to waste. Scratching her eyebrow, she tried again. "I have been to the Icelands, I am the only one other than Queen Bryanna and Rhyah to do so and survive. He knew about my accidental journey and felt I was the one who would succeed in going there again, but I would have to go directly into the caverns to get the Fang and return. Otherwise," she began afore she was cut off.

Alyssa was outraged. "Otherwise, you would die! Anastasia, we know not for certain Bryanna is alive, only that Rhyah is. And we know not for certain where he has been. I know you trust the Wolf, but I do not. Not with my daughter's life. This mission you propose is more dangerous than anything I can think of. What if he gave you the coordinates to lure you into the middle of an Ice Rain, to take you hostage, to kill you?" The look on Anastasia's face made it clear that those possible scenarios were absurd. Her Empathy would have told her if 'twas so.

Kevon stood silent as Alyssa continued grasping for straws. "What if you cannot survive, even in the caverns? 'Tis only Rhyah's theory that you'd be protected there. And what if you cannot direct a portal to that point, and if you are successful, what if you cannot return? After all, 'twould seem clear by now, that only those who Shift, can do so!"

Ana felt Kevon's hand on hers, encouraging her to be patient and understanding of Alyssa's feelings. "Mother, I have been in many dangerous situations," she stated, reminding the Queen of the part she'd played to Draw the Dome o'er the Bog Lair. "This is no more dangerous than that. And just think of the possibilities! Rhyah is convinced I will be able to survive in the caverns! You know the skills and talents of the Ice Dragons, their forte Magic of Mesmerizing, their stealth capabilities. Their chameleon characteristics allow them to stand next to even a Highland, and not be noted. The Battle Commander needs such allies. WE need such allies. Besides, we are at war, and the Black will stop at nothing. Rhyah has disclosed a way to get to the Ice Dragons, and if we can, so too the Evil One, and then they will be lost to us. They are the gentlest, the most delicate of the Dragon Races. They are also the easiest to kill. They'd never accept him, evil is not in their nature. But by so refusing, he will destroy them. We cannot let that happen. They must be protected. They must be brought into the Resistance."

Queen Alyssa was torn. But her daughter was of age and if she decided to go anyway, she could not stop her, not just for her right to make up her own mind, but for the fact that she no longer fell under Alyssa's rule. If Ana chose to go on this mission without her approval, Alyssa would have no real say. Lowering her eyes, she swallowed hard then looked back at her daughter. She'd taught her well. The girl was near full grown. She had a good head on her shoulders. And her Magic was strong.

Alyssa also knew Ana was correct. Everything she'd said, was truth. Glancing to the floor and then back to Ana with a sigh, she asserted, "At least don't try to portal from here. The shorter the portal, the more accurate 'tis. And the Keep is closer to the Icelands than is the Wyrdritch. Mayhap you are correct to want to return there and speak with Darque. You can make your jump from St Swiftyn's with as much safety as is possible. IF the Battle Commander so orders such AFTER you present your evidence!"

Ana shut her eyes and gave silent thanksgiving, then rapidly closed the distance 'tween them. Hugging her daughter hard, Alyssa had to wipe tears from her own eyes, for she was bidding Anastasia farewell once more and knew not when, or if, they would meet again.

Return To King's Gate

WYNDSYR FOREST WEST OF EVANNTYR
NEAR A MOON AFTER LEAVING DREKINN
~~~~~ THE RUINS OF THE HOME OF THE PAINTED ONE ~~~~~

The Stealth Team had made a dark camp close to the old ruins. Artemis was a skilled Healer of the Daggogh, and like all the Healers of the People, held the knowledge of the potion along with the process that could transport one's spirit into the Otherworld. Known as the Painted One for her spiked hair, dyed skin designs and tattoos that identified her tribe and prowess, she now lived at Drekinn Lair with her Night Beast Ryygg, and her kinsmen, Larken and Matana.

When Artemis was taken in for questioning by the Sorcerer, his Agents burned down her home and everything in and 'round it 'til little but char and rubble remained. Now nature was reclaiming the area, changing the appearance for those who knew not its history to the point that one would not recognize what once had been.

But the Stealth Team knew. And after traveling for near a full moon, 'twas here they'd chosen to finalize their plan and launch the mission. Not having to use Dia's Magic to create a glamour for the men would save her energy for other needs, and they were grateful for Larken's help as they donned their disguises, using the makeup he'd also provided. The distinctive, dark brown, ankle length, supple, oiled cloth cloaks had arm slits to give them full range without hindering their weapons, and large hoods allowing them to see, but not be seen. With multiple pockets and loops inside, they were well armed.

These were not the cloaks normally worn by the Warriors, nor were they peasant garb. These were the cloaks of a Bounty

Hunter. They'd asked not how Larken had procured them, merely thanking him for his assistance. He'd smiled slyly, accepting their gratitude, but said not a word.

Pyth and Dyrth had come along for the adventure, meeting up with them at the ruins, and were hanging out at the nearby stream waiting to play their roles as required. They were most excited.

Dawn would soon break, and the mission would be completed within a mere few marks. The Team had their entrance, search, and exit strategies ready to put into action. They should be on their way home again by mid-day. That is, if all went as planned.

LESS THAN THREE MARKS LATER

~~~~~ EVANNTYR ~~~~~

</div>

And here he was. Bastyen leaned on his sword, panting, and praying to his ancestors that no one had seen him entering the Grand Hall. He held his breath as he peered 'tween the hinges of the barely open, oak plank doorway, to watch as the King's Agents ran past, listening to their booted feet disappear into the distance.

Bastyen had laid the trail then circled back through one of the passages to get here, hoping Graasyn had disappeared safely as well, while Bastyen led their pursuers away from the alcove. Dia had already been taken to the Pits and leaving that alcove was the last time he'd seen his father. All he could do now was hope Graasyn had entered the passages and had found Sarai's lab.

Bastyen's chosen hiding place would not last long. 'Twas a massive open space with several entrances on this level as well as multiple entrances above via the Grand Staircase. But 'twas also the only other way to get to Sarai's lab. The doorway, once the 'front door', lay behind a most ancient tapestry that hung in a shadowed corner on the third-floor landing of the stairs. The tapestry depicted the Battle Commander and her sister Storrm, a work of prophesy designed by Sarai herself and completed long afore either was birthed. If he could get inside, the rest would fall into place.
~~~~~

With no cover 'tween where he now stood and where he had to go, he must hurry afore the Agents circled back. If he were seen, he'd have to abandon the mission and fight his way out, an effort which would probably get him forced Past the Veil, for the lab entrance, its very existence, could not be compromised. 'Twas the lives of his father and his woman at stake, not to mention the many secrets within, advancing the cause of the Resistance.

Grasping his sword once again, he turned and raced to the stairway just as his sensitive ears picked up the sounds of heavy boots hitting stone floor. The Agents were on their way back.

LESS THAN A QUARTER MARK PRIOR
~~~~~ AN ALCOVE 'CROSS FROM THE KITCHENS ~~~~~

Bastyen pushed his father back into the shadows. Their plan had gone awry. 'Twas not anyone's fault, 'twas truly the Fates intervening. Now they were on the run and Dia might be lost to them. Gulping back his despair he stated dryly, "I believe our contingency plan has just been activated." Graasyn nodded in agreement. They'd rarely had to revert to a contingency plan and this one was devised of pure desperation and depended upon the Water Dragons. But 'twas their only chance now and 'twas the main reason they'd had the beasts tag along. Bastyen continued, "We get what we came for. Return to the passages and find the lab. I'll lead them away!" And afore Graasyn could protest, Bastyen ran down the hall, the Agents quickly following.

Their initial plan was good. The 'Bounty Hunters' had arrived at the gates of the castle with Dia in chains and were quickly escorted to High King Shytin. They told him they'd found her wandering in Wyndsyr Forest and knew nothing of the men who had accompanied her when she'd escaped. They'd asked for the price on her head. 'Twas their expectation that she'd be taken away and would use her Magic to Suggest they let her go, meeting up with the men in the passages within moments.

All was going well 'til Shytin leaned o'er and listened intently to a messenger just arriving. His eyes narrowed and he stalled on payment. He insisted he be allowed to take Diadranei to the Pits of Hades while the Hunters waited for their bounty.

They'd been made. Someone had tipped the King to their identities. The room was well guarded, and the Agents began surrounding them in a tightening circle as Dia was abruptly snatched from their grasp. Just as she was dragged out of sight, the Sorcerer sauntered into the audience chambers with two real Bounty Hunters shadowing his steps. He stopped, turned to them, and with much melodrama, placed a heavy bag of precious gems into their hands, never taking his eyes off Bastyen and Graasyn. Without a word, the Bounty Hunters then turned and walked out.

But the two Warriors were not the kind to give up against an enemy, no matter the odds. Maddened with Battle Lust and the anger of losing control of the situation, as well as losing Bastyen's lifemate, their swords sang through the air, striking and clanging and bloodletting. Gaining the upper hand by sheer force, aggression, and skill, they managed to make their exit afore disappearing 'round a corner down the hallway where they gained entrance to the passages just afore the Agents chasing them, rounded the same corner.

Their destination was the alcove 'cross from the kitchens in the lower levels of the castle, nearest to the old Witch's Dungeons, the hallway ending abruptly in that direction from the damage and subsequent repair. But this was also the alcove closest to the only entry to the Pits of Hades. As Bastyen ran past, rising from that stairwell came the muffled voice of Diadranei.

SHORTLY PRIOR
~~~~~ THE AUDIENCE CHAMBERS ~~~~~

As they'd entered the chambers Diadranei could sense the betrayal with which they'd soon be confronted, but everything happened too quickly. With all eyes upon them, she had not the
~~~~~

time or ability to warn her companions. Besides, such a warning might throw off their contingency plan. Everyone knew the risks. Everyone had to act according to the plan. She would do what must be done.

And so she'd allowed the Agents to drag her all the way to the Pits of Hades, dumping her down the stairs, not even bothering to chain her to the walls as for some reason they believed she was too weak and would give them no trouble, along with the implanted notion that the Sorcerer would be disappointed if she were to Pass the Veil afore he could 'examine' her.

Immediately after they left she shifted her Magic from their easily controlled minds to the removal of the chains on her wrists afore she sent forth the Call. Broadcasting her voice as loudly as possible into the cosmos, the Humans heard only a muffled cry. She was concerned that Bastyen would hear her from above, his mostly Elven blood giving him very acute senses, and that he'd try to rescue her too soon. She should not have been so concerned. Regardless of his love for her, Bastyen was a highly trained and disciplined Stealth Ops Warrior and knew this plan was their only hope to leave Evanntyr alive.

As Dia Called to the Water Dragons, guiding their furious excavating activity to her location using their spit, strong talons, and jaws to bite, scratch, claw, carve, and cut through from the cliffs of the Southern Slippes afore going upwards at a sharp incline to the dungeons, she also used her Magic to cover the noise from those walking past along with the Standing Guard in the hallway above.

The Water Dragons had created the wells throughout Kadoor as their gateways into the mainland, for they were awkward on land yet incredibly fast and efficient in water. Adding an enzyme from glands inside their jaws, they typically used their spit to create a strong mortar to maintain the walls even as they carved their way through.

The wells had survived all attempts by weather, time, or deed, to wear them down or destroy them. They appeared as if a burrowing animal were pushing upwards through the ground, the rock opening up and pouring all 'round a massive hole that would provide clear fresh water wherever 'twas. Usually they took great care in making a well, building up the sides at the top to about hip or waist height of the average Human male, even to the point of creating an aesthetic design like a signature, with the native rock. After the Last Holocaust, the wells were what kept the Humans alive and gravitating to them, their true purpose and method of creation unknown, they'd built their villages 'round the endless source of life-giving water.

But with the rise of Synahmarr and the destruction of the Well of Evanntyr, the only other well in the area was in the town square of King's Gate Village. Such would do them no good. Knowing they might require another way of escape, Pyth and Dyrth were recruited to dig into the castle to rescue them if required but had to wait 'til Dia Called to guide them to where they were needed.

However, this time the Water Dragons were not planning on leaving a well for the use of others. They meant to destroy it once they made use of it as 'twas intended, and so they worked together, sparing nothing for aesthetics, using minimal 'mortar', and not caring if they carved through from the underground river system. Their main concern being function and speed, they also had to plan ahead for their descent and build accordingly.

All in all, 'twould take near a mark, therefore, when Bastyen heard Dia's voice, he knew he had just less than that mark to get what they came for and then join her and Graasyn in the Pits of Hades to make their second escape by Water Dragon.

Dia split her attention 'tween the Call and Suggesting no one above could hear the digging and had no desire to descend the stairs. At the same time she was praying the Sorcerer would be in no hurry to meet his newest guest as she suspected her Magic would have little to no effect upon the Black's necromancer.

~~~~~ SARAI'S LABORATORY ~~~~~

Bastyen was quick but 'twas by the mercy of the Fates alone that he found himself ducking under the tapestry just afore the Agents returned. He'd run swiftly 'cross the Grand Hall to the stairs and then up three flights with barely a whisper of sound. Using a special tool, he managed to pick the lock on the door. He was tall and the top of the doorway only came to his chest, forcing him to crouch through, carefully shutting it behind. The tapestry was heavy and 'tween that and the Agents filing into the Grand Hall on their search, all sound was muffled.

'Twas dark and he began to step in the direction of the fireplace for the torch. But afore he could get halfway 'cross the room, the torch flared to life, and he nodded to his father who had just arrived via the passages. Graasyn stepped quickly to him, grasping his arm, and pulling him closer, grateful he was alive. Neither said a word about Dia, and as Graasyn walked to the desk, Bastyen looked about him in amazement.

There were no outside windows. The only obvious entrance was at the landing. A long, wide countertop ran the length and width of the room along three walls, and above and below were floor to ceiling shelves of bottles and small boxes and containers and vials, books and scrolls and parchments, pestles and mortars, incense burners, tabletop grills, magnifying glasses of all shapes and sizes, quill pens and inkwells, along with an abundance of items he could not identify.

Everything was neatly labeled but 'twas not a language he'd ever encountered afore. There were old cobwebs in every corner and a heavy layer of dust lay o'er every surface with the exception of the desktop which was much less than elsewhere. This kept in line with the story they'd been told of when Aalanna and Larken met here during her escape and that 'twas where she'd left the Fang.

Now standing shoulder to shoulder, Bastyen took a half step back and allowed Graasyn to pick it up. Dusty and covered with
~~~~~

bits of Blood Wax, the Fang of Solvyngarr lay in the middle of the hand carved desk.

'Twas in amazement they noted that the Fang felt warm to their touch, not as the cold steel expected. For although 'twas Magically disguised to appear as metal, 'twas in reality a living thing. Pushing the blade into the sheath at his hip, Graasyn turned to find Bastyen had stepped 'round to the opposite side of the desk and was searching the bookshelves behind. Curiously, he asked, "For what do you seek?"

"Shayla's notes. She requested we bring back her research notes. But I have no idea what they look like, 'twas to be Dia's task."

Graasyn remembered Larken telling him about what they would find when they entered the lab. He'd described it in painstaking detail. He wished he had time to fully explore its wonders, but the mark was getting short and they had to get back to the Pits to meet up with Dia to make good their escape. Still, those notes were also important, and 'twas unlikely they'd ever get another chance.

"Not there! Larken mentioned he'd attempted to read from the notes but could not decipher the language." Graasyn started pulling open the drawers as he mumbled to himself, "He put the folder and the books inside one of the desk drawers." Then triumphantly he raised the book up in one hand, a thick bundle of notes tied together with twine in another as he exclaimed, "One of these has to be what she wants!"

Turning back to Bastyen, he noted his son had another thick journal of handwritten notes. Which were they to retrieve? Neither could read them. 'Twas puzzling. Though they did not read or speak Ancient Tongue they'd have recognized it, and this was not true Common either, yet there were some familiar words, and all were written in the distinct hand of the Healer. Squinting, they looked at each other and then with a shrug of his broad shoulders Bastyen tucked the journal into one of his pockets while Graasyn did the same with what he had in his hands, and together they sprinted to the passage entry through the fire-place, taking the torch with them.

There was no passage entry directly into the Pits of Hades and once they were back at the alcove, they found themselves in a new predicament. Guarding the stairwell to the dungeons were half a dozen extremely nervous Agents. Of what did they think Diadranei was capable? Listening carefully, they soon learned that strange scuffling and snorting noises had been heard coming from the Pits and when one of them finally worked up the courage to go see what was causing them, his mangled and bloody body had been tossed back up into the hallway as if 'twas an empty sack of flour. Of the nine original guards, two had taken the body to the Sorcerer and the remaining Agents were waiting for them to return with new orders, not to mention that they were terrified the Sorcerer would send them all to the same fate.

Superstitious and wary, the guards stood near shaking. 'Twas a most dangerous situation. Fighting against irrational and fearful men, left one unable to predict their movements. Strictly speaking however, all they had to do was engage the guards and let them think they'd been o'erwhelmed and forced down into the dungeons, without getting killed in the process.

With any luck (of which they'd been running a tad thin lately) the Agents would not follow them into the dungeons afore the Sorcerer arrived. And they had to think that the noises were caused by the Water Dragons having broken through. This was probable as the description of how the guard had been killed was more likely Pyth and Dyrth's doing than Dia's Magic. If 'twas Dia, however, she'd be spent and have nothing left for her defense. Or theirs. They'd have to carry her. But such action was not her style.

In the distance, they heard others coming their way and 'twould be with the Sorcerer. Preparing themselves, they each took a deep breath and a firm grip upon their swords, afore the two men yelled and burst forth from the alcove charging straight into the huddle of Agents.

Swords swinging, clanging, and clashing, Graasyn and Bastyen forced their way through the men to the open stairwell afore diving headfirst down into the darkness below, yelling wildly as if 'twas not at all what they'd wanted to do.

They could sense the expectation of the laughing Agents as they rolled downward to land flat on their backs at the bottom of the stairs. When they opened their eyes, they found themselves nose to nose with Pyth and Dyrth, whose quizzical expressions made them snort out loud. Choking on sheer mirth, they leaped to their feet as soon as the Water Dragons shuffled backwards, grabbed Diadranei's hand and mounted, the Sorcerer's angry voice now echoing down the stairwell, his booted feet descending the steps rapidly.

Without hesitation, the Water Dragons pushed off from the stone floor and dove through the hole in the middle of the stone floor. They'd dug mostly through solid rock and although they had some difficulty, they managed to collapse the opening in the floor of the dungeons, along with most of the tunnel behind them so no one could follow.

The steepness of their descent had them near flying through the shaft, even though 'twas dry, and other than being in total darkness, the initial dive reminded the Team of their leap off the cliffs not so long ago. However, this tunnel had been designed to end halfway up the cliff and certain only that they were moving ever downward, twisting, and turning, and looping, the Water Dragons moved quickly, sliding on their oily bellies. Using the walls to push against, they gained incredible speed.

Soon enough they saw what they thought was a light in the distance, and to their utter astonishment, they were suddenly catapulted out of the tunnel into the sunlight, hurled through the air gripping onto the Water Dragons as they stretched forth their leathery wings. Soaring for breathless moments, they splashed into the Ocean of Fears and disappeared 'neath the murky surface.

~~~~~~~~~~

Within a sennight, the Stealth Team arrived at Drekinn Lair with their treasures. Shayla was ecstatic with the extra notes and clutching them tightly, the lump in her throat making it impossible to speak, she'd nodded her sincere gratitude and then led them to the clinic where her Apprentices tended to what minor injuries had yet to heal, while she locked herself in her office to spend some time with her 'old friends'.

As soon as they'd been triaged thoroughly, Diadranei, Bastyen, and Graasyn were flown by Free Dragon to the Keep to deliver the Fang. Darque was just as ecstatic to have them return safely, mission successful, and assured them that Caleichante would also return soon, though she knew not if 'twas truth.
~~~~~~~~~~

CHAPTER SEVENTEEN

The Fang And The Alliance

NEAR THREE DAWNS LATER
~~~~~ THE KEEP OF ST SWIFTYN'S ~~~~~

Myrrdin and Caleichante had arrived the previous evening, making report and handing o'er the Fang. Taking a deep breath, Darque accepted it, and knowing the history of this Fang, she'd held it to her heart reverently. And by the Ancients, she was grateful that she'd not lied when telling the Stealth Team that Calei was safe.

To celebrate, Darque and Gunnarr planned an outing this morning with some of the Free Dragons to fly their guests. A picnic in the mountains. Gunnarr was delighted. And then less than two marks past, just afore they'd been scheduled to meet up in the Ward, the Gatekeepers announced the arrival of new guests.

"My treasure, surely we can still leave the Keep for a short time?" Gunnarr questioned hopefully, despite knowing the answer in his heart.

"I have to take care of this, 'tis important, 'tis my duty as Commander." Her Voice softened as she Felt the frustration of her lifemate with her response. *"We'll go later."* Gunnarr Answered her not, leaving in a huff the likes of which the Gatekeepers had never seen afore. Darque sighed at his hot headed temper tantrum. But he was a Dragon after all, and sometimes an emotional one. His hunt would be aggressive, venting his frustrations in the kill, and when he returned all would be well. She sighed, for likely not. 'Twould not be like Gunnarr to vent his anger upon another creature, unless 'twas in battle, and the hunt would not change their situation.

Still, Darque promised herself that she'd make it up to him as soon as 'twas feasible. She so longed to spend time with him again. It seemed like winters past since they'd made love. With that thought came the sensation of increased moisture 'tween her thighs, the warm tingling of their Shared experience, the sensuality, the raw sexual need. Darque swallowed hard and struggled to return her focus to her duties. Her lifemate was not only fiery tempered as was she, their physical drives matched as well.

'Twas now a mark since Gunnarr left, and Princess Anastasia and Prince Kevon stood afore the Battle Commander in her office. Caleichante and Myrrdin stood side by side near the bookshelves on the far side of the room and although they refrained from speaking, they continued reading as did she.

After succinctly making report on all the recent happenings in the Wyrdritch, including Aiisabeau's successful mission, the capture of the spy and his cohorts, and the security of the Spell Dome making it now safe to plan the Call to Return, Ana and Kevon had carefully and methodically shown Darque, Myrrdin, and Calei their evidence. Now they waited for the Battle Commander to say something. Anything. The silence was becoming deafening and they could scarcely breathe.

The journey to the Keep of St Swiftyn's had not been easy, and they'd chosen to Dance instead of traveling o'er ground as they felt time was of the essence. Yet 'twould be impossible for the pair to Dance with so many books and scrolls and therefore they'd used a Spell to copy and then recreate a visual of those written references to show to the Commander. They knew that Darque could read and speak Ancient Tongue as General Gunnarr had taught her. Darque's diligence to the learning of such an archaic and complex language was as highly respected in the Resistance as was her swordsmanship. And so they'd not required any translations of the texts, which greatly reduced the energy to maintain the Spell.

The ghostly visuals were still scattered o'er the floor, the desk, the table, and hung in the air surrounding Darque as she'd read each one of them very carefully, passing them along to Myrrdin and Caleichante. Finally, she looked at Ana and Kevon, then leaned back in her chair, cocking her head, and fingering the Fang that had been handed to her last evening, as she considered what she'd just learned.

There was no doubt that Rhyah had been trying to tell them the Fang was in the Icelands. After all, 'twas what Tegrynn, Rygyl, Fryya, and Walkyr reported as well. But was she to believe that the Ice Dragons actually built the Keep of St Swiftyn's, living there for a time afore retreating to the Icelands? Was she to believe there was yet a place in the Keep filled with blocks of ice-pack where they'd stayed when visiting the Rashei? And was she to believe that 'twas the Ice Dragons who had 'deeded' the Keep to the Fay to give to the Rashei when the Island of Rienne was destroyed? Were the Ice Dragons the original 'scholarly residents' referred to in the Clan's histories?

'Twould explain much. The carving of the Keep's many halls, banquet rooms, personal living quarters, meeting places, as well as the library, was not only vast but precise and clean, just as was the carving done by the Water Dragons using their stream of water. 'Twas understood that the Ice Dragons used their spit in much the same manner, only as a stream of frost or ice, Brewing the Magical substance known as Freezyn in one of their guts as did the Highlands with their Flame. It could have happened that way. Which might lead one to also believe that they could have carved livable space in and under the massive glacial icepack in the farthest northern region of the world, providing enough insulation that it might sustain their Magic and their lives.

Three Fangs now lay side by side upon her desk. Diadranei was more experienced than Anastasia with their forte Empathy Magic but she was extremely fatigued from their mission and they'd have to give her time to recuperate. Darque needed to be ready to perform this ceremony by the winter solstice and that meant they had not long. But what put her o'er the edge of indecision was twofold. One, 'twas the only lead they had on the location of the last missing Fang. And two, the Ice Dragons were a comparatively fragile Dragon Race, easy to kill, and would not be able to survive an Ice Rain for long, any more than any other living creature. Therefore, they had to have a safe place to go when such occurred, and such occurred at an alarming frequency.

The Ice Dragons existed. Of this, she was certain. And if they existed, 'twas also certain they had a home that protected them from the Ice Rains and therefore 'twould be relatively safe from the extreme cold as well.

Darque hoped her reasoning was sound and not merely influenced by the need for the Fang. But putting together all the information available to them, the mission was a go. Anastasia would make the jump. Tonight.

<center>~~~~~ WITHIN THE MARK ~~~~~</center>

The Spell Domes required a Gatekeeper, and to be a Gatekeeper, able to open and close the portals, required the ability to handle the Magic of the Spell, to manipulate it and make it work. This in turn required at least some Magic bearer blood and after Graasyn and Bastyen reported their mixed heritage, due to unexplained Gifts many others came forth to see if they too, carried the blood of the Elves, though most had not been aware prior. These mixed bloods had a variety of aptitudes for the portals, presumably due to the percentage of Magic bearer blood in their ancestries, and the strongest of them were chosen to become Gatekeepers.

Mardesha was the chosen Gatekeeper for Anastasia's jump. She was an original, learning and then teaching others for the past few winters since the Spell Domes were drawn down. Although she knew not her own heritage, 'twas surmised Mardesha was at least a quarter Elven. She had the most seniority and was efficient, quick, and precise.

Darque had impressed upon Mardesha the need for all these things. Not only were they trying to portal the girl further than any other thus far, they had to keep the portal open to allow Ana to return the same way she left. But this presented a major problem. Such had never been done afore. The portals had always been used for a single trip in a single direction with the one being portalled always starting out within the sight of the Gatekeeper (though they need not end within their sight). Thus far portals were opened outside the Dome to bring one inside, or opened inside to send one outside, or opened outside to send one from one close location 'cross to the other side of the Lair or another location (still outside) to give the one so portalled the impression that the Lair could not be found or no longer existed.

But 'til Anastasia told her tale, 'twas thought that no portal had ever been used in reverse. Yet, Darque was still not sure 'twas even possible. To the Gatekeeper's fascination, Ana revealed her initial experiments when the Spell was erratic, unable to accurately predict her destination. But she'd always been able to return. While they discussed her travels trying to find a solution, Darque listened as Anastasia described using her Magical Hearing talent, to Hear the Song of her surroundings, both organic and not. She'd managed to find a rhythm to which she thought she could Dance. After many such journeys she found 'twas not true Dancing, as it had nothing to do with the energy of organics nor of their shadows, but that the rhythm she Heard was the opening or closing of a portal.

Darque knew that only Anastasia could succeed in this quest, for only Anastasia through her unique Magic, would be able to find the portal in Crystal Caverns and return safely should it close prematurely. But given the distance to the provided coordinates, 'twould be weak. Calling for Bryynn, they discussed the mission, the creation of the portal, recruiting his support to increase the distance, the solidity, and the accuracy, along with keeping that portal open 'til Ana returned.

Looking up, they realized the night had waned and dawn was breaking o'er the far horizon of the Talons. Taking Anastasia by her shoulders, Darque stared at the girl. She'd grown so tall! And she'd changed. No longer a child, she was of age, ever wiser, her Magic more powerful. Ana's Elven eyes shone with determination and with the certainty that she would succeed. The Battle Commander smiled and nodded as she remembered another with such brash self-assurance. Looking to Bryynn and Mardesha she questioned needlessly, "You understand what you must do?"

THE ICELANDS

~~~~~ LESS THAN HALF A MARK LATER ~~~~~

</div>

Anastasia stood knee deep in snow and she wiggled her toes in disbelief that the cold was already penetrating her heavy leather, fur lined boots. She was not her mentor, Diadranei, her senses not as powerful, but this situation could only mean that she'd misunderstood the Wolf and the coordinates she'd been given. And although this was the Icelands, this most definitely was not Crystal Caverns. She tugged the heavy cloak tight 'cross her shoulders and peered out from the fur lined hood into the whiteness of the near constant blizzard conditions, the chill seeping through the leather and fur as if 'twas paper.

She refused to give up, yet she knew not where she was and had but a few heartbeats to choose 'tween trying to locate Crystal Caverns through the white curtain of constant snowfall or diving back through the portal to go home. But the cold was affecting her senses and with dismay she realized the portal was not where it had been. Should she start searching, or should she start walking? Shivering uncontrollably, she began to feel as if 'twould be a study in futility either way.

And then, just as the thought that she might see the end of her span of days floated to consciousness, she saw the Ice Dragon flying in her direction. 'Twas similar to her memory. Bryanna was not riding Bronwyn, but the Ice Dragon had seen her! She'd made it!

As they flew away from her landing site, the magnificent glacial ice laid out beneath her, Ana discovered she'd been off her coordi-
~~~~~

nates by about half a league, and with that notion came the sensation that she was forgetting something very important. But the cold of flight coupled with the cold of the environment seeping through her clothing, shifted her focus to other things. Like were the Elven Queen and the Fay Wolf, really living here? And what was she going to say to the Empress to get her to agree to ally the Ice Dragons with the Resistance? And would her teeth ever stop chattering?

<center>~~~~~ SHORTLY LATER ~~~~~</center>

Anastasia opened her eyes to those of a Highland staring back at her. The crystalline beauty, the fracturing light sparkling throughout, the mesmerizing prism effect was all so wondrous. Squinting, she suddenly appreciated the eye was much too large to be that of a Highland. She tried to reach forth and touch it, but 'twas too far away and now waking fully, she found she was staring at the high vaulted ceiling of the ice palace. The similarities of the ice crystals to the eyes of the Dragons she knew back home were remarkable. Except for the depth of color. In the Highlands, the color was deep, bold, bright, but although the colors reflecting through the ice were softer and more pastel, they were just as rich and no less beautiful.

Sighing, she attempted to regain her bearings and sat upright. Then remembering what Rhyah had said about having been 'altered' to survive here, she near panicked, patting herself frantically from head to thighs trying to determine if she felt any different. Had she been 'altered'?

Looking 'round, she noticed a section of the wall tremble, and then it clarified itself, still awash with the same crystalline colors of the surrounding ice. But now she could see its shape, her vision picking up the chameleon camouflage of an Ice Dragon. Then there was another, and another.

They were breathtaking, as breathtaking as was the cavern itself. Stunning, delicate, with gossamer wings, long graceful necks, and slender muzzles with long fangs top and bottom, their enormous jeweled eyes missed nothing. These were the first Ice Dragons, other than in pictures, that Anastasia had ever seen. And those pictures did them no justice. She wondered who the idiot was who'd had the audacity to try to capture such beauty in a mere painting.

Ana felt vaguely dizzy. Then she laughed for she realized how few others had ever seen an Ice Dragon, and how had a painter even known how to begin? Her laughter started as a giggle, quickly progressing 'til her stomach hurt. The Ice Dragons moved not. 'Twas as if they were frozen. And that mental image made her laugh even harder.

As the tears began to roll down her reddened cheeks, Rhyah walked briskly into the room followed by Queen Bryanna, followed by an even more beautiful Ice Dragon, who must have been Bronwyn. Ana tried to stop laughing but she couldn't. Her heart was pounding, her head was aching and suddenly she was sadder than she'd ever felt in her life. The tears were solidifying on her cheeks and she felt sick.

Concerned, Rhyah stepped quickly to her and placed his hand upon her forehead, pushing her gently back down to the bed where she closed her eyes, extremely sleepy. She heard him ask angrily, "A side effect of the cold, the near-death experience, the lack of oxygen here, what?" She heard someone reply apologetically, but 'twas muffled, and the last thing she heard him say was, "NO! She cannot be altered. She must survive on her own."

<center>~~~~~ DAWN ~~~~~</center>

Bronwyn was the one who realized what had happened. Softly she whispered to the girl, a Mesmerizing Song to help Ana believe what she was Hearing, what she was sensing. Or rather, what she was NOT Hearing and sensing. 'Twas as being o'erwhelmed in reverse. Under-whelmed. Ana's senses were different from even her Elven brethren. A throwback Magic originally considered 'weak', the fact that she could Hear the Song of everything 'round her, and being an Empath as well, she also felt every emotion with which she'd been surrounded from her birth, adjusting as she'd matured to the tumultuous levels, the chronic background noise both pleasant and grating. She'd learned how to read those sounds, those feelings, how to cope, moving through them like swimming through a thick bed of sea kelp without becoming entangled and drowning. But the Icelands were near silent in comparison, and Ana's system knew not how to regulate the change. 'Twas as being thrust into sensory deprivation, her senses screaming in panic at such an unfamiliar world.

With Bronwyn's assistance, Ana fell asleep to the soft and gentle melodies she Heard all 'round and the lack of emotional chaos. She felt as if thousands of skilled musicians were playing the loveliest lullaby just for her, and a thousand butterflies covered her as a blanket of warmth and security. There was no evil here, 'twas as the cleanest most uncluttered space upon the entire world, and she'd rested as she'd never rested afore. Her Empathy picked up nothing, and there was no discordant sound to spoil the Song. She'd never felt more at peace.

And then she felt love. A tidal wave of emotion 'tween Rhyah and Bryanna, that seemed near ancient in its origins. 'Twas that sensation that woke her. It had been near a full day since Anastasia made her jump to the Icelands, and breathing deeply, she'd never realized how chaotic to her senses was her own world. The world to which she must return.

As soon as they noted she was awake and obviously well, they'd taken Ana on a quick tour of part of the castle. Crystal Caverns was larger than the Keep of St Swiftyn's and would take far more time than she had, to fully explore. But what she did see was remarkable. Most everything was made of ice. She wondered how her body warmth did not cause melting and was told 'twas Magically protected. Every remaining Ice Dragon left in the world, lived in Crystal Caverns. The Magic contained here was ancient, extremely concentrated, and all encompassing.

There were many similarities 'tween her own castle and this one. The main differences were the materials of construction, and of course, none of the rooms had fireplaces. She'd smiled when Rhyah joked about that one, informing her that the temperature within the castle was constant but neither he nor Bryanna could feel the sensation of cold now anyway.

As for the similarities, they had conference rooms, woven rugs, paintings, flowers in vases, draperies, tapestries, tables, chairs, beds, blankets, most made of b'Spelled water then quick frozen by the breath of an Ice Dragon, with some of these items having been clearly collected from outside, as 'stash'. She noted the total lack of any living organics and so it must be true that the Ice Dragons actually fueled their Magics from the cold itself. And that observation led to another. There seemed a lack of dining facilities. For that matter, there was no evidence of food.

But the castle was huge, and she could not possibly see everything. And she'd not had time to ask all the questions that came to mind. They had business to conduct. Entering a large conference room, with ice crystal chandeliers reflecting the b'Spelled light in rainbow colors, they sat, Empress Bronwyn at the head of the table, two other Ice Dragons at her shoulders, with many more surrounding the room along the walls. Blending into the background, Ana was not intimidated but she kept a watchful eye upon them as everyone settled. Then came Rhyah and Bryanna to sit in chairs on either side of Bronwyn. Anastasia was directed to sit at the end of the table, facing the Empress.

Abruptly she felt the weight of the entire Resistance riding upon her shoulders. So much was depending on her success, her powers of persuasion, her logical presentation, her ability to gain their trust, and her tact. Well, she wasn't much on tact, taking after her mother and grandmother in that side of her personality. She'd have to rely on her other attributes.

Taking a deep breath and licking her suddenly dry lips, she sat up straight, laced her fingers together, leaned her elbows on the table, looked Bronwyn straight in the eyes, and began.

~~~~~ THE KEEP OF ST SWIFTYN'S ~~~~~

Darque was livid. There'd been no word since Anastasia had set foot in the portal. No word in near two days. She'd agreed to return within one dawn.

Bryynn was certain he and the Gatekeeper had been true to the coordinates with which they'd been provided, but now no one was certain that Ana had been. She may not have heard them correctly. Diadranei had come to speak with the Battle Commander when the Elf missed her initial return window, raising just this concern.

Since then, Darque and Gunnarr had Regynn studying the coordinates Ana insisted she'd been given for Crystal Caverns, against the only maps he could find of the region, which Regynn had dredged up while trying to find similar references in the library to what Ana and Kevon had presented. Without stopping to eat or sleep, they'd all been comparing and figuring, trying to get as accurate a scale as was possible. Now they were convinced she'd landed short of the goal. Mayhap far short.

Diadranei felt awful. She should have been there, mayhap she would have understood. Ana must has missed something in her interpretation of the Wolf's message. Their Empathic senses were not the Link, 'twas not true communication through telepathy.

And then Kevon spoke aloud what none of them had wanted to face. If Ana were portalled somewhere outside of the caverns, even if she'd survived her landing the likelihood of her being able to return by that portal now was slim to nil, for how would she find it, not to mention how would she survive the search? And how much longer could Bryynn and Mardesha maintain it afore it collapsed anyway? They were struggling now and 'twould
~~~~~

not be long, a few marks at best. Even with Bryynn's Magic, the Gatekeeper was merely a quarter Elven, after all, and the Spell was not designed for this purpose.

Darque leaned back in her chair, her arms crossed o'er her chest, boots resting on the desk, ankles crossed and eyes narrowed, biting her bottom lip trying to devise a plan, working with the only 'factual' evidence they had: even if Bronwyn, Rhyah, and Bryanna had found Ana afore she froze to death, Ana may not be able to get back, forever stuck in the Icelands. And 'twould be all her fault.

<div align="center">~~~~~ CRYSTAL CAVERNS ~~~~~</div>

The meeting was lengthy but went well. Anastasia was elated with the progress in their negotiations. Now for the other reason she'd made this daring journey.

The Empress Bronwyn was anxious, for no outsider had ever seen her stash, considering not the resident Elf and Fay as 'outsiders'. She walked elegantly along with Rhyah and Bryanna, leading the newcomer down the halls, winding their way deeper and deeper into the caverns. It reminded Ana of St Swiftyn's. In fact, 'twas so similar in places that she felt she knew where they were going.

Soon enough, they approached what was known at the Keep as the Lost Room, where the Rashei had kept the Dragon Sword of Darque Abriya D'Rienne, the Fangs of Solvyngarr, and the Book of the Conqueror, among other treasures. As she stepped into the room that seemed to go on and on into the distance out of sight, she saw piles and stacks and bundles of every imaginable treasure known and unknown. There were weapons and armor of all kinds, trinkets, statues, mounds of precious metals and glittering gems to include what must have been every single Desert Crystal in the whole of the world. Her eyes widened in shock. She'd thought she'd been prepared by the Wolf for what she'd encounter, but this was so much more.

During their discussions, they'd reminded Ana of the fact that Bronwyn would not hand o'er the blade, as she'd given it as a gift to Bryanna. Rhyah could not carry it as the Wolf, and neither could hand it o'er to another living being, for they could not touch them. But then Ana had furrowed her brows, reminding Rhyah that he'd touched her, placing his hand upon her forehead, and gently pushing her down to sleep. Rhyah had appeared dazed as he recalled the act, and then he and Bryanna became delighted.

With this revelation Bronwyn said not a word, her posture stiffened, her face unreadable. But the lovers saw this not. 'Twas true then, they could touch others but what were the parameters? Only inside the castle? Was it because of the cold or the close proximity of the Ice Dragons? Rhyah hoped more would be revealed while Ana was their guest. They would have to do further research. Mayhap those in the Resistance could help. 'Twas another notch in Ana's belt for convincing the Ice Dragons to become allies.

Now descending the stairs with confidence, she recalled the first few stilted steps she'd taken in the castle thinking she'd slip and fall at any moment upon the slick surface. But soon discovering her steps were sure, though she was walking on ice, 'twas not slick. As she looked about she saw the Fang had been given a place of honor, prominently displayed upon an ornate pedestal near the bottom of the stairs as one of the first items one would see when entering.

<center>~~~~~ THE KEEP ~~~~~</center>

Darque stared unseeing at her sister's Dragon Sword on the bookshelf, her meal untouched on the plate upon her desk. Four dawns and the portal was long lost. She'd shut down their efforts to try to reopen it as 'twas a waste of Magic in her opinion, and she had a bad feeling the high energy expenditure of Allure would become a beacon to the Hoard, leading them to the Keep if not directly to the Icelands.

Kevon had begged her to try another portal location, mayhap to move them from place to place, leaving it open for a few marks at a time. Mayhap if a pattern was established 'twould give Ana a chance. If she could Hear it, she could still find it. Darque had let the young man ramble on uninterrupted and the more he'd talked the more he knew he was wrong, and the Battle Commander was correct. There was no hope this way. And without knowing the real coordinates, finding Crystal Caverns would be against phenomenal odds.

Sighing, she returned her attention to the others, all sitting or standing 'round a table in the office, studying their predicament. 'Twas Regynn, Caleichante, Myrrdin, Diadranei, Kevon, and the Dragons Sydrayyah and Gunnarr, all doing their best. But their best was not good enough and they knew it. All they could do was wait. Wait for Ana to send some kind of sign giving them her location, wait for the Wolf to return with the true coordinates, wait for something. Anything.

Early that afternoon, Aalanna came to see her daughter. "I've found something," she told Darque, beckoning she follow as she described the vast open space in the bowels of the Keep, in a previously unexplored area. She'd passed by the corridor leading to this area many times on her way to and from the Lost Room, but there was always so much to do. However, a memory had been sparked with Ana's story of the Ice Dragons having once lived here, and acting upon instinct, she'd gone down that corridor.

There were no torches along the way and no brackets for holding them, but they were not needed as the corridor made its own diffused light, keeping up with her as she walked, twisting, and turning, and eventually reaching a dead end at a large doorway. The doorway took up the entire corridor, but 'twas itself not locked or b'Spelled to stay closed, and as Aalanna pushed it open, memories flooded through her.

The first thing she felt was intense cold that near took her breath away. Though 'twas evident the space had been shut down for centuries, 'twas open, well lit, clean, and sweet smelling. In the far corners were small pieces of ice and signs of old melt throughout. 'Twas then Aalanna remembered her mother telling her stories of how the Ice Dragons once visited the Keep after the Rashei became residents, making regular diplomatic visits for many winters, becoming less regular and then stopping altogether shortly afore the Last Holocaust.

'Twas ancient history but if true this area could again become a place where the Ice Dragons could stay, allowing them to return to the Keep. That is, if Ana was successful. Darque chewed on her bottom lip. This had become a game of patience. Patience had never been her strong point, waiting was most difficult, but 'twas all up to Ana now. Darque could do nothing to assist her.

<center>~~~~~ CRYSTAL CAVERNS ~~~~~</center>

Shortly after she took the Fang from Bronwyn's stash, they'd decided Ana must leave to avoid being trapped. The Empress was becoming agitated and pushing for her to leave soon, for they knew not how long Ana could safely stay in the Caverns. The Ice Dragons would discuss her offer of alliance with the Resistance. Bronwyn could travel to speak directly to Darque at some time in the future. Nonetheless, soon after that decision was made, Ana realized she was indeed, stuck.

Rhyah and Bryanna tried to help Anastasia find an exit portal for marks, searching all o'er the caverns despite her protests, and even had Bronwyn fly her quickly to the place she'd been found. No portal. But that flight had taken its toll upon the girl and near frozen they'd been forced to return, unable to do a more sweeping search outside. Such would be fruitless, and Bronwyn could not find it for her.

Now Ana recalled thinking she was forgetting something important as they'd flown away from her landing site to the castle. She was so upset. Why had she not thought of this afore? "NO!" she cried in frustration. Rhyah said not a word. Then still agitated but regaining her control, Ana continued, trying to explain her unique talents, and the function of the portals. "I Hear nothing of a portal within the Caverns. Besides, they no longer appear randomly. Now all portals are focused and created by the Gatekeepers. There will be no portal to find, unless they send one to me, and to do that they'd have to know the correct coordinates! I'm not even sure they can create one to reach this far into the Icelands, and the Magic concentrated here might prevent the creation as well."

But Rhyah was adamant. He'd not surrender to failure. Too much was riding on the success of Ana's venture. Afore Rhyah made his journey in Shift to find Ana, he and Bryanna had also discussed the possibility of them flying outside the Icelands, mayhap maintaining contact with Bronwyn. Rhyah felt 'twas a strong possibility they could do so as themselves without need to Shift, but Bryanna had become uncharacteristically frightened, and since there was no proof 'twould work, Rhyah chose to do his exploration on his own, as the Wolf.

Abruptly they noted that Ana was showing signs of aging. 'Twas the same symptoms Rhyah had shown in Shift, leading him to return or die. It seemed the process was working in reverse. 'Twas clear that if they didn't find a way to get Anastasia out of the Icelands soon, she could die.

Ana sat on the couch and listened to the discussion but was beginning to feel out of touch. Not like in the beginning, but as if she just didn't care what happened to her anymore, and her memories of afore she came, seemed so long ago. The only person she could really see clearly in her mind's eye, was Kevon. For some reason, she knew she had to hang onto his memory, or she would be lost forever.

~~~~~ WITHIN MOMENTS ~~~~~

Bronwyn's love for these two 'outsiders' outranked their fear of 'outsiders' in general and she made her decision. She would tell
~~~~~

them the truth. She must, there was no other option, she could see it happening afore her eyes and 'twould soon be too late. She would not be the cause of such sorrow.

But mayhap she could still dodge full disclosure. Her long neck arched and then she leaned down to face Rhyah. "I must return to the Keep of St Swiftyn's. I must fly this one back home. She does not belong here." Then she remembered she had not one, but two who needed immediate help. Turning her slender muzzle to Bryanna, she stated, "You must guide me."

But while hoping not to be forced to reveal their secrets, Bronwyn had procrastinated for too long, and her sudden demand pushed the Elven Queen o'er the edge. Bryanna's eyes widened and she began to shake in fear, blurting forth in near panic, "Why me? Rhyah has been outside, he can Shift, and you can fly the girl. He can guide you, he's been to the Keep afore!" Becoming clearly illogical, she sat on the floor and scooted in fear into the corner like a Cave Rat, much to Rhyah's shock.

But the Empress answered Bryanna not, turning to face Rhyah once more. She had no choice, 'twas now or never, and she'd accept the consequences. "Bryanna is also sickening here, as will you eventually. I have seen it growing in her for many winters. I thought 'twould change with your arrival. I thought she would return to her former self. The Elven Queen is a strong force with whom to be reckoned. She is not one to be fearful. But the longer she has been in the Icelands, the more she has withdrawn into herself. Now even her senses are affected. If this is allowed to continue, she will ultimately lose her ability to see, hear, speak, think… love."

Rhyah ran to Bryanna, huddling in the corner as if trying to get away from some invisible force attacking her. He hugged her hard, and no longer thinking about Anastasia he asked, "You have to save her. What can we do?"

"We must leave the Icelands."

"But you told us she would die!"

"Is she not doing that now?"

Rhyah shook Bryanna's shoulders to get her attention. "Do you hear me? Do you feel my hands upon you? I love you, please look at me!"

Bryanna stopped shaking and tried to focus on Rhyah. "What is wrong with me? Why is this happening?" she whispered in horror.

Suddenly Rhyah turned on the Empress. He remembered her reactions, her dismissals of their doubts, and that she'd not even attempted to stop him from touching Ana, ignoring the action later as if it never happened. He remembered Bronwyn's past hesitations and now felt her deception most strongly. Stepping toward her aggressively and with total disregard for his own safety, he growled, "What are you not telling us? What have you done?"

CHAPTER EIGHTEEN
The Ice Box

Five days. There'd been no word of the fate of Princess Anastasia for five days. Darque had taken to chewing on strips of leather to save her bottom lip, thinking, strategizing, trying to come up with a plan to effect a rescue from Crystal Caverns. All the others were still with her, spending every moment of these past five days working together in her office. But 'tween them, no plan they'd devised had any real chance of success.

Abruptly she Heard Mardesha breathlessly announcing incoming. Jumping to her feet she raced to the Ward, followed by the others. When she got there, she could not believe her eyes.

As the others fanned out behind Darque, there in the Ward standing in front of the massive gate from the bridge was an Ice Dragon and sitting atop her shoulders were three people. The tall slim beast stretched wide her long delicate wings for just a moment afore she laid them to her flanks gracefully as if she were the most elegant dancer. Darque could near see through her wings with the light from the eastern skies, her scales radiant and soft as of a prism rainbow, reminding her of the icicles that hung from the walls through the winter. These clear images made Darque shiver.

Kevon suddenly broke into a huge smile and ran to them as Anastasia slid off first. While they embraced and jumped up and down, Rhyah the Fay and Queen Bryanna slid off to stand side by side upon the stone of the Ward.

Kevon exclaimed excitedly to Ana, "You did it! You did it! You did it!" To which Ana repeatedly responded with equal excitement, "I did it! I did it! I did it!"

Rhyah laughed at their antics, and then with his arm 'round Bryanna to help steady her, they began to stumble toward Darque while the Ice Dragon simply stood as if frozen, so perfectly still that 'twas near bizarre. Her very presence would have been ignored by all if not for Rhyah stopping midstride, glancing o'er his shoulder and yelling, "Come, Bronwyn, there is no need for that Magic here. You are the guest of honor! This is your moment! 'Tis your party!" And as his arm swept dramatically toward the Commander, "And this gorgeous creature is Darque Aalanna Grifynn, Battle Commander of the Dragon Clan, the Resistance Armed Forces, and the LifeBond Teams!" Then with brows furrowed, he questioned, "Or would that be considered egotistical?"

As Darque set her jaw with fire flashing in her eyes, Kelseacyr and Chynnar strode quickly forward and hustled the travelers off to the clinic, the Ice Dragon following.

THE NEXT AFTERNOON

~~~~~ DARQUE'S OFFICE ~~~~~

</div>

'Twas as if they were all drunk. But after finally getting them settled Darque learned much. First, 'twas a sensory flood for Rhyah and Bryanna as well as Ana on their landing, precipitating their cavalier attitudes, which they were able to stifle in less than a mark with the assist of the Healers. And there was the extraordinary concentration of Magic that prevented Ana from becoming hungry or needing any nourishment 'til they'd arrived at the Ward at which time they became quite ravenous.

Second, 'twas the Empress Bronwyn herself who flew the trio from Crystal Caverns to the Keep, and with that revelation came many more questions from the Battle Commander. Questions that Rhyah took upon himself to try to answer.

"Yes, the Ice Dragons are shockingly strong, and can fly three or four persons with ease despite their delicate appearance. However, along with that strength they have only their chameleon characteristics and their ice breath to protect them. And they can be killed as easily as a Human for their scales are not like those of the Highlands. Any blade can penetrate. 'Twould seem their Kind
~~~~~

traded heavy armament for speed of flight, and they can fly faster than any of the Dragon Races. As for their association with the Keep of St Swiftyn's the story actually begins long ago, when the Ice Dragons lived here. They built the Keep as a 'summer palace' and then abandoned it when they were betrayed, no longer trusting any but their own Kind. They moved further north into the Icelands where none could follow, thinking such isolation would also provide perfect security. But the environment in the Icelands was harsher than even they were prepared for and through the many centuries that passed they discovered that living in Crystal Caverns became a problem of another kind. The sheer concentration of Magic and ice created a delusion to the point of eating and drinking not. Eventually even they require fresh air and real sustenance and found if they did not make regular trips out of the area, they would starve. 'Tis no different really, than the fact that the Water Dragons must breathe of the air eventually, even though they live and thrive in the water. But the Ice Dragons would also show signs of aging and loss of their reasoning capacity as well as the ability to use their Magic if they did not make these forays. The cold and ice which had always fed their Magics, failed them in the extreme and they would weaken. But with frequent journeys outside to meet their needs, they were rejuvenated. 'Twas as when I stayed away too long I began to show the same phenomenon, only in reverse to theirs. Bryanna and I must have the cold to rejuvenate our systems, while the Ice Dragons must have the cold to fuel their Magic. We can both live without it but we will become weak and defenseless after a period of time."

He paused for a moment as the others pondered what he'd said thus far. Then he continued, "When Bronwyn found Bryanna, she'd fallen through the portal into the middle of an Ice Rain and was quickly near the Veil. Even the Magic of the Empress was not enough to bring her back from that edge. She had to alter her by creating a similar Tie as with the LifeBond, or the Ties of the Sprites to the Water Dragons. But the Ice Dragons had never attempted this type of Magic. Her alteration allowed Bryanna to heal her wounds and share her Magic, making her infinitely tolerant of the cold. But the Empress soon learned that Bryanna was no longer tolerant of other environments for 'twas a system adjustment that she found could not be reversed. Nonetheless what no one knew, including Bronwyn initially, was that if we did not leave regularly our tolerance would fade, and we'd begin to age and lose our sanity, as did they."

Darque was nodding her head in understanding. Feeling confident, he tried to continue his explanation. "But given their fear of betrayal and of being discovered, Bronwyn made us fear leaving, for the Ice Dragons remember everything, they have perfect memories. Not just able to access the Memories of their Ancestors, the Ice Dragons have eidetic memories, they recall everything they see, touch, smell, or hear. Yet despite her trust in us, they did not trust us not to betray them, even unwittingly. If someone saw us outside the Icelands and followed, they might be discovered. Bronwyn is Empress, but she could not go against the will of all her Kind. So, still not understanding fully the consequences of the alteration, she planted the notion that we'd 'turn to a pillar of ice' if we set foot 'cross the border and that we could never leave, to keep us there. You see, originally they thought the intolerance phenomenon only affected them. They didn't believe 'twould affect us. Even when Bronwyn began to notice Bryanna changing, they still did not believe. And then when I returned and reported that I was affected in that same way, she became very suspicious. But the clincher was the change in Ana. If Anastasia had not arrived and such had not occurred in their own sight, both of us would have died. So, both Bryanna and I must leave the Icelands from time to time, to increase our tolerance for our new home. After all, one cannot be hot or cold all the time and appreciate the heat or the cold when it happens."

Darque had been very quiet listening to Rhyah speak, followed by Queen Bryanna, and then Anastasia afore she'd listened for several marks to Empress Bronwyn. She was astounded with how close they'd all come to the Veil, and how stupid she felt about letting Ana go without having done more research. But as Rhyah pointed out, Ana's timely experience saved the Fay and the Elf. It seemed all had worked out well, and in fact, Darque could forgive the Ice Dragons, for she understood exactly how they'd felt when they were betrayed, needing to protect themselves as she needed to protect the Clan and the Resistance. Nevertheless, the Ice Dragons needed allies. And thanks to Princess Anastasia and her negotiation for an alliance, they were ready to bend knee to King Gabriel.

Bronwyn confirmed the area Aalanna found in the roots of the Keep was once their 'guest quarters' for 'twas easiest to maintain huge frozen blocks of pack ice there for long periods of time. They need not themselves be freezing to maintain their Magic, but the availability of the ice allowed them to stay longer with no ill effects. This also included Rhyah and Bryanna. In fact, as long as they could sleep in the 'Ice Box' as it became known, they could wander about the Keep and go anywhere as did others, needing about half of each day in the cold, in exchange for the other half of freedom. And since 'twas not the extreme of the Icelands, if one wore sufficient winter attire, others could visit them in the Ice Box.

<div align="center">~~~~~ NEAR A SENNIGHT LATER ~~~~~</div>

Shortly after arriving, the Empress swore allegiance to King Gabriel and officially made the Ice Dragons allies of the Resistance. She immediately began renovating the Ice Box, other Ice Dragons flying in carrying enormous blocks of pack ice to line the floors, walls, and ceiling. Using the ice and their Freezyn, she also designed and created a comfortable living space for up to fifty Ice Dragons at a time as well as giving Rhyah and Bryanna special quarters, and then she set up a rotation for them all to visit and train in Stealth Ops techniques, learning about each other, the Resistance, and their new roles in the war effort.

Bronwyn told Darque that the Ice Dragons had not fought in the Last Holocaust, having already secluded themselves in the Icelands, but they'd fought with the other three Dragons Races in the War of Chaos. Their roles suited their attributes. They were natural spies. With their unique characteristics, their forte Magic of Mesmerizing so no one would even know they'd been seen if they HAD been seen, they were extremely effective. And they could go to the source, simply 'ask' for the information, erase their memory, and then retreat with no one the wiser.

Still, 'twould take stealth, for if they were caught by another, they were finished, therefore, they'd have to work alone or at the very most, in pairs, to prevent disclosing their presence. 'Twas a most hazardous occupation, and Darque could not help but feel anxious about putting these beautiful creatures in such danger. For in doing what they did, they'd be closer to the evil than any other. But she was also grateful for such valuable support. What the Ice Dragons offered, gave the Resistance a most powerful advantage.

As Darque walked out of the Ice Box that morning after another intense discussion with Bronwyn, she felt something nagging in the back of her mind. Then it came to her. Spinning 'round, she near ran back down the hall and burst through the door. Startled, Bronwyn turned away from her creations to gaze at the Commander curiously. Darque's voice indicated her disbelief in what she'd heard. "Wait! You said the Ice Dragons fought with 'the three others' in the War of Chaos. Are you telling me there are FOUR Dragon Races?"

LATER

~~~~~ **DARQUE AND GUNNARR'S QUARTERS** ~~~~~

</div>

Darque laid in the cradle of Gunnarr's paws, looking up at his brilliant crystalline eyes as he cocked his head toward her. She'd been quite upset when she'd found him but did not think she should talk to anyone else 'til she'd spoken to her General. His
~~~~~

deep rumbling voice filled her heart as he spoke, "I must apologize for not mentioning them earlier, but there has been no word of the Sand Dragons since the Last Holocaust and 'tis widely believed they've gone extinct. They were about the size of the Water Dragons at full growth but with much larger wings, short but wide and very strong. From the ground, a Sand Dragon in flight would appear similar to the shape of a stingray in the ocean. They once lived in the sands of the Dragon's Breath, their 'castle' at the Oasis. But the desert only enlarged upon the devastation, making the legendary Oasis in the middle even more inaccessible." He snorted at the similarity of the Sand Dragon castle, to Crystal Caverns in the middle of the Icelands. "I once tried to Contact them but Heard nothing for many winters. I never attempted to travel deeper into the desert for I saw no need. I thought, as did others, that the Sandies had perished. And as you know, the Highlands had committed themselves to keep Mankind from slipping into that same fate. At the time, I was quite busy."

Darque could hear the sadness in his voice. The Sand Dragons were his cousins, as were the Water Dragons and the Ice Dragons. They all had their forte Magics, their survival skills in their chosen homes. But she knew if any Dragon Races were still out there, the Sorcerer would try to recruit them and if such effort were not successful, the Black would destroy them. If the Sandies still existed, she needed to know.

But not now. She was exhausted. The Resistance had gained a very strong ally in the Ice Dragons and their association was moving along swiftly. She had to focus on making that transition as smooth as possible. Shortly after Bronwyn had flown in, Myrrdin and his brothers had spent much time with the Fay and the Elven Queen. 'Twas a glorious reunion. They all approved Bryanna and Rhyah's mating wholeheartedly and Myrrdin shared his adventures since he'd been forced to escape from Haven so very long ago. In return, Bryanna shared what had happened after he'd left, and then all that had happened since she'd been 'lost'.

Eventually even glorious reunions must end, and Myrrdin knew he had to continue to another reunion, though this one would not be 'glorious'. He must go to the Wyrdritch to help in the Call to Return. But Bryanna refused to go with him. She would play no part in the ceremony. The Wyrdritch was no longer her home, the Elven Nation no longer her people, and had not been for a very long time. She had her sons at the Keep to visit with, and Myrrdin agreed to tell the others so they could come to visit as well. She planned on staying at the Keep for some time and if not, she could arrange to be there when they arrived. Such information could easily be passed along through the Communications section, for Maakayyel had already set up his Link with Bronwyn and the Ice Dragons and had confirmed his reach all the way into Crystal Caverns.

Bidding farewell the next dawn to Myrrdin and his companions, Darque reveled in the fact that she now had the last Fang. Now, she and Abriya had their own planning to do.

<p style="text-align:center">~~~~~ THE WYRDRITCH ~~~~~</p>

Lord Rohar and the rest of his entourage were well ensconced in Haven when Myrrdin arrived with Ana and Kevon. As expected, the initial meeting did not go well. Upon seeing the Heir Apparent the Council of the Elves demanded he take the throne, while Alyssa was forced to sit to one side of her usual place. Then after hearing of Bryanna's survival, they made the audacious demand that SHE return and take her rightful throne, even if Myrrdin had to force her to do so. 'Twas a ridiculous notion and unable to tolerate the ensuing chaos, the Prince had simply walked out of the meeting, despite their loud, pompous protests.

His angry and thunderous voice heard o'er his shoulder as he disappeared down the corridor, they cringed at the knowledge that his word was now law, even if he hadn't officially been crowned. "I shall hear no more of this! Alyssa will lead the Call to Return with Persephone at her side! This shall happen within the sennight!"

Myrrdin had expected such behavior and mayhap had made it worse by trying to avoid it for so long. But 'twas what 'twas and now he had to figure out how NOT to be forced to take the throne. 'Twas a topic that had consumed his thoughts for the past few moons. And suddenly a plan came to light. All he had to do was prove to the Nation that Alyssa deserved to be Queen, that she had the strength, the skill, the passion, and the right to keep the throne. To that end, she must perform the Call to Return successfully.

But therein lay doubt. For such a Magical Communication had never been performed afore. 'Twould be the first time for any of them. Alyssa and Persephone had been studying, practicing, strengthening themselves, in preparation. Alyssa was determined not to fail. And this had nothing to do with keeping the throne. This was her duty to her people. If she lost the throne afterwards, so be it. She just wanted to be successful in helping the Nation as her last act.

Since his return Alyssa and Lord Rohar had become quite close, sharing as much time together as they dared. The Lord was quite attentive, and so very handsome. And he wore his heart on his sleeve when it came to the Queen. After admitting to herself and then Rohar that she felt the same toward him, she no longer cared if she lost the throne for she was seriously thinking of leaving the Wyrdritch anyway and moving to the Island of Dreams with her daughter.

'Twas during one of their more intimate rendezvous' that Alyssa lost her glamour in the passion, and Rohar saw not only her Human shaped eyes, but the true color of her hair. She was a magnificent blonde. But the Lord refused to allow her to retreat in horror, simply showing himself as he really was, his hair dark brown. He too, used a glamour to hide from his own Nation. He assured her that such anomalies were more widespread than she knew and could only have been handed down from afore the

Separation. Therefore the fact that their people had been proven to be one Race must be true.

CHAPTER NINETEEN
The Call To Return

'Twas dusk and all was ready. Lord Myrrdin and the rest of the royal brood stood near the tree line while the remnants of the Elven Nation within the Wyrdritch filled the forest surrounding the clearing. Myrrdin stepped forth and as the Elves parted to allow Queen Alyssa and Princess Persephone to enter the clearing opposite, he lit the bonfire with a flick of his wrist, fingers pointing to the elaborately laid wood.

At dawn, the logs had been cut from old growth oak and blessed for this effort, laid in a precise pattern of interlocking ends, all while those who'd prepared it, chanted nonstop in Ancient Tongue, calling forth the authority of their Ancestors to this place.

Now while the surrounding Nation took up the rounding chant, they tried not to gasp at the beauty of their Queen and Princess entering. They were dressed alike, wearing diaphanous gowns of forest green, flowing freely about their lithe bodies without sash or clasp, swirling with each step and turn they made, as barefoot in the grass, the pair began to dance.

Elven dances and songs elicited power, drawing energy to them from the surrounding organics and such would send their Call to the world, if done correctly. Precision was required, but more so, passion. As the Nation watched and listened, their chanting providing melodic background to the performance, they gazed wide eyed upon the pair, chills running up their necks and arms as the energy intensified. The air was charged as with lightning, they felt as if they could not move, and the pair danced on, their song drifting away upon the gusts of wind beginning to whip through the clearing, the fire crackling and leaping to the skies.

With each pirouette, long legs stretching high and sweeping 'round, skirts flying and clasping hands, with each dip and bow, each spin with their backs elegantly arched, the eyes of the Nation were glued upon them.

And then, the Magic tingling and sparking throughout the area, they saw it join with the fire reaching into the night skies, afore fanning outward similar to an umbrella being forced open as had the Spell Domes themselves. The dancers now upon their knees on opposite sides of the fire, their bodies alight from within with the strength of their Magic, they raised their arms upwards as if pushing the Call to the far corners of the world for all Elven ears to hear. Come home! The Wyrdritch lives! Come home!

<center>~~~~~ TWO DAWNS LATER ~~~~~</center>

Myrrdin had refused to sit at the head of the Council 'til Alyssa and Persephone recovered but 'twas in reality his effort to stall. And it worked. Within the first few marks, having Heard the Call to Return, the Elves who had been living outside for centuries began to appear, crying with their joy, heartily welcomed home. Not all would stay but some would, and all were being educated in their new reality, the Alliance with the Resistance, the Black War, and the Spell Dome. The returning Elves had been as a steady stream since the first ones straggled in, and from their reports the Call had covered their world. Alyssa had been successful. 'Twas all Myrrdin needed to face the Council.

One major event that had happened during the Call was the loss of Alyssa's glamour. There afore the entire Nation she was exposed, but it had taken these past two dawns for such to be realized for what 'twas.

Now Myrrdin sat and faced the Council. Raising his hand to quiet the protests, the vile comments being whispered by some about their Queen's heritage, he had difficulty controlling his celebrated temper. Harshly, he addressed the rumors. "You know the truth. The Queen and Lord Rohar have proven such. Our Races are not separate, they never were. The Sprites and Elves are ONE." His tone brooked no argument, and though all were aware 'twould take some time to be accepted, and that some would never accept such knowledge, they could not deny the truth now. They'd seen it with their own eyes.

Also, 'twas truth that even though Alyssa might not be pure Elven, with the morphing of the Protection Spell o'er the Wyrdritch at the time of the Last Holocaust any such 'defect' had to be from the long distant past. Mayhap all the way to the War of Chaos when Elf and Man stood shoulder to shoulder as allies. And the success of the Call proved she had more than enough Elven blood to fuel her Magic. Myrrdin made this a very strong point while preparing to make his next arguments.

Clarifying Bryanna's status and refusal to reclaim the throne, he pointed out that Alyssa was of royal family with long and well-known history and when Bryanna was lost, Jeeryd took Alyssa as his lifemate, subsequently crowning her Queen at his side. She took the throne outright upon his death, had kept the Nation safe through dark times, and had been faithful to the Elves, even to the point of imprisoning her own. She saved the Nation from the Sorcerer's evil infiltration scheme and secured the Spell Dome. She was wise and perceptive. She was fair, and though tact was not her forte, she was honest and trustworthy, and one need not guess for all knew exactly where they stood with her.

Myrrdin paused briefly afore adding, "Not to mention, but I will, that Bryanna was declared dead when she disappeared which removed her from the royal lineage, and that I, as Heir Apparent to the throne, was cast out of Haven, also out of the family, my bloodline cut off forever by order of the King when he placed a death sentence upon me." He cleared his throat and reminded the Council that such sentence had since been revoked, but that strictly speaking it still did not clear his way to the throne. 'Twould take some effort and time to change that ruling, along with much paperwork to include fixing his succession and voiding Alyssa's.

As Alyssa halfheartedly listened to Myrrdin building his case, her mind drifted to Lord Rohar sitting alone in his chambers, awaiting word on the decision of the Council. His emotions were just as tumultuous, for if she retained the crown, they might indeed be torn apart.

And then Alyssa heard Myrrdin's voice again. "In conclusion I know everyone here wants to avoid a lengthy and obviously complicated process to 'correct' the succession." This statement brought a quick round of enthusiastic approval from the Council members afore he continued, "Therefore, I offer this suggestion."

LATER

~~~~~ **THE ROYAL GARDENS OF HAVEN** ~~~~~

</div>

Sitting next to Persephone, Myrrdin once again wore his Mariner's garb, looking every bit the dashing Ship's Master that he was. A loose fitting white silk blouse with a deep V-neck and thin lacing barely hid his smooth muscular chest. 'Twas tucked into skintight pants of soft black leather with matching knee high boots. With his sword in its scabbard at his hip and his long brown hair pulled back in a single tail, most had to look twice.

Myrrdin's dark eyes glistened as he discussed leaving soon. "How can I ever thank you, my sweet sister? I shall return when I can. 'Twill not be forever this time."

Her soft voice replied, "Not forever? You will return to your mistress, the Krakken, and forget all about us. Of course, 'twill be forever!" Her contagious laughter filled the air as the jingling of wind chimes in the breeze. Still, she could not hold the act o'er his head, and she'd come to see the need for her skills not only for the Nation, but in the Resistance. She'd grown with her Magic and was no longer the weak and timid Elf she'd been made to believe from the past. Having once thought such was not for her, with the
~~~~~

recent events, including the loss of her brothers and Thyrazin's betrayal along with seeing how well Alyssa held the throne, gave Persephone courage that she might do the same one day. Now confident and assured in her own power, she'd agreed to take on the responsibility.

But such agreement required the official abdication of that position in line by the one currently holding it, and that was Myrrdin. The Elven Nation had undergone much turmoil of late and they needed solid leadership and few changes with which to deal. Seeing the logic, the Council had agreed that the relatively simple paperwork involved with Myrrdin abdicating the throne to Alyssa and placing Persephone as Heir Apparent, was the only thing to do. His suggestion receiving no opposition, 'twas quick, easy, and done. The royal lineage would go on without him.

Nevertheless, Myrrdin could not deny his bloodline and therefore he retained the title of 'Prince of the Elven Nation' by decree of the Queen, giving him royal privileges and a vote on the Council, should he ever care to exercise those rights.

It hadn't taken long for the Queen and Lord Rohar to make arrangements for her to travel to the island as soon as possible, leaving Persephone in charge, and 'twas not just for personal reasons. They were preparing for the Reunion of their people and such would require frequent and lengthy visits both ways. And everyone knew that Prince Kevon and Princess Anastasia had already been groomed to rule the island in Rohar's absence. And though they'd had no real experience yet, rumors were spreading that such would soon change.

CHAPTER TWENTY

The Long-Awaited Reunion

Darque had spent the past two days supervising the latest updates to their census. 'Twas no doubt the Call to Return had been successful, as after dropping their glamours several dozen Elves, both male and female, turned themselves in to her from all three Lairs. These had been previously unknown to the Clan, long time neighbors, friends, kitchen staff, and Masters, representing a variety of professions.

After interviews, one thing stood out amongst them all. Their loyalty to Darque, the Dragon Clan, and the Resistance was steadfast. Although since the Black War began they'd remained hidden behind their glamours, 'twas out of a sense of habit and a watch and see attitude, for they were afraid of exposure. And the longer they waited, the more afraid they were of being accused as spies. But when the Call came, instead of simply answering it and leaving for their homeland, they banded together and turned themselves in to Darque, putting their very lives in her hands.

Once they bent knee to King Gabriel, they were given the choice to remain or return to the Wyrdritch. Without hesitation, every last one chose to stay with the Resistance, their families, and the lives to which they'd dedicated themselves. But the Call drove them to visit their homeland first, after which they would all return. Darque had approved.

~~~~~~~~~~

Compared to the Call to Return, the ceremony to reunite Darque Abriya D'Rienne and Solvyngarr was more than subdued. 'Twas determined that Abriya would have no difficulty leaving Ardyth's body once she was reunited with Sol, and there-
~~~~~~~~~~

fore Ardyth had already channeled her to help with the few preparations necessary.

All they required were the Fangs, the altar bowl, and the ability to perform the conjure, which would be facilitated by the potion being brewed by Artemis. While waiting for that to be completed, they arranged the Altar Room for the ceremony and during a rest break Darque asked Ardyth/Abriya about something that had bothered her for some time.

When Darque was Claimed by Gunnarr, he'd told her that Dragons mated for life, and she'd felt awful that they could never have offspring. Yet through the many winters since, she'd wondered. Gunnarr was the 7th son of a 7th son and although he'd been first hatched, becoming High Prince, he was actually last laid, giving him a most unconventional and shared status with his youngest brother, the first laid and last hatched named as 7th Prince, Bryynn. That situation had given her many marks of confusion afore she finally just pushed it to the back of her mind.

Then came Abriya and the whole ancestry of the Highlands returned to further confuse her. Abriya mated Solvyngarr, her LifeBond partner, as had Darque mated Gunnarr. But Solvyngarr was a 7th son of a 7th son, giving o'er his seed to the lives of his brood, Avyndarr being his 7th son, who was Gunnarr's sire. If Dragons mated for life and only had eggs with their lifemates, then how had that happened anyway? Solvyngarr Claimed Abriya the way that Gunnarr Claimed her and by what she'd understood, could not have done so if he'd already Claimed another, which he must have done to have had offspring.

What then was she to believe? Solvyngarr was still lost in the Otherworld and she couldn't ask Avyndarr as he'd been forced Past the Veil in the War of Chaos shortly after mating with Maahayyel, who eventually took the Matriarchy when her sister Kaahayyel abdicated, Maahayyel's children taking their current positions, replacing Kaahayyel's. And she couldn't ask either of them for they too, were now Past the Veil. Gunnarr knew nothing of the controversy, and seemed just as confused as was she, beginning to doubt his own history, what he'd always believed. Even searching his Memories, the answer eluded him. Mayhap he was too close to the situation.

So, who could she ask? 'Twas Ardyth/Abriya who supplied the answers. She had listened as Darque spoke and had been somewhat surprised that such was a problem. It seemed simple enough to her, but then she had to admit that she was from a time long past and things had changed, much had been forgotten, and traditions once started were hard to break.

Even for the Highlands with the Memories of their ancestors, such would create confusion through the millennia, for such Memories still required accessing. If one did not keep up with one's history, then that history would be forgotten, and such was what Abriya noted now. "When Solvyngarr recruited me for the High Races Council to represent Mankind, he already had offspring. But he'd not Claimed the mother. You see, the Dragons were quite… active, then." She smiled noting Darque's blushing understanding, and then continued. "Solvyngarr Claimed me as his lifemate. Yes, Dragons take on a lifelong commitment but 'tis out of a strong sense of loyalty and honor. Such could not possibly be biological. And therefore they need not make that Claim to have eggs. 'Twas their seclusion, the loss of so many of their lifemates as well as so many unattached Dragons, that led to such a belief, led to the notion that only the Matriarch could continue to have eggs, when in truth, any female Dragon could mate and have eggs."

Darque pondered this information. 'Twas logical and 'twould also explain how Avyndarr came to be. She'd have to tell Kelsey and they could inform the Matriarch. All female Dragons were capable of having eggs. Claimed or unclaimed. So even those whose lifemates had Passed the Veil could mate again and have eggs, which gave rise to yet another question. A very disturbing one. Slowly she asked, "So, with whom do you enter the Beyond?"

Ardyth/Abriya smiled meaningfully and without hesitation replied, "With the one you truly love. Your soulmate." Darque's quizzical expression made her pause and then she went on, "You can care about another, you can love them, you can be intimate with them, but there is only one soulmate, and you either connect on this side of the Veil, or the other."

MIDNIGHT

THE WINTER SOLSTICE

~~~~~ THE ALTAR ROOM ~~~~~

</div>

'Twas quiet, and unlike the Call to Return, there were few attending this ceremony. Yet the intensity of raw excitement and true anxiety remained unmatched.

Darque would play no role, neither would those few present to stand witness, for this required only Ardyth/Abriya to perform the conjure. Her strength, both physical and emotional would be tested, and under the influence of the potion of the Healer of the Daggogh to help her build the bridge 'tween the Otherworld and the Altar Room, she would Call to Solvyngarr. Drawing him out of his solitary existence, the Fangs would become her anchor and his beacon to follow, to escape the imprisonment of so many centuries.

After drinking the potion, Ardyth was afraid the First Warrior would forget the words she'd need to chant, or the rhythm, or the inflections, but Abriya assured her that such had repeated itself in her mind every day of her span, both living and as a spirit. All she required of Ardyth was her physical presence, her strength, her voice, and her ability to hold the Fangs. Ardyth need only let go and allow Abriya full control. She wanted so much for her friend's success.

Wearing leathers designed as an exact duplicate of those once worn by the First Warrior, Ardyth/Abriya stepped into the room, walking past the few who had been allowed to watch and to support her, without seeing any of them. Her presence was com-
~~~~~

manding and everyone near held their breath so as not to be a distraction. She was beautiful.

Ardyth/Abriya's voice began rising and ebbing, flowing, and chanting. 'Twas as a song she sung, calling out to her beloved, her long lost partner. The anguish she exuded, the courage, the authority, was astounding. She demanded that Solvyngarr look for her, come to her call, sense the Fangs, and not be afraid 'twas a trick of the Hoard, for 'twas truly her, the love of his life, his soulmate.

Darque had to swallow hard. 'Twas all coming to an end. Nevertheless, once Abriya and Solvyngarr were together, she could find and open the Book of the Conqueror. The Fangs would assure her success and be even more powerful once Sol was out of his long imprisonment and back with his LifeBond.

<center>~~~~~ THE OTHERWORLD ~~~~~</center>

Solvyngarr opened his eyes to the strange forest in which he lay. He'd lain here for many centuries, unmoving, always listening, hoping. 'Twas here he'd Heard the last echoing vestiges of her voice, but he'd been unable to determine from whence it came and eventually he knew he was lost. Not in the Void as he'd originally thought, he understood now that he was in the Otherworld and his lifemate was Calling to him elsewhere. He could not grasp onto the Magical thread from his own Fangs to guide him back, to reunite them. Miserable, he felt his own failure. And worse, she would blame herself for all eternity.

But suddenly, after so many eons, he heard her voice. He shook his great head. This could not be happening. His black and silver scales shone with his rising emotions as he stood up and swung his huge head slowly back and forth, trying to catch the sounds again, needing to know which way he should move. 'Twas so faint if he moved in the wrong direction he feared he'd lose her again. Only if he could determine which way to go, could he locate and then grasp the thread, allowing her to guide him to her side.

~~~~~ THE ALTAR ROOM ~~~~~

Darque noticed the sweat beading upon Ardyth/Abriya's forehead. The channeled pair were showing signs of weakening. 'Twas as if they were in a battle, a brutal tug of war, and she likened it to the LifeBond ceremony itself. All were quiet as the struggle continued, the chant becoming more emotional, the sounds enthralling.

Please my love, please come back to me, Ardyth/Abriya implored, all the while chanting perfectly, for any mistake in the words or the sequence could spoil the conjure. They were beginning to tremble with fatigue but Ardyth would not give up and filled Abriya with encouragement, willing her to keep going, and telling her she would not fail if Ardyth had anything to do with it. In response, Abriya was bolstered and they carried on with renewed vigor.

Holding two of the crossed Fangs in each of her small hands Ardyth/Abriya lifted them toward the bowl, offering them as beacons to Sol, using them to create a thread of love that would draw him back to her. The ceiling and walls melted away from view and in their place was the starlit sky surrounding them. As Ardyth/Abriya pushed her way as close to the Otherworld as she could, she heard a distant voice. 'Twas a voice she'd not heard in many centuries and near made her choke. She had to force herself to continue the chant, for 'twas the voice of her true love.

~~~~~ THE OTHERWORLD ~~~~~

Now Solvyngarr believed, now he understood. Roaring his excitement to the surrounding forest, Sol stepped this way and that, searching for what he could not see as yet. Somehow, Darque Abriya had the Fangs and she was calling to him again. Abruptly he saw the thread of light emanating from them and he grasped onto it like a lifeline in the middle of an ocean, following it ever onward toward the brightest light he'd ever seen, knowing 'twas the Fangs and his beloved was there, waiting for him. Gritting his teeth, he began to run. Nothing would stop him this time.

~~~~~ THE ALTAR ROOM ~~~~~

Without warning, a huge apparition came into view. 'Twas as if he'd burst in from another world and falling through the skies he'd landed on all fours in the middle of the bowl. But Solvyngarr was no longer this side of the Veil as Abriya had Passed long ago and therefore he was not a true physical presence, he was a spiritual one.

As his form took shape to the naked eye of those witnessing, the Dragon was a magnificent beast. Huge even for a Highland, with randomly scattered patterns of silver upon his black scales, he glittered in the torchlight. And the expression upon his muzzle was one of such yearning that Ardyth/Abriya leaped into the water to hold him. However, since Ardyth was alive, Abriya could not touch her lifemate. Confusion became anger and frustration led to turmoil and afore the situation exploded, Darque stepped up to intervene.

And then just as the atmosphere settled, 'twas with astonishment that Darque watched the Fangs disappear from Ardyth/Abriya's hands and reappear in their rightful place. Solvyngarr's massive jaws.
~~~~~

CHAPTER TWENTY-ONE

A Lesson Learned

~~~~~ DARQUE'S OFFICE AT THE KEEP OF ST SWIFTYN'S ~~~~~

After the conjure, Ardyth/Abriya had delayed separating so she could explain. She'd felt an obligation to do so, and with deep humiliation, she'd admitted to Darque the truth: they needed not the Fangs to open the Book of the Conqueror. 'Twas long ago, but Abriya had been a member of the Council of the Rashei both afore and after she'd been chosen to be the representative for Mankind to the High Races Council. Her duty was then, and would always be, the protection of her people.

After Beryl had used the Book to destroy the Island of Rienne, Darque Abriya suggested to the Council that they use the Fangs in a ruse to keep others from trying to open the Book. Along with ensuring their safety for all time, there'd be no way anyone could figure it out, because there wasn't anything to figure. The Council of the Rashei knew the Book would only open to the Conqueror himself, and since some of their people, mayhap a handful throughout the ages, could channel spirits, they needed to ensure its safety and security. If the Fangs were ever stolen, 'twould be clear someone was trying to open the Book and the threat could be neutralized.

But Abriya was afraid to tell Darque this. She'd been sworn to secrecy of their ruse. Was she to break that oath? Mayhap Darque would still try to help her use the Fangs to reunite with Solvyngarr, but once she learned the truth would the Battle Commander place Abriya and Sol's needs above those of her own people? Abriya had struggled with this, not knowing for certain if she'd kept the oath of secrecy out of duty or to get Darque to help her perform the ceremony.
~~~~~

Abriya's admission had been mindboggling, and Darque knew not what to think. She wanted another's opinion. She called for Tammra Dayo, Commander of the Ancients and now of the Kreegaren Elves. Standing afore her desk, the tall dark-haired Elf was mysterious as Darque asked her why Abriya hadn't told her the truth about the Fangs. Was she to believe what Abriya had confessed? Such affected how they were to continue.

Tammra's Elven voice rang though the office, echoing back softly from the bookshelves as she spoke. "Darque, do not chastise Abriya, for she did not lie to you. She merely redirected and omitted some critical information. 'Twas an oath taken by the entire Council of the Rashei. She did her duty, to the end, to her own suffering. To keep your Warrior Oath, you would have done the same."

Tammra spoke with the confidence of certain knowledge. Darque wondered why she felt so. "How do you know all this?" she asked.

Winking she grinned and stated, "I was there, remember?"

Several breaths slipped past them as they faced each other. Finally, Darque nodded. "Of course, how could I forget?" Slightly envious, she continued, "You knew her personally. You were part of her life." With the acknowledgement came questions unbridled running through her mind that she'd wanted to ask the First Warrior and now might never get the chance. Like just who was the one the Rashei had warned them against: 'the bastard Fay' of Myriam's note? If she'd known, mayhap so too, the one standing afore her now. But such questions could wait, for once they found the Book and released the Rashei, they could simply ask Darque's grandmother Myriam. If she yet lived.

Tammra's smile softened as she replied. "I considered her a friend. As are you." Gazing at the Battle Commander, she could sense the turmoil. Tilting her head quizzically, she asked, "Darque? What's really bothering you?"

Her drifting thoughts refocused, clarity reigned, and she now understood why she'd been so agitated. 'Twas naught to do with the Fangs. She took a deep breath, for the admission was most difficult. "The two people who should have trusted me enough to tell me the truth, lied. I would've tried to help, I would not have chastised them, but they didn't trust me. What kind of Commander prompts lies from those closest to her, from those who need her the most?"

Licking her full red lips, the look on her face was sad as the tall Elf answered quietly, "I'm assuming you speak of Darque Abriya and your sister, Storrm."

Darque's voice was equally soft in her reply. "Yes."

A knowing expression came o'er the Elven Commander as awareness struck. "Darque? You were named after a great leader and warrior of her time. But she was a diplomat, a chosen representative for Mankind who had no idea she'd soon be thrust into the thick of battle. When she took the position, she had little training and no experience. She just did the best she could, day to day."

Darque's eyes hardened with the echoed words from her past. Would that sentiment haunt her the rest of her lifespan?

But Tammra took no notice as she continued, "However, you are not her. Not to minimize her successes, but you are a better leader, a better warrior than she ever was, or could ever be. You've been trained from birth for this position, BUT you still didn't have any real experience when you took Rank."

Darque nodded her head. She thought she knew where Tammra was going with this. Had her recent insecurities, her pondering notions, been that obvious to others? The Kreegaren Commander continued, "What I'm trying to say is this. There's only one other person in all Kadoor who could be as good a Commander as are you." Tammra turned her back to Darque as she reached for two glasses from the shelf and began to fill them with the soft amber glow of Drekinn Whiskey.

Tension now gleamed in her eyes and Darque set her jaw, her nostrils flaring. Did Tammra want to command the Resistance? Thinking about her failures with trust, she'd actually brought the

Elf here to find out if she had such aspirations. But now that 'twas a possibility, she knew she could not just hand it o'er. Being Battle Commander was her prophesy and she'd fight for it, anyone, anytime, anywhere. Someone else had the capacity of being as good as was she? Sarcasm oozed as her brows furrowed and with her infamous temper rising she asked, "And just who might that be?"

Turning 'round, she said, "You're lookin' at her." Tammra chuckled. "And she doesn't want the job," she emphasized with a grin, handing one of the glasses to Darque. Acknowledging her understanding of Darque's prior thoughts, she continued, "And you wouldn't have offered it to me at any rate. Surrender is not your style. The heights of your brilliance are higher than most, you know. You're one tough woman, you've become the Hoard's worst nightmare, and together we make a good team. Trust me, even with my skills, I wouldn't want to meet up against you in a fight. But my place is at the head of the Kreegare, and yours is leading the Resistance."

With a snort and complete release of all her personal doubts, Darque responded, "The heights of my brilliance may be higher than most, but the depths of my idiocy have set records."

"'Tis the bane of every good commander, my friend." Tammra sighed, tipped her glass toward Darque, and stated, "May we fight well…"

Darque's relief was evident as she reached forth her glass, tipping it toward Tammra's. "And may the Fates be with us."

Tossing back the whiskey in a single chug, they each set their glasses down, the clinking sound against the desk surface, filling the room. Then Darque watched the Elven Assassin glide smoothly out of the office, leaving her with the ever-growing mountain of paperwork in the middle of the huge desk.

Abruptly, Abriya manifested in front of her, and having been unaware that she and Ardyth had separated, Darque was uncharacteristically startled, exclaiming, "Abriya!"

Although she was there merely to apologize and say her farewells, there was irritation in her voice as she replied slowly. "The name 'Abriya' means, 'Warrior'. 'Twas not my given name. My name is Darque."

The Battle Commander hesitated when an o'erwhelming sense of sorrow washed through her. 'Twas an emotion with which she'd become far too familiar o'er the past few winters. Inhaling deeply, she questioned, "Darque?"

Her eyes a'gleam with her own emotions, Darque Abriya's voice was gentle and filled with forgiveness in her response. "Yes?"

Darque licked her lips and swallowed afore she could speak. "I understand why you told me not about the Fangs."

"And I am sorry for my deception," Darque Abriya apologized sincerely.

"Truly, 'tis nothing to forgive. I would have done the same," Darque assured her, biting her bottom lip afore she continued. "Will I ever see you again?"

The First Warrior could sense her namesake's doubts, the loneliness that threatened to drown her, despite her resolve to push such into the past. Having lost her sister only last winter, the Battle Commander now felt she was being abandoned by everyone, even though she still had her lifemate. Yet Darque Abriya understood those feelings. Looking down in her 'tell' of discomfort for she thought the chances were slim, she replied, "Mayhap."

Then she glanced back at Darque with a slight smile afore changing the subject and returning to why she was here. "I can never repay you for what you've done for Sol and me. You are my namesake, but more than that. We've become friends and I do not wish to leave you, but my blood runs through your veins and you need nothing more. As Tammra said, you are stronger than I ever was, and already a better fighter and leader than I could ever be. And, you are not alone, Darque. Remember. Spend time with those you love whenever and however you can, and don't stand at the Veil looking back upon your span of days with regrets."

Darque nodded as the First Warrior began to take her leave. Again, the many questions she wished she had time to ask her ancestor rushed through her mind, but she could not keep her from her full reunion with Sol any longer. Still, 'twas one of most immediate importance she did need answered afore they parted. She'd yet to hear from the Team sent to Tupry and finding Koryl might never happen. As of now, the Queen Mother was their only hope. There had to be another. "Wait, please! Since you can't help me open it, can you at least help me find the Book?"

Darque Abriya would have sighed if she were still capable. The Battle Commander was going to be fine, her thoughts already forging ahead to her duties. But had she learned anything from their experiences other than how to fight more effectively? Life wasn't all about fighting. Relenting, she stated, "Ask Ardyth. She has seen it."

"She's seen the Book of the Conqueror?" Darque asked incredulously. "But why hasn't she told us?"

Shaking her head, her long thick mane of red hair brushing the floor, Darque Abriya replied, "She knew not what 'twas and has forgotten the event. 'Twas a childhood memory and associated with much trauma."

Darque chewed on her lip as she tried to think of a way to evoke such a painful memory for doing so was in her experience, most difficult. Not that anyone tried to hide such, but they seemed to be unable to bring them forth to consciousness when required.

Darque Abriya winked. "Ask her where she got the pearls," she whispered.

Darque's brows furrowed. Then she recalled the Vision Walkyr had just a few moons past, of the little girl and the pearls. It had to be Ardyth. Her Gift of being a Seer of the Dead led her to the ability to channel spirits. But there was so much more to

Ardyth. An Outlander born into a fishing community that had once been a thriving though small village along the dangerous Southern Slippes of the Ocean of Fears, Ardyth was the only survivor of their destruction by order of High King Shytin. She suddenly recalled that Ardyth owned a bag of unusually large, rare, and multi-colored pearls, the origins of which she'd never revealed. 'Twas adding up to be a most interesting conversation.

Noticing that her ancestor had started to leave again, she caught her attention by calling softly, "Darque!"

The fading wraith looked back curiously. "Yes?"

With much sincerity, she made her final farewell. "Good travels to you and Sol. May your paths never part again."

Darque Abriya D'Rienne near glowed in joy and with a quick wink and slight nod of acceptance, she turned about. Reaching forth into the cosmos, she took the glittering black and silver scaled elbow of the giant Dragon, Solvyngarr, as they walked into the Beyond together, fading away to nothingness. The Battle Commander watched them 'til they'd completely vanished even from her enhanced vision.

Feeling quite deflated, Darque sighed and looked down at the pile of paperwork on her desk, seeing it but not seeing it for several long moments. Her mind drifted through her conversation with Tammra, then to the new intel about the Seer of the Dead and the pearls. Rubbing her forehead, she wondered how they were to use pearls to locate the Book, and once found, she still knew not how they were to open it if not with the Fangs. And there was the need for the next LifeBond, a task for which the Matriarch was preparing now. They'd be ready within a moon. And where in Hades was Koryl? So much to do. Would it never end?

With sudden clarity she realized that no, 'twould never end. No matter how fast or how hard or how long she worked, her administration and other duties would always be there, there'd always be more to do, there'd always be something. Shaking her head decisively, she stood up, grabbed her Sword, and vacated the office. She could work later. For now, the sun was shining, and though 'twas cold, the skies were clear. 'Twas the perfect time to go for a ride. She Called to Gunnarr, who was delighted to be able to spend some time with his lifemate. Just some time together, with nothing at all that they must do. Such was guaranteed to no one, and Darque wanted to enjoy life as much as they could, whenever they could, while they could. 'Twas a lesson learned.

The Wall of Valor

~~~~~ **THE TRAINING PITS OF THE DRAGON'S DEN** ~~~~~

'Twas chilly and Fryya's breath came in frothy puffs. But heavy snow had yet to fall and the sands of the Training Pits were warmed by Magical Spells, for the Highlands liked not the cold.

Fryya walked slowly 'round the walls, reading the names with much respect. They'd fought and died bravely, Legend Song immortalizing their deeds. But Fryya was frustrated. She'd not been able to find the Fang, marking her first mission a failure in her opinion, and although Walkyr had tried to console her, she was not to be consoled.

Stepping from one section to the next, her eyes beheld the neatly carved names of so many Warriors lost as she continued to chastise herself o'er the fact that she'd not been the one to find the Fang. Nor had she been the one to get the Dragon Sword. Surely there was some way she could make her mark, earning her place here amongst the valiant at the end of her days.

Whispering aloud, she noticed not Walkyr, as he stood at the entry to the Pits watching her, hearing the heartbreak as her soft voice lifted to the heavens, "M'Liege, what CAN I find? How can I impress Darque, impress the others? What can I DO?"

'Twas not a Vision that gave Walkyr his understanding of what Fryya was thinking. 'Twas her abrupt halt, the lift of her chin, her posture. The lost Warriors. Shaking his head, he knew she was far too brash for her own good. Or for his. Despite the fact that they had yet to come of age, and although they'd been deployed on one mission, they had yet to reach their full growth and needed to continue to train, he knew in his heart that with or without orders, he'd likely be following his partner into the Outlands to try to locate the missing Warriors and bring them home again.
~~~~~

Sighing loudly, she finally realized he was there and ran to him. Lifting her off her feet, he hugged her hard, wishing the depth of his love alone would be enough to make her feel complete. But he would never stop trying, for 'twas all he could do.

JUST PAST MIDNIGHT

THE RAZOR'S EDGE

~~~~~ TUPRY ~~~~~

</div>

Near four winters past, Darque had deployed the brothers to Tupry, the outlaw village where one could procure anything for a price. Populated by thieves and cutthroats, one had to always be aware to avoid losing one's life, let alone one's coin. There was little order here, and no one trusted anyone. Still, 'twas not total chaos. Though there was layer upon layer of immoral activities, there were still rules to follow and breaking them would lead to severe consequences.

Tyrak and Tybryn had spent much time and effort cautiously and steadily insinuating themselves into the lives of the worst of the worst, and finally this very evening they'd succeeded in hearing something that suggested more than rumor about the Queen Mother, Koryl. At last! 'Twas the information for which they'd come.

Still, the information was not fact. What they did know was that Koryl had disappeared many winters past, about the time the True King, Gabriel, now in the protection of the Resistance since the imposter Shytin still sat the throne at Evanntyr, had gathered thirteen winters and joined the Daggogh for his own protection. Soon after, the Queen Mother could not protect herself from her own newly crowned son and his advisor and was forced to flee for her life. At the time the rumors suggested she'd traveled to Tupry.

'Twas imperative they find Koryl. She was a most ambitious witch, thought to be a full-blood Rashei, and she was responsible for the curse that sent her own people into another existence.
~~~~~

'Twas probable that she'd used the Book of the Conqueror to do so, with help from the Sorcerer to accomplish this amazing feat. If the Sorcerer had the Book, they'd know. And if Koryl had used the Book then, she likely knew where 'twas now.

Not a mark earlier this evening, the brothers had found one of their associates lying in a puddle of his own blood, near the Veil. Beside him lay the one who'd struck the fatal blow. The man had always steadfastly denied any knowledge of Koryl, as had they all, but as Tybryn leaned o'er him, the man suddenly grabbed his cloak, yanking him closer. Wheezing his confession, he'd shoved a pouch into the Warrior's hand. "I know not who you are, but you're in much danger. There are many who would like to find Koryl. Her bounty is high on every side. The others know of your search but have given you free rein so you might do their work for them to locate the witch." He'd taken a ragged breath afore he continued. "Koryl came to Tupry many winters past and established herself as a traveling Oracle. But even in disguise the Queen Mother was known, and after she fled Evanntyr and returned here, 'twas not long afore she was forced to flee again. Nonetheless, a few winters later she returned once more, saying she'd located the Dranahh of the Dragon's Breath and that with enough mercenaries she could march on the Oasis to conquer them, giving her a vast army of followers and Sand Dragons at her beck and call. She produced this pouch as proof that she'd found the nomads of the great desert and not only did they exist, so too, their riches of Legend Song. For those who would follow her now, she promised a share in those riches." His breath stuttered and he coughed up bloody spittle afore he was able to continue. "But Koryl failed to convince them and since she still carries a price on her head, she was once again forced to flee. There are those who believe she went back to the Oasis claiming she'd have nowhere else to go. But I believe there's another possibility in the distant south." Again, he took a breath, but this time his voice was near a whisper, the pain in his eyes, clear. Instead of offering his suggestion of just what that possibility was, he wheezed, "Take the pouch. Inside… is…" His eyes glazed o'er, and his hand went limp, releasing Tyrak from his grasp.

Leaving the man where he lay, they'd disappeared into the night, heading to the tiny room they'd shared for so long o'er the tavern in the vilest part of the village. Once there they discovered that the pouch contained a single, perfectly clear crystal the size of Tyrak's thumb but was like nothing he'd ever seen afore. Still, the brothers knew from their earliest Training, from whence this crystal came. There could be no doubt. Once, long afore the Last Holocaust, the mines of Kadoor were active and prosperous. Known as Desert Crystals now, the most perfect gems such as this one were only found at the Oasis and were once known as Dymins. They were rumored to be as hard as were Dragon's Eyes, and just as sought after, just as valuable. But none had been seen since the Last Holocaust.

'Twas time to leave, they could wait no longer. Not only had they found the evidence for which they'd come, but also where Koryl might be hiding now. With such knowledge came the escalation of their own danger and they were acutely aware of the need to end their mission. 'Twould be prudent to leave afore dawn if they were to return to make report to the Battle Commander.

Tybryn had insisted Tyrak have the honor of carrying the 'evidence' since he was the elder. Tyrak patted the pouch at his hip to make certain 'twas still there. Such was their death sentence in Tupry. In mutual confirmation of their need to leave post haste they downed their drinks in one gulp, when suddenly they heard the sound of heavy booted feet running up the stairs. Clearly came many men who cared not if they were heard, which spoke of their intent. Standing rapidly from the table and knocking it o'er in their haste, they grasped arms and nodded. Tyrak winked and said, "May we fight well."

Ever armed and prepared for emergencies, his free hand upon the hilt of his sword hidden under the long black cloak that matched his brother's, Tybryn replied, "And may the Fates be with us." 'Twas a twinkle in his eye even though they both knew their odds of getting out of Tupry alive had just dropped dramatically. 'Twas the challenge all Warriors faced at one time or another in their careers. The greater the odds, the stronger their determination. They feared not the Veil, for 'twas their chance to claim the honor of Legend Song, but they would do everything they could to fulfill their mission. Turning as one, they crashed through the window, grabbed a branch of the tree outside, and dropped to the ground effortlessly, just as their pursuers broke through the locked door. With their cloaks billowing behind them they raced away under cover of the darkness of the new moon and disappeared into the back alleys of the village.

~~~~~ THE DOORWAY TO SHAHANALAA ~~~~~

'Twas precisely as in Adryanna's scry near three winters past. The sound of the Dragon Sword had stopped. The constant rhythmic clanging of steel on stone suddenly ceased and the quiet that permeated throughout the land was deafening in its absence. Rushing to the door, the remaining Rashei, ten including the child, simply stood, staring in amazement. Then mutely they glanced from one to the other to confirm they were yet this side of the Veil afore touching each other to confirm they had not become cursed spirits.

'Twas Adryanna who climbed up the roughhewn steps to the stone door, peering into the darkness of the hole carved through winters of constant hacking to confirm one more fact. The Sword was gone.

~~~~~ THE PRIVATE QUARTERS OF THE
BATTLE COMMANDER ~~~~~

Darque had finally fallen asleep. Exhausted but with much burden lifted from her shoulders, she simply crawled into

Gunnarr's arms, cradled and safe, and with a deep breath, she'd closed her eyes less than half a mark past.

When the Warrior banged insistently upon the door she near leaped out of her skin. While she grabbed her leathers, Gunnarr tore open the door and glared at the Warrior standing there, with an expression that told him this better be good.

Having sprinted through the Keep, near panting with the effort, the Warrior made report. "Shahanalaa, Sir! 'Tis open! The door has been breached from the inside!"

Darque peeked out from behind Gunnarr's elbow, already strapping on her bracers and weapons as she prepared to see the Warrior. "Breached from the inside? You are certain?"

They'd long suspected the noise they heard was the Dragon Sword trying to answer Darque Abriya's Call, and since the first sounds Darque had guards posted. But confirmation of such filled her with mixed emotions. Catching his breath, the Warrior nodded and then continued, "A Dragon Sword broke through and flew out, disappearing down the corridor. I came to make report while my partner followed it." The man glanced to the still irritated countenance of the General afore he finished, "As per your orders, Commander."

Just as Darque and Gunnarr stepped out their door to join in the search, the second Warrior came running up behind the first. His hand held up to stop them, he stated, "No rush, Commander. Follow me, I know where 'tis."

<center>~~~~~ FRYYA'S QUARTERS ~~~~~</center>

After she and Walkyr had returned from their first deployment they were each granted their own quarters, which was a wonderful improvement from the Warrior's Barracks. Fryya had been sound asleep, having made her decision earlier and feeling good about it. They would crash the 4th LifeBond to be held within the next two moons. Not only would this save Walkyr's life as she was convinced that a 'Bond partner could and would control the increasing violence of his Visions, but she and Walkyr would then be able to deploy with the approval of the Battle Commander, to find the lost Warriors. Walkyr had reassured her that surely Kydra and Ragnyrr could use some help as they rarely made report and had not brought in anyone. Thus far. Once she and Walkyr took the 'Bond, Darque would have to see reason, deploying them on the mission. She could feel it.

While in the Training Pits last evening, she'd come to terms with Walkyr having a Dragon Sword when she did not. Ariel's Sword was a perfect fit for him, although the grip was a bit large, but he'd grow into it. 'Twas a graceful design, though not at all feminine, and the Sword would help him in the fight. She had her Gift of protection and would manage with her sword of Clan steel. After all, Warriors had been making their mark for eons with no less.

Waking groggily from a most vivid dream, she thought she was still dreaming. She'd felt the slight movement of air 'cross her face, and if she'd been out in the field she would have leaped up, weapon in hand. But she was NOT in the field and she did NOT appreciate this interruption.

Wearily she rubbed her eyes, then opening one slowly with her fingers still pressing down upon the other, she tried to focus. At the end of her bed, the stuffed down mattress lying on a wooden frame of her own creation, she thought she was seeing things. Even with excellent night vision, what she saw there simply could not be.

Squinting, she blinked several times and then widening both eyes, the view shocked her. Floating there, was a Sword. Not just any sword, for ordinary steel did not float, and 'twas not her own sword for it still leaned against the head of her mattress within her reach. No, she knew this one had flown here for she'd felt it, 'twas why she'd wakened.

Incredulously, she crawled forward on her hands and knees, reached forth and gingerly took hold the hilt, breathlessly waiting to wake up from this dream, or have the thing jerk out of her unworthy hand. Why would Ariel's Sword change allegiance? Dread filled her heart as she knew no one would believe she had nothing to do with it.

But then another thought occurred to her. Storrm's Sword still lay atop the bookshelf in Darque's office. Her breath stuttered. Yet the Sword did not move from her grasp and with much guilt, she pulled it to her in amazement. 'Twas stunning but 'twas not Ariel's, nor to her shock was it Storrm's. Then full awareness hit her, and her jaw dropped, eyes glued to the ancient runes running the length of the blade.

At that moment, the two Warriors who'd stood guard o'er Shahanalaa, along with Walkyr, Darque, and Gunnarr, came striding into her room. Fryya slapped one hand o'er her mouth and her eyes filled with tears of astonishment as Walkyr grinned ear to ear, Ariel's Sword strapped to his back. Darque appeared dazed while Gunnarr and the Warriors laughed loudly, the sounds of their approval reverberating through the chamber. The Dragon Sword of Darque Abriya D'Rienne had chosen.

THUS ENDS THE FANGS OF SOLVYNGARR

Look for further adventures in:
THE BOOK OF THE CONQUEROR
Coming soon!

Long Live Darque and the Dragon Clan!

Lifebond Rosters

THE FIRST LIFEBOND/FIRST FLIGHT

1. Darque (sister of Storrm and Fryya) and Gunnarr (male, High Prince)
2. Storrm (sister of Darque and Fryya) and Mystynn (male, Second Prince)
3. Kydra (female) and Ragnyrr (male, Third Prince)
4. Axyl (brother of Daxx) and Haniyyah (sister of Linayyah)
5. Daxx (brother of Axyl) and Linayyah (sister of Haniyyah)
6. Yanais (male) and Shykiyyah (female)
7. Rolf (male) and Nalwynn (female)
8. Rygyl (male) and Tegrynn (female)
9. Tyndall (female) and Fyndarr (brother of Zaydarr, cousin of Gunnarr)
10. Apryya (female) and Dannyrkyn (male)
11. Zoe (female) and Kyrlayyn (male)
12. Ethynn (brother of Daylyn) and Makayyd (sister of Makyyan)
13. Ariel (female) and Zayddarr (male sibling of the children of Kaahayyel: Fyndarr, Shraadarr, Krynnarr, Synahmarr, and cousin of Gunnarr)

THE SECOND LIFEBOND/STORRM FLIGHT

1. Regynn (male. An Elder Warrior and Clan Historian) and Sydrayyah (female)
2. Astraa (female, sister of Aspynn) and Kaygynn (male, Quad Prince)
3. Tannah (female, sister of Tiyya) and Synddarr (male, Fifth Prince)
4. Daylyn (female, sister of Ethynn) and Makyyan (brother of Makayyd)
5. Tiyya (female, sister of Tannah) and Shasynn (male, Sixth Prince)
6. Thorrn (male) and Taniyyah (female)

7. Barynn (male) and Shraadarr (female sibling of the children of Kaahayyel)
8. Hannah (female) and Izayyah (male)
9. Mikkal/Gabriel (males) and Daynahmyn (female)
10. Rakkah (male) and Petrayyah (sister of Pelayyah and Sydrayyah)
11. Loryyn (female) and Krynnarr (male sibling of the children of Kaahayyel)
12. Daayn (male, elder brother of Tonn) and Kashiyann (sister of Krydann who has been missing since the time of the Last Holocaust)
13. Tannyr (eldest brother of Tonn and Daayn) and Kaahayyel (sister of Maahayyel. Mother of Fynddarr, Zayddarr, Synahmarr, Shraadarr and Krynnarr)

THE THIRD LIFEBOND/MACE FLIGHT

1. Aspynn (Astraa's sister) and Maakayyel (brother of Maahayyel and Kaahayyel, uncle of Gunnarr and his siblings, and of Fyndarr and Synahmarr)
2. Soryn (male) and Pelayyah (sister of Petrayyah and Sydrayyah)
3. Drysalyn (female) and Danniagg (brother of Korriagg, cousin of siblings Radryagg and Hadryagg)
4. Prysym (female) and Rasparyn (male)
5. Valkyn (male) and Zymaalynn (female)
6. Alyyse (female) and Kyralayah (female)
7. Paydynn (female) and Korriagg (brother of Danniagg, cousin of siblings Radryagg and Hadryagg)
8. Kytahna (female) and Dylordynn (male)
9. Hadyn (male) and Delfyyan (female)
10. Maddyx (male) and Varrdayyn (male)
11. Mace (male twin of Mynx) and Maddokyn (female)
12. Darrtan (male) and Illsyyah (female)
13. Baylis (female) and Maklarynn (brother of Lyrriynn)

Author's Bio

Born in Connecticut and raised in the Midwest, Derrien Relyea grew up fascinated with mythology, Viking lore, and Dragons. Her vivid imagination was kindled by her highly creative family, encouraging a love of writing and fantasy. She worked her way through Oklahoma City Community College with degrees in Occupational Therapy and Therapeutic Recreation, and later graduated from the University of Oklahoma Health Sciences Center with a degree in Physical Therapy.

Taking her cue from an exciting genealogical history and such authors as Anne McCaffrey, Edgar Rice Burroughs, Jules Verne, and Sir Arthur Conan Doyle, she has embarked upon a new adventure in her life. Please join her at:

https://thedragonwarrior.com

Kudos and credit to my friend and
accomplished artist, Lisa Dixon:

https://lisadixonart.com

www.ingramcontent.com/pod-product-compliance
Lightning Source LLC
Chambersburg PA
CBHW031941110726
47902CB00001B/257